ENCRYPTION

Encryption

Richard J. McLeish

I dedicate this book to the loving memory of my dear friend Terry Hollohan. During your courageous two-year battle with cancer, you never gave up on me becoming an author. You never quit Terry, so how could I? I just wish you could have seen the book finished. Then again, you probably have.

Today should be a sad day
My friend has gone away
Today I should be mourning
The man who walked my way
But I cannot grieve his leaving
For he is with me still
Every time I think of him
His words, I recall at will
"I have lived a good life
I have fought the good fight
Now carry on and celebrate
My life of which you were part."
Our friendship is eternal
As you are in my heart
We will be together in a little while
And share the stories once again
Which always made us smile.

God bless and keep you my dear friend.

ACKNOWLEDGMENTS

I wish to thank all those who have encouraged me in this endeavor, especially during the times I was about to give up. I wish to offer a special thank you to my editor, Ashley Rayner. Without her help, this book would never have happened. I also wish to thank Jenn Bell for her help with the final read-through. I especially want to thank my daughter, Megan, who didn't stop believing in the "old man" and whose ideas at a critical point were invaluable.

PROLOGUE

It is surprising that a venue that receives over four million visitors per year could be so tranquil; however, that is the way I found these undulating grounds this lovely March day, just as the other times I had visited them with my dad. There are already two members of the Hanson family buried at Arlington National Cemetery: my great-grandfather James T. Hanson whom I am named after, and Edward R. Hanson my grandfather. Today my father became the third.

I have always thought of Arlington as a book with a story to tell, with each of its 400,000 pages denoted by a simple white stone marker. Each leaf holds the story of the individual's life journey to their own piece of these 624 acres of lush, green Virginia countryside, rolling on toward the horizon, the stone markers like white caps on breaking waves. For Captain Robert E. Hanson, my father, the journey ended here this beautiful spring day with full military honors. The soldiers who made up his Honor Guard wore dark blue uniforms that were perfectly fitted, starched, spotless and resplendent with gold trim. A horse-drawn caisson bore the flag-shrouded, oak and brass coffin to the grave next to his father and grandfather. The playing of "The Last Post" and the firing of the 21-gun salute brought tears to the eyes of all who beheld this poignant ceremony. The soldiers, with practised hands, folded the flag cloaking my dad's coffin to a perfect triangle. The Sergeant leading his Honor Guard stepped forward to where I was sitting with my mother, Dolly, and my two children, Jason and Jennifer. He saluted, bent forward, and presented the flag to my mother with the words heard by the families of too many sons and daughters who—as President Lincoln said—had given, "the last full measure of devotion."

"From a grateful nation."

1

As I sat with my family, my mother leaning her head on my shoulder, I found myself staring at the mast head of the Battleship Main, which adorns its memorial, as I tried to make sense of the last two weeks, but the words of a poem kept intruding, interrupting my thoughts. I was concentrating so much that I was unaware of the events around me. My uncle George had been talking to the mourners who had remained after the service. He was the first to notice the small convoy of four SUVs that had stopped on the path below the grave site. About a dozen men got out, each with a radio bud in one of their ears, and began to survey the area. It was one lone figure, however, who made everyone stop and stare. She was a tall woman, about fifty years old, and walked with confidence up the hill. Her perfectly tailored dark blue pant suit accented her trim, fit figure and was accessorized with a simple white pearl necklace and matching earrings, all appropriate for the occasion. She approached us from behind and came around to where we were sitting. Addressing my mother she said, "Please excuse my intrusion Mrs. Hanson, but on behalf of my family and the people of the United States, I wish to offer our deepest condolences."

Mom was startled at first, but quickly recovered and took the lady's hand as we all rose. Mom smiled and said, "Thank you very much, Madam President, and we appreciate very much your coming, especially with all you have been through. I hope you are feeling better."

"I have a few bumps and bruises, but I'm doing just fine."

"Madam President, I know I speak for all Americans when I say, after seeing that video, how proud we are to have you as our president," she said with great passion, still holding the president's hand.

"That is very kind, Mrs. Hanson."

To say I was stunned was an understatement. Fortunately, Mom was handling things perfectly.

"May I introduce my son, Jim, and my two grandchildren Jennifer and Jason?"

I shook the hand of President Kathleen Galbraith as she offered her condolences. She then turned to Jenny and Jason.

"Now here are two young people I've wanted to meet. How are things in the history department at Georgetown, Jason?" she asked, shaking his hand.

The surprise on Jason's face matched Mom's, mine, and Jenny's as to how she would know, or more importantly, why she would bother to find out, where Jason went to school.

"We're all just living in the past as usual, Madam President," Jason responded, drawing a grin from her.

She continued with Jenny.

"Now here is a young lady who is quite the rising star in the world of computers," she stated while taking her hand. "I understand your doctorial studies are going well at MIT, Jennifer."

"Yes, Madam President, and thank you," she replied, flashing an infectious smile.

"I was born and raised in Cambridge. Is Flannigan's Pub still as nice as I remember?" Kathleen replied while matching her smile.

"Now, Madam President, I would have no knowledge of such a place!" Jenny responded laying on a mock look of surprise to accent her smile, which gave Kathleen a chuckle. "I am just a hard-working student."

"I know you're hard-working, Jennifer, you specialize in mass data, I believe."

"That's correct, Madam President."

They stood there looking at each other for a moment, much as two people who each knew the same secret, but knowing it was one they could not discuss. Kathleen excused herself and went over to meet the other mourners, while we formed a huddle.

"She seemed to know all about you," Dolly observed addressing her grandchildren.

"What's going on here, Dad?" asked Jason.

"She's been well-briefed," stated Jenny.

I could only think of one thing.

"She just delivered a message; I hope we will get the rest of it before she leaves."

"By the way," Jason asked with a look of concern, "has anyone seen Emily?"

Three shaking heads soon gave him his answer.

Kathleen greeted each of the mourners and finally came to my Uncle George. She gave him a long hug. The love and deep affection my uncle has for his former law clerk was very evident.

"Well, Judge Grayson, what can I say? He was a good man."

"The best, we both saw him practice law. He was very proud of you Kathleen … pardon me, Madam President."

"Imagine, your second-best law clerk getting this far," was the laughing response from Kathleen.

"I just wish I could remember the name of that lady who was my best clerk," was the reply; they both laughed.

It had been a running joke between them over the years, with Uncle George never being able to remember the name of his best law clerk, the woman who was now president always having run a close second. Kathleen and Uncle George finished with the other mourners and she returned to my family. I sensed she wanted to say something, but didn't know how. Mom sensed her reservations as well and, as usual, knew just how to handle the situation.

"Jim, if the president has a moment, why don't you show her the memorial your father put up for his squadron?"

"I would very much like to see that, Mrs. Hanson."

Taking the cue, we started down the path, shepherded by a number of Secret Service agents.

"Your father was a very brave man, Mr. Hanson," Kathleen remarked as we strolled along the pathway between my dad's grave and the amphitheater.

"Thank you very much for that, Madam President. He showed us all great courage in all five of his battles."

Kathleen tilted her head, looking as if she was listening but wanted more.

"First, he fought as Captain Robert E. Hanson, United States Air Force in the Korean War. Next, he fought against the memories and guilt he felt losing most of his squadron in that horrible battle in 1951. Following the war, he fought as a lawyer, for justice, especially in the civil rights cases of the 1960s. Then came Alzheimer's disease, and of course, this last battle which brings all of us here today."

"It is the last battle I need to talk to you about, Mr. Hanson. I know this is probably the wrong time and place, but events are moving so fast and I need to get ahead of them, so I have to know what happened."

"Why would you think I would know anything about what happened, Madam President?"

Kathleen stopped and fixed her eyes on mine. She was a woman of great beauty, with high cheekbones and fine features. It was those eyes, however; TV did not do them justice. They were deep blue and spoke volumes, and right now, they were saying, *Don't even think about trying to jerk me around, guy.*

"So how did you figure it out?"

"We have good computer people, Mr. Hanson."

"The attack was too well-executed, too well-covered; your people would have needed more time to even have a chance. With all due respect, I am calling the president's bluff."

"Remind me never to play poker with you, Mr. Hanson."

I was now standing almost nose to nose with the most powerful person on the planet, and she was one who I could see was ready for a fight if I was going to start it. But she didn't have to deliver a blow; I did it myself when I figured out how she knew.

"Uncle George called you."

"Damn right he did."

The bolt of fear that hit me was almost paralyzing. I did not know how to react. I turned away and meandered further down the path; I needed a few moments to think. Kathleen finally strode over.

"George is worried sick about you and your family," she continued.

"If any of this gets out, even a hint, they'll kill me and my whole family along with anyone else they think is involved."

"Who is the 'they' you are talking about, Mr. Hanson?"

"Well, have your pick, Madam President. We took down three cartels for about a trillion dollars, several terrorist front organizations for about ten billion, not to mention all the tax evaders and dirty politicians with their offshore accounts for about another trillion. After we dropped into a few questionable super PACs, our ATM card reached its maximum."

Kathleen stared at me vacantly, her eyes glossed over as though she was trying to fathom what she just heard.

"Pardon me, Mr. Hanson, but what I am hearing challenges all credibility. How could you possibly move trillions of dollars from offshore accounts ..."

She struggled to grasp the enormity of our achievement.

"Well, money doesn't really exist anymore—it's just zeroes and ones on computer bases—so that made it possible. Also, the use of that second Internet you guys built really helped. It's very fast."

Now the president's face turned pale with anger.

"Mr. Hanson, 'net-2 is a national secret, how the hell did you find out about it?!"

Now it was my turn to stand my ground.

"May I remind the President she has yet to answer my question? Who else knows about my family's involvement besides you?"

"Just me; your Uncle made me promise. He said given the circumstances I should assume there was no one in my government I should trust. Coming from the man who was the closest to a father I ever had, well, frankly, that hurt. Then, in the next twenty-four hours, all those financial statements started arriving at the media outlets showing the people in the government, as well as others who had offshore accounts, which confirmed his information was accurate—as usual."

"Please Madam President; we did a much more thorough job than just supply you and the media with financial statements and names. You got the amounts of the funds given that individual, where they came from, and why they were given and where they were hidden."

"Well pardon me, Mr. Hanson," Kathleen replied with no little sarcasm in her voice, "I do stand corrected. Further, I do thank you for helping me cement my place in the history of this great nation; not only will I go down as the first woman president but as the chief executive of its most corrupt government."

"Well Madam President, look at the bright side."

Kathleen raised her eyebrows.

"The history books will give you more ink than they ever gave Millard Fillmore."

Kathleen's reaction to my little joke was unexpected. She gave me a long, hard stare and then started to laugh. She laughed so hard her whole body shook.

"Thanks, Mr. Hanson. I needed that, it has been a rough forty-eight hours."

With that she took my arm.

"Now show me the memorial your dad made while we talk."

*
**

"George, did I just see the president laugh and take Jim by the arm?" asked Dolly.

All the other mourners had drifted off, leaving the Hansons and George, now joined by Dominique Deselva and Jake Connors, at the gravesite. George started to chuckle.

"Okay, Uncle George, come clean, what's going on here?" asked Jennifer, smiling broadly.

"George Michael Grayson, I have known you for over sixty years, so don't try to fool me; are you trying to do some matchmaking here?" Dolly asked.

"Dolly, as you know, Jim is the son my dear Rachel and I never could have. Kathleen is the daughter. I know the character of these two fine people. Jim has the answers that Kathleen needs, not only to save the United States from the worst financial and political crisis ever to befall it, but to save her presidency. As far as Jim is concerned, I am hoping he will see just how much he needs to help her. As far as anything else, I think they'll discover it on their own."

"Just think Jenny, the president could be our new stepmother!" exclaimed Jason.

"Jason!"

"What's your problem here, sis? A nice, white house comes with this deal!"

Dolly and George just shook their heads and laughed.

*
**

"So Madam President, what is the body count now?" I asked as we strolled along the path.

"So far twenty-one Senators and ninety-eight from the House have resigned, plus two Justices of the Supreme Court. You can add to that two assistant directors of the FBI, and now the director himself, a good man, has tendered his resignation for the scandal in the FBI you exposed, which he had no part in."

"You might want to hold off accepting the director's resignation; he's one of the good guys. They're a hard find."

"And you know this how?" she asked, giving me another stare and squeezing my arm.

"First things first Madam President. Are your computer people hot on our trail?"

She stopped dead in her tracks and turned to me.

"The truth is, Mr. Hanson, no, they aren't. We have some of best computer minds in the world at the FBI, NSA, and Homeland Security all looking at this and all they can say to me is 'if you find out who did this, hire them.'"

I started to laugh, causing her to look annoyed as she placed her hands on her hips, like a mother about to scold a child.

"Well I am glad one of us finds amusement in all of this, Mr. Hanson, but I need to know what happened. Right now our financial and political system has been turned on its head. We're getting reports that millions of people all across this continent and Europe have had money turn up in their bank accounts and I—we—need to get a clear understanding of all these events or there will be chaos. Will you help me, Mr. Hanson?"

I could see she was sincere; her concern was genuine. As she looked at me, I could see the strain on her face. It was amazing how people who become president aged so quickly.

"My president is standing in front me asking for my help; of course I will help, it's my duty. However part of me wants to tell you to ..."

"You do not have to finish the sentence, Mr. Hanson, I get the message. You're angry; in fact—do pardon my language—you're pissed off. Wanna tell me why?"

We were practically nose to nose again and there was no doubt about it, as the world saw in the video, this lady was a person who did not back down from a fight.

"Remember 2008, Madam President?" I asked sarcastically, only to be stopped cold by her response.

"How could I forget it? It was the year my husband died."

I felt the anger drain out of me as I turned slightly away from her and cast my gaze down the tree-lined path.

"I am sorry, Madam President; I shouldn't let myself get angry. I know what you've been through."

"Yes, you do. How long has it been since your wife's passing?"

"Almost three years."

"I am very sorry, Mr. Hanson, and I think I know why you're angry. You're in the insurance and investment business. You saw a lot of people get hurt in the financial meltdown of 2008 and the government did nothing."

"Madam President, I know this was before you were in office, but your colleagues at justice saw the biggest theft in the history of this planet take place and all they did was toe-tag the bodies, let the thieves throw some coin at the Security and Exchange Commission in the form of fines and no one went to jail while a big piece of America died. Well, Madam President— and do pardon my language—payback is a bitch."

"So that's what this is about, revenge for 2008?"

"No, that's the side benefit; it was more about the six murders and the attempted murder of my family."

"I am sorry, you're losing me … murders, what murders?"

"Let's go over here and visit Major Murphy while I tell you about a war."

We went to the grave of Audie L. Murphy. While the president read the inscription on the headstone, I took a coin out of my pocket and placed it with the others on top of it.

"I know this name," Kathleen said. "Why the coins?" she added.

"Major Audie L. Murphy, America's most highly decorated soldier of the Second World War. As for the coins, it's a tradition here at Arlington. They like to know someone stopped by for a visit. My dad built this special memorial over here to his squadron mates who were lost in Korea."

Kathleen read the inscription on the four-foot-high marble headstone that was standing a few feet away from Audie Murphy's grave, partially shaded by a willow tree that was just starting to turn green in response to the gentle bathing of the spring sun. It bore the outline of a P-51 Mustang fighter plane under which were the words "Still on Patrol" followed by the seventeen names of the pilots who did not make it home from my dad's squadron.

"It is very touching, Mr. Hanson, and a lovely act of kindness by your father to memorialize these men's sacrifice."

"Thank you very much, Madam President. It is probably time I started talking."

"Please do not leave anything out, especially about the murders," she said as we sat down on a bench by the willow tree.

"First of all, Madam President, please call me Jim, and I will call you …"

I paused as she smiled, waiting for my next statement.

"… Madam President."

She laughed, then replied, "Thank you for the courtesy, Jim."

"Now, let me see if I can gather my thoughts here, it has been hard today. The words of a poem keep running through my head."

"I can certainly understand that."

"I guess this all started on the day Jenny drove me in the Camaro to the regional office of the New Times Financial Group …"

" Capitalism is the
  legitimate racket of
  the ruling class."

—Al Capone

CHAPTER 1

Virginia, USA; Present Day

"Remember, Jenny, she isn't like any car you've driven before. She's got lots of power," warned Jim.

"Now listen here, Dad! What is it with guys? Why are cars, boats, and airplanes always 'she'? The car is an 'it.' *It* is not female," Jennifer ranted as she got behind the wheel.

"This 'it' you're referring to is a perfectly restored 1969 Camaro convertible your grandpa and I put a lot of time into. Whether it's an 'it' or a 'she', I don't want it bent," Jim replied as he slid into the passenger seat. "This … let's call it a vehicle, is a lot older than your humble twenty-five years. It has a 454 big-block V8 in it, putting out over 500 horsepower. You need some pointers before we drive off."

"Big-block? Do they call it that because guys who are into cars are usually blockheads?" Jennifer inquired with a cheeky smile.

"I'll answer that one," Dolly said as she walked up to the car.

"Whether it's cars or airplanes, these two are blockheads," she said, gesturing to Jim and Robert, who had just joined them.

"Are we going to stand for that, Dad?" Jim asked.

Robert smiled, hesitating before speaking, as though choosing his words.

"So Jennifer, you're driving our special baby girl today."

Jennifer gave her father an icy stare as he broke out with a wide grin.

"It could be worse, Jenny," Dolly observed. "You could have your name on the side of an airplane, like I do, next to a painting of a half-naked woman."

"C'mon, Mom! I think *Dolly Girl* is a lovely name for a P-51 Mustang fighter, and you've had your name on two of them!"

"Lucky me," was the dry response.

Jennifer turned back to Robert. "That's right, Grandpa. Dad has to go to Freelton for a meeting. My friend Tracey is meeting me there for some shopping."

"That's nice. You girls have fun. I got a letter from my old buddy Steve Fowler and I can't find it. Have any of you seen it?" Robert asked.

Jim, Jennifer, and Dolly exchanged glances.

"I'll help you find it later, dear," Dolly said hurriedly, then leaned over the side of the car and smiled at Jim and Jennifer. "Have fun, you two."

"I'll see you later, Dad. We'll take *Dolly Girl* out," Jim called over Jennifer revving the engine.

With that Jennifer and Jim headed to the highway. It was spring break in Virginia. The cherry blossoms were just starting to come out and the air had that certain scent that only spring could bring. The top was down and the warm sun was on their faces under a radiant blue sky.

"I didn't know what to say about the letter," Jennifer murmured.

"Your grandmother handled it best. It's not good to always be correcting him—it just causes frustration for both us and him. I sure didn't want to be the one to remind him he gave the eulogy at Steve's funeral. Here's the on-ramp, watch your speed, remember we have over 500 horses and if you floor it, that Edelbrock six-pack will …"

Jennifer floored the pedal, shooting the Camaro up the on-ramp and into the right-hand lane, behind a truck. She expertly changed lanes, hammered the accelerator, and passed it at ninety miles per hour.

"Is that a six-pack like Brad Pitt has, Daddy, or one you buy at the grocery store?"

"Okay, Jennifer, very funny. Now back in the right lane before you give me a coronary."

"You sell life insurance, Dad. I figure you have a big policy on yourself. How did you say your heart was?" The smile on her face was ear to ear.

No doubt about, she took after her late mother: the same quick smile, the same bright eyes glinting with a hint of mischief. Jennifer also possessed something else: a brilliant mathematical mind, which had led her into computer sciences and a full scholarship at MIT. Jim and Elizabeth couldn't have been more proud.

Fortunately for Jim, the rest of the trip was uneventful, and they arrived at the New Times regional office, where Tracey and her ten-year-old Toyota were waiting.

"Well, honey, at least Tracey can't do to you what you did to me," Jim quipped, smiling at the sight of the junker.

"Oh yes, she can," Jennifer replied. "Our first stop is the Ferrari dealership for a test drive." She pecked Jim on the cheek. "Thanks for letting me drive."

Jim smiled as he waved to the young ladies, but Jennifer knew it was just for her benefit. She understood how her father loathed sales meetings and the business he was in. She appreciated the fact her dad had left his profession as a photographer—which he loved, but it paid little—for his present one in order to support his family. Jennifer threw him a big wave and smile as she and Tracey left the parking lot.

Jim probably wouldn't have noticed at all if he hadn't managed to drop the car keys while retrieving his briefcase from the backseat. It was very small, only about two inches long and about half an inch wide, but there it was, right behind the left front tire of the car parked next to his Camaro. Jim picked it up and read the label: "Herbert & Hector Data Pal 128 Plus." It was a memory stick, as he called it, better known to the tech whizzes as a flash drive, similar to the one he used to back up his own computer. Not being raised on this computer technology, Jim was confounded by it. It was a world beyond his understanding. The fact something so small could hold the same amount of information as a library was incredible. One of his follow agents must have dropped this one. He'd turn it in at the office.

"Morning, Ralph," a familiar voice said.

"Morning, Sam," Jim replied to the man who just pulled up in his Mercedes-Benz SL550 convertible.

It was a running joke Ted Bayden and Jim shared. Ted and Jim had started with the company at the same time. They always seemed to be the first to arrive at the office in the morning and the last to leave at night. It reminded them of the Ralph and Sam cartoons they'd watched as kids, with Ted playing the part of the calm sheepdog to Jim's cunning wolf.

"It's a beauty, Ted. Did you just get it?" Jim asked as he checked out the lines of the sleek sports car.

"Just picked it up two days ago."

"Business must be good."

"Never better, my friend. Well, I see you and your dad finally finished her," Ted said as he looked over the fine crimson lines of the Detroit classic. "No doubt about it, she's a beauty."

"So, are you looking forward to learning the virtues of New Times's new wonder life insurance policy, the MAX 2000 Universal Life?" Jim asked, sliding the flash drive and his car keys into his coat pocket as he and Ted crossed the parking lot toward the office door.

A sarcastic smile crossed Ted's lips. "You know head office has all the answers to our problems, Jim, so it will be a great meeting."

Jim chuckled dryly. "If only it were so."

When Elizabeth died, Ted and his wife, Martha, had been a great help to Jim in the days following her passing. During the week Jim and the kids took Elizabeth back to Richmond to be buried in the family cemetery, Ted and Martha came over every day to feed and walk Rusty, their Dachshund, water the plants, and look after their home.

Elizabeth had been so much more than a great wife and mother; she had been a solid, steadying influence in Jim's life. She had given to the community. She'd been a great supporter of Habitat for Humanity, helping the underprivileged build their own homes. Many weekends had found Jim and Elizabeth alongside his Uncle George and Aunt Rachel out on the job site, building a house. Tragically, his uncle had lost his dear wife of fifty-two years to the same cancer that stole his Elizabeth two months after her passing.

As Elizabeth had grown weaker, Jim took more and more time away from his business—not only to support her, but to care for her. Elizabeth had always been the strong one, but as she became more frail, Jim knew he had to adopt her strength to get the family through this terrible time. Finally, after three agonizing years, while Jim gently rocked her in his arms, she passed away, but not before whispering to him something that touched him deep down, in a place that had been secret even to him.

"Jim, you have so much love in you. Don't wait too long."

Jim returned to a business in shambles. He almost had to sell the family home to make ends meet. With all the memories of the last couple of years attached to it, there were times he wished he had. As fortune would have it, his parents were looking to downsize and moved in with him and their grandchildren. With his dad ill, it proved a good move.

"How are Jennifer and Jason doing these days?" Ted inquired.

"I'll have to send them a text and find out," Jim replied. Ted quirked an inquisitive brow.

Jim shook his head. "They've got their faces stuck to their computer screens 24/7 these days. Being in college was never like this for us, Ted. We at least took time to drink beer and chase girls. All kids do today is date their computers and text on their cell phones."

"I think all I did was drink beer in college," Ted said, laughing as he patted his ample stomach. "I left the chasing girls part to good-looking guys with all the money," he added as they opened the door and entered the foyer.

"So, which one of you do I bug to sell the first Max 2000 policy?" Janice Collins asked as she approached them.

"I didn't think it was your job to bug us about sales, Janice," Ted replied. "I thought that was Sharon's job."

"Yeah, it is. But I'm her assistant, and I can bug you too. Unless tribute is paid."

"Thank God, I have tribute!" Jim exclaimed in mock relief, opening his briefcase and removing a one-pound Hershey chocolate bar. Janice's eyes went as wide as saucers; she was a notorious chocoholic.

"Take me, Jim, I'm yours," Janice laughed and licked her lips. "Ted, buy a Max policy on yourself if you have to. Jim, you don't have to be first. You're off the hook," she informed them, raising the chocolate bar up high like a trophy and retreating to her office.

"You must have been a great Boy Scout: always prepared," Ted observed.

Jim raised his hand with three fingers up as a response.

"Let me guess, Eagle Scout?"

"You got it."

"I got to see Sharon before the meeting. Let's grab a coffee next door after."

"Works for me Ted, especially if you're buying," Jim retorted.

*
**

"Two coffees, black," Jim said to the waitress as they sat down following the meeting.

"Make mine with a jelly donut," Ted added as she darted off.

"You look like you've got a lot on your mind, Ted."

Ted paused as the donut and coffees were delivered. He watched the waitress head back to the counter, then said, "Jim, do you feel we've done good work for our clients?"

"I think most of us do."

"How about the management team?"

Jim raised his eyebrows. "Yeah, things have sure changed since we got sold."

"Damn right they've changed, Jim. Now everything is about shareholder value. Make a profit, to hell with service. Keep the money coming so the management team can line its pockets!"

"Ted, I'm not a big fan of stock options. It's nice when everyone in the company gets the right to buy stock in the company at below market-value. But when it's just the management team, and they're buying for pennies on the dollar, just to flip it for full value and make lucrative profits, it's an abuse of the system. So yes, Ted, we're living in an Enron world. Too many companies are being ripped off by their managers and their directors do nothing about it. What's your point?"

"So when do we get ours, Jim?

"What do you mean?"

Ted's expression steeled. "Look at the average working man. If he isn't being laid off because his job has been sent offshore, then his company is cutting his health benefits and stealing his pension—if he even had one."

"I know. There's been too much of that going on. But what does this have to do with 'getting ours?'"

"Are we really doing our clients a favor by keeping their money in this country? You and I both have been successful selling both life insurance and mutual funds. We're both certified financial planners. Most of our clients depend on us for all their financial needs. Maybe it's time we help them, by helping ourselves."

"You want to take our clients' money out of the States?"

"In the next few years, trillions of dollars will be passing down from the old generation to the baby boomers. On top of that, the boomers will be unloading their big houses to downsize as their kids leave home, creating more wealth. We can't stop taxation on all of it, but if we leave it here, the government and their corporate buddies will find ways to get their hands on it."

"Ted, you're talking about tax evasion here. They put you in jail for that, you know."

"I prefer the term tax avoidance: avoiding the government stealing my hard-earned money and pissing it away making a few congressmen and their buddies rich. We deserve something out of this too, Jim. Let's get ours while there's still something to get."

"How do we do that?"

"There are firms that have offshore accounts and they pay a very good commission."

"We'll have to take this up later when I have more time." Jim glanced at his watch. "But I think you're playing with fire and I don't wanna get burned, especially not now."

"I understand. No doubt about it, you've had a rough go of it the last couple of years, what with Elizabeth passing, and now your dad being sick. How is he, anyway?"

"He has his good and his bad days. But there's no cure for Alzheimer's and it's a cruel disease, destroying the mind before the body. He'll eventually have to go to a home. It could get to the point where he doesn't recognize me anymore."

Jim found himself suddenly feeling all alone at this thought, the same way he had when Elizabeth died. Ted dropped a few crumpled bills on the table and they stood to leave.

"Right now, he's upset about giving up his flying license. He can't fly *Dolly Girl*, so I've been taking him up in it every once in a while. Seems to make him happy."

"I thought the Mustang was a single-seat fighter."

Jim looked confused for a moment. "Oh, that's right, you've never been up in it. You've been in the two trainers—the Stearman and the Texan—but not the Mustang. We took out the middle long-range fuel tank and the old radio equipment to make room for a small rear seat. I'll have to take you up. But if you keep eating those jelly donuts, I don't know if you'll fit."

They laughed and said their goodbyes, Ralph and Sam again, and headed to their cars. As Jim pulled out of the parking lot, he gave Ted a final wave. Ted paused with a hand on the door of his Benz and waved back.

"Do you think we have another recruit?" a voice from behind Ted asked as he opened his door.

"Too early to tell."

"His clients have over a hundred million on deposit with us. We need him on board, 'Sam.'"

"Don't push. I'm working on it." Ted slammed the car door and sped off.

Ted and Jim weren't gone five minutes when two people rushed out of the office and started to search the parking lot, looking under cars and on the boulevard.

"How could you let this happen? It's your only job! Watch and carry the stick!"

"It has to be here somewhere! I couldn't have lost it."

"You better pray to God you haven't. Culper depends on these memory sticks. That's what gives our clients the sense of privacy they like. But now it's lost and can't be replaced."

"What do you mean, can't be replaced? We'll just call La Vella and get another update."

"Call La Vella! Have you lost your mind? They don't tolerate mistakes like this! They bury mistakes like this! Now find the stick!"

"I wonder what they were looking for?" Dominique Deselva looked at his buddy Jake.

"I dunno, but I got it all," Jake Connors replied, hefting up a Nikon camera equipped with a large telephoto lens. He and Dom were in a small office across the street from the New Times building.

"Did you get the plate on that Camaro?"

"No problem." Jake checked the images on the camera's viewing screen. "Nice ride. You know, I think I've seen this guy before."

"Better call it in and find out who it belongs to. I'm sure McWilliams will be glad to find out we may have a new player in this case."

"Dom, how long have you been in the FBI?"

"About ten years."

"Have you ever known the regional director to be *happy* when a case got more complicated?"

"Jim, are you okay?" Kathleen's voice brought me back to the present. I had been staring at the amphitheater.

"I am sorry, Madam President, I just got lost in thought thinking back on that day and the drive home. The conversation with Ted Bayden bothered me and it wasn't the part about the offshore accounts."

Kathleen raised an eyebrow.

"It was in that conversation I first vocalized my worst fear: my father would soon forget all about us. The little league games he'd watched me pitch, the hiking and boating we did when he was an Eagle Scout leader, but especially the flying. There was always the flying. As you know, Uncle George flew Mustangs with my dad in Korea. He bought two surplus in the 1960s and they became the terror of the air show circuit for years, putting on dogfight displays. As for me, I was the envy of every ramp rat out there. How many teenagers get to fly war birds?"

Kathleen was listening very intently. Her face had softened from its earlier combative state. She was truly lovely, a fact I was starting to find distracting.

"I'm sorry, Madam President, I digress."

"Don't be sorry, Jim. I understand fully. So the FBI already had this company under observation."

"I wish they'd come out of hiding and arrested me. Maybe it would have prevented me from making the biggest mistake of my life."

The president leaned forward, looking very concerned.

"What was that, Jim?"

"The flash drive. I gave it to Jason …"

*
**

As Jim opened the door to his house, Rusty ran to greet him with his usual sloppy "hello." Dolly followed him down the hall.

"He's always glad to see you," she said.

"Sometimes, he's the only one. Where is everyone?"

"Jim, you know that's not true. Your father is still napping and the 'net-o-holic is in his usual place. And on such a beautiful day, I might add."

"I hear ya," Jim replied, shaking his head and reaching into his jacket pocket to grab his car keys. He wrapped his hand around something small and metal. The memory stick! He'd forgotten to hand it in!

Jim went into his office. Jim loved his office, partly because his father had helped him install the rich oak paneling, but mostly because of the special photographs hanging from the walls. Not only were there some reproductions from his favorite photographer, Ansel Adams, but others that Jim had taken himself. It was nice, at certain times, to come in here, pour himself a scotch, sit back, and enjoy the rich black-and-white tones of the lovely prints. But today, his sanctity has been invaded. Jason was perched at the desk, typing on his notebook computer.

"Hi Jason. I've got something here you may find interesting." Jim handed him the flash drive.

"Hi Dad. Oh, for me? You shouldn't have. It's not even my birthday."

"It's not a gift. I found it in the agency parking lot. I thought you might be able to look at what's on it. Maybe the owner's name is there somewhere; that way I can return it."

"Are you sure it's not a gift? This one's expensive."

"Really?"

"Yes, Father. Let me introduce you to the Hector & Herbert Data Pal 128 Plus, the Rolex of flash drives. A hundred and twenty-eight gigs of memory, stainless steel impact resistant case, which is …" He pulled the cap off with a pop, "… both dust- and water-proof."

"You sound like you sell these things."

"No, dear Father. I just like to be well-informed, unlike other people in this room …"

Jason was quite the satirical wit. They would often verbally spar with each other like this. Jim had always enjoyed Jason's sense of humor and Jason reveled when Jim played the straight man for him. But Jason had become more solemn and withdrawn after his mother's passing. Jim had tried to talk with him more, but he usually got one-word answers. It was just in the last year that Jason was starting to come around.

"A gig. Isn't that what musicians call a job?"

Jason rolled his eyes in disbelief. "No, Father." Jim went from "Dad" to "Father" whenever Jason swung into the role of a teacher with a particularly dumb student. "Gig is short for gigabyte. Say it with me now, gig-a-byte. Which is one thousand megabytes. In simple terms, you could store a thousand books in one gigabyte of memory. This thing can store a hundred and twenty-eight thousand books."

"And to think there's a whole library in that itty-bitty thing there," Jim drawled in his best hillbilly accent, putting his hands on his hips. "What'll they think up next?"

Jason just shook his head as he plugged the stick into one of the USB ports and clicked the computer icon. "Okay, I now have an E drive. Let's see what's on here," Jason murmured, clicking his mouse again.

Jim peered over Jason's shoulder as two icons popped up. One was labeled "Photos"; the other was an archive file. Jason clicked on the photo file and up came two photographs of Italian sports cars, complemented by scantily clad models.

"Wow. Is that ever beautiful," Jason exclaimed. "And the Ferrari and Lambo look pretty good too. I dunno who owns this stick, but they've great taste."

"Stop ogling the ladies. What about the file with the zipper through it?" Jim asked.

"Encrypted," Jason said.

"Is that bad?" Jim asked, hoping playing "dumb" would really get Jason going.

"It means, Father, you don't get to peek inside that folder unless you have the key. The password. Understand?"

"You mean it's like if you belong to one of those secret societies, and have to knock three times on the door and say 'Homer sent me?'"

"Sit down, Father, and I'll explain encryption to you."

Jim took a chair as Jason wandered over to the whiteboard on the office wall. He picked up a marker and scrawled "encryption" on it. "Encryption, Father, is the term used to encode some data, or in simpler terms, make text unreadable. In order to read the data, it must first be decoded. The process involves a key, which is only known to the sender and the receiver of the data. That brings me to cryptography, which is the process of encryption and decryption. Let's start with the Caesar Cipher, named after Julius Caesar, who used it. It's one of the best examples of early cryptography."

"Caesar. Wasn't he the guy who invented the salad?" Jim tried to keep a straight face.

"I'll ignore that one. Here's how it works."

"Am I going to have to sit through two thousand years of history to learn about encryption?"

"You sire a history major, you suffer the consequences," Jason replied. He scribbled out the alphabet twice; the second one started with the last two letters of the alphabet:

A B C D E F G H I J K L M N O P Q R S T V W X Y Z
Y Z A B C D E F G H I J K L M N O P Q R S T V W X

"Judging by that last alphabet, I'd say you flunked Sesame Street 101 and I wasted a lot of money on your education," Jim chuckled.

"I'll continue," Jason said stoically. "Now we write our message."

Jim bristled as Jason wrote "Photography is not an art."

"You can see I've lined up the two alphabets, but they're two letters out of sync. For every letter in our message appearing in the top line, we write down the corresponding letter from the bottom one. Therefore our message becomes ..."

He jotted something else on the board.

NFMRMEPYNFW GQ LMR YL YPR

"Our message is now encrypted, and the key is the number two. By moving two letters forward in the alphabet, and using the key to encrypt the data, we created an algorithm. In this case, we're substituting one letter for another, which is two along the alphabet. If the person receiving our message has our key and uses the algorithm, they can decrypt our message."

"In all seriousness, Jason, this code seems easy to break," Jim observed.

"It is, but what if you changed the algorithm so that for the first letter the key was six, the second, nineteen, the third, thirteen, and so on."

"But with a computer, you must be able to make more complicated codes, way more complex than this," Jim said.

"Which brings me to World War II and Bletchley Park!" Jason announced triumphantly.

"I did it again, didn't I, Jason?" Jim groaned, his face pinched in mock agony. He'd probably just set Jason off on another historical lecture.

"You always do, Father."

In fact, Jim was proud of his son, even if the lectures pained him. Jason's interest in world history was insatiable. In a subject Jim and many others found boring, Jason found solace and possible answers to the problems of the present day. He was always pointing out historical parallels to current news stories. His favorite quote was from President Truman: "There is nothing new in this world, just history you have not read yet."

"At the beginning of the Second World War, Nazi Germany had a coding machine they called the Enigma. It looked like a typewriter, but was actually a complex electromechanical cipher machine. You typed your message in and as each key was pressed, it went through a number of spinning rotors, which substituted different letters, just like the Caesar code does. This would have meant a fancier, but still very breakable, substitution cipher. However, when they added eight rotors and some electronics, they came up with a polyalphabetic substitution cipher."

"A poly what now?" Jim scratched his head.

"Let's put it this way: a much more complicated situation. The Germans thought Enigma was unbreakable. They put the odds at billions to one of anyone breaking it. Which brings me to Bletchley Park."

"Where is that Jason?" Jim asked, getting up to get a cola. "Would you like something?"

"Not while I'm lecturing." They both laughed. "Bletchley Park is in England. The Poles had already being working on breaking Enigma before the war. In fact, they had even built some deciphering machines called Bombes. By the time Poland was attacked by the Nazis, the Poles were reading seventy-five percent of the German military radio traffic. They managed to get their decoding technology out to England before they were occupied. The British set up a special code breaking center at a place called Bletchley Park."

"So did the Brits do as good as the Poles?" Jim sipped on his drink thoughtfully.

"They had to. The Germans made Enigma even more complex. The British brought in everyone they had that could work on ciphers: cryptologists, mathematicians, even people whose only claim to fame was they were good at doing the London Times' crossword puzzles. By the war's end, over ten thousand people had worked on the project known only as Ultra."

"So how did they do?" Jim repeated, and then stared at the bottom of his empty glass.

"They built better deciphering machines and were soon reading some of the German signals even before the German commanders were. But the British were after the big prize: Lorenz."

"Okay, Jason, give me a clue."

"Lorenz was Hitler's personal cipher, which he used to communicate with his High Command. It was very complex and required the building of a very sophisticated deciphering machine, which they named Colossus. The machine they ended up with was bigger than this room, weighed over a ton, and had over 2,300 vacuum tubes in it. A fellow of your advanced age should remember those."

All Jim could do was fix Jason with an icy stare as he got up to refill his glass.

"In the end, it worked and probably shortened the war by two years. It also gave the British something else."

Jim gave Jason an inquisitive look now.

"One of the world's first programmable electronic computers."

"I suppose modern computers have encryptions that are unbreakable," Jim said.

"Just the opposite, Dad. Anything can be cracked."

Jim stopped refilling his glass and stared at Jason for moment with a look of disbelief. "How so?"

"Look at what goes over the 'net. A software company comes out with a new program. Within days, it's available on the 'net, along with the 'cracks' to break their encryptions so you can steal it. But people should be more concerned about their computers being hacked and their identities being stolen. Same with businesses and their records, even if they are encrypted. There are programs out there to break any encryption on anyone's computer. But the easy way to attack a person's computer is not to break the encryption, but to get their passwords, which you can find on the computer. That's why you should never use obvious passwords, like your kids' names or the street you live on, or your birthday."

"So what can you do with this memory stick?" Jim asked.

"Well, the expert on anything computer-related is Jenny. I'll forward her the files and let her have a go at them if no one at your office claims the stick." Jason copied the files onto his computer and returned the stick to Jim.

"I hope you're not gonna spend the whole of spring break working on that essay about those two Canadian doctors. You're allowed to have some fun," Jim said.

Jason was working on an essay about "unsung heroes of history." He'd chosen the doctors who had discovered insulin, Frederick Banting and Charles Best.

Jason shrugged. "I should be done in a couple of days."

"Well, good luck. I'm off to the airport with your grandfather. Thanks for the lecture."

"Feel free to come and drink at the fountain of knowledge anytime."

After Jim left, Jason forwarded the files to Jennifer with the message "Brilliant Historian to Geek-Head, see if you can crack this one. If you know any of the women in the car photos, I want names and phone numbers."

Later that day, Jennifer would forward Jason's challenge to her classmate at MIT, Angie Borello; and to a colleague at the University of Waterloo in Canada, Steven Bertrand. Steven then forwarded it to a friend at the Institut National des Sciences Appliquées in Lyon, France, Gerard Tremblay; all challenging each other to be the first to break the encryption.

"So you see, Madam President, it all started with a simple challenge, but within a week, this challenge would prove fatal for three of them."

"What are you saying, Jim? Something on this flash drive killed people? That sounds fantastic, utterly unbelievable."

I had to get up and walk around for a moment. The sun was high now, just past noon. I could hear the birds chirping while the occasional squirrel ran to fetch some lunch then scramble up a tree. I found myself staring down at the Audie Murphy's grave.

"In some ways, it was a bit simpler for you wasn't it, Audie? When you jumped up on that burning tank destroyer and used the turret 50 cal to hold off the German infantry so your men could retreat, you could see your enemy. We couldn't see ours; we didn't even know we had one."

"I am sorry Jim, I'm not following you."

"Ever heard of the Trojan war, Madam President?"

Jason Hanson had all the abilities to be a fine historian. If someone asked him about the Trojan war, he could have given you all the details of this piece of ancient Greek mythology, including how the ancient Greeks had built a giant wooden horse and left it outside the city of Troy. The Trojans brought the horse inside the cities walls, thinking it was a prize. Of course, hidden inside the horse were Greek warriors, who crept out in the middle of the night and captured the city, making Trojan the perfect name for the virus now in Jason's computer. If Jason had checked the size of the photo files, he might have noticed they were unusually large. That was because they weren't ordinary photographs. They were *steganographs*, photographs with data hidden inside them. As Jason and Jim talked, one of these modern electronic warriors came out of the photos and scouted Jason's computer. Not discovering the keys it was programmed to find, it moved itself and a large file of other viruses out of the photos, squirreling themselves away on Jason's computer, avoiding the anti-virus programs. There they would wait, as the Greeks of old did, for the proper time to strike.

" It is well enough that people of the nation do not understand our banking and monetary system, for if they did, I believe there would be a revolution before tomorrow morning."

— Henry Ford

CHAPTER 2

It was a quiet ride to the airport for Jim and Robert. Jim had observed that his dad had become quieter as the months rolled on. Today, he was dressed as usual for flying: brown leather flight jacket and his "lucky"white silk scarf, adorned with bright green shamrocks, protruding from the collar. But he sat in silence, just looking out the window of the car, as the Virginia countryside rolled by.

"Sure is a beautiful day to go flying, Dad," Jim volunteered.

"Sure is, Jimmy. I was just saying to Elizabeth this morning, today is a great day to go flying. Your mother agreed too."

Jim tensed up. "I don't think you were talking to Elizabeth, Dad."

Jim regretted his statement almost instantly; the look of confusion that crossed the older man's face was almost painful. Then Robert got agitated. "Yes, of course," he huffed. "I'm sorry, Jimmy. I meant … It must have been Jenny. Damn this memory of mine! Bastards took away my flying license, can't remember stuff. And people are starting to bug me about things. Even when I know I've taken my pills, your mother will say I haven't! The other day, I got a letter from my old buddy Steve Fowler. I put it on my dresser. Now it's not there. I asked your mother about it and she says she never even saw a letter for me."

Jim had already broken the cardinal rule in dealing with someone with Alzheimer's: it usually wasn't worth correcting them because it upset the patient. Jim generally just ignored Dad's errors. He was ignoring the fact Robert had called him "Jimmy" today, like he had when Jim was five. He wasn't going to mention that Steve Fowler had been dead for six years.

"It's okay, Dad. We'll look for the letter tomorrow. Today, we have a date with *Dolly Girl*!"

Fenton County Airport was a small affair. It was designed to handle small, private aircraft. Jim drove toward the control center and was just in time to see George Grayson pull up in his golf cart. After a distinguished career as a lawyer and then judge, George had retired to teach law part-time. He spent his spare time flying. After his wife, Rachel, died, George had spent more and more time at the airport. Besides keeping his own aircraft in top condition, he was around to help anyone who was having trouble. So much was he appreciated by "the airport crowd," that everyone had chipped in to buy him a golf cart for his eightieth birthday.

"Just what I needed!" George exclaimed as Jim and Robert stepped out of the car. "Someone to buy me a coffee!"

"I think it's your turn to buy, Uncle George," Jim retorted, shaking George's outstretched hand.

"He hasn't bought a coffee in twenty years," Robert added.

"Now sir!" George cried in an exaggerated Southern drawl. "As a gentle-man, those statements appear to be impugning on my honor. If this be the case, my seconds will be calling."

As they headed into the coffee shop, which was part of the control center, the good-natured debate between George and Robert as to who had bought more coffee over the years continued. By the time they sat down, George threw up his hands in mock despair, crying, "All right, Bob, you win, just like you always did in court. I therefore capitulate to the coffee question before the court and agree to a fine of one round of coffee."

Jim was happy to see his dad laugh. He was very touched by the gentle way in which George handled conversation with his old friend. He seemed to make it a point not to bring up events from the past unless Robert did. One could easily see George was not going to do or say anything that would embarrass his friend.

It had always been fun for Jim to be around his dad and Uncle George. They had always been blessed with good health and looked twenty years younger than most men pushing hard on ninety. Every year they'd passed the physicals to keep their pilots licenses. Well, every year except this year, when his dad didn't get his. Jim felt guilty about this, for it was he who'd informed the medical board about his father's memory issues, which had led to investigations and the diagnosis of Alzheimer's. Jim knew he'd done the right thing, but it hurt to see how not being able to fly broke Dad's heart. To help, he made it a point to take Dad flying whenever possible.

They'd just started their coffees when Jim saw something that surprised him. From their table, he could see through the glass wall of the coffee shop to the front counter of the control center. Sharon Turner was there, filing a flight plan. Excusing himself from the table, Jim trotted over to the counter. "Hey Sharon," he called as he approached.

Sharon whipped about. The look of surprise on her face was the first genuine expression he'd ever seen on it. She'd taken over as the agency branch manager five months ago after the previous manager, Frank Belarus, died. Jim found her cold; the typical "head office" type: the lips smiled, but the eyes never did. He never knew what she was thinking.

"Why, hello, Jim. How nice to run into you," Sharon said, regaining her composure. She still looked like a child who had just got caught with their hand in the cookie jar.

"What brings you out to our little airport, Sharon?"

That cold smile again. "Well, you're not the only flyer in our office, Jim."

"I didn't know you flew. You should've said something. We've got a really active flying club here. I could introduce you around."

"Thank you, Jim. I'll have to take you up on that sometime. So, why are you here and not out selling our new Max Life?" Sharon kept smiling, but her eyes were still dead.

"I'm taking my father up for a ride in that Mustang over there." Jim pointed to *Dolly Girl* out on the tarmac.

"Well, you've a nice day for it. Look, I have to run, Jim. Enjoy your flight." With that, she rushed out the door and across the tarmac to a Piper Twin Comanche.

Jim meandered back to the coffee shop. Robert looked at him expectantly as he flopped into his seat.

"Who was that?" Robert asked at last.

Jim could see that his father was hoping it was someone he didn't know.

"You haven't met her, Dad. She's the new manager where I work."

"That is interesting, Jim," George said. "Her name, Bob, is Sharon Turner and besides being a beautiful woman, she is one hell of a pilot."

"She is?" Robert asked.

Jim leaned forward so as not to miss a word.

"How do you know that, Uncle George?"

"Remember about three weeks ago, when we had that big storm?"

"I sure do, that was the day my car decided to die," Jim replied.

"As you know, the Piper Twin Comanche, like she flies, isn't designed to fly in the weather we had that day. It's mostly for the amateur pilot market, so you can imagine our surprise when about three in the afternoon, we're about to close 'er up 'cause of the high winds, and the tower gets a call from a Comanche requesting immediate clearance. They tried to send her to another airport where the winds weren't as bad, but she said she was outta fuel and coming in. We all held our breath as we watched her land."

Jim and Robert held their breath as George took another sip of his coffee.

"I tell you, she did something I thought you couldn't do in that plane. She slipped it in for a perfect landing."

"You're kidding!" Jim exclaimed.

"I wouldn't have believed it if I hadn't seen it," George stated. "She stuck the nose of that Comanche into the wind so it wouldn't flip over, then flew it sideways down the runway to slow down, and then turned and dropped it for as good a landing as you're ever gonna see."

He shook his head. "Well, I hopped into my cart and drove out to meet her, get her out of the rain. She was carrying a small aluminum case. I went to take it from her, but she wouldn't let go of it. I congratulated on her landing, but she just shrugged it off, like it was a walk in the park. Another thing …"

George paused while he drained his cup.

"The next day while we were cleaning the place up, Johnny, our fuel guy, gets a call to gas up her plane. I noticed him doing it when I went for a coffee, but he was still doing it when I returned. So I asked him about it and he tells me it holds twice as much gas as a regular Comanche, and then he tells me to check out the engines. Her plane is like having a Toyota Camry with a V8 under the hood and extra gas tanks in the trunk and backseat. If her name was Lindberg, she could fly it to Paris. The landing gear has extra reinforcing too."

The waitress came by to refill the coffee cups and to chat with Robert and George, a conversation Jim did not join as he was watching Sharon Turner out the window. He observed her do a thorough pre-flight check of her Comanche, which was parked near *Dolly Girl*. There was something about the confident way she moved around the plane, checking out the engines, landing gear, and control surfaces that evidenced an experienced pilot. At last, she taxied out and took off, and, despite the crosswind, the plane never flinched. Jim now knew he had been watching a professional pilot.

After coffee, Jim and Robert went out to do their own pre-flight check of *Dolly Girl*. Robert worked with Jim as they checked the control surfaces and landing gear. Jim made it a point to ask his dad his opinion of the condition of the P-51D model Mustang's many components. Robert's opinion was so concise and correct, it almost belied the fact he was suffering from a disease that would soon rob him of the ability to make these judgments. However, that was not today. Today, Jim would make sure his dad was shown the respect of being asked his opinion and having that opinion valued. Jim helped his dad up onto the port wing and into the small rear seat, a position he was still not accustomed to as evidenced by his fussing with the seat and harness. They put on their headsets and were ready for the final checks.

"Hey, Dad," Jim said into the microphone. "Want to take me through the cockpit check and engine start up?"

"You got it, son, know it by heart," was the reply in Jim's headset.

The instructions started to come swiftly and accurately.

"Ignition switch off, set parking brake, generator and battery switch to ON, open throttle one inch, mixture control in IDLE CUT-OFF ..."

Some nineteen instructions in all and Robert did not miss one, a fact that made Jim beam with pride. The last command was the one they had always greatly anticipated no matter who was in the pilot's seat:

"Lift guard on starter switch and press switch to START."

With that, the big, four-bladed Hamilton-Standard propeller started to turn. As the third blade crossed the wind screen, the Packard-built Rolls-Royce Merlin engine came to life, placing over 1,500 horsepower at Jim's command. Jim radioed for clearance, and in a few minutes, *Dolly Girl* was lifting off the runway into a Virginia sky so blue one would think Jim and Robert ordered it. They climbed to about 5,000 feet and were enjoying looking down at Virginia, roused from a long winter slumber, transforming to fields of green crisscrossed with blue streams and rivers, when their tranquility was interrupted by a loud voice roaring over their headsets.

"BANG, BANG! YOU'RE DEAD!"

Jim looked to his right and what he saw sitting off his starboard wing was something he knew was going to cause trouble. It was another Mustang, but this one bore the name *Lady Rachel*. It was clearly identified by the painting on its nose: a beautiful, black-haired woman in a shapely, flowing gown. Their headphones became live again.

"Bob, I thought you raised that kid of yours up right. But here I am able to come right up on his six and cut him a new one." George chuckled.

"Jimmy, we're not going to stand for that, are we?"

"Not for one second, Dad," exclaimed Jim as he hit the radio transmission button.

"Uncle George, prepare to get a good ole Virginia ass-whuppin," Jim called out as he rolled *Dolly Girl* into a dive.

The battle was now on. For the rest of the afternoon, *Dolly Girl* and *Lady Rachel* put on a display of dogfighting that was a pleasure for those who witnessed it. Robert was in the fight and Jim loved it. All Jim could hear in his headset were instructions.

"Watch it, Jimmy, he's coming in at ten o'clock high!"

"Break right, Jimmy, he's back on your six!"

At last, the fuel gauges said it was time to end the combat and head for home.

"Isn't that just like George Grayson," Kathleen remarked. "He wanted to make the afternoon extra special for you. You know, I owe him my career. The hours he spent with me going over different points of law when I was his clerk …"

Kathleen was standing on the pathway as she shook her head, reflecting and looking back up the pathway to where my family was sitting by the graveside.

"I believe you were the daughter he never had."

She looked down. A moment later her eyes met mine and I could see they had moistened; my remark had touched her.

"As I said before, he is the father I never had. It's a shame he and Rachel never could have children of their own, but with the Hansons around, he's not short of family. I know you're not actually related, so it's especially nice you call him your uncle."

"Growing up, they were always my aunt and uncle. As far as I am concerned, they were always family."

She smiled at me as she nodded her head. Those eyes were speaking again, this time with words of approval.

"Well, Madam President, back to that afternoon ..."

All of a sudden, I could not speak; I was standing there with my mouth half-open. When the words finally came, I didn't remember formulating them.

"It was the last time my dad and I flew together."

It just happened. I couldn't control it; I started to cry. I quickly turned away from the president, striding over to the memorial and leaning on the cool, strong stone for support. I wasn't able to control my tears. After a moment, I felt an arm around my shoulders; I then heard Kathleen's voice, softer and gentler than before.

"You haven't had any time to mourn, have you?"

"I guess not. Look, I'm sorry—"

"Don't you dare apologize, Jim!"

I was starting to regain my composure. She led me back to the bench. We sat very close to each other and she actually held my hand.

"What just happened there?" Dolly asked.

"I think Jim got upset, but he appears to be doing okay now," George stated.

"It looks like the president is holding his hand," observed Jennifer.

"This is starting to look promising," added Jason. "Isn't there a swimming pool in the White House?"

"Jason!" shouted three voices in unison.

*
**

We sat on the bench for a few moments, neither of us speaking. Most people, when dealing with a distraught person, would tend to look away from them, perhaps embarrassed or not wanting to make the other person uncomfortable. This was not the case with Kathleen Galbraith. She looked right at me, as if wanting to share my feelings while comforting me with her touch. I was looking into those eyes again, and now I saw my sorrow mirrored there.

"Jim, as I said before, I know this is the wrong time and place for us to talk. I shouldn't be intruding on your grief like this. I—"

"Perhaps it isn't the best time," I said, "but it is the best place. In fact, it is the only place that truly understands."

"I'm not sure I'm following, Jim."

"You don't always get to choose the time and place for your battles, but when they come, there can be no substitution for victory. Major Murphy here understood this and certainly the man we laid to rest here today understood it too. All of those here understand. Unfortunately, sometimes a battle can start and you don't even know it's started, as it did on that afternoon ..."

*
**

Jim, George, and Robert were back at the airport enjoying some cold drinks, but the dogfighting was never over. It had been going on for years, and showed no signs of ending.

"How can you possibly say you won this afternoon? I got the drop on you from the first and never let it go," exclaimed George.

"Jimmy got out of that sneak attack of yours in a second and waxed your ass," Robert retorted.

"Are you accusing this gentleman of doing something sneaky?!" George responded in his mock Southern accent. "For if you are, sir, you know the dire consequences of such a remark!"

"I do?"

It was not certain whether it was Robert's intention to make a joke or not, but they all broke out laughing, with Robert laughing the hardest. The laughing quickly stopped as a woman approached the table.

"It sounds like there's been some serious dogfighting going on around here this afternoon," Sharon Turner said.

Jim quickly recovered from his surprise at seeing her again and introduced Sharon to his father, who shook her hand then proceeded to stare at her.

"My dad and I were just giving my uncle here a lesson on the finer points of dogfighting," Jim said.

"Now don't you start, Jim. Please join us, Sharon," George offered. "Can we get you something?"

Sharon sat down and ordered a coke, while Robert seemed to continue studying her.

"I take it I shouldn't ask who won this afternoon's combat," Sharon said.

"Probably a good idea," George volunteered.

"So, Mr. Hanson, you and Mr. Grayson flew Mustangs in Korea?" Sharon asked, taking a sip of her soda.

Robert paused before answering.

"That's right. I got shot down."

"I am very sorry to hear that, Mr. Hanson."

"Got tricked, the Russians had that new jet of theirs out ... can't think of the name, swept-back wings ..."

"The MIG 15," Sharon volunteered.

"Got jumped by a bunch of them just south of the Yalu River. Lost most of my men and I crash landed in *Dolly Girl*."

Jim and George squirmed in their seats; they hoped Sharon would drop the war talk quickly, as this could upset Robert. Sharon, however, surprised Jim by showing some sincerity in her next statement.

"I am very sorry for your loss, Mr. Hanson. Further, I want to thank you and Mr. Grayson for your service to our country."

"Thank you very much for that, Sharon," George responded, touched by the comment. "You're most welcome."

Robert did not reply at first; he continued to stare at Sharon. When he did speak, it surprised everyone at the table.

"You're a fighter pilot," he said.

Jim and George exchanged worried glances, both thinking Robert's illness was affecting what he was saying.

"I beg your pardon, Mr. Hanson?" Sharon replied, her big, brown eyes showing genuine surprise.

"You're a fighter pilot," Robert repeated.

They stared at each other like two gun fighters, each waiting for the other to make the first move. It was Sharon who shot first.

"That was a long time ago, Mr. Hanson."

"Really, Sharon! What did you fly?" Jim asked.

"F-16s."

"Wow, that's a hot fighter!" George exclaimed.

"As I said, that was a long time ago," Sharon reiterated, then added, "I have to get going. Thank you for the drink."

Sharon shook hands all around, then left.

"What do you make of that, Jim?" George asked.

Jim stared down into his glass, stirring the ice cubes with his straw, then tilted his head and looked up at George.

"I don't know, but there's a story there for sure. How did you know she was a fighter pilot, Dad?"

Robert had both hands on his glass while transfixed with the black liquid within. He then looked up at his son with great concern.

"I didn't say something wrong, did I?"

"No, Dad, you didn't," Jim said, shaking his head. "Just surprised us."

Robert let out a big sigh before saying, "Just a hunch, Jimmy. But I know one thing for sure: that woman has seen a lot of pain."

Jim and George exchanged knowing glances. They both knew—from their extensive investigation of Alzheimer's after Robert was diagnosed— that people with the disease could have great moments of insight and clarity. They both felt this was one of them. They left the coffee shop, and, after saying their goodbyes, George got in his golf cart and left, while Robert and

Jim headed for the parking lot. As they walked, they saw Sharon Turner examining *Dolly Girl*. She ran her hand along the wing edge and then just stopped and looked at her.

"She's quite the beauty, isn't she?" Jim said as he and Robert walked up to her.

"She certainly is. First P-51 I've seen up close."

"Care to sit in her?" Jim asked.

"You bet!"

Jim helped Sharon and his dad get up on the port wing, then he ran around to the starboard. Sharon climbed into the cockpit. Jim noticed her right hand fell automatically on the joystick while her left quickly found the throttle.

"Where's the gun sight?" Sharon asked.

"We took it out," Jim responded. "It's large and blocks the front windscreen."

"I noticed the gun barrels sticking out of the wings are wooden dowels. You should give this lady back her claws, guys. She is a fighter, after all."

"C'mon, Sharon, all the extra weight of six 50 cal. Brownings and a big gun sight blocking the windshield. What's the point?" Jim asked.

"We just fly it because it is a great airplane," Robert added.

"But what made it a great airplane was the fact it was a great fighter," Sharon stated.

"I think you got that the wrong way around," Jim replied.

"However it may be, Jim. I see, Mr. Hanson, that you have nine little red stars on the side of this Mustang, making you one short of double ace. You did your killing the way it should be done, Mr. Hanson: up close and personal. Not like today, where we just fire a missile at some target over the horizon and your target doesn't even know what hit him. The way you did it, you had the satisfaction of knowing your enemy knew he had lost before he died."

Robert brow wrinkled as he tried to comprehend what Sharon said as she sat in the cockpit pulling the trigger on the joystick while staring blindly through the windshield at some imaginary enemy.

"Remind me never to expect mercy from you in a fight, Sharon," Jim chuckled, almost nervously.

Sharon whipped around to face Jim. Her lips formed a sardonic grin before she said, "That is a good thing to remember, Jim."

They were just getting down from *Dolly Girl* when George pulled up in his golf cart.

"Well, Sharon, I see they gave you the grand tour of *Dolly Girl*," he said.

"Yes, they did. What are those, Mr. Grayson?" Sharon asked, pointing to five silhouette drawings on George's cart. There were two garbage cans, a cat, a car, and what appeared to be a blind person led by a guide dog.

"Those are my 'kills,'" George chortled. "Some person, or persons, of unknown origin, painted those on my cart. There are vicious rumors around this airport about my reckless driving. Now, I will admit to knocking over two garbage cans, and yes, I did scare Patches, the cat, and perhaps there was a small confrontation with a car. But as for hitting a blind person and their guide dog, that is pure mischief on someone's part!"

"Well, at least they put five on the cart. That makes you an ace," Sharon pointed out, flashing an empty smile.

George laughed, but noticed Jim and Robert did not join in. Sharon said goodbye again and left for the parking lot. Jim filled George in on their conversation.

"Jimmy, we never took satisfaction like she said when we got a kill. But if she did it, I think she would enjoy it," Robert stated.

"Jim, what authority does she have over you?" George inquired.

"Well, it's not like I'm an employee," Jim replied. "The agents work as independent brokers and contractors. But I suppose she could make trouble for me if she wanted."

"Do yourself a favor, stay out of her way," George advised.

It was 2:30 AM in the Hanson household. Everyone was asleep, including Rusty, who was curled up in his usual place: Jim's chair in the office. For others, their workday was just beginning. The Trojans on Jason's computer had detected the keyboard and mouse had been idle for several hours. This fact, including the time on the system's clock, told them the moment had come to strike.

The only one who was aware of Jason's computer turning on was Rusty, who startled when it booted up. He, however, quickly returned to his slumber. The computer connected itself to the 'net. The invaders next started a search of Jason's files, gathering his name and home address, his passwords, and the type of computer they were sitting on. Over the course of the next few hours, the same process would occur on Jennifer, Angie, Steven, and Gerard's computers. All of this information was then bundled and sent to Pakistan. There, it was automatically forwarded to a computer in the Caymans, then on to Bermuda, and finally to Europe, specifically the small nation of Andorra. Their job complete, the Trojans were supposed to destroy themselves after creating programs to help trace the location of the computer or any "smart" devices attached to it. But for some reason or another, their suicide did not take place.

In the capital city of Andorra, Andorra La Vella, spring was just starting to break. There was still enough snow in mountains to keep tourists happy with their skiing in this tiny nation-state nestled between France and Spain, deep in the Pyrenees Mountains. These beautiful mountains, with their snow-capped peaks etching a clear blue sky, had witnessed much change in the economy of this thousand-year-old principality. Originally, the raising of sheep sustained its people, but today on its streets, besides the many tourists who made up a large part of the Andorran economy, were employees of its newest business: banking. Billions of dollars were now flowing into this tiny state to take advantage of its tax shelters and other investment vehicles. Their clients, confident of discrete handling of their investments, were steadily increasing in number, adding to the wealth of the various new banks, insurance companies, and investment houses which now made up a large part of the Andorran economic landscape.

On one small, cobblestoned side street was a large eighteenth-century home, which, like many in this part of town, had been converted into an office. Displaying the woodworking artistry of this era were the intricate carvings on the doors and shutters of this stone building, which helped conceal the security cameras. Next to the oak front door was a simple brass plaque that bore the name of the firm occupying the premises: International Predictive Analytics. As quaint as the exterior appeared, the inside of this building gleamed with the best of modern digital communication hardware.

It was information on a large LED computer screen that was holding Gaston Leroux's undivided attention. He'd been transfixed by this high-resolution monitor for over twenty minutes now. He was having trouble comprehending what he was seeing. Over the years, he'd had to deal with the occasional security breach, but nothing like this. Most had been minor incidents: a misplaced flash drive, a misdirected file. All had been recovered. But here, all within twenty-four hours, five complete breaches had happened, in three countries on two continents. Gaston picked up the phone on his desk and pushed a button. "I need to see Culper. It's urgent."

A few days later, Jim went to see a client in Freelton. After the call, he stopped in the agency office with the intention of picking up some literature and dropping off the memory stick to Janice. Not seeing her around, he dropped into Peter's office.

"How's the car business?" Jim asked.

"Always on the move," was the reply, followed by a smile.

"I knew I shouldn't have asked."

Peter was one of those unique characters in life that stop it from being boring. He had a bent sense of humor, which Jim really appreciated. One agent was always complaining about files and other items always "going missing" off his desk and blaming others instead of his own disorganization. One morning, he'd arrived at the office to find his entire desk, with its contents, had been shrink-wrapped, courtesy of Peter (though he'd never actually confessed to being the culprit). Peter was also the go-to guy around the office if you had any problems, especially with computers. Jim had made use of this skill many times, especially in the last six months. New Times had introduced a new computer program that was supposed to help the agents manage their clients. Jim, and many of the agents, found it very complex. It was known only as APYN; Jim wasn't sure what the acronym stood for, but he was sure the first two letters meant "awful programming". It was a program that ran on cloud computing, which meant he had to be connected to the head office computer to use it. Jim thought it was very inconvenient; he'd had to get a smart phone so he was always in the cloud, no matter where he was. Peter's passion, however, was for cars. Models and photos of exotic sports cars decorated his office. Ask Peter about any car from a classic Bugatti to a Corvette and someone was in for a lecture; his knowledge was encyclopedic.

"What unusual instrument was on the dashboard of every Duesenberg?" Jim asked in continuing their contest of Jim trying to stump Peter.

"Oh, please Jim! Will you ever ask a hard one? An instrument you are most familiar with, an altimeter."

"You win again."

"And I always will."

"Sorry you weren't here the other day when I was in for the meeting, because I drove *it* in."

Peter's face lit up with a big smile.

"You finished it! Please tell me you have it outside Jim."

"Would I disappoint you?"

Within seconds, they were outside and Peter was practically drooling on the red, metallic custom paint that adorned the Camaro.

"Can I marry her, Jim?"

"You can't even date her, Peter."

They both laughed as Peter went into a lecture on the whole history of the Camaro. Finally, Peter ran out of steam and Jim asked, "So, are you holding down the fort today?"

"Looks that way. Janice and Sharon don't appear to be in today. Of course, Sharon's hardly ever here."

"Interesting you should say that, Peter. Did you know she's a pilot?"

"Funny you should mention that," Peter said with a furrowed brow. "She was in a meeting the other day and called out for me to get something for her out of her office. She had left her monitor on and what caught my attention was the unusual display. It was some kind of navigational program; I'd never seen anything like it before."

"It's common knowledge I'm an avid pilot and she never mentioned it to me. Pilots are like fisherman or you car guys, you meet one and you talk shop."

He paused. "But what I found really curious is the fact she is ex-Air Force."

Peter's eyes widened. "Now that is interesting! Might explain her management style."

"Really?"

"She does not ask, she tells. No discussion, my way or the highway."

"Oh! Before I forget, I found this memory stick in the parking lot the other day." Jim fished around in his pocket for it and found nothing. "Damn it! I must have left it back in my office. Would you put the word out in case one of the guys lost it? It had a funny brand name on it ... Yes, Herbert and Hector."

"No problem, I'll send out an e-mail," Peter replied.

"Herbert and Hector, sounds like a comedy team," Jim added.

At that moment Peter's cell phone rang. He glanced at the screen. "I have to take this call, Jim."

"That's okay. I've gotta go anyway. See ya."

Neither of them knew it at that moment, but this would prove to be the most fortuitous telephone interruption in history. After a long conversation with his mother about her sister's deteriorating health, the call ended. Peter sat alone in his office, thinking about his favorite aunt. He simply forgot to send the e-mail about the lost flash drive.

"Enemies are people whose story you haven't heard, or whose face you haven't seen."

— Irene Butter

CHAPTER 3

The last thing Nathan McWilliams wanted was to hear was another knock on his office door, but there it was. Between his cell buzzing, his landline ringing, and people knocking on his door, his plans to get any work done this morning were shot. It was days like these that made him wonder why he'd taken the job of Regional Director in the FBI's Richmond office three years ago.

"C'mon in. You might as well, everyone else has," he exclaimed as he turned off his monitor.

"Good morning, Director," Agents Deselva and Connors said as they settled into chairs in front of McWilliams' file-strewn desk.

"Only if you have good news for me."

"It's the New Times case, sir," Jake responded. "We've discovered a new agent who reports to the Freelton branch."

"Oh, yes, that life insurance and investment company we're looking at for money laundering and offshore tax sheltering. Tell me again, why we are looking at this and not the IRS?"

"It's due to the possible involvement of organized crime, specifically several cartels," Dom replied.

"So we have a new player here. Who is he and why did you not know about him before?"

Dom pulled out a file from his briefcase and handed it to McWilliams. He looked at the photographs showing two men talking to each other in the New Times parking lot.

"Those were taken a few days ago. The one on the left is James Hanson," Dom informed him. "The other is Ted Bayden. We've told you about him before."

"Yeah, the one with all the offshore accounts," he murmured as he laid the three photographs side by side on his desk.

"We hadn't picked up on Hanson before because he rarely comes to the agency office. He has his own office in Gradon. He only shows up for special meetings."

"Is that all you have on him?" he asked incredulously. "I thought you two were good at your jobs."

"No, we ran him through some of the databases."

"I don't recall approving the request."

"You didn't, Director. We asked a contact at Homeland Security," Jake replied cautiously.

McWilliams sat up straight. "You did what?"

"I know it doesn't look good," Dom volunteered, "but you were away and we needed fast answers. So we used Jake's contact to get some more info."

McWilliams flattened his lips and stared at them for a long moment. Inside, he was seething. One agency did not contact another agency without going through the proper channels, especially when it came to Homeland Security. Homeland Security was a slap in the FBI's face as far as McWilliams was concerned. It was another unneeded layer in a network of intelligence operations that already numbered more than a dozen. On top of that, they stole a lot of the FBI's best agents to staff it.

"I'll deal with this run around the FBI later," he said at long last, coolly. "Now what did you find out?"

"As you know," Jake began, "Homeland can get at online info faster than we can."

McWilliams narrowed his eyes. He'd heard the rumors about Homeland being connected to every database out there. There was a reason they were known as Big Brother in intelligence circles. It was also the reason if they asked for your help, it was best to give it.

"James Hanson has no priors. He is a certified financial planner and is licensed to sell life insurance and investment products. There are no complaints on file with the respective licensing bodies. He is a widower with two children, and a licensed pilot. His father is Robert Hanson, who was a big time lawyer around here before he retired. Robert Hanson was also a law partner with Judge George Grayson before he ascended to the bench."

"Grayson, I have heard of," McWilliams stated. "That's where our president did her law clerking. So is this guy clean?"

"There isn't any indication he has facilitated moving any of his client's money offshore," Dom answered stiffly.

"Then why are we here, gentlemen?" McWilliams asked, glancing at his watch.

"We need someone connected to this branch of New Times working for us. We want to approach him," Jake stated.

"But he hardly goes there and don't we already have people on the inside?"

"Yes, we do, but they're at the corporate head office. We need someone at the branch. The fact he doesn't come in much is the beauty of it," Jake explained. "He's involved enough to get the kind of information we want, but because he's not in the building, he's less likely to get caught if he screws up."

"And how are you going to feel him out about this?"

"By going through Judge Grayson," Jake answered.

McWilliams raised his eyebrows. "You know him?"

"Let's say an acquaintance. I've been taking flying lessons and Judge Grayson is quite well known around the airport. Since his retirement, he's become the go-to guy around the place and knows everyone. As far as Jim Hanson is concerned, I have seen them together a lot."

"Give it a try, but get his commitment to keep the matter confidential first," McWilliams cautioned. "He has a reputation as an honorable person; he should cooperate."

He picked up another photo.

"Who are the women and what are they doing?"

"The blonde is Sharon Turner. She recently became manager of the branch. The brunette is Janice Collins, her assistant. They seemed to be looking for something in the parking lot. We don't know what," Jake replied.

"What's the latest from our people at corporate, uh …"

"Black and Decker," Dom replied.

"I see someone thinks they're a comedian," McWilliams commented dryly.

"Black works in their investment area and was the first to bring this case to our attention. He spotted the unusually large number of transactions involving foreign banks after New Times was bought out."

"Hadn't he worked with us before?"

"That's right, sir, he did some consulting," Dom said with a nod of his head. "That's why he knew enough not to go to management when he saw the transactions and came to us. To answer your first question, the transactions have increased in number. He hasn't been able to ID the head people running this operation, but it has to be one of the cartels."

"Decker is in IT," Jake stated. "Apparently New Life has introduced a new client management program for their agents, which is designed to integrate with their other systems. We got a copy of it and our people are looking at it. It appears very complex."

"Okay, guys, keep me posted. I have to get back at it."

Dom and Jake left the office as McWilliams turned on his monitor and stared at the aggressive lines of the Corvette Stingray C7 sports car that made up his screensaver.

No doubt about it, Aleix Caba had been one of Andorra's best furniture makers, if this desk was exemplary of his work. It dominated Culper's office. The nineteenth-century oak masterpiece, with its inlays of ivory, cherry, and ebony, looked as if it belonged in a palace rather than in its present location under Culper's elbow as he watched Andorra La Vella's five o'clock traffic. His glasses dangled from his right hand as he contemplated the events Gaston had briefed him on. As usual, Culper's white hair was immaculately groomed; his Armani suit was perfectly tailored to his lean, hard frame, which belied his sixty-five years.

"How could this happen, Gaston?" he asked at last, breaking the dragging silence. "I thought there were safety features built into our flash drives to prevent this."

"There are," Gaston replied. "If the flash drive is plugged into a computer which doesn't contain the proper recognition software, the hidden programs on the drive are supposed to send us two messages: one that the incident occurred and another confirming all the encrypted software has been erased, including the programs hidden in the photographs. We received the first message, but not the second."

"What's the purpose of those photos anyway?"

"I thought it was clever," Gaston answered shortly. "Most of our information comes from our associates. Many of them work in general business offices where a passerby could look over an office divider or pass by their desk and see their screen. By having our communications camouflaged in photographs, if this should happen, all they would see is a harmless photograph."

"So what went wrong here, Gaston? Why didn't we get the second message?"

"I can only assume a corrupted file caused the program to fail. We're running simulations."

"What does Tallmadge say our risk exposure is?"

"Ninety-eight point seven percent chance of them breaking the encryption. Sixty-two point six percent of our eventual exposure," Gaston rattled off mechanically.

"Anything over sixty percent requires a full sanction. No exceptions."

Culper's voice was even as he ordered the deaths. Gaston's insides twisted painfully. "Sir, we're talking about five murders in three countries. That's bound to attract attention. The targets all know each other; hell, two of them are brother and sister! It won't take Sherlock Holmes to figure out there's a link."

Culper spun about in his chair, fixing his piercing blue eyes on Gaston. "How have we remained undiscovered for almost two hundred and fifty years, Gaston?"

"We've always operated in small cells. Always covered our tracks and kept our numbers small," Gaston replied cautiously.

"Correct!" Culper cried, walking around the desk. He perched on a corner and faced Gaston. "We've always covered our tracks and these five targets have left large footprints. How many computers are involved?"

"Five notebooks," Gaston replied. "And two smart phones," he added.

"Backups?"

"All in the cloud."

"Perfect," Culper said, smiling. "We'll have no problem handling those. Now, what do we do about those two spies at New Times?"

Gaston thought for a moment. "We'll keep isolating them from any real information. We could even use them to plant false information for the feds to find," he offered.

"Or," Culper said softly, "we could eliminate them along with the rest."

Gaston turned pale. "Sir, you're now talking about seven murders! It's much too risky. These are FBI informants. You take their people out and they'll increase their investigation of New Times."

"I want the slate wiped clean here, Gaston. Use our connections to kill the investigation."

Gaston felt sick.

"I know we have a good team for these matters here, but, tell me, what do we have in the States?"

"He goes by the name Darien," Gaston murmured. "We've used him for jobs in the past, but nothing on this scale." He paused, then added, "There's danger for us all in this operation, sir."

Culper looked at Gaston as if he were a student who was not bright enough to grasp the lesson he was teaching.

"You really don't understand the correlation between money and power, do you Gaston?"

Gaston turned his back for a moment as he walked over and leaned on a chair. He did not want Culper to see his quivering lips. He hated being talked down to and it was hard for him to conceal his contempt.

"The wealth is ours, Gaston, the ruling class. Others may become rich—an athlete, a lottery winner—but they will never know wealth. For wealth occurs when money is combined with power and transforms to energy. And if you remember your physics, energy can be neither created nor destroyed, but it can be controlled. And *we* control the energy of the nations, not the temporary holders of public office, the politicians; they are but servants to our wealth. The puppets we choose to give the people the illusion they are free to choose. But the only choices they have are the ones we allow them. What did that comedian say… 'you have a choice in this country, paper or plastic.'" Culper leaned forward until his face was mere inches from Gaston's. His voice was quiet, almost a whisper, but his words rang in Gaston's ears. "So no, Gaston, there's no danger for us all in this operation. We *are* the danger."

Within an hour of their meeting, a special encrypted e-mail was sent to the New Times office in Freelton, Virginia, as well as to the office of another insurance company in Lyon, France. When the message was opened in Virginia, a picture of a Lamborghini Murciélago appeared. But after the entry of a special decryption code, the photo delivered its steganographic message. A special cell phone was then picked up and the pre-programmed number called. The message was simple. "This is 355. We have an order for you. Contact me the usual way."

"Excuse me, Madam President, but I just have to stretch my legs," I said as I got up from the park bench.

"Good idea."

I extended my hand, helping Kathleen up. We started to walk along the path.

"As I understand things so far, the FBI is investigating New Times for money laundering and offshore tax sheltering, this Sharon Turner is flying around the country—why, we do not know at this point—and your friend Ted Bayden is placing his clients' money offshore. Add to this the mysterious flash drive and its hidden software … Well, Jim, if you should ever decide to become an author, this sounds like it would be a good book."

"If I was writing this one, Madam President, I think I would leave out the murders. We didn't know it at the time, but seven of us in three countries were now marked for death, including Jason and Jennifer. My parents and I would be added to the hit list later."

"What countries, Jim?

"Canada, the United States, and France. We would involve more countries as events progressed."

Kathleen stopped and looked me.

"Yes, I guess you did, judging by the reports I'm getting," she stated with a wrinkled brow, shaking her head. "Just what I need; more international situations to deal with."

"Again, Madam President, you are not looking at the positive side here."

"I'm going to regret asking 'what is that,' aren't I?"

"I can just about guarantee that."

She laughed, showing me that alluring smile, which I was finding so very attractive. Maybe it was the way her eyes sparkled, the way she turned her head. It was becoming very distracting and that was just fine. She raised her hand and waved her fingers towards herself, saying,

"Lay it on me, Jim."

"They can only impeach you once, so why not throw in a few international incidents into the mix with the whole 'most corrupt government' thing? You'll always be known as the 'First President'—the first woman president and the first to be impeached."

The president stood there with her hands on her hips for a moment and just looked at me. I figured she was thinking, "I can't believe this idiot just said that to me." Then she started to laugh.

"I guess I'm just going to have to get use to this bent sense of humor of yours," she said with a smile. "The only problem is you're probably right."

"Well, we all have our coping mechanisms, Madam President. Humor beats drink and drugs."

Then I said something that had been on the tip of my tongue since I had met her.

"For the record, Madam President, I think you have been a damn fine president."

She looked startled at first; then her face softened and, looking me in the eye, she spoke.

"Thank you, Jim."

I offered her my arm which she took as we walked the path.

"It's nice strolling with the 'First President,'" I said with a smile, which was returned. "The next part of this story involves killing, in which there is not one bit of humor."

"Amen to that, Jim. So who was behind it?"

"That, we would find out later, but we did learn the name of the killer they sent. His name was Darien."

"It was almost painful to be different."

— Shannon A. Thompson

CHAPTER 4

Darien had always known he was different. Even as a child, when the other kids told jokes, he didn't find them funny. They'd bully him and he wouldn't get mad. He'd even watched his dog get run over by a car and still he felt nothing. His father died when he was twelve. He wanted to cry, but he couldn't. He'd accepted the fact he was a sociopath. He thought it was fascinating. He had read everything he could on the subject, trying to understand why he could not feel. He saw people in love and he wanted to feel what they felt, but now, at forty-two, he knew he never would. If he had ever felt any sort of love at all, it was for his profession: master watch and clock repairman. It wasn't the job that made him the most money, but he especially liked old clocks and their beautifully crafted cases, remnants of a bygone time when true craftsmen took pride in their work.

But he reveled in the movements, the gears, the levers, and the springs all working in perfect harmony. Maybe their harmony brought logic and sense—regulation—to his chaotic life. If there was a problem, it was usually easy to find. Fixing was easy; it just took time. His approach to clocks could also be applied to his other job: killing.

It all started back in New York with Mr. Caramello. He lived across the street when Darien was growing up. He was always nice to Darien and his parents, bringing them vegetables from his garden or the occasional loaf of bread or cake that his wife, Adona, had baked. In return, his parents always made sure Darien kept the Caramello lawn cut and the garden weeded.

Mr. Caramello took a liking to Darien. Perhaps it was because his own children had grown up and had moved to California. After Darien's father died, the Caramellos took a special interest in him and his mother, often having them over to dinner, especially Darien, during the holidays. Mr. Caramello employed him after school to do odd jobs at his watch repair and jewelry shop. Everyone knew that shop was just a front for his real business. Yes, Mr. Caramello was "connected."

Darien swept the store, kept the counters clean, and did deliveries, but it was the watch and clock repair that really interested him. Observing Mr. Caramello looking through glasses with magnifiers on them at the fine movements of wristwatches or the larger movements of hundred-year-old mantle clocks, Darien learned how an old-school craftsman worked. Mr. Caramello was only too happy to teach Darien his craft and take him on as his apprentice. When Darien finished high school, he was fixing watches and clocks on his own and Mr. Caramello believed he had someone to pass his store onto. It was the other "business" that worried Mr. Caramello. Darien saw the men come into the shop. He heard the whispered conversations, saw the manila envelopes exchanging hands, and heard the ringing on the private line. Darien never asked and Mr. Caramello never brought it up.

It was a rainy Tuesday morning. The shop was quiet and Mr. Caramello had just gone into the bathroom with his newspaper, a daily event that made for at least twenty minutes of goofing off for Darien. Darien was at his bench studying the beautiful movement of a 1959 Omega Speedmaster Chronograph wristwatch when the men burst into the store.

There were two of them. One came through the front door, the other through the back. Darien recognized them both; they'd been into the shop several times before. But they'd never brought the sawed-off, double-barrel shotguns before.

Darien's workbench was an antique with a copper top, one that had been in the shop for years. It wasn't the best shield, but it made a good ram as Darien, instead of fleeing, hefted the bench and charged the backdoor shooter. Darien caught him in the solar plexus. A blast screamed past his left ear, almost deafening him, but not before Darien knocked him back against the now-closed door, sending the shotgun skidding across the floor amid the scattered contents of the workbench. They dove for the weapon, their hands landing on it simultaneously. Darien spotted his narrow, long-shafted screwdriver on the floor. He fumbled for the tool as his assailant tore the gun away. Darien shoved the screwdriver through his attacker's left eye and deep into his brain.

All the while, Mr. Caramello was in a life-or-death struggle of his own. Mr. Caramello had exited the bathroom as the door banged open, but he was caught, literally, with his pants down. But his timing couldn't have been better. The hallway from the store to the backroom was very narrow, given that the building was over a hundred years old. So when the bathroom door flew open, it smashed into the assassin, knocking the shotgun out of his hands.

Against a man less than half his age, he did not stand a chance. As the assassin wrenched the gun from his hands, Adolfo Caramello knew he was done.

The sound a twelve-gauge shotgun made in an enclosed space was enormous. Mr. Caramello could attest to that. He also knew what double-aught buckshot does to the human abdomen at point-blank range; he'd seen it before, and he saw it again as the assassin's mid-section exploded. Darien was standing in the doorway, holding a smoking shotgun.

Mr. Caramello was shaken, but his face was one of controlled determination and rage. He turned toward the front door. The would-be assassin had locked it and turned the sign on it to "Closed." He investigated the bodies on the floor.

"Macchi's men," he said, "they have gone rogue. There's still time, Darien." He looked up. "You did well here, but now I have to ask you to do more. I never wanted you involved in this business, but I am afraid you are now."

"They were going to kill me too," Darien replied.

"They still might. We must act fast," was Mr. Caramello's reply as he went back into the bathroom. He pulled down the mirror, which had, Darien thought, always been bolted to the wall over the sink. It, in fact, revealed a concealed compartment. Darien was rapt as his employer removed a rolled up umbrella, a cane, and a small, brown leather case. Mr. Caramello exited the room and looked toward the front window.

"Good. It's still raining. I need … We need you to go to Mario's Eatery, that deli two blocks up Court Street. We will use the umbrella. Today is perfect for it."

Darien was lost.

"This is a weapon, Darien," Mr. Caramello said slowly as he twisted the decorative collar near the handle of the umbrella. Darien had seen concealed swords in canes and umbrellas in movies but nothing like this. Mr. Caramello pulled the handle away from the umbrella revealing not a blade, but what looked like a gun barrel.

"This is essentially a rifle," explained Mr. Caramello as he handed it to Darien. "But it does not shoot bullets. It fires these."

He reached into the leather case and held up a small glass bottle for Darien's inspection. It contained about a dozen small ball bearings resting in a thick, clear fluid.

"That's right Darien. One-point-five millimeter ball bearings. But these are different. Each one is hollow and has two small holes in it. That allows the contents of them to escape."

"Poison?" Darien asked.

"Like no other," Mr. Caramello chuckled darkly. "Seconds after it enters the body, the person will have a fatal heart attack."

"I don't have the time to explain how everything works. You have to trust me. Macchi goes to that deli every day at eleven AM. He runs his organization from there. He will arrive in his dark blue Cadillac. He will park in his private spot in the alley. He will enter by the front door."

"How do you know all this?"

"Because he is my brother-in-law. I've known him for thirty years!"

Darien stared at Mr. Caramello for a few minutes. At last, he spoke.

"Is he that fat guy who comes in here every few weeks with the envelopes and wears the flashy rings?"

Mr. Caramello nodded. He took back the rifle from Darien. "We will talk later."

Pressing a small lever where the barrel met the handle opened up a small breach. Taking a pair of tweezers from the leather case, Mr. Caramello opened the bottle and extracted one of the bearings.

"Always handle these with tweezers. The poison is sealed into the bearings with a special wax. The fluid keeps the wax from melting, but just the heat of your fingers could dissolve it."

Mr. Caramello dropped the bearing into the breach, which snapped shut. Next, he unscrewed part of the handle, reached into the leather case, and extracted something Darien recognized: a CO_2 cartridge.

"I built this to use off-the-shelf parts. This cartridge will provide enough force for the bearing to penetrate even the thickest coat."

"You built both of these?"

"Every piece."

Darien should have guessed: the precision work, the flawless way everything fitted; it all smacked of Mr. Caramello's handiwork.

"I would do this myself Darien, but he would see me coming from a mile away. You, he hasn't noticed."

"Why not just shoot him?"

"You shoot a man, everyone knows he has been murdered. That starts a war. A man has a heart attack and dies, it is an unfortunate incident and everyone gets to go to the funeral and tell lies about what a great guy he was. I prefer the latter. You get fed after, especially at Italian funerals."

Mr. Caramello finished assembling the umbrella. "Now here is what you must do. Make this look like an accident. It is raining. You are walking along with the umbrella over you. Hold it forward, so it blocks your face when you approach him. Then collide as if you did not see him. Before you bump into him, pull this lever down." Mr. Caramello held up the umbrella handle and pulled down a recessed lever from the shaft, just in front of the handle. "This arms it, pulling it the rest of way fires it," he explained. "Just jam the umbrella tip into his side, back, leg—it does not matter. Then fire. Say 'excuse me,' and keep walking. Do not come back here until after three and ..."

Darien saw something in Mr. Caramello's eyes he had never seen before: fear.

"Thank you and good luck."

Fifteen minutes later, Darien was in front of a small store near the deli, under its awning. He was watching for Macchi, pretending to window shop. The rain fell steadily, a thick curtain of water.

He didn't have to wait long. The dark blue Caddy pulled into the alley. Darien opened the umbrella and pulled down the arming lever. He walked toward the deli. Macchi was rounding the corner. Darien lowered the umbrella, took two quick steps. He stabbed and fired just above the man's left kidney.

"What the hell!"

"Excuse me," Darien murmured and walked off.

Macchi could not move. He leaned against the wall, then slid to the ground; the last thing he saw was a familiar young man looking over his shoulder as he walked down the street.

When Darien arrived back at the store later in the afternoon, he couldn't believe it. He never would have thought there had been a gun fight on the premise. The bodies were gone. All the blood was cleaned up. The glass of a shattered counter had been replaced. The backroom was as neat as a pin.

Mr. Caramello was in his office.

"How did you get the place cleaned up so fast and the ..."

Mr. Caramello held up his hand. "Nothing happened here today. My dear Adona has just called. Her brother had a fatal heart attack right in front of the deli this morning." He reached over his desk to retrieve the umbrella.

"I have to leave now to be with her. Please look after the store."

With that, Mr. Caramello was gone and Darien was alone with his thoughts. He'd come very close to dying; he had killed three men. Now he was alone in an empty store. And none of this bothered him. He felt a stranger unto himself.

Over the next few months, Darien learned there were two forces behind Mr. Caramello. One was the mob; the other was known only as "355." It was still Mr. Caramello's wish to leave Darien out of his mob business. As far as he was concerned, that business retired with him. It was the 355

business that could not be ignored. If 355 called, the job took priority over all else. Darien was under the impression even the mafia respected this 355. As the years went on, Mr. Caramello turned all of his hits over to Darien. Fortunately for Darien, the Swiss bank account into which 355 made their payments for his work was also passed over. As for Mr. Caramello, he did retire from the business, but not the way he wished. One Wednesday morning, Darien came into the shop to find him slumped over his desk, dead from a heart attack. Darien fully appreciated the irony in the way the man who had become his father and mentor died, but still he felt nothing, a fact that bothered him. Again he stood alone in the shop, still a stranger unto himself.

Tomorrow he had a mission. He would be going to airport in Virginia, where he would meet a woman known only as Sharon. She would fly them in a small plane to Canada, to the city of Waterloo.

The old grist mill on the edge of Silver Lake in Waterloo often caught Dr. Steven Bertrand's eye. He would jog his lean, six-foot frame along part of a trail known as the Uptown Loop to help clear his head when his work at the Perimeter Institute proved too intense. But his jogging would always end at the grist mill where he would clean his glasses, refresh from his water bottle, and reflect on the mill's nineteenth-century architecture and how it contrasted with that of the very modern Perimeter Institute just a few hundred feet away. At twenty-eight, Steven was working at the world's leader in the study of theoretical physics, especially quantum theory, and one of the institutions that had given the city of Waterloo its nickname, Quantum Valley. Here he was making full use of his doctorate in computer architecture, hoping to be part of the invention of the world's first quantum computer.

It wasn't the work that was troubling Steven today; rather, it was a matter of the heart. He sat on one of the boulders at the water's edge while Canada geese tended their nests and the water from Silver Lake ran down the mill race, forming a white current—a scene almost reminiscent of post-cards in dozens of tourist shops.

Tonight was the night. He had been building his resolve all day and was still doing so when his cell phone rang. Emmanuel's number was splayed on the screen. Steven glanced at the time, frowning. It was odd for Emmanuel to call while he was at work; Blackberry certainly didn't discourage their employees from making calls, but Emmanuel was usually so absorbed in his work that he didn't.

"Well, a call during working hours. Is it to tell me to sell my Blackberry stock and buy Apple or Samsung?" Steven asked with a laugh.

"Bite your tongue, bro," Emmanuel replied with gusto. "We'll be buying those companies in no time!"

"Make me a believer, buddy, so I can hit up Blackberry for a donation to the Institute."

"I am on the advisory board and you want money too? In all seriousness, Steve, tonight is the night … right?"

"It is. I even got the ring."

"Arissa Thompson is a great girl, Steve," Emmanuel said in a serious voice. "Don't worry. She'll say yes. She understands ugly guys need love too."

They both laughed. The joke was just what Steven needed to help him relax.

"You are still going to be my best man?"

"You bet. I will get a tux and we'll shine up the ol' wheelchair here. Maybe trick it out with some sweet rims. But remember your prime duty as the groom."

"Yes, yes I know. Make sure there are plenty of lovely single women at the wedding for the best man."

"I love what I am hearing, bro."

"I am sure Jennifer Hanson and Angie Borello will come up from MIT if there's going to be a wedding."

"What do you mean 'if,' man? Am I detecting a lack of confidence here?"

"Well, she hasn't said yes yet. Remember, buddy, I had zip experience with women before Arissa. I'm that nerdy guy no girl wants to be caught dead with—will she really wanna bind herself to me for the rest of her life?"

"She hasn't said yes because you haven't asked her yet. Now, remember buddy, this is not all about you. I have checked out Jennifer and Angie online and they're gorgeous and brilliant in mass data. I am handsome, charming, and *very* available. So get your butt over to Arissa's and get this job done. There are bigger issues at stake here!"

By now Steven was laughing so hard he could barely hold his phone.

"Thanks for the laugh, buddy. I needed it."

"Anytime, catch ya later."

Despite Emmanuel's clear support—and his sardonic humor—Steve's heart was still pounding as he climbed into his car, intent on seeing Arissa at the University of Waterloo where she was earning her doctorate in advanced computer systems. As he gripped the wheel with sweaty palms, he couldn't help but remember the words Stephen Hawking had given to him when he'd visited the Institute: "Women, they are a complete mystery."

Steve laid his head against the wheel, groaning, "If one of the greatest minds on the planet can't figure them out, what chance do I have?"

At the east end of the Fenton County Airport, there was a distinctive hangar made from a surplus Second World War Quonset hut. The arched steel building was painted the usual military olive green, with the notable exception of the hangar door, which instead bore a large painted American flag, below which was written in block letters "5th AIR FORCE." As Jake Connors drove up to its side door, he spotted the golf cart—George Grayson was here. Jake rapped on the door and then pulled it open a fraction and stuck his head in.

"Is this the home of the Mighty Fifth?!" he yelled.

"Darn right it is! Advance and be recognized!" George bellowed back.

Jake stepped in and shut the door behind him. He glanced up to find George lubricating the port aileron of *Lady Rachel*.

"Hello Jake! How are the flying lessons going?"

"Just great, Judge Grayson."

"Judge Grayson? Haven't been called that in a while. Why so formal?"

"Well, frankly Judge Grayson, I am here on official business. As you may recall, I'm with the FBI," Jake responded, producing his ID and shield. "I need to talk to you in confidence about an important issue that's come up."

"Most certainly," George replied, putting down his tube of lubricant and wiping his hands on a rag. "Come into my chambers." He gestured to a small side office that looked more like a storeroom than anything else. Aircraft parts were strewn on every possible surface. The beat-up future was all army surplus; Jake perched gingerly on a chair that looked like it had seen service on Omaha Beach. George scuttled behind the ramshackle desk, which was littered with enough parts to build another engine or two.

"So Judge Grayson, who's your decorator? Pratt & Whitney?" Jake asked with a smile.

George guffawed. "Don't have clerks to do all the grunt work anymore. So how can I help the FBI? And call me George."

"Again ... George, I cannot stress how important confidentiality is."

"I understand."

"Ted Bayden. He's a friend of Jim Hanson?"

George looked puzzled. "What about him?"

"Have you met him?"

"A couple of times. He works with Jimmy at that insurance place. He helped out a lot when Elizabeth was sick. What is this all about?"

"We are investigating what may be some very large, improper financial transactions over the last seven months involving the New Times Financial Group and Mr. Bayden is ..."

"A person of interest," George finished. He glanced about furtively, then leaned forward over the pile of plane parts. "You don't think Jimmy is involved, do you?"

Jake was silent.

"Jim and I are very close. You know his father and I were law partners," George stated.

"Yes, Robert Hanson has a very fine reputation, as do you."

"I'd stake that reputation, my life, that Jim's as honest as they come. Besides, you said you've been looking at them for the last seven months. Well, Jimmy's been having a helluva time for the last several years, first with Elizabeth, and now with his dad ..."

"All that had to affect his income," Jake said flatly.

"Yes, it did," answered George. "Big time."

Jake raised his eyebrows.

"Don't pursue that one, Jake. There's plenty of money in the Hanson family. I was concerned so I asked Jim if I could help. Said no, he's got good insurance. Besides, that Mustang parked out there"—George gestured to the door—"is worth millions."

"But doesn't it belong to his father?"

"Yes, I suppose it does." George was getting flush, a sure sign he was frustrated. "What's going on here?" he asked sharply. "Is New Times dirty or just Ted?"

"George, we're not accusing anyone of being dirty. We are just investigating."

"That brings me back to my original question: how can I help the FBI?"

"By setting up a meeting between my partner, me, and Jim Hanson."

"Can't you just call him yourself?"

"Can't risk exposing our operation. This may sound paranoid, but we do not know what surveillance New Times may have in place on its people. I know what I am about to suggest sounds very … circuitous, but perhaps you could call Mr. Hanson to meet you here at the hangar, regarding a problem with one of the planes. We could be here and meet him then."

"Hold on here, Jake. You are not talking circuitous—you're talking devious. The Hansons are my family. Do forty pieces of silver come with this job?"

"Look, Jim is not 'a person of interest' here. We are hoping he can fill in some holes in our investigation. If you wish, you may be at our meeting as his council, but as I said, we are not looking at him as a criminal."

Jake could see George was very uncomfortable with the idea.

George inhaled sharply. He clasped his hands and fixed Jake with a cold look. Jake held up his hands.

"George, I know I've taken you out of your comfort zone here. Please understand we would not consider this route if it wasn't important. This is vital."

George took a long look a Jake, then slowly reached across the desk to the phone.

*
**

For Sharon Turner and Darien, the flight from Fenton was northwest to a small airport near Butler, Pennsylvania, where they topped up the fuel tanks. During the flight, Sharon took stock of her passenger. Sharon felt any woman would be attracted to that face with its square jaw and accenting features, which belonged on a magazine cover. She figured him to be about forty, with dark brown hair and a very athletic build. Normally, he would be the type of guy she would like occupying half her bed, but he was very quiet, the sort of quiet that made her uncomfortable.

"Have to watch those clouds to the north, could have some storm cells," she said, glancing out the window.

"Hm," Darien replied. Silence pervaded the plane for a moment.

"I got all the information from 355," Sharon said, glancing over at her passenger.

"So did I," Darien said flatly, then pressed his lips together as though physically sealing his mouth shut again. Sharon took a deep breath.

"Are you always this quiet?"

"Yes."

Sharon decided to push a little further.

"Too bad, I like to get to know the people I work with."

"As do I," Darien replied. "If I had in this case, you wouldn't be here."

"What the hell do you mean by that?" she snapped, just barely containing her rage. "I wouldn't be here?!"

"Let's review," Darien drawled in an almost professorial tone. "Right off the bat, you're beautiful. You accentuate that with perfect makeup and a flattering hairdo. The style exposes your ears, to better showcase the quarter-carat, brilliant cut, D color, IF-quality diamond earrings in platinum and gold settings. You add the Albert Nipon pant suit, the Nanette Lepore blouse, and that antique Faberge pendant around your neck, and you are a perfectly turned out woman who will be noticed—and, more importantly, remembered. In this business, that will get you caught."

He glanced down at her hands. "Furthermore, you're wearing something that doesn't go with your ensemble."

"What?" was her dumbstruck reply.

"That Brietling vintage aviator chronographic watch. It doesn't match your outfit, is large, and looks very complex. All it does is broadcast that you're a pilot."

"Are you finished?" Sharon snarled.

"I could mention the Bausch & Lomb sunglasses."

"Anything else?"

"As matter of fact, yes."

"Oh my God, I think I liked you better when you were quiet!"

"I usually work alone, which is probably why I'm not rotting in prison. So when I do work with someone, they need to understand how I work."

"Okay, let's hear it …," she groused, then flippantly added, "and to think I was going to offer you a nice little 'cuddle' when all of this was over." She glanced at him again.

He didn't blink. Darien's good looks had attracted many women over the years, but he usually spurned their advances, preferring the anonymity of prostitutes. But watching Sharon Turner, he felt an attraction he did not fully understand. He knew from her look that she wanted him to say something. He'd never been good at conversation, but he did remember a line from a TV show.

"It's been a while for you, has it?"

Sharon startled, but the look faded into a warm—almost devious—smile. Now they were playing on her terms. "Honey, it's been so long, I forget which one of us gets tied up."

Darien did something he rarely did: he laughed. It was only for a brief moment before he went silent, surprised by his own reaction.

Sharon, clearly more at ease now, kept smiling. "Okay, Darien. Let me know your playbook."

Darien held up a hand. "Here's how I work: one, always use a disguise; never appear in the same place twice without changing your looks. Two, insertion. Get into place for the hit interacting with as few people as possible, especially women, as they have very good memories for detail." He glanced at Sharon. "Especially for other women. Leave no trail."

He continued to count off his fingers. "Three, preparation. Scout out the kill zone carefully. Look for security or traffic cameras. Make sure all equipment is fully functional. Track the target to make sure it is alone and not armed."

He paused. "Four. Repeat rule three."

Sharon was still smiling.

"Five, execution. Quick and clean, drawing little, or better still, no attention."

He took a breath. "Six, extraction. Have an escape plan fully prepared with at least two options in case the primary plan fails."

Sharon's smile turned sarcastic.

"Can I get all this in writing? I'm liable to forget."

Sharon could feel Darien's gaze boring a hole through the side of her head. She sighed.

"Okay, I get it. I have an old hat and jacket in the back I'll wear if I have to leave the van in Waterloo."

Their flight plan showed them going to a private airstrip on a farm near Jamestown, New York. After landing the Piper Twin Comanche, Sharon, with Darien's assistance, set about altering its appearance. Using self-adhering vinyl, they changed the color of the wing flashes from red to blue. They also added a blue stripe to each side of the fuselage. Finally, they altered the plane's registration number to a Canadian one. Before taking off, Sharon switched off her transponder, making them undetectable to radar. Any traffic controller who had happened to be tracking them would have seen them make it to the farm, their stated destination, but not notice that they'd taken off again.

They crossed Lake Erie and entered Canada illegally at under 1,000 feet to avoid any air traffic control facilities that might have had primary radar operating. Primary radar could still detect them even with the transponder off and since they didn't want to leave a trail, they didn't want to encounter any border checks. They wanted to be invisible.

The flight to Waterloo ended in a field at a farm just north of the city. The prearranged minivan was waiting. Darien loaded his cane and a small case containing makeup and a wig. It was a short drive to the heart of Waterloo, seventy-five miles northwest of Toronto. As they drove, Darien applied the makeup and wig. When he was finished, he looked about fifteen years older.

***

For Dr. Steven Bertrand, the day dawned as beautifully as it could for any man in love. He was lying in bed holding the love of his life, Arissa Thompson, in his arms. Her long, light brown hair cascaded across his shoulder and offered up the gentle sent of lilacs while her peaceful breathing in slumber caressed his cheek. The firm softness of her breasts pressed against his chest while his hand tenderly outlined the contours of her body in long, slow strokes. The morning light streamed through his bedroom window catching the diamond on the engagement ring adorning Arissa's finger, bright and vivacious as the new day. Steven was taking this morning for himself and Arissa. He had an appointment in the afternoon to interview a prospect for the Institute at the university, but that was all. This morning was for them, a morning where he did not have to think, a morning where he could just experience something other than the cold, hard sciences he worked in; something soft and yielding. The non-quantifiable sensation of love.

***

Waterloo was the home of a second university, Wilfrid Laurier, which was just a few blocks away on University Avenue (a name perhaps all too fitting). In the early afternoon, Sharon dropped Darien at the corner of King Street and University to scout out his "kill zone." She continued on to University of Waterloo to confirm the target's location. This was very easy, as the target carried a smart phone with its location tracking turned on. Once ensconced in a small alleyway, using codes and software supplied by 355 on her notebook, Sharon was able to hack the Facebook page of Steven Bertrand. Sharon studied his picture so she could confirm the target's identity but couldn't keep herself from reading his profile:

"Degrees in advanced computer engineering and quantum mechanics, works at Perimeter Institute, picture of him with Steven Hawking ... Yes, you are a bright boy," Sharon said to herself.

What gave Sharon pause, however, was a photo of Steven with a pretty young girl, which had just been posted the night before announcing their engagement.

"So why are we killing you this day, Dr. Bertrand, and breaking this young woman's heart?" Sharon wondered aloud.

Yes, Steven made it easy for Sharon to find him with the location setting on his phone turned on. "Smart phones, stupid people," she chortled. She put on her old flight jacket and baseball cap and tracked him to the library. She observed him discreetly from a distance and confirmed his ID. She watched him shake the hand of someone she assumed was a student as they said goodbye. She was able to confirm his notebook computer was with him. She already knew from text message interceptions that he was going to meet his fiancée, Arissa, for coffee at a cafe on King Street at three PM.

As for Darien, he didn't know why this guy had to die nor why it was so important for his computer and cell to be recovered. It was none of his business. He was just the executioner. Darien had selected a certain sixty foot stretch of sidewalk on the west side of King, just south of University, which he had determined wasn't under surveillance.

At 2:15, Sharon watched Steven slide his notebook computer into a small leather briefcase in preparation to leave the library. She hurried back to the minivan in time to watch him leave the building while sending a text and walk across campus toward University Avenue.

For Steven, this was a great day. The sun was out and the spring air had that certain ambiance of new life that only this season brings, with flowers rising from a long winter and birds building their nests. This was the soundtrack to his memory of last night, the single most elating moment he'd had in his life, and he could see it all unfold again as he strolled toward University Ave.

He and Arissa had walked across campus to the Modern Languages building, where they sat down under the watchful gaze of Porcellino, the bronze statue of a boar who stood guard at the entrance. For Steven, the moment had come, and he turned to Arissa as he told her what was in his heart, words he'd been rehearsing for a week straight. And he heard his voice, the words pouring forth strong and sure as he said, "And now the time has come for me to get down on one knee," and he knelt before his lady love, "and to take your hands in mine and look into the eyes of the woman I love and hope against hope she will accept my proposal of marriage."

And he saw again Arissa's eyes—God, he loved her eyes!—brimming with tears, and he heard her voice and felt her breath again, almost a whisper in his ear as she leaned as she gave him her answer. "Yes."

⁎

Sharon made careful note which pocket Steven put his cell phone in. Then she climbed into the minivan and trailed him. She picked up one of the two disposable cells she and Darien had purchased earlier. Darien had the other phone and he picked up on the first ring. "Subject five minutes out, cell in left coat pocket, computer in briefcase. He is wearing a brown leather coat over a blue, pinstripe dress shirt."

⁎

That single joyous syllable! He'd swept Arissa into his arms and held her as tight as he could, overwhelmed, overjoyed. He kissed her once, then twice, and then he took the ring box out of his pocket. He slid the ring onto her finger, breathing, "Now and for always."

⁎

Darien used his phone to log into an e-mail account. He wasn't checking for e-mails; he was checking out the drafts folder. He always thought this was a clever way to communicate with someone without creating a record of e-mail traffic between you and another. You create an e-mail account with a provider. You would both have the same address and password. To send a message, you went into the account, typed up an e-mail, but instead of sending it, you saved it under drafts. When the other party logged in, they'd look under drafts and there was the message. After they read it, they'd just delete it, no record. Darien was looking for a draft with two special words in it: an order to abort the mission.

It wasn't there; the mission was a go.

Steven paused at the crosswalk of University and King, shutting his eyes. He could still feel the lingering warmth of Arissa's lips after that first kiss; he knew he'd always cherish how her face had lit up as she gazed at the ring wrapped around her finger. And he could still feel the cold metal of Porcellino's shiny snout against his fingertips; he almost laughed at the memory of it—two grown people, giddy, rubbing the statue's snout, just as students did for luck before an exam. They needed luck; they'd just signed up for the most difficult test of all. But unlike all his exams, Steven felt no fear; only calm confidence that Arissa would always be by his side.

**

Sharon watched as Steven came around the corner and started down King. A half-block away, Darien ducked into a convenience store. As Steven passed, he exited the store and followed behind Steven, pulling down the arming lever of the cane.

Sharon marveled at the careful way Darien stalked his prey, waiting for the exact moment when there would be the fewest number of people in his kill zone. When it happened, it was so fast she almost missed it. Darien took a few quick steps and poked Steven in the back of his leg with his cane. Steven spun about as Darien put his arm around his shoulder like an old friend greeting him. As he fell forward into Darien's arms, the briefcase slid into his hands. He plucked the cell phone from Steven's pocket and let the body slide to the sidewalk. And then Darien slid into the role of shocked passerby, shouting, "Oh my God! Help! Somebody call 911!"

Once the crowd had gathered and the ambulance and police were seen, Darien melted away. He met Sharon a block away. As he entered the van, Sharon said, "You are very good at what you do."

"Is it, how did you put it, cuddle time?"

Darien could not believe he said it. Sharon just looked at him and smiled. She was quiet all the way back to the farm. After they pulled up to the Comanche, Sharon turned to Darien.

"It's cuddle time now," she proclaimed, wrapping her arms around Darien.

*
**

Kathleen strolled further down the path and leaned against a tree with her hands in her pockets and her head down while the Secret Service detail spread out a little further. She was clearly in deep thought. I gave her a few minutes, then strolled over.

"So these people killed a brilliant young man with a great future before him who had just gotten engaged … and for what, Jim?"

"At this point, we didn't know he had been murdered. We wouldn't have known at all if a local retailer hadn't been remodeling."

*
**

The Hollohan Stationery Shop had been a fixture on King Street for over thirty years. As a provider of the finest papers and writing supplies, Terry Hollohan had built up good business over the years. Unfortunately, with the progression of the digital age, expediency had replaced elegance. E-mail had replaced letter writing, leaving Terry with services the public no longer required. This would have left most men bitter, but not Terry. His positive attitude and indomitable spirit showed him opportunity instead of defeat. Terry owned the building, which afforded him the opportunity to retire into the role of landlord. New tenants would soon be occupying this space, which was why Terry was at his old store that day. His new tenants were opening an internet cafe. They loved the location, close to the universities, but the location was also something else: right across the street from Darien's kill zone. When Darien checked out this part of King Street, he had been very careful to make sure there were no security cameras about. He did notice Terry's old store, but it was closed. If Darien had looked a bit closer, he might have noticed the back of a white van parked down the narrow alley next to the store. If he could have seen the side of the van, he would have noticed it bore the name S&E KW Security Services. What had brought Sam Carson of this company to Terry's store was the installation of a new security system that Terry had bought to protect his property. This system included high definition cameras to watch not only the interior, but the exterior of the building as well. It was Terry who first noticed the commotion across the street.

"I wonder what's going on over there," Terry mused, observing the crowd that had gathered around the body of a young man. Two police cars had arrived and one of the officers was administering CPR. The ambulance's arrival blocked Sam and Terry's view of the scene.

"I didn't see what happened, but I've been running tests on the new security cameras. Maybe they caught something."

Sam went over to his notebook computer, perched on the counter and started typing. Terry stood beside him as they watched the images of the commotion in the street unfolded before their eyes.

"Oh my God! That guy stabbed him! I'm gonna get one of those officers," Terry cried as he hurried out the door.

Jim's mind was racing as he drove home from his meeting with his Uncle George, Dominique Deselva, and Jake Connors. He was not happy with the way his uncle arranged the meeting, but after George apologized and they'd talked with the two FBI agents, he understood the reason for secrecy. 'New Times possibly involved in money laundering, just great,' he thought. 'First the crash of 2008 and now this. If this gets out, I won't have a client left.'

Was this what Ted was trying to tell him about the other day? He hadn't told the FBI agents about that conversation. He needed time to think. What was he supposed to say to them—"Oh yes, my dear friend Ted. He and his wife, Martha, who were so helpful after Elizabeth died, are probably laundering money. Better check out Martha too."

Jim had ended the meeting early, using an appointment as an excuse. They'd agreed to talk later. Jim arrived home and went straight to his office, followed by Rusty. Jim poured himself a drink and patted Rusty on the head.

"How about you, Rusty? Doing any money laundering? Got any bones buried where you shouldn't?"

Jim flopped down in his chair and fixed his eyes on his print of Ansel Adam's iconic photograph "Moon Rise." Jim often pondered it when he needed to think. He'd just taken a sip of his drink and put his feet up when Jennifer burst into the room, tears streaming down her face.

"Daddy, I just got some horrible news! My friend Steven. He–He's dead!"

Jim dropped his feet to the floor. "What! What happened?"

"I dunno, Daddy! I just got this text from Arissa. She said he just dropped dead and they had just gotten engaged last night!"

"Oh no, Jenny, I'm sorry," Jim said, pulling her into a hug. "If there's anything I can do, if you need to go to her, let me know. I'll make the arrangements."

"Okay, Daddy," Jennifer sobbed. "I have people to call."

With that Jennifer ran back upstairs and Jim found himself standing in his office wondering what he could do to comfort Jennifer. He looked over at the portrait on his desk of Elizabeth. The one he took of her on their first anniversary. He glanced at Rusty. "Well, pal, if she was here, she would know what to do."

*
**

The following day proved to be a busy one for Sharon and Darien. 'The three earlier hits, the two FBI informants at New Times, and Angie Borello at MIT in Cambridge, went very well,' Darien thought. 'Especially as they've been followed by a nice … "cuddle" from Sharon.'

That Angie Borello certainly had been a pretty young lady, a shame really, but business was business. What was a bit unusual, however, was that something was clearly bothering her even before he'd arrived on the scene. They'd tracked her right across campus from the Computer Science and Artificial Intelligence Laboratory on Vassar Street down to the Dr. Paul Dudley White bike path near Harvard Bridge.

She'd gotten off her bicycle. She'd sat on a park bench and she was texting. As Darien meandered down the bike path, he observed her get up and walk around the bench shaking her head. Then she sat down again.

The hit went as planned: a tap on the shoulder with the tip of the cane; a surprised look on her face; the rolling back of the eyes. But this time

Darien found himself doing something he could not explain. He closed her eyes and propped her up on the bench facing Harvard Bridge. 'She looks as if she's asleep,' he thought as he ran a finger down her cheek. "So lovely. I wonder what upset you?" he said aloud. Darien picked up her cell phone, turned it off, grabbed her backpack, and left.

*
**

"But Madam President, Angie wasn't texting when he stabbed her with his cane. She was Skyping," I said as I walked down the path with Kathleen on my arm.

"But why Jim? Why was he killing these innocent students? The FBI informants makes sense if murder ever does. But students? I don't get it."

"Understanding would come later. I had another problem at this point."

Kathleen stopped and looked at me with a wrinkled brow in anticipation of my next words.

"When Angie was stabbed, she dropped her cell phone and it fell, landing against her backpack at the perfect angle for the person she was talking to, to watch her friend die on her computer screen."

"So who was Angie talking to?"

I found myself not being able to answer for a moment as the shock of that day came storming back to me. My silence answered the question.

"Oh my God, Jim. No!"

"There are only two things we should fight for. One is defense our homes and the other is the Bill of Rights."

— Smedley Butler

CHAPTER 5

Jim was still working in his office when he heard Jennifer scream. He dashed to her room. Jennifer had a hand clamped over her mouth. She looked helplessly at her father, then pointed to her computer screen. Jim glanced at the screen just in time to see a hand stretching over the screen, blocking out all the light. The screen then went blank.

"He killed her, he killed Angie!" Jennifer's voice trembled under the force of barely restrained fear.

"Oh my God, Jenny! What's happened?"

"What's going on?!" Dolly cried, poking her head into the room, eyes wide. Robert followed her in.

Jennifer slumped onto her bed. "I told her about Steven, and while I was talking to her, I got an e-mail saying Steven was murdered!"

"I told Angie. She walked around. I could see the background moving. She sat back down and then she dropped her phone and I saw him, and then I saw Angie, and she was just staring—she!"

She wailed long and loud. "She's dead!"

"Do you know where she was calling from?"

Jennifer nodded. Tears were streaming down her face. "She answered the phone and said she was in our conference room."

"Which conference room is that?" asked Jim.

"It's a joke. It's a park bench at the bike path near the Harvard Bridge. We'd meet there a lot."

Jim raced off. Dolly sat down on the bed with her granddaughter. Robert hovered nearby.

"The murderer—he—touched her face, he said she was lovely, he asked what was bothering her." Jennifer's voice was choked.

Robert didn't quite understand what had happened, but he did know his granddaughter had seen something terrifying. He put his arm around her and pulled her close to him. "It's okay, Jenny," he said gently. "We're all here for you. It will be all right."

Jim came back, toting the phone with him. "The campus police are checking it out. They said they'd call back."

Rusty had wriggled his way between Dolly and Jennifer and put his head on Jennifer's lap. She began to pet him with a shaking hand.

"I don't understand any of this. First Steven, and now Angie ..."

She took a shaky breath. "We had our own little support group: Steven and Arissa up in Canada, Gerard over in France, and Angie and I here. It's been working so well for us; they've helped me solve so many problems with the AIM-DAT program."

"It's nice that you help each other out," Jim said softly.

"We helped them with issues on some of their projects," continued Jennifer. "Angie and I had just written some programming for Waterloo's SPAUN project. We had even developed some new programs together and were thinking of forming an online company to market them. Arissa and Steven had just gotten engaged and ..."

The phone rang. Jim grabbed it up and stepped into the hall.

They waited.

"Okay. Okay. Thank you." Click.

Jim's face was grim when he stepped back in. Jennifer shut her eyes tight as the tears started anew.

"I am so sorry, honey."

Jennifer started to shake.

"You ever see anything like this, Detective?" Dr. Richards glanced up from his tablet.

"Not in my twenty years with the Waterloo Regional Police," replied Detective Sutherland. "I'll bet no one else has either."

"It's a first for me, but I've heard of it," Richards mumbled.

They stared at the small ball bearing lying at the bottom of the test tube.

"There was a case back in the late '70s. There was a Bulgarian dissident named Markov living in London. The KGB wanted to get rid of him. They used an umbrella the same way our guy used a cane. But the poison used was ricin. It took Markov a few days to die. This was so fast. That's what I can't get my head around: what poison was used here. We've seen the video. Death was almost instantaneous," Richards muttered.

"Here's what I don't get," Sutherland said. "This guy is a professional and, judging by the hardware he's using and his technique, probably an expensive one. This begs the question, why does someone want to pay thousands of dollars and risk going to jail to kill a kid who doesn't seem to have an enemy in the world?"

Richards pondered his tablet for a moment before answering.

"They say murder requires three things: motive, means, and opportunity. We know the answer to two of those. It's the motive that's missing. I don't envy you your job. I wouldn't know where to start."

"I know where I'm starting. I'll be looking at airport surveillance videos from the last couple of days. We're looking for a man with a cane."

"You're assuming this guy isn't local?"

Richards could see the reflections of the video in Sutherland's glasses as he studied it for probably the twentieth time on his laptop. He answered Richards in a slow analytical voice, as if he were speaking to the killer himself.

"No, you're no local boy, are you? You're international and you came in and left by air. You wouldn't risk detection by being on station for too long. It's quick in and quick out. It's not the kill that turns you on, is it, buddy? It's the execution of a well-planned operation that gets you off."

"How would you know that?" Richards huffed.

Sutherland froze the image on the screen at the point the killer stabbed Steven Bertrand.

"He came into our city and murdered one of its citizens on its main street in broad daylight. That's beyond gutsy; that's arrogance. Arrogance brought on by self-confidence honed by lots of experience. This guy is smart and a planner."

Sutherland looked down, thought a moment, then glanced up at Richards and stated, "Smart or not, I am going to make this sonovabitch sorry he came to Waterloo."

*
**

As they approached the Fenton airport, Darien knew tonight's job was going to be different than any he had ever done before. Five people, all in the same house, a family named Hanson. There was no disguising that as simultaneous heart attacks. This would definitely be a job for Ivan, his Russian-made revolver. As a general rule, Darien did not like firearms— too messy. But in the rare cases he had to use one, his primary rule—leave nothing behind—was paramount. He couldn't understand why others in his profession chose to work with semi-automatic pistols. They could carry more bullets, sure, but every time the pistol fired, the shell casing was ejected. That meant running around looking for casings if they didn't want to leave any evidence behind. With a revolver, the shell casings stayed in the cylinder. However, they had a different problem. The cylinder had to rotate to allow each chamber to stay aligned with the barrel, which meant that there had to be a small gap between the cylinder and the barrel. It was this gap that allowed some of the propellant gases to escape. So powerful was the loss that if someone had their hand wrapped around the cylinder of a revolver when it was fired, they could lose their fingers. It also made the weapon louder, even when using a silencer (which Darien always did).

The Nagant M-1895 solved all those issues. Every time the revolver was cocked, the cylinder moved forward, creating a seal. Furthermore, the 7.62-millimeter bullet, instead of sticking out of the cartridge casing like most bullets, was actually recessed in its casing below the rim. That meant that when the cylinder went forward, part of the cartridge casing sealed to the barrel as well.

But that wasn't enough for Darien. When he acquired his Nagant, he dissected it. Using his watch-making skills, he polished and honed every piece so that even when he cocked it, there was hardly a sound. The bullets he used weren't jacketed; they were pure lead. When the bullet hit someone, it distorted, a feat with two advantages: the wound size increased, thereby increasing the odds for a kill; and it made it all but impossible to match the bullet to the revolver. Nevertheless, Darien made sure to never handle the weapon without wearing gloves; he didn't want prints. That applied to the ammunition as well, an oversight which had put many of his colleagues in jail.

What concerned Darien the most about tonight's job was not the fact he had five people to eliminate. It was the sixth target that troubled him: the Hansons' dog, this one named Rusty. Dogs were always a problem. If he didn't get them first, they'd get him, either directly or by barking and waking everyone up.

*
**

Arissa Thompson sat on a bench. She'd been walking for hours, lapping the entire campus several times, trying to make sense of what had happened. Now she sat, as dusk fell, staring at the blank eyes of Porcellino, on the very bench on which Steven had proposed just forty-eight hours ago.

"Of all the guys out there, why him?" she whispered, finally giving voice to the question ever since … it. The internet had been buzzing between the universities. Rumor said it was a murder, he'd been *killed* … but he was dead all the same.

Arissa had never really dated. But Steven had been different. They had worked on projects together before he went to the Perimeter Institute, feeding off each other as they crafted the next generation of software. They were already being scouted by Microsoft and Apple, and others were coming. Computer engineers and their abilities were always in need.

Arissa glanced at the diamond ring on her finger. Some of her friends thought it was quaint she was getting engaged, as most of them were content just to live with their boyfriends and forgo marriage. But Steven was old-school, and frankly, she realized, she was too. She stared at the cold eyes of Porcellino.

"Well, Porcellino. How do we find out who did this … and why?"

Being dressed to kill in Darien's world meant donning a black jumpsuit and double-latex gloves taped to his sleeves, and taping his pant legs to his running shoes. A balaclava, backpack, and night-vision goggles completed the ensemble, which ensured none of his DNA would be left at the scene.

Tonight's location was the Hanson home. The house was protected with an alarm and security cameras inside and out. Darien smirked. He knew this particular system had a feature that permitted someone to log onto their security service when they were away and have a look around their property. Offering clients a key fob or an app for their cell phones that would turn the system on or off remotely was also very convenient for the security companies' clients; and for Darien, making his job so much easier. In this case, 355 had supplied him with the codes. Getting into the Hanson home would be effortless.

The Hansons' backyard was surrounded by a ten-foot cedar hedge with a small gate in the middle, which led to an alley that ran behind most of the properties in the neighborhood. Darien's first challenge was to get up to the house without being spotted. Once he was in the backyard, the tall hedges would prevent any neighbor from spying him. The plan was to have Sharon drive the alley without stopping. Darien would be in the back with the door partially open. As they passed the rear gate, he would roll out.

The mission would take place at 3:30 AM. It was a cloudy night—no moon, making the darkness deeper. Sharon pulled into a convenience store parking lot. Darien logged in to the e-mail account and checked the drafts for the abort message. There was none. Next, Darien logged onto the Hansons' security provider and scoped out the house using the security cameras. Darien now found his first target. The dog was in his usual place, curled up in the office chair. All looked peaceful; it was time to go.

Sharon drove down the alley slowly; Darien rolled out as they passed the gate. Crouching near this entrance, he worked his way partially into the hedge for concealment before entering the Hansons' backyard. He turned on his night-vision goggles and scanned the back of the two-story, Tudor-style home with an enclosed deck. Then he spotted them on the roof: two motion-sensor light fixtures, each with two spotlights. Darien pulled Ivan from his backpack. 'Now we'll see if all that practice on the twenty-five-yard range was worth it,' he thought.

Four silent shots, four spotlights broken. Darien slipped past the gate, only to slide and nearly fall in the dew-laden grass. Regaining his composure, he proceeded to the screened deck, pausing to reload Ivan. He placed the spent cartridges in a zippered pocket of his jumpsuit.

The door to the deck was unlocked. He proceeded to the back door. Peering through the decorative window, he spied a red light glowing on the wall-mounted security keypad. Pulling out his remote, Darien keyed in the security code and watched the light turn green.

Darien next went to the southeast corner of the building. All the services for the house ran four feet underground from the alley and under the back lawn. A conduit pipe sprouted up out of the ground, joining up with a junction box mounted on the corner of the house. Plucking a screwdriver from his backpack, Darien loosed the cover off the box. With a pair of insulated wire cutters, he severed the telephone, TV cable, and electrical service lines. The house was now dead.

He tiptoed back to the door. 'Always the same,' he thought with an idle smirk. 'Thousands of dollars for a security system, but only twenty bucks for a lock.' Before picking the lock, Darien checked his phone. "No signal" flashed at him. 'Well, 355 has kept their word,' he mused. 'They'd said the towers in this area would be offline at 3:30 AM. for a half-hour.' He yanked open the door and stepped into the hallway. Rusty's ears perked up at the sound of the door. He hopped off the chair and padded out to the back hall. Darien heard the distinct click of dog nails on hardwood flooring. He knelt down, assuming a classic shooting position with one elbow on his knee, steadying Ivan for the first shot. He could see the dog coming now; its eyes glowed an eerie green in the night-vision goggles.

Unfortunately for Darien, it wasn't Rusty who was in danger here. It was him. For Darien had lost something. If he were a fighter pilot, what he'd lost would be called "situational awareness due to target fixation." In aerial combat, many a good pilot had lost his life by tunnel-visioning a single target, becoming so fixated he saw nothing else. Unbeknownst to Darien, Rusty had a wingman, and he was about to execute a perfect deflection shot and blow Darien and his mission right out of the sky.

*
**

It was raining in Andorra La Vella. Culper enjoyed the rain, the way it created a sense of motion in the colors of the elegant eighteenth-century stained glass that adorned his office window. He liked to stand in front of the ancient glass and think, as he was doing now.

"What's the situation?"

Gaston startled. He hadn't realized Culper had noticed him. "Nothing has changed since our last briefing. The Waterloo police have labeled it a homicide, but haven't stated the means of death."

Culper sat down at his desk.

"We'll continue to monitor the local media," Gaston added.

"How did the police discover it was a murder?"

Gaston was silent.

"How about Lyon?"

"Our people there do lack Darien's … finesse."

"How so?"

"Tremblay met his end about an hour ago: knifed in a mugging, computer and cell phone stolen. Crude, but effective. A small complication, however."

"I'm listening." Culper's mouth twisted in a frown; a bad sign, Gaston knew.

"Tremblay's brother, Maurice Tremblay, a professor of advanced software architecture here at the University of Andorra."

Culper leaned forward on this desk. "You see that as a problem?"

"I don't like coincidences, especially not in our own backyard. They make me paranoid."

Culper grinned wolfishly. "You mean more paranoid than you already are, Gaston?" His eyes flashed. "How are things in Cambridge?"

"So far, listed as a death, but the coroner is investigating. There was a complication there as well."

Culper fixed Gaston with cold stare, but remained silent.

"The target was on a video call when she was killed. Whoever she was talking to saw Darien kill her. We've erased all traces of the call from the pertinent servers. The police will find nothing."

"Do I dare ask who she was talking to at the time of her death?" Culper drummed his fingers on the desk.

"Jennifer Hanson," replied Gaston. He glanced at his watch. "She'll be dead in a moment or two along with the other four members of her family."

"I didn't authorize that. Just her and her brother."

"Another complication, I'm afraid," Gaston said. "The brother and sister don't seem to be out much. He thought it best to stage the murder as a robbery gone bad where the whole family dies."

"How about those two spies at New Times?"

Gaston looked down and walked over to the stained glass window while shaking his head. Culper could see the colors from it wash over his face when he finally looked up, giving him a surreal appearance.

"Regrettably, two middle-aged men with bad hearts passed away early this morning: one in a grocery store, the other while out jogging."

Robert Hanson had taken to wandering at night. He couldn't sleep. Dolly told him it was 'cause he was sick—but he wasn't. He felt fine. He was just ... restless. He'd wandered into the living room and he'd been looking out the front window, trying to remember *what* he'd come in here for, when the lamps on the side tables blinked out. He stumbled into the hallway. The light from the streetlamps coming through the windows was hardly enough to see by. "Dang fuse box, always was faulty ..."

He paused. He was sure a man had just walked into the hallway and knelt down. He had a gun. Robert didn't hesitate longer; he charged straight at the man, sending him into a small table in the hall. A vase crashed to the floor. Rusty started to bark.

Darien had been just about to pull the trigger to kill the dog when he was knocked sideways with such force that he dropped Ivan. A fist slammed into his face; his head snapped back, night-vision goggles crashing to the floor. He could see Ivan and reached to retrieve it when searing pain rushed up his arm. Rusty clamped his jaws around Darien's hand and wouldn't let go. He slammed Rusty against the wall. "Let go, you little mongrel—"

He swung at the old man, shoving Rusty into him. He stumbled back and Rusty released. Darien scrambled out the back door. Rusty chased him into the night, barking and howling. He leapt and tore at a flailing hand. He hung on for dear life, but Darien managed to get his right hand, despite its injury, around the screwdriver. He struck blindly at the dog, catching him in the hindquarter. Rusty yelped loudly and Darien pulled free, fleeing through back gate.

Jason dashed into the backyard as he heard a man yell followed shortly by Rusty's yelp. It took Jason a few minutes to find Rusty in the dark. When he did, Rusty was whimpering and hobbling toward the gate. Jason knelt down over him.

"It's okay, buddy. You've done enough."

Jason reached down to pick him up, but stopped when he felt something warm and sticky on his hands. A flashlight illuminated the yard.

"Over here! Rusty's hurt!"

"He got a piece of him! You should've heard the yell, Rusty got 'im!"

"So did your grandfather," Jim replied, crouching down over the dog.

"How is Grandpa?" asked Jason.

"He's bloodied up, but he'll be okay. Jennifer's across the street at the McGills' to call 911. Our phones are out."

The sound of sirens rent the air. Robert was sitting at the kitchen table, holding a cold compress to his head. Dolly was sitting next to him, cleaning blood off his face from a split lip and a cut above his eye. The fear and concern on her face matched what Jim felt as he and Jason came in with Rusty.

Everyone crowded around Rusty as Jason laid him on the kitchen table.

"Let me see my friend," Robert demanded.

Rusty, upon seeing Robert, tried to get up and lick his face.

"It's okay, Rusty. You'll be all right. We got him, didn't we, we showed him! You did good, boy. You did good." Robert stroked the dog affectionately.

The police arrived, along with the paramedics and the house was soon bustling.

"Jason, the Cornwall Animal Clinic has a vet on overnight. You and Jennifer should take Rusty there," Jim said.

"On our way, Dad," Jason replied lifting Rusty carefully.

"Nothing but the best for Rusty," Robert called after them.

"I'm Officer Gilbert, and this is Officer Edwards. I understand you had a bit of trouble here tonight."

"Trouble is an understatement, sir," Robert grunted. "Shine that flashlight of yours down the hall there and tell me what's on the floor."

The officers moved into the hall. They examined the abandoned Nagant revolver and night-vision goggles. Jim and Dolly exchanged glances. Robert hadn't been this lucid in months. It was if something had taken him over.

"You know, officers, that sonovabitch is lucky he ran away," Robert said as he was loaded up on a stretcher.

"Why is that?"

"Rusty and I don't take prisoners." Robert grinned.

"Mom, would you accompany Dad to the hospital? I'll finish up here with the officers."

As they left the house, Dolly looked down at her husband with the love and understanding that only comes to those who have been together so long.

"You know honey, they don't give you a Purple Heart for injuries sustained while fighting bad guys that invade your home," she said whimsically.

"Well, they should and to dogs too."

"An elderly man and his Dachshund fought off an armed assassin. My God! They're lucky to be alive." Officer Gilbert shook his head.

Officer Edwards had been out in the yard and now returned. "We're gonna need a forensics team out here," he reported. "There's a lot of blood on the back gate. It looks like your dog did get a good piece of him."

As a gourmet, Culper could tell you a vintage glass of red Châteauneuf-du-Pape served in antique Belgian crystal, such as the one he was holding right at that moment, paired well with most things. As with most things in life, there are exceptions. One being a course of bad news, which he assumed he was about to be served, if the look on Gaston's face was anything to judge by. The note had just been delivered and was commanding Gaston's full attention. He read it and went stock-still. He started to tremble.

"What is it?" Culper snarled.

Gaston slumped back into his chair. "We seem to have a complication in Virginia."

***

"Three brilliant young people, two brave citizens of this nation who were trying to help the FBI—all dead—and then almost your entire family too! My God, Jim!" Kathleen exclaimed as she sat down on the bench. We were back at the memorial. I could see she was upset but trying not to show it, trying to look "presidential," gracing me with her best "nothing can shake me look" that the media thought we demanded from our presidents.

"I saw surveillance video of the young man in Canada on TV; it was horrible. I had no idea it was tied into all of this. My God, Jim! If it wasn't for your dad and your dog ... a man in his eighties ... and a little dog ..."

"A fighter pilot and his wingman, Madam President."

Kathleen smiled, reached over, and gave my hand a squeeze.

"Well, God bless them both, Jim."

"There are mysteries which men can only guess at, which age by age they may only solve only in part."

— Bram Stoker

CHAPTER 6

Maurice Tremblay was in his office. His hand was on the receiver of the phone, resting in its cradle. It had been over ten minutes since he'd hung up, but he couldn't bring himself to move his hand, as though letting go would mean what he'd heard would become true. His sister Marie had called. Their brother Gerard had been murdered. Maurice couldn't fathom what she'd said. This couldn't happen, not to his family. He couldn't stop staring at the phone. 'Now what do I do?' he wondered.

'I'll call Chantal.'

Maurice's fiancée answered almost immediately. Chantal LePage's comforting words were what he needed to hear. They talked for a while, before she said, soothingly, "We will get through this together, Maurice. Your family needs you now. I will make the arrangements to get us to Lyon."

After he hung up, he logged into a chatroom he knew was frequented by computer students at the Institut National des Sciences Appliquées. The room was abuzz with at least a dozen posts about Gerard's death … and two others, Angie Borello and Steven Bertrand. Maurice knew the names. Gerard had been working with students in Canada and the United States on some projects.

Maurice frowned, then dredged up an old message—a programming question from his brother. Steven and Angie were copied on the e-mail, as were two others: a Jennifer Hanson and an Arissa Thompson. Steeling himself, he began to write an e-mail, informing them about Gerard's death.

The sun was rising when the forensics team departed the Hanson home, leaving Jim all alone in the house. He'd just received a phone call from

Dolly, telling him the doctors wanted to do more tests on Robert. She didn't know when they'd be home. When Jim went to put on a pot of coffee, he discovered he was trembling. He could not stop it. He sat down heavily.

"My God, he was gonna kill us all! We could've been dead!"

He needed help. He ran to his office and plucked Jake Connors' business card off his desk. He whipped out his cell and rattled off a text. He had just sent the message when the front door opened. Jason and Jennifer had arrived home with Rusty. Jim took a shaky breath.

"How's our gallant warrior?" Jim asked, trailing them into the living room. They laid Rusty down on his dog bed. He licked Jim's hand when he reached out to pet the pooch.

"The vet says the wound wasn't too deep. Didn't think it was a knife, something blunt." Jason adjusted the bandage wrapped around Rusty's hindquarter.

"He needed some stitches and the vet gave him a shot," Jennifer added.

"How's Grandpa?" Jason asked.

"He's still at the hospital. More tests."

"What now? Do we just wait here?"

Jim looked at his children, their hollow eyes and the deep, dark rings marring their faces. "Get some sleep. We've got a lunch date and I need you on your game."

The pain was unlike any he'd ever known. His right hand had two deep puncture wounds from the damn mutt's fangs. He couldn't even feel two of his fingers. His left hand was worse. His little finger dangled limp and lifeless above the first knuckle.

Sharon had taken him to meet a certain doctor at her country home; 355 retained a physician just for such emergencies. This doctor was a very skilled practitioner, but with one little weakness: she loved to gamble, something that Sharon and 355 exploited every chance they had. The result was a very cooperative doctor. She worked on him for almost two hours, first re-attaching his little finger, then stitching the lacerations. Darien watched her work, a dark thought brewing in his mind like a storm, boiling through him, twisting through his insides.

Could he still be a watchmaker? He was like a surgeon: without his hands, he was useless.

"You've suffered nerve damage to both your hands," the doctor told him flatly. "Five of your fingers aren't responding: three on your left hand, and two on your right. You'll need more treatment and physiotherapy. I dunno where you people are going—I don't want to—but a big center is your only chance to get the kind of help you need."

Darien nodded.

"Physiotherapy can't wait if you want to have full use of those hands again." She dropped some white pills into a container and handed it to him. "Take two of these as needed to deal with the pain. Don't take more than eight a day."

Darien nodded again.

"Must've been a big dog," she said after a pause.

"A Dachshund," Darien growled.

This statement almost brought forth a laugh, but the look on Darien's face told her discretion was a better, if not a healthier, choice. She bit her lip, then turned away so he couldn't see her smile.

It was early morning when Darien got back in the van. "Where to?" Sharon inquired without glancing up from the morning paper.

Darien weighed his options. He needed money. He needed a place to stay, to lie low, and to ponder how to settle the score. And he needed a place from where he could easily travel to a big city to get his hands treated.

"Bermuda," he replied at last. Sharon folded up the paper.

"So much for a morning cuddle," she simpered, giving him a wink.

Dr. Richards led off the news conference. "We believe the death of Dr. Steven Bertrand to be a homicide," was his opening statement. "He was poisoned. The poison used—which we found traces of—causes cardiac arrest almost immediately."

He glanced at Sutherland. "Roll the tape."

The audience stared at the footage in stunned silence. Then they exploded into a barrage of questions.

"What poison was used?"

"Was this a random act?"

"Do you have any word on the killer?"

"Why Steven Bertrand?"

"Did he feel any pain?"

"What does his family think?"

Sutherland had to face the reporters with no leads, no information … All he could do was ask the public to report anything they'd seen, and the press nearly rioted. They clamored, their questions becoming more numerous, more shrill. Richards and Sutherland retreated to their respective offices.

"Well, *that* went swimmingly," Sutherland huffed.

"Do you *believe* some of the questions they ask? What a buncha …"

"Heard one, heard 'em all. Well, doc, I'm stumped. I dunno if this news conference did any good or not. I just hope releasing the video might shake up some action."

Jim, Jennifer, and Jason were already at the restaurant when Jake and Dom arrived, shaking hands as they were introduced to Jennifer and Jason for the first time. George joined them shortly thereafter in the private dining room Jim had secured so they could talk confidentially. It was obvious to George that something was very wrong: the Hansons looked like zombies, their eyes bloodshot and their skin pale.

"What's going on here?" he demanded.

"Well," Jim started, glancing at his kids. "We—"

"Hold on a second," Dom said, and it was then that Jim noticed a hush had fallen over the restaurant. He glanced out at the public dining room. Every eyeball in the building was glued to the TV over the bar, now playing a grainy black-and-white video.

"Oh my God," Jennifer breathed, and they turned to her. She shook her head. "It's Steven. And—and that's the guy that got Angie!"

"Sit down," Dom said.

Jim put a hand on her back to guide her into her chair. Jennifer's cell phone buzzed.

"Ignore it," Dom advised. Jennifer glanced at him, but took the phone out anyway and read the message.

"Oh God!" she cried. "Gerard's been murdered too!"

Most people could never be a coroner. Death was something most people never even discussed, let alone fathomed dealing with every day. Dr. Patricia Fellows was willing to face fear and learn from it. Good coroners hated mysteries. Dr. Fellows was staring down a mystery with this autopsy. She'd seen in the report that there was a witness, whom the deceased was on the phone with when she was attacked, but no trace of the call could be found and no cell phone was found at the scene. There was no physical evidence of an attack. It appeared the victim had died of a myocardial infarction; in other words, a heart attack. But Angie Borello appeared perfectly healthy. A heart attack was implausible.

Dr. Fellows went to the lounge to get some coffee. The last couple of days had been tough: two children and now this young woman. As a coroner, she was supposed to remain detached and, for the most part, she had. But the young ones were always rough. It was on days like these she was glad to have Howard and the twins, Carolyn and Catherine, in her life. Howie was able to read her moods the moment she walked through the door. The girls would tell her about school, their homework, their friends—a welcome distraction from work.

As Patricia sipped her coffee, she glanced at the reeling news, the ticker-tape scrolling by—and now, grainy footage of a security camera played across the screen. She left her coffee on the table. It took her fifteen minutes to find the tiny puncture wound. She probed the wound and extracted the small ball bearing. She placed it in a plastic sample container.

"Andy, come here please. I want a second look for toxins on these samples, including electron microscope scans. Get the pathologist handling that murder case in Waterloo—in Canada, the one on the TV—get him on the phone."

*
**

Richards didn't recognize the name on his call display when his phone rang, but he picked it up anyway.

"Dr. Richards, I've just extracted a ball bearing out of the shoulder of a twenty-five-year-old lying on my autopsy table."

It was a moment before he could reply. "I'm gonna ask you to hold for a moment."

Richards called for Scott Sutherland. He set his phone to speaker.

"Dr. Fellows, does the victim show signs of a myocardial infarction?"

"Yes, she does, but with no cause."

"There's a cause. You just found it. Any idea what toxin was used?"

"I was hoping you could tell me."

"We're still running tests," he sighed.

Sutherland had come into the office and now joined the conversation.

"Dr. Fellows, I just got off the phone with our victim's fiancée. Our victims knew each other. Furthermore, there's been another murder—one of their colleagues in France. In addition, there was an attempt on another colleague's life in Virginia.

Detective Sutherland looked over at Dr. Richards as he removed his glasses in contemplation of the situation.

"I suggest we coordinate our investigations."

"Good idea," Dr. Fellows stated. "I'll have our detective in charge of this case call you."

*
**

The Hansons and their guests had finished their lunches and the dishes had been cleared when Jennifer's phone came to life again, displaying a name and number she did not know. She was going to let it go to voicemail but found herself answering it anyway.

"Hello Jennifer, this is Detective Scott Sutherland of the Waterloo Regional Police in Canada. I am calling you on the advice of Arissa Thompson."

Detective Sutherland explained the conversation he'd had with the coroner in Cambridge and how they believed Steven and Angie had been murdered by the same person.

"Detective Sutherland, may I put you on speaker?"

"I'm not sure that's a good idea, this is highly confidential—"

Jennifer glanced up. Jake and Dom were shaking their heads. Dom mimed zipping his lips.

"I think we're all right," she said. "There's nobody here except my family—and we're all aware of the situation."

"I understand you texted Arissa that you were attacked today."

"First of all, Detective, I can confirm Angie and Steven were killed by the same person. The person on the surveillance video is the same as I saw on the Skype call. As far as today is concerned …"

The Hansons quickly reviewed the day's events: the attack, the heroics, the hospital trip, and the investigation. Detective Sutherland then asked the million dollar question, the very same one they'd been asking themselves all day:

"Have you got any idea why someone would want all of you dead?"

"We were hoping the police could come up with a motive, as we can't," answered Jim.

"I'm sure they'll be in touch," Detective Sutherland added. "Good luck, and stay safe."

The line went dead. Jim turned to Jake and Dom. "What was that all about?"

"I'll explain," answered Jake, "but first, I've got some questions for Jennifer and Jason." He frowned at them. "Are you in contact with the other three students by e-mail?"

"I'm not," Jason replied. "They're Jenny's friends."

"Were," Jennifer corrected.

Jason snapped his mouth shut.

"It's okay," Jennifer said. "We were in touch mostly by e-mail."

"Have you been in touch lately?" Dom inquired.

"Not really," Jennifer answered. "A couple text messages here and there. The only e-mail I sent them lately was that encrypted file you sent me, Jason." She looked at her brother.

"You sent them the files that were on the flash drive Dad found?"

"I didn't know they were Dad's. I thought you sent me a cracking challenge so I forwarded it to my friends. We love breaking those things."

The room went silent.

"Oh, c'mon people!" she cried. "A good encryption's like a crossword puzzle to us!"

"It sounds like everyone here has a piece of this puzzle. Let's start putting it together. Let's start with you, Jim," Jake stated.

"Well, I found a flash drive in the parking lot at work ..."

"Was that the same day Jennifer drove you to New Times Financial in a red 1969 Camaro?" Dom asked.

"How do you know that?" Jennifer spluttered.

"Yeah, same day. And how *do* you know about that?"

"Just continue, Jim. Sorry I interrupted."

"I know you well enough to know something is bothering you," George huffed, all but glaring at Dom and Jake. "There's a family here that deserves an explanation."

"I'm going to ask them to indulge us just a bit longer," Dom replied. "Jennifer, do you have the files?"

"I do," she said with a nod. "They're on my laptop at home."

"I still have the flash drive," Jim volunteered. "I kept forgetting to hand it in to the office. It's in my car with my notebook. I'll go get them."

A few moments later, Jennifer opened the photo folder with the two pictures of the cars with the models. "I'll just have a closer look at one of these skank-o-graphs."

"Hey now!" Jason huffed. "No need to be rude. Just 'cause you lack, how to put this delicately ... the natural assets to be a model ..."

"Now hold on there, Jason," Jake interjected. "Your sister has all the assets to be a model in that photo, but she has something else —class—which is why she isn't."

Jake's comment caught Jennifer by surprise.

"Why, thank you very much, Jake," she said, while giving him one of her infectious smiles, which transformed to a sneer when she turned to her brother.

"These files are huge. I think we're looking at steganographs."

"Don't look at me, Jim," George chuckled. "She lost me at skank-o-graphs."

"Time to get cracking," Jennifer announced with a grin. She reached into her purse and pulled out a large key ring with at least half a dozen flash drives attached to it.

Silence again.

"What?! No woman today could possibly consider herself properly accessorized without her ring of favorite crack ... I mean APCs," Jennifer mumbled.

"APCs?" Jason asked.

"Alternative Program Choices," Jennifer replied haughtily.

With that, she plugged in two of her drives and let her fingers fly over the keyboard.

"Jennifer, I have to ask you. Just how many these 'APCs' do you have on that ring of yours?" Dom asked with a smile. "You know that even one could land you in jail, right?"

"Uncle George, do I have to answer that question?"

"If you were my client, Jennifer, I would say no. But as your uncle, I say yes because I was about to ask you the same question."

"If it will solve the mystery, there will be as many APCs as it takes."

"Don't worry, Jenny. Uncle George here'll bail you out."

It took Jennifer about ten minutes before the photographs suddenly dissolved into several hundred lines of code.

"Can you make any sense of that, Jennifer?" Jim knew he sure as heck couldn't.

"Not yet. It'll take further study. Let's have a go at the zip file while we wait. I wanna see just how good these guys write."

"Why?"

"They're about to be slammed with the JAAGS crack."

"JAAGS crack? Give me a hint, please," George begged. "I swear, I am going to have to keep Bill Gates on speed dial just to understand half this stuff."

Jennifer sobered. "It's a project the five of us worked on together," she said softly. "We were trying to write a better encryption program. We also, almost by accident, came up with a better crack. We called it the JAAGS crack: Jennifer, Angie, Arissa, Gerard, Steven."

She bit her lip.

"Seems fitting," George said after a moment. "Let 'er rip, Jenny."

She smiled through her tears.

"Of course, Dom here may have to arrest you."

Everyone laughed.

"Uncle George, now would be a good time to remember the name of your best law clerk. I may need a lawyer."

A few moments after Jennifer's fingers returned to the keyboard, the zippered file disappeared.

"It's loading data onto your computer, Dad. A lot of data." Jennifer's eyes widened. "This is huge."

The minutes clicked by agonizingly slow. At last, it finished and they were looking at something none of them comprehended, except Jim. There were hundreds of lines of names, addresses, phone numbers, Social Security numbers, professions, classification codes, and the name of their agent. They were looking at New Times Financial's client database.

"It's basically the same database I use," Jim observed, "But this one is so much more detailed."

Jennifer clicked on a name and a drop-down menu appeared, allowing them select to display various investment information. But the menu that caught Jake's and Dom's eyes was the one that said "O/S Accounts." Clicking on any given deposit brought up the name of the institute, the amount in the accounts, and a plethora of other information. Another click opened up a tab called "Notes." The reason for the transfer was detailed there. One client read "hidden funds from divorce settlement;" for another, "capital gains from stock sale." Many simply said "corporate bonus" with deposit dates in January.

"Just what are we looking at?" George asked.

"I'd call this the mother lode—a list of tax evasions." Dom's eyes were glued to the screen. "My Lord, just look at it! Names, dates, amounts. A prosecutor's dream come true."

"Too bad a jury will never see it," George muttered.

"What do you mean!?" the other five cried.

"Where's the search warrant?" George snapped. "I'd throw it out."

"But I found this thing," Jim started.

"Doesn't matter, Jim. Let me show you. Pretend we're in court. You're on the stand and I'm the defense. I would probably say: 'Mr. Hanson, when you found the flash drive, you did not turn it in to your company or the police. You turned it over to your daughter, a computer expert, who proceeded to hack into it. Further, Mr. Hanson, when you did identify the files on the drive as being property of the New Times Financial Group, you again failed to turn the drive over to New Times, but proceeded to share the confidential client information it contained, in violation of the laws of this state and the ethical tenets of your profession, with five other individuals, including your son and daughter, a retired Judge, and two FBI Agents.'"

Jim shrank back a bit. "Oh …"

But George was on a roll. "Therefore, Your Honor, I'd ask this court for five things. First, to set aside all evidence garnered from the flash drive as the search was illegal. Second, with regard to Mr. James Hanson, I would ask this court to write a letter to the appropriate state licensing authorities advising them of his actions in this matter and suggest further legal action be taken. Third, with regard to the conduct of Ms. Jennifer Hanson, I would ask this court to write a letter to the Massachusetts Institute of Technology advising them of her conduct should they wish to expel her, with a copy to the District Attorney for any further legal action."

He paused for a breath. "Fourth, with regard to Special Agents Jake Connors and Dominique Deselva, I would ask the court to send a transcript of these proceedings to their superiors so they can review their conduct. Fifth, with regard to Judge George Grayson, I would ask you show him great leniency in recognition of his years of fine service to the community. With that Your Honor, I rest my case."

Everyone was applauding and laughing when he finished.

"Unfortunately, George is right," Jake sighed with a tired smile.

"What I don't get," George said, "is where they got all this info."

"From people like me," Jim replied. "We have to ask clients about their net worth and stuff, to see if there is really a need for life insurance. If you want to invest money in a mutual fund, we have to do a financial analysis then as well. Every time you apply for a credit card or a loan, financial information is taken and put online. Of course, where is your banking info? All online—not to mention what all the government agencies have on file."

"So if you want info about anyone, hacking an insurance company, or having someone on the inside giving you the information, is a good place to start," Jennifer concluded.

"No more hacking, young lady," George admonished, waggling a finger at her.

Jennifer responded with a smile and a look of mock guilt.

"But there have to be safeguards," Dom insisted.

"They're called firewalls, Dom," Jennifer answered. "For the most part, they do a pretty good job of keeping hackers out."

"I know about firewalls," Jason grumbled.

"I don't," George interjected. "But I have a question which I know you'll answer honestly. I don't know anything about computers, chips, or firewalls. Heck, my radio still has vacuum tubes in it and I fly seventy-year-old airplanes. But I do know people, and basically people never change. Could these firewalls stop the JAAGS team?"

The question hung in the air for a moment. All eyes were on Jennifer.

"No," she replied, head held high.

George just smiled and nodded.

"Jenny, what do you think the purpose of this flash drive is?" Jim asked.

"Good question," Jake said. "And why would they risk having something so damning, just in case they got caught?"

"You'd think it'd have some kinda self-destruct software built into it," Jason added.

"I'd use the flash drive to update a larger database," Jake stated. "It's too risky over the 'net—too easily hacked—so they're couriering the drives to where they have to go, probably to feed a 'standalone.' And Jason, I'm sure there's a self-destruct code on the drive. I can only guess it malfunctioned."

"Standalone? Help me again Jennifer," George implored.

"It is a computer that's not hooked up to the 'net. It therefore cannot be hacked; not from the outside anyway. It's where organizations would store their most sensitive information."

"The mule in this case is Sharon Turner," Dom said.

"What?!" Jim cried. "My manager?!"

"It sure would explain all her flying," George said. "She was at it again this morning, bright and early, but this time she had a man with her. She was having some problems getting him in the plane with his hands being all bandaged."

Jason and Jim snapped to attention. George looked at them.

"Say, didn't Rusty bite the intruder on the hand at least once?" George asked idly.

"Yes!"

"I'd say this Sharon and whoever's with her should have an appointment with a needle at the Greensville Correctional Center," George mused.

"They'd just walk," Jason sneered.

"True, Jason, even though they've killed five people," Dom said.

"Five?" Jason asked. "But only three—"

"I guess it's time to explain," Jake said, glancing at Dom.

Dom clasped his hands, leaning forward on the table. "We ran the investigation on a need-to-know basis. We have had Jim's branch office under watch for a few weeks, which is why we knew about the trip with the Camaro. A few days ago, after a meeting Jake and I had with him, I was asked by my immediate superior for a full report on the New Times case and he wanted the entire file, which included the identities of the informants we had in New Times' head office. Both of our informants were found dead from apparent heart attacks yesterday morning."

"Does that mean your boss is in on the murders?" Jim asked.

"Jennifer, is there a Nathan McWilliams on the list?"

"Here he is. Last transaction was two weeks ago, two hundred and fifty thousand transferred to an account in Bermuda from an account in the Caymans, under the name of Tillman Consulting. Notes … 'For services rendered.'"

"Well, that explains why he shut the New Times case down."

"He shut it down?!" Jim exclaimed.

"Dom and I got the e-mail this morning. Apparently there's not enough evidence to bring charges." Jake held his hands askance.

"Well, there won't be now. He made sure your main witnesses would never talk," George said. "In all my years, I've never seen anything like this. They have so much info on everyone …"

"Uncle George, I think you just hit the nail on the head," Jim cried. "This is all about information! Think what you could do with all this info! People could be blackmailed to do anything you wanted."

"Like supply you with more information," observed Jason. "It's how spies have worked for years."

"It will be interesting to see what the Cambridge and our local police come up with," George stated.

"If it all gets swept under the rug, we'll start to get an idea just how big this thing is," Jake observed.

As they were talking, Jennifer switched out to another flash drive and started typing away on the computer, a mischievous smile fixed firmly upon her face.

If Gaston had been at his computer, he might have seen his screen flicker slightly. Even if he had, he probably would have ignored it. But he wasn't even at his desk; he was in a meeting with Culper. Culper's placid smile was truly terrifying.

"You're telling me that Darien failed. He got his ass handed to him by an old man and his Dachshund?!"

"That's what the police reports say," Gaston replied meekly.

Culper cracked his neck. He didn't stop smiling. "And what has become of our intrepid Darien?"

"He's in Bermuda. He's out of commission; his hands are allegedly chewed up."

Culper looked incredulous. "Just what type of Dachshund was this?"

"One that apparently punches above his weight."

Gaston got up and stared at the Monet on the wall. "The police have linked the death in Cambridge with the one in Canada."

"And those two spies at New Times?"

"No word on those at all. We're monitoring the situation."

"Do you think they'll link the death in Cambridge and Canada with the one in Lyon?"

"Tallmadge puts it at seventy-eight percent."

Culper, for the first time, looked uneasy. "That high? What can we do about it? If they link all of the deaths, even we could have a problem."

"The best way to stop an investigation is to not have it start in the first place. But now that it's begun, we let it disappear."

"What are you saying? We do nothing?"

"No. We use our assets. We monitor all telephone traffic, both cell and landline, to anyone connected to this case. We've stopped the FBI investigation and the one in Cambridge will go nowhere, as will the one in Virginia."

"What are we going to do about this family in Virginia, what's the name …?"

"Hanson."

"Yes, Hanson. We can't hit them now. It would bring too much publicity, more than we could control."

"But we could discredit them. Make them look like 'nut jobs' looking for their fifteen minutes of fame."

"Make it happen. What about Canada?"

"We don't have any assets in Waterloo. Besides, with the hit being caught on tape and being played on all the networks, the genie is out of the bottle."

"Some good could come from the city of Waterloo yet. You know, Gaston, I was there once."

Gaston started.

"Very busy place. Lots of computer engineering going on," Culper mused. "Google is there, as well as many others. And we do have an asset there. A very good asset." He spun his Blackberry about on his desk, then glared up at Gaston.

Gaston furrowed his brow. "I don't—"

Culper grinned.

"Oh no," Gaston gasped. "God, no—"

"What did you just do?" Jim asked, peering over Jennifer's shoulder.

"I want to know who I'm dealing with. I just launched JAAGS track."

"Let me guess. Another 'alternative program choice' invented by the Fantastic Five," Jason drawled.

"I really am gonna need to get Bill Gates on the phone, aren't I?" George stated.

"Oh, I think you'll get it, Uncle George. It's not that complicated. All I did was take our program for tracking hackers and hid it in their message program."

"But Jenny, when the message gets back to the sender, won't it identify my computer? So they'll know we're onto them." Jim frowned deeply.

"Relax Dad, I write better than that," she replied as a house appeared on the screen.

"Look at this place." Jennifer turned the computer around. The screen displayed an old stone building, very well preserved, accented with intricately carved shutters.

"This is 82 Carretera de Santroma in the city of Andorra La Vella, the capital city of Andorra, between France and Spain. The flash drive originated here."

"You've led us right to them," Jake said, shock and surprise buried in his voice. Jim beamed.

"Let me try to understand," George said. "You and your friends developed a computer program that can not only track a signal back to origin, but also pinpoints the building the computer that generated it is in?"

"Well. Google Earth was a lifesaver for that part ..."

"Dom, what are our options here?" Jim asked. "We know where the flash drive came from, but what do we do about it?"

Dom paused. "We become silent. Absolutely silent."

"Using Emmanuel was never part of the deal!" Gaston barked. He could feel the fire of his face, the trickle of sweat on his skin.

"Gaston." Culper's voice was placid. "Let's be calm."

"When it comes to dragging your own kin into *ruin* for this sick little …
game! I can't be calm! He has suffered enough. For God's sake, he's in a
wheelchair!"

Emmanuel Cartier had been in a car accident when he was twelve. His
parents had been killed. Emmanuel had survived, permanently crippled,
bound to a wheelchair for the remainder of his days. If it wasn't for Gaston,
Emmanuel—his *nephew*—would have had a much poorer life. Even still, he'd
had enough misery—no "opportunity" could override that.

"We've done so much for him—isn't it time to repay us? Summer jobs,
private tutors … he even got to work with Tallmadge one summer."

"Culper," Gaston growled. "But he has a life now, his own—"

"Which he owes to us," Culper said. "His bachelor's, his master's, even
his Blackberry job—all because of what we did for him."

Gaston glared at Culper. He knew where Culper was going with this.
He hated it. He ground his teeth. "And now you want him to give all that
up to bail *us* out? He's free, Culper—leave him out of it."

"Why?"

"He's innocent! He doesn't even know what we do!"

"Only six people know what we really do, Gaston. What is our real job,
Gaston?"

He paused. "We gather information on people, especially important
people. We find their weakness; who they're sleeping with, what their medical problems are, their addictions, and where they hide their money."

"And why do all these people stay with us?"

"We have the info."

"And information is power. We can make them do whatever we want.
People, the banks—even the power companies."

"It's blackmail and we don't do it to family!" Gaston cried. "Emmanuel
will not hack into the Blackberry cell network."

"He will help us," Culper countered.

"Why now?! We're already able to read most e-mails of our targets!"
Gaston snapped.

"But we have never cracked an entire network. We will start here and
if it works, we will go for the others. Besides, Blackberry is going to carry

everything from automotive diagnostics to medical records. I want us in on the ground floor. It's within our grasp."

Gaston was suddenly very calm. He saw clearly that Culper was a combination of genius and insanity, the type of person who became so fixated on a goal he lost sight of everything else. Then it hit him, what he was really after. Terror seized him but he stayed outwardly composed. When he spoke, it was slow and deliberate; he wanted no misunderstanding of his question.

"Do you honestly think you can hack the President of the United States' cell phone?"

"An idea that is not dangerous is unworthy of being called an idea at all."

— Oscar Wilde

CHAPTER 7

"What did Agent Deselva mean, 'we become silent?'" Kathleen inquired as she leaned against a tree just off the path. I could see the concentration on her face in the story I was telling her. She wasn't missing a word.

"He and Jake realized the people we were up against had some immense power. They were both shocked to find out their boss had gone dirty and they figured, if this person or group or whoever was strong enough to corrupt senior FBI directors, they'd probably gotten to other people—a lot of other people, some with a lot of power themselves. But who?"

"A very good question," Kathleen commented as she joined me back on the path and continued our stroll.

"They explained that they felt we were up against an organization with great computer systems skills, proven by the fact there was no record of the call Jennifer was on when Angie was murdered. Further, when we were attacked, our home security codes were known to the attacker, and finally, when the attack was taking place, our cell phones were out of commission."

"Therefore you would have to assume you were being watched and monitored," Kathleen concluded. "So they wanted you to stop e-mailing, texting, faxing, and telephoning anything to do with this case," she added.

"Precisely. They also wanted us to be wary of strangers and new people trying to befriend us."

Kathleen stopped walking for a moment and turned to face me.

"You know, Jim, you really are an extraordinary group of people. Within a few hours of being attacked, you'd managed to pull yourselves together and go on the offense. You shouldn't have had to do that; that's the FBI's job. Our job. *My* job. As president, my first duty is to protect the citizens.

Now I find out there's still another organization out there trying to hurt us. Needless to say I am ashamed we weren't there for you."

"I will hear none of that, Madam President. The FBI remains one of the finest police and investigative forces in the world. Okay, we found some bad apples—there's probably more—but we'll get them. It can happen in any organization. If we checked Jennifer's list again, I'm sure we'd find people from every profession. Except financial planners, of course," I added with a smile.

"Thanks, Jim. Did you find out who was in the house in Andorra?"

"You bet we did: a company called 'International Predictive Analytics.'"

"Sounds important. What exactly is Predictive—what did you say?"

"Analytics. It's the study of trends in markets and other fields using mathematical modeling utilizing present and historical data. It was a good cover for them."

"'Them' being…"

"Ah-ah, Madam President, you're getting ahead of the story. We hadn't found out yet. But we were going to find out. To quote John Paul Jones, 'We had not yet begun to fight!' So the meeting continued …"

"As this investigation has been compromised by the Regional Director, and who knows who else, we are going to have to run it under the radar with something we have no right to ask you for," Dom stated. Everyone looked to him and Jake in anticipation of the question—one that evidently had a great deal of gravity, as Dom hesitated, as though searching for the right words. He looked over at Jake, who was staring at the floor for help and found none.

George could see they were dealing with two men with strength of character and a sense of honor, not to mention pride in working for the FBI. He could see something else though: anger. Anger that they had been betrayed by one of their own. Anger that they couldn't use the full resources of the FBI to defend the citizens they were sworn to protect. Anger that greed was casting a shadow on an organization with such a proud heritage. George decided to spare them any more discomfort.

"Dom, Jake." Everyone turned to look at George. He spoke in a slow, deliberate voice, which displayed a sense of strength Jim had not seen since his uncle last addressed a jury.

"If you are looking for our help, I know I speak for everyone here when I say you have it fully," he said.

That sentiment was quickly endorsed by everyone as they nodded their heads.

"George, this family was almost murdered. To have to ask them to get right back in harm's way again …" Jake said.

"That issue has already been resolved, Jake," Jim interrupted, pouring another coffee. "Now let us talk strategy. If we go silent, won't that tip them off to the fact we're on to them? They'll expect us to be using our cell phones."

"Fortitude," Jason blurted.

Everyone looked at Jason with raised eyebrows and half-formed questions on their tongues.

"Operation Fortitude," Jason said. He glanced at Jennifer, then continued, "For the historically illiterate, that was the name of an operation the Allies conducted before D-Day in World War II. We had to convince the Germans we were landing in France at the Pas de Calais instead of Normandy. To accomplish this, we created a fictional army around General Patton. To make it seem real to the Germans, they flooded the airways with phony radio traffic. They even put inflatable tanks and trucks in fields and bases for the Kraut spy planes to see."

"So what are you saying, Jason?" Jim asked.

"We keep our cell phone traffic at normal levels so as not to raise suspicion. When we talk about the murders, it's to express impatience with the investigation as there are no answers or to convey false messages to throw them off. We never mention the FBI or Dom and Jake. We don't want these guys to know they're involved. We especially never phone them."

"But we have to talk to them if we're going to help with the investigation," Jennifer protested.

"The only one who phones them is you Jennifer, and only to Jake," Jason stated emphatically, causing Jennifer to look confused.

"Why that exception, Jason?" Jim asked.

"Well, Father, I don't know what it was like in the Stone Age, but now when you're dating someone, you should call them once in a while."

"What are you talking about, Jason?!" Jennifer cried.

Jake smiled broadly. "I can guess where you're going with this."

"It's the perfect cover story. If we're under surveillance, they'll see you two at restaurants, movies, or wherever you go on dates," explained Jason hurriedly, fidgeting under the weight of Jim's concerned stare.

"That way they can brief each other without using any electronic media."

"Have her home no later than eleven PM, Jake," Jim ordered, grinning from ear to ear. "She has a curfew."

"As the elder person here, Jake," George chimed in, his Southern accent rolling about the room, "I must insist you purport yourself a gentleman at all times with this lady, as I consider her under my protection. As such, the curfew is now ten PM."

By this time, Jennifer was turning different shades of red and laughing with everyone else, while Jake just continued to smile.

"I would date you too, Jennifer, but my wife might object," Dom chuckled.

"I must say, it's a good cover, Dad," Jennifer said. "It works for me if it does for you, Jake."

Jake gave his positive acknowledgement while the waiter delivered the check.

"Should we have your Nathan McWilliams foot the bill, Jake?" Jennifer asked.

Jake threw her a perplexed look.

"It's all here, Jake: account numbers, passwords, transfer codes. Anybody wanna be a millionaire?"

"You mean to tell me, Jennifer, from the list you uncovered today, you have enough information to reach into these accounts and steal all the money?" George asked with astonishment.

"Every nickel," was the reply.

Jim could see Jennifer wasn't suggesting they do this, but she was displaying some serious attitude. He knew his daughter was upset from events of the last few days and wanted some payback.

"Jenny, surely, if you could get past one of these bank's firewalls, reach into one of their accounts and transfer the money out, it must leave some type of electronic trail as to where it went?"

A very sly smile crept across Jennifer's lips, one her family had never seen before—one with great malevolence. It actually scared Jim, and, glancing about, he could see it concerned the others.

"Generally it does, but that could be dealt with," she replied.

"I don't like where this conversation is going," George grumbled. "Or do I have to explain the term 'grand larceny?'"

"I do not think anyone here was suggesting we actually steal the money, Uncle George," Jason said. "Although it would be good rough justice for these people."

"May I remind everyone there are two FBI agents and a judge present?" Dom commented.

Jim had become very silent in the last few minutes; he was very deep in thought. But now he spoke.

"Let's break this up. Mom is probably home with Dad and I want to see how they are."

"Dad, I hope you backed up your computer today. I'm stealing your hard drive in case this flash drive left some files on it I don't know about. I'll pick you up a new one on the way home," Jennifer said.

"Jennifer, I would like a copy of those lists. I want to check out these offshore banks and who is hiding what," Jake said.

With that Jennifer reached into her purse and pulled out a new flash drive still in the bubble packaging from the store.

"You even carry new ones in there?" Jake laughed.

"A girl never knows when she will run into a program she likes and can stea ... I mean borrow."

"Yes, Gaston, just think of the possibilities: hearing the president's cell phone conversations, reading her texts. You see, Gaston, when I asked you 'what do you view our real job is?' you forgot to mention one very important point. We gather information, but we sell it too. What do you think Iran would pay to know when their nuclear facilities were going to be bombed? What do you think a country like China would pay to know the American strategy going into a trade negotiation?"

"Culper, it's one thing to deal in trade secrets, blackmail politicians to vote a certain way on a tax bill or help people launder and hide money, but when you graduate to espionage ... that's a whole new game."

"How is it really any different than what we already do, Gaston?" Culper asked as he strolled over to the ornate antique crystal decanter sitting on a 200-year-old cherry side table and poured himself a glass of port. "Care for a glass?" he added, tone almost congenial.

"No. Thank you."

"Too bad. Hundred-year-old Seppelt Para Port won't be around forever."

"It will certainly last longer than us if you want to go head-to-head with the United States in a game of espionage. You'd do well to remember, as I read once: 'If you twist the tiger's tail, you better have a plan for dealing with his teeth.'"

Culper seemed unmoved.

"Do you really want to face the prospect of SEAL Team 6 kicking in our doors and hauling you off to spend the rest of your life in Guantanamo Bay?" Gaston implored.

Culper grinned, took his glass of wine, and walked over to the window he was so fond of gazing out. He raised the glass to the light and studied the color of the port. Finding it satisfactory, he took a sip and resumed peering out the window.

At times like these, Gaston didn't know what to expect. He had seen him stand like this for over an hour or more, sipping wine and thinking. But this time Gaston didn't have to wait that long. Culper turned from the window and faced Gaston; this answer was short.

"I want in to Blackberry."

The Hansons arrived back at home feeling very weary, only to find Jim had forgotten about one aspect of the attack that none of them had prepared for: the media. The new security guards had managed to keep the various reporters from entering the front yard and knocking on the door, but as soon as the family pulled in the driveway, the scavenging journalists swarmed the car. Jennifer and Jason managed to escape into the house, while Jim held back the reporters, trying valiantly to field the questions that crashed down like the incoming tide.

"Mr. Hanson, can you say who attacked you?"

"Why did they target your family?"

"Was this an act of terrorism?"

"Does this have anything to do with al-Qaeda?"

Jim was surprised to see one reporter in particular: Holland Day. He thought Day was too big a TV personality to cover a home invasion. Holland Day had a syndicated news/opinion show that appealed to those folks that didn't trust government and saw left-wing conspiracies everywhere. Whether it was the moon landing having been faked or 9/11 being an inside job, Holland Day preached the gospel of paranoia well and the ratings just kept climbing, which, of course, was all that seemed to matter in his world. Jim sometimes found him entertaining, but mostly just too off-the-wall for his tastes. His colleagues in the news field seemed to share Jim's view, having nicknamed him "Howlin' Mad" Day, a label he had made no bones about detesting. No doubt some of his fellow reporters were envious, if not bitter, about his success, as Day had started at the top. His father-in-law was very wealthy and owned several TV and radio stations so his place at the top of the heap had been assured.

Jim knew Holland Day had become a master of the "I got you" interview. Anyone foolish enough to allow themselves to be interviewed by Day would probably not recognize the interview when it aired after the tape was edited to reflect what Holland Day wanted you to say. One TV critic wrote, "If Holland Day had taped Jesus reciting the Lord's Prayer, after it aired, you would think Jesus was an atheist."

It had been a long day for Jim as it had been for all his family and he found the questions very irritating but he handled them as best as he could. He ended the interview saying, "I am sure you can appreciate what my family has been through and we need time together and some rest. Thank you for your attention and have a good day."

Unfortunately there was still one more question to come. Jim turned, only to find the cobblestone path blocked by Holland Day and his cameraman. Jim knew what was coming—he'd seen Day in this type of situation before—and he was in no mood for it. The other reporters and the cameramen knew something was about to happen and turned on their cameras and their recorders. Jim decided to be polite.

"Excuse me, Mr. Day. I wish to go into my house now."

Jim knew the question was going to be vile, but it was a new low even for Holland Day.

"What are you people hiding? You must have done something to warrant an attack like this if it occurred at all. Do you really expect the public to believe a demented old man and some mutt could take down an armed intruder? Why don't you tell us what's really going on here?"

The other reporters and the cameramen were stunned by the question—a couple of them lowered their cameras, and someone dropped their phone in shock.

"Hit him!" someone yelled.

But Jim kept his cool.

"I will not dignify that question with an answer. But it does answer a question for me; I now know why they call you Howlin' Mad Day."

Day turned pale with anger, especially as he could see and hear the other members of the news media laughing at him and that it was all being recorded. Jim, however, was not finished. He turned to the other reporters.

"The gentleman Mr. Day has so crudely described as 'demented' is Robert E. Hanson, a man I proudly call Dad. He suffers from Alzheimer's disease, as too many of his fellow Americans do. If you look him up, you'll find he has had a distinguished career as a lawyer, having tried three cases before the Supreme Court and winning them all. Further, he served on the boards of several charities in this community which benefited thousands. Last, but certainly not least, he served our country as a fighter pilot in the Korean War where he was decorated with the Distinguished Flying Cross and the Silver Star for his courage under fire. Last night's circumstances called Captain Robert E. Hanson back to active service, this time to defend his home, along with his wingman, Rusty the dog, who is small in stature but great with the courage only known to a few."

By this time, tears were forming in Jim's eyes, on display for the rolling cameras, along with the passion of his convictions. The reporters also witnessed Holland Day and his cameraman trying to sneak away, but they stopped when they Jim addressed them.

"You see, that is the difference between you and my dad, Mr. Day. My dad has something you will never understand. Honor. He never lied, never falsely maligned anyone, and always stood his ground. And that is the basis of another thing you do not understand, something called character. Thank you for your attention ladies and gentlemen."

Jim turned and went into the house while Holland Day and company beat a hasty retreat to their van. His cameraman would later swear that, as they drove off, he heard Day say under his breath, "Enjoy your fifteen minutes Hanson, but it will be me who writes your epitaph."

Holland Day, within a few hours, had reason, in his mind, to hate Jim Hanson even more. Every news channel aired the confrontation and Jim's speech. A few hours later, it went viral on YouTube.

When Jennifer and Jason entered the house, they found their grandmother snoozing on the living room couch. As soon as they came in, she woke up, greeting them with a yawn that spoke of the long night at the hospital with Robert. Jim had instructed his children on the way home as to what to say to Dolly about the meeting. They did not want to lie to this very special lady, nor did they want to cause her unnecessary worry or concern, so it was decided to omit the part about the Hansons working actively in a clandestine operation with the FBI. They therefore informed her that the police were investigating and would be contacting them when they had more information. When Jim joined them, they went upstairs to look in on Robert—and found him asleep with Rusty curled up beside him.

"So there they are, the two warriors," Jim observed.

"We owe them our lives," Dolly stated. "But I still don't understand why anyone would want to hurt us."

"We are going to find out, Mom," Jim replied.

Jim, Jason, and Jennifer decided the idea of a nap was a good one after the night they'd experienced. But Jennifer couldn't rest, as her mind was reeling. She couldn't get the idea of a large standalone out of her head, one tucked away in a quaint house in Andorra. If that computer contained information similar to what she'd already seen—information that was worth killing five people for—she had to hack it. 'But how?' she wondered. 'How do you get to a computer that isn't connected to the 'net?'

And then it hit her so fast she had to sit straight up in bed. But she had to talk to Arissa first, which meant a phone call. Remembering not to use her own phone, she grabbed her purse, checked to see if she had enough coins, and headed out the door, muttering, "Where am I going to find a pay phone in this day and age?"

"I saw what you said about your father on TV, Jim," Kathleen commented. "It was lovely. It's always moving when someone speaks so honestly, from the heart. And I give you full marks for not clobbering Day."

"It was tough not to."

"You know, he accused me of murdering my husband."

"I seem to recall something about that. Now I regret that I didn't punch him when I had the chance."

"He said I got the drugs to give Jack a heart attack from my son, who is a physician. He said I did it because Jack didn't support my running for president."

"And to think some people believe that crap," I said.

"Would you believe the emergency department of the hospital where Mark was interning did a special audit of their pharmacy to make sure certain drugs weren't missing?"

"You must be kidding!"

Kathleen shook her head.

"The power of the media," was my only comment.

She reached forward and took my hand again. I studied her face. I could see the strain of her presidency in the crows' feet that were starting to form, the puffiness around her eyes from lack of sleep. As I looked into her eyes, I could tell she was an exceptional person. Exceptional because of the compassion that I was seeing. Exceptional because of the caring I could see. Exceptional because of the pain I could see. I was drawn to her like no other woman since Elizabeth, a fact which made me feel some guilt.

"Why didn't George call me?"

"Because I asked him not to."

She stared at me, perplexed.

"I didn't know if we could trust you. We didn't know how far up the chain this thing went. You, the vice-president, and the chief of staff weren't on the lists, but who would you call? George finally relented, saying if this thing all went south, at least you would have complete deniability."

"Well! Thank you for that much, at least," she exclaimed. She looked somewhat annoyed, but she wasn't releasing the tight grip on my hand.

"Something else was happening during all of this with Jenny and Jason."

"What's that, Jim?"

"Let me ask you this. When did you first notice Mark was a man and no longer your 'little boy?' We parents tend to forget they grow up and become their own persons."

Kathleen looked over at me and I could see her eyes starting to fill up.

"Gosh, Jim! That's a question that touches the heart. I can tell you the exact moment I saw the man my dear Jack and I gave this world. It was this time of year, March break in 2006. I was still a senator and Mark was doing his residency. Jack was driving the three of us to a family event back in Cambridge when we came upon it. My God, Jim, it was the worst thing I have ever seen."

I felt her release my hand, bringing both of hers to her face. She started to cry. Forgetting all protocols, I put my arm around her and drew her close.

"I am so sorry, Kathleen. I didn't mean to bring up a bad memory."

She looked up at me while wiping tears away.

"It's okay, Jim. It's a story that should be told. It was a terrible car accident. Three cars and a truck. Mark fortunately had his doctor's bag with his luggage. He was out of the car in seconds and took charge. One woman had cut an artery in her arm. Mark had me push my thumbs into the wound while Jack made a tourniquet. We watched Mark use a tracheotomy kit to open a man's throat so he could breathe. When the police and paramedics arrived he directed them. He went in an ambulance with one badly injured little girl with an open chest injury. I never saw so much blood and suffering!"

"Do I believe my eyes? Am I seeing our Jim holding the president?" Dom asked.

"I believe we are," stated Jake.

"I think this has become one serious discussion," George observed dryly.

"Do not say one word, Jason!" ordered Dolly.

"Not even 'yes, Grandma?'"

"It sounds like the Galbraith family did some fine work that day."

"We found out later that no one died. If history brands me a lousy president, you know Jim, I can live with that because I know I helped give this world a good doctor and an even better man."

"For me, it was seeing Jennifer and Jason coming up with ideas to fight this menace. There was never any thought of quitting or not doing something. It was only what and how."

"So what did our intrepid Jennifer come up with?"

"Oh, it was a beauty ..."

"Now let me get this straight, Jenny," Jim said as he put down the copy of Ansel Adams "Bridal Veil Fall" he had just had reframed and was about to hang. "You want me to just walk into the branch office in Freelton and hand in that flash drive like nothing happened?"

"Think of it as your contribution to the Operation Fortitude part of our campaign, Dad," Jason said.

"Thank you for the historical perspective, son. But, Jenny, these people aren't stupid. They will take that flash drive and subject it to every virus scan on the planet, which I'm sure will find that program you plan to stick on it. And when they do find it, they'll know who put it there. What makes you think they'll send it to Andorra anyway? Why would they risk it?"

Jennifer knew her dad raised some very good points, but she also knew she had to do something.

"Dad, they killed three of my friends and two other people, not to mention almost murdering all of us. I just can't sit here and hope Dom and Jake will come up with something."

Jim could see the fight in his daughter's eyes. He also knew something else: she was right.

"Jennifer, tell me more about this, I believe you called it 'virtual wi-fi.'"

Jennifer explained that Arissa had mentioned to her a few months ago there was a contest at the University of Waterloo to see who could come up with the most original computer program. One of Arissa's friends had won the contest by coming up with a program which, when loaded onto a computer without one, would instruct the computer how to make an internet card virtually, from components already in it, and then log onto the 'net.

"That computer in Andorra is most certainly a standalone, not connected to the 'net. The only way we can talk to it is if we can get it to make its own internet card and log on."

"This just sounds too fantastic, Jenny. But we still have a problem: how do you get it past their virus detection programs?"

"That's where John Riley and Bill Franks at MIT come in. They're two of the best programmers in mass data situations. They're also two of the best guys in the world at hiding ..."

Jennifer paused, choosing her words carefully.

" ... programs in other programs."

"You mean virus makers," Jim accused.

"The difference between a virus and a well-written program is only a matter of perspective, Dad. Would not a beautiful rose growing on the eighteenth green at Augusta be considered a weed?"

Jennifer then flashed the smile that always made Jim's heart melt. Even as a little girl, when she'd been caught doing something naughty, all she had to do was flash that smile.

Jason was laughing so hard by now that he doubled over. All Jim could do was put his head down on his desk, murmuring, "Lord, give me strength."

He lifted his head. "Okay, Jennifer. Where are we now with everything?" Jim asked stoically.

Jennifer explained how she had used computers at the library to avoid detection to get the program from Arissa. From there, she had forwarded it and the program from the found flash drive to her friends at MIT. They would send it back to her in a couple of days.

"Did you tell them why we needed it?" Jim asked fretfully.

"They asked me, of course, but I told them I couldn't discuss it. They did finally ask if it was for Angie. I said yes. They said that was good enough for them."

Jennifer looked down.

"You and Angie have loyal friends," Jason noted.

"Dad! Are you ready for the coincidences of coincidences?"

"I hope so," was the reply.

"I telephoned Dr. Maurice Tremblay, Gerard's brother."

"Jennifer! I can understand that you want to extend your condolences, but we're not supposed to make phone calls!"

"He's a professor of computer science at the University of Andorra."

Both Jim and Jason looked stunned.

"Not to worry guys, I found what's probably the last payphone in town, and we had a long talk. Lucky for us, his English is much better than my high school French. He and his family are devastated by the murder. Dad, you and Jason may be upset with me, but I took him into our confidence. I told him everything."

Jim and Jason flopped back into their chairs.

"My God, Jennifer!" Jason exclaimed. "If this guy opens his mouth to the wrong person, we're all toast."

Jennifer went on to explain that Maurice fully understood they all had to assume the authorities had been comprised and they were on their own. Maurice had also informed her that many of the students at the Institut National des Sciences Appliquées in Lyon had already linked the murders of Steven Bertrand, Angie Borello, and Gerard Tremblay. The conspiracy theories were rampant on the 'net. He'd also offered the full resources of both universities to the Hansons and their allies.

"Finally," Jennifer said, "Maurice said he'd observe the house at 82 Carretera de Santroma. Discretely, of course."

"Jennifer! That's dangerous—what if he gets caught?"

"What if he rats?" Jason asked.

"Dad, we need people over there who know the lay of the land! Maurice can find out what these people are doing. If my bug is successful, we need someone close by to read the signal and get the standalone online so we can see what we are up against."

"But how do we get around the fact they could be monitoring our computers?" Jason asked.

"We'll use a dedicated one at MIT."

"Of course, MIT will know you are doing this and give their full approval, right?" Jim asked sarcastically.

"I'm meeting Jake tonight for dinner. I'll discuss all this with him," Jennifer said.

"Don't forget that ten PM curfew your uncle laid down," Jim stated with a smile.

"Now, Dad! You know I'd never disappoint dear Uncle George!" Jennifer cried, returning the smile in kind.

As Jason and Jennifer got up to leave, Jim said," "That person who designed that wi-fi program must be some kind of genius."

"Yes," Jennifer responded. "Arissa told me about him. He's been confined to a wheelchair ever since a car accident when he was a kid. But he's brilliant; he got a full scholarship to Waterloo and now he works for Blackberry."

"No battle plan survives
contact with the enemy."

—Helmuth von Moltke

CHAPTER 8

"Now, Jim, I have to ask you something, and please don't take offense," Kathleen stated.

I looked at her and nodded my head.

"Jim, after all you and your family had been through, Jennifer was looking for a way to break into these people's computer, which would put you all at risk! How could you let this happen!?"

"Well, that's my girl!"

"This is not funny, Jim. These people are killers!"

I felt her squeeze my hand harder. We were sitting on the bench. I turned myself so I was facing her more directly and, looking her right in the eye, said, "So who's laughing, Madam President? What were our options? Sit back and wait until they sent another Darien? We couldn't go to the police. We knew they were being monitored and watched. We were on our own— or so we thought. I did not realize it at the time just how many allies we had until the plan started to come together. I also didn't know who the enemy was yet …"

"Well, it looks like your esteemed Mr. Holland Day is the one who got discredited, Gaston, not Mr. Hanson," stated Culper.

"Mr. Day is not finished yet, Culper. That was just round one. When it comes to the art of the smear campaign, he is a virtuoso."

"I will look forward to the next instalment," Culper replied. "In the interim, we must discuss the Blackberry operation."

Gaston could feel his anger rising again.

"As far as I am concerned, there is no 'Blackberry operation' if it involves Emmanuel," he said as he rose from his chair in front of Culper's desk and walked to the center of the office.

Culper could see Gaston wasn't going to cooperate so he had to be prepared for the response he was going to get from his next statement.

"As a matter of fact, Gaston, there is—and it's already in full swing."

Fear suddenly gripped Gaston.

"What have you done, Culper?"

"Is it not Emmanuel's birthday tomorrow? I sent him one of those delightful animated birthday e-cards. I'm sure it will amuse him."

Gaston felt the blood drain out of his face.

"You sonovabitch! You put a sniffer virus in it, didn't you? Let me guess, you're trying to steal passwords."

"I see you understand my strategy."

"And if you're successful, what next Culper? Hit with a worm that uses the computer network to replicate itself?"

"Very good, Gaston! And what is the payload our dear worm is carrying?"

"A program to give you a backdoor into the Blackberry network."

"Excellent thinking. That will make the Blackberry network ..?"

"The ultimate zombie. An entire cell phone network controlled by us without Blackberry knowing."

"Of course, we don't want to do the network any harm; we just want to eavesdrop, run a few sniffer programs to detect certain data, oh, say, anything from the White House," Culper pontificated while pouring Remy Martin cognac into the antique Belgian crystal snifter. He paused, a strange smile coming across his face. "Here we are talking about sniffer programs while I'm holding this beautiful snifter. There must be a pun to be made here."

Gaston just stood there, fixing Culper with a hateful stare. He was now so angry, he could hardly speak.

"You have put ... my son ... in great danger," he ground out.

"Not at all," Culper replied while rolling his cognac around the snifter as he returned to his desk. "This virus is virtually—I think I just made a pun—undetectable. It combines both the sniffer and the worm virus into one tidy and discrete package, which, we are most confident, will slip past any anti-virus program Blackberry has. If it doesn't … well, someone sent Emmanuel a card with a virus in it. It gets found and erased. How does any of this fall back on Emmanuel? He would probably send me an e-mail warning me about the e-card site and instructing me to improve my anti-virus programs and firewalls."

Gaston could not refute Culper's logic, but he was still angry with the way Culper was using Emmanuel. Then it hit him.

"Developing a virus of the sophistication you just described would take months, if not longer. You've been planning this for a long time."

"Yes, Gaston, I have been. And this is why I was given the title of Culper after our predecessor died and you were not. They knew I was just the sort of bastard they would want to make the hard decisions. I won't let sentiment get in the way. Sure, I like Emmanuel, but I knew, once I saw his brilliance with computers, he was an asset worth investing in. I also knew Emmanuel would get into a position where he could help us. And now he has."

Gaston knew Culper was right about one thing: he was a bastard. Nothing Culper did was without a purpose. Gaston decided it was better to let him ramble for now.

"When you and I discussed our real job, perhaps I should have reminded you of our purpose. For over two hundred years, we have created economic order. Even through two world wars and the Great Depression, we made sure the right people got the wealth and the power. Doing so has brought some stability to an unstable world and has made us both very rich."

Gaston could not deny Culper's facts, so he decided to bring the conversation back to the point at hand.

"When Emmanuel goes to open that e-card tomorrow at Blackberry, you had better hope a dozen anti-virus program alarms do not go off."

"So, how's our date going so far, Jake?" Jennifer asked with a smile as they sat down at the restaurant.

"I think it's going very well. I managed to pick you up on time, our table was ready, and no one has tried to kill us."

Jennifer was taken in by his smile, how genuine and honest it seemed. He really was a straight-shooting sort of guy, or so she figured.

"I don't know if your brother was playing master strategist or match-maker. But I'm not going to complain about spending my evening in the company of a beautiful woman."

Jake could see the surprise on Jennifer's face as she blushed and realized he'd put his foot in his mouth for what was probably about the hundredth time already.

"I'm sorry, Jennifer; I didn't mean to embarrass you! Whether pretend dates or real ones, I'm not just bad at them, I'm horrible. I always say the wrong thing. At least I'm consistent."

Jennifer watched him shift uncomfortably; grinning mischievously, she said, "This I have to hear more about. Tell me your best war stories."

As their drinks were consumed and the hors d'oeuvre were sampled, Jake regaled Jennifer with tales of how he'd blown one date after another by saying exactly the wrong thing at exactly the wrong time. By the time the main course had arrived, Jennifer was laughing so hard she didn't know if she could have her meal.

Jake and Jennifer really looked like a couple on a date. At least, they did to the gentleman at the bar who finished his scotch and left. He had a report to make.

"Anything from the coroner in Boston on the Borello case, Dr. Richards?"

"Funny you should ask, Sutherland. Dr. Fellows called me this morning, wondering if we had anything on the Bertrand case," was the dry reply.

"So they're in the same position as us—with nothing."

"More to the point, Detective, according to Dr. Fellows, the police aren't even trying. Apparently, as the case has been linked to ours and possibly to another crime in Virginia, it's been turned over to the FBI as it crosses jurisdictions."

"No one from the FBI has contacted me," Detective Sutherland pointed out. "How about you?"

"Not so much as an e-mail."

"Am I the only one who feels there is something amiss here, Dr. Richards?"

"Not at all, Detective."

*
**

"We're almost ready for dessert and we still haven't talked business, Jennifer," Jake pointed out.

Jennifer had been enjoying her time with Jake very much. She'd heard all about his graduating from college with a degree in criminology and gaining a position with the FBI and the extensive training he'd gone through.

"I don't think you'll like what I have to report," she said

She explained all about wi-fi plan with the flash drive.

"You're right, Jennifer, I don't like it," Jake stated, giving Jennifer a look at the inner strength she knew was there. "This is very dangerous. If this virus is discovered, they'll know who sent it. Then they'll come for you and I might not be there to stop them."

"Any idea who 'they' are, Jake?"

Jake took a long pause before answering.

"No."

"Then let's go find out."

*
**

It was a late work day for Emmanuel Cartier. He had been working on a special project with regard to the Blackberry BB10 operating system so the evening found him still in his office. Sitting behind his specially designed, wheelchair-accommodating desk and working at his ergonomically designed keyboard had proven fruitful. Before he left, Emmanuel decided to check his e-mail. He was pleasantly surprised to find a message from his old boss, Mr. Culper. Opening the link to what was obviously an e-card brought up an instant virus warning from a new detection program Arissa had given him. She told him she'd developed it with four other programmers and they'd called it JAAGS Keep. It was strange, though, that his other anti-virus programs hadn't detected anything. That meant one of two things: the virus had fooled the other programs or JAAGS Keep was malfunctioning. Emmanuel had to find out. He had noted a few moments ago that a colleague of his—the head of systems security—was still in the building. A quick phone call brought Matt to his side.

The first thing Matt did was disconnect the internet. He then backed the computer up to a new flash drive. Next, Matt took Emmanuel's internet line and plugged it into a small black box with a different flash drive attached to it. He then ran a line from the box to Emmanuel's computer.

"Okay, Emmanuel, click the link again and tell the anti-virus program to ignore," Matt instructed.

A red LED light flickered on the flash drive for a few seconds.

"All right, I got it. Let's go to the standalone. Bring a copy of the program that found this thing."

Emmanuel followed Matt where a tabletop computer sat, loaded with over a dozen virus detection programs. It was about to get one more.

"Well, JAAGS Keep," Matt said, glancing at the label on the flash drive. "Let's see what you found."

Matt loaded both the e-card and JAAGS Keep programs into the computer. After a few moments, an amusing animation of three dogs wearing French berets singing "Happy Birthday Emmanuel" graced the screen. All the while, JAAGS Keep not only flashed warnings, but spat out indications of the type and location of the virus. It took several minutes, multiple programs, and careful guidance from Emmanuel and Matt, but they extracted the hybrid virus program. "Well, this is one for the books. What say we find out what this thing does?"

"I'm with you, Matt," was the reply.

The drive home from the restaurant was a quiet one for Jennifer and Jake.

"I know you're concerned, but give me an alternative," Jennifer said at last.

"I guess that's what has me pissed off. I don't have one, Jennifer. I keep thinking about a line from a book I read."

"Oh?"

"If you twist the tiger's tail, you better have a plan for dealing with his teeth." Jennifer smiled.

***

"This is as slick a piece of programming as I've ever seen. You're the expert here, Emmanuel. What do you think?"

Emmanuel didn't answer; he just stared at the lines of code on the screen. He was truly shocked; he didn't know to what say. He was angry, he was disappointed, but most of all, he was hurt.

"Can you tell me who wrote this?" Matt asked.

"You know that most programmers, like writers of literature or music, have their own style and this one is very familiar to me. I think I know who wrote this. But before I tell you, I need to make a phone call."

Emmanuel took out his phone and pushed a couple of buttons.

"Hey, Arissa. I know it's late, but could we meet tomorrow at my office? Say around noon. It's really important. I'll let security know you're coming."

***

"So they wanted to read my e-mail," Kathleen said. "We should have let them; it would've bored them to death."

We were back to strolling the pathway. "Jason would have loved that contribution to Operation Fortitude. We could have faked me having an affair with some mysterious foreign banker, then leaked it out to Howlin' Mad Day. He would've gotten so excited; he would have had a heart attack and we would've killed two birds with one stone."

We both laughed.

"You are absolutely right. I could've played the part of the mysterious banker."

Kathleen shot me a sly look and grinned before she said jauntily, "So Jim, the Hansons made the decision for you to drop the 'loaded' flash drive off at your branch office. Do I dare ask how that went?"

"Well, Madam President, it proved a very interesting and fortuitous visit ..."

*
**

Jim walked into the branch office and could not believe his luck. Peter Thompson was in Sharon Turner's office, along with Janice Collins. The door was open, as it appeared to be an informal meeting, so Jim just walked in. Sharon was the first to speak.

"Why hello, Jim! What brings you in today?"

Greetings quickly followed from Janice and Peter.

"Just dropping in to pick up some forms, and to make two important deliveries."

Reaching into his briefcase, Jim pulled out a chocolate bar and handed it to Janice.

"You are such a sweetheart, Jim!" Janice exclaimed.

"What, no candy for me Jim?" Sharon asked, feigning hurt.

"But aren't you sweet enough, Sharon?" Jim asked with a forced smile, pretending to enjoy the banter.

"What you're saying is that I'm not sweet enough?"

"No, Janice, what I'm saying is that you're an overachiever and I just wanted to help," Jim replied with a laugh.

The laughter continued until the moment Jim pulled the flash drive from the briefcase. Janice and Sharon exchanged quick glances as their faces went hard.

"Oh my God, I forgot to send out the e-mail!" Peter exclaimed.

"What e-mail?" asked Sharon.

Peter explained how Jim had come into the office to turn in a flash drive he'd found in the parking lot, but had left it at home. He'd asked Peter to send out an e-mail to see if anyone was missing one. Jim explained how Jason opened it looking for any clue to the owner only to find two car photos and an encrypted file and without Jim's knowledge forwarded the files to his sister.

"Apparently these computer geeks just love to try to crack these encryptions. Once I found out about the forwarding, I put a stop to all that. I hope the owner shows up," Jim stated.

"The drive's mine. I've been looking everywhere for it," Sharon said.

"Oh good. I'm glad I was able to give it back then," Jim replied, looking her right in the eye and seeing nothing, no clue to what she was thinking, just emptiness. Jim thought he'd see if she could handle a ringer.

"I never knew you were a car fan, Sharon. Those are nice photos on that flash drive."

Sharon didn't even bat an eye.

"I'm not, but a guy I know is. Came across them on the web."

'No doubt about it, you are good,' Jim thought. 'What would you expect? If you could land a small plane in a storm the way Uncle George described, you would have to be one cool lady.'

Jim needed one more thing from her.

"Sharon, is that the new mutual fund report?" Jim asked, pointing to a glossy magazine on the side of her desk."

"I believe it is."

"Would you have an extra copy?"

"You can have this one," she replied, handing it to him.

After saying the appropriate goodbyes, Jim left Sharon's office. As he passed Janice's desk, he extracted an empty paper coffee cup from the trashcan next to her desk. He then slipped down the hallway to the men's room. There, he opened his briefcase and carefully slid the magazine into an envelope and wrapped the cup with a paper towel to assure the preservation of any fingerprints.

He was about to leave when he heard Janice's and Sharon's voices as they came down the hallway to the ladies' room. The two rooms were side by side and appeared to share a common ventilation duct as Jim could hear their spirited—though hushed—conversation.

"You do realize, Sharon, that we might have killed five people for nothing!"

"We don't know that, Janice. Besides, the orders came down from Culper directly according to 355. All of this because I dropped a drive."

"Apparently, Tallmadge put the risk of exposure at over sixty percent."

"We still need Hanson's client money in the offshore accounts. Ponzi accounts need constant cash flow."

"Yeah, I know. Damn! We should have left the Hansons alone. Killing a whole family was much too risky. All we got out of it is Darien with chewed up hands parked in Bermuda," Janice pointed out.

"Is he coming back anytime soon?"

"Yes, next week he's going to Atlanta to get his hands worked on. You'll never guess the doctor's name."

"Let's hear it."

"Dr. Barker."

As Janet and Sharon laughed, Jim could feel his anxiety rising, knowing that at any moment the men's room door could open and he would be found out.

"So are you coming over tonight?" Janet asked.

"Now, you know I wouldn't miss our special cuddle time."

"Stop that," Janice giggled. "Not here, someone could come in."

"Okay, let's go."

Jim waited for a few moments and quickly left through the back door. He sat in his car for a few moments trying to process all he had learned. In the end he just shook his head and drove home.

In Jason's world, there were four types of girls: regular-looking, pretty, beautiful, and Veronica Parker—Veronica Parker being the young woman whose presence had just graced the local library that morning as Jason was working on his paper. By any measure she was a stunner, with a honey complexion complimenting her brown hair with blond highlights and a figure most women would kill for. Add to this the designer clothes, backpack, and high heels, and Jason was thinking, as he took in this vision, 'There is a student with great beauty and a *very* good allowance.'

As she moved into the library, it was all the guys could do not to stare. As for the girls, it was the usual up and down glance followed by a derisive whisper to a friend, usually about attire—something Jason had observed in the past whenever a beautiful woman entered a room. Jason enjoyed the view for a moment before returning to his paper. He hadn't been working on the bibliography of his essay for five minutes when he heard a woman's voice behind him.

"Isn't that the newest MacBook?" Veronica asked, pointing to Jason's notebook computer.

Jason turned and was struck by something he had never seen. It was Veronica's green eyes. All he could think was 'This has to be the most beautiful woman I have ever seen.'

This observation aggravated his natural shyness when around women, especially good-looking ones, which left him with a problem: he had to think of something to say. Perhaps something witty, clever, or intelligent would impress this goddess. What he did say wasn't any of these, but at least it was accurate. "Yes, it is."

"I was thinking of getting one; how do you like it?" Veronica asked, sitting down next to him.

They talked about computers for a few minutes in hushed tones so as not to disturb others at the library. This compounded Jason's issue in comprehending what she was saying; the other factor was that he found her great beauty very distracting. Despite this, introductions were made and they started discussing their studies, music they liked, movies they had seen. All the while, a little voice in Jason's head grew louder and louder. Jason had learned an important lesson from his dad: always trust your gut; if it doesn't feel right, it most likely isn't. They'd been warned about strangers who might try to befriend them.

Jason didn't have a lot of experience with women. He knew he was an average-looking guy that most girls would find pleasant and nice. The girls Jason had pursued had all given him what Jason called the "NGB" when dumping him: he was a "Nice Guy, But ..."

The little voice was saying loud and clear, 'This woman could have any guy she wants—why is she talking to me?'

Jason was pondering how this attitude could reflect a lack of self-confidence; when Veronica spoke and the little voice in his head turned into a scream.

"Are you one of the Hansons that were all over the news the other day because someone tried to kill you?" she asked.

"One and the same," Jason replied.

"Wow! What happened?" Veronica asked.

Jason forced himself to stare right into her eyes as he explained. Suddenly his shyness left him. He now knew she had no interest in him; he was being played and he didn't like it. Now he was mad. Jason finished his story and reached into his backpack, pulled two bottles of water from it, and offered one to Veronica.

"Thank you. It's dry in here," she said, opening the bottle and taking a sip. "So what happens now, did the police catch the guy yet?"

"No, we have no word yet," answered Jason, calculating his next move.

Fortunately, he didn't need a next move: the ringtone of a cell phone erupted from Veronica's purse, exonerating him. She glanced at the phone. "Excuse me, Jason. I'd better take this outside. I don't want to disturb anyone."

Jason could still see Veronica through the large window next to the desk. He quickly got his own cell phone out and took several photographs of her, discretely. When she returned, she informed him there was an urgent matter she had to look after.

"I've enjoyed talking to you. Let's get together and have coffee soon. Maybe in the next couple of days," she stated.

"That sounds great," Jason replied.

Veronica reached over and picked up Jason's cell phone, entering her number into his contact list, a fact noted by several other male students in the library. As she left, he could see them look at her and then back at him, all wondering the same thing:

"What's he got that I don't?"

That made him smile, but it faded as he put the bottle Veronica was drinking from carefully into his backpack. 'Another opportunity for Operation Fortitude,' he thought and the grin came on anew.

" You can fool some of the people all of the time, and all of the people some of the time, but you cannot fool all of the people all of the time."

— Abraham Lincoln

CHAPTER 9

"On *Today with Day*, another look at the Hanson case. As you, my loyal viewers, may recall, when I asked Mr. Hanson about the alleged break-in and attempted murder at his home, I got this reply."

The screen cut to Jim saying, "I will not dignify that question with an answer."

"As you know, ladies and gentlemen, Holland Day doesn't take that for an answer—I keep digging until I get the truth. I want to ask Mr. Hanson some questions: are the police still investigating this alleged crime? What's his daughter's relationship with FBI agent Jake Connors? Are there any issues with your clients' accounts, Mr. Hanson? We all know you're a financial planner with his hands in hawking investment products—maybe the Security and Exchange Commission's got some dirt on you, Hanson. You'd be better to come clean here and now, before it all comes out.

"I know my viewers are waiting for your reply, just like I am. This is *Today with Day*, where the truth's heard first."

"You should have punched him in the mouth when you had the chance. No one would have blamed you. And as far as the ensuing assault charge and trial, my summation to the jury would have had them in tears."

"I can always count on you, Uncle George, can't I?"

"You are my favorite nephew, Jim."

"If I recall correctly, I'm your only nephew. Unless you have something to tell me?" replied Jim with a smile.

"By the way, what you said on TV the other day about your dad was very touching, Jim," George grinned. "And I'm glad you didn't forget his wingman."

"Thanks, Uncle George. I was just stating the truth. Unlike this guy."

Jim had dropped by the airport after he left the branch to pick George up for lunch with the rest of the family. He'd found George at the coffee shop and he'd arrived just in time to see the report by Holland Day on the TV behind the counter.

"Clever smear job, Jim, not one libelous statement. He framed them all as questions," noted George.

"He's the master of the game. To hell with truth, all that matters is ratings," Jim grumbled.

"I do miss Cronkite," George sighed. "Now that was reporting."

"Let's get going. I want to get home before the media show up looking for another statement."

When Jim and George arrived, they found Jennifer was settled in Jim's office, typing furiously on her laptop. She was smiling that same mischievous smile, the one Jim knew all too well.

"All I want to know, Jennifer, is if what you're doing is going to mean I need to start pulling together a legal defense team," George said, putting on a voice of resigned apprehension.

"Are you familiar with the expression 'dream team,' Uncle George? I would expect the best," Jennifer replied with a smile.

"Okay Jennifer, what are you up to?" asked Jim.

"Giving one Howlin' Mad Day a lesson in the power of the blogosphere," Jennifer responded.

"The more I see of my lovely niece, the more I realize I should be taking a night school course in 'computer lingo 101,'" George stated dejectedly. "Help me out again, honey, a blog-o-what?"

Jennifer explained the term "blog" to George. She further explained that it was interactive and people could answer back.

"Mr. Day has one, a fact he's about to regret," Jennifer said. "No one questions the integrity of anyone in my family."

George could see the fire in Jennifer again. He knew at this point Holland Day was in trouble.

George took a breath and was about to lecture Jennifer, when Dolly stepped into the room, closing the door behind her carefully. The look on her face gave George pause.

"So how is Dad, Mom?" Jim asked.

"He's resting right now. Where's Jason?" she asked.

"On his way, he just texted," Jennifer replied.

Dolly looked down, hesitating, then lifted her head. She took a deep breath, then said, "I have a question to ask everyone and I'm hoping for a straight answer."

Her tone was uncharacteristically harsh, forceful even, and the room fell silent. Every eye was fixed on her.

"What is going on here? The hushed tones you speak in when I'm around, the meetings you have to which I'm not invited. I know it has to do with us being attacked, but for some reason, my family doesn't trust me." Her voice was strained, breaking under the weight of her grief. Her face was etched with sadness.

Jennifer leapt up and hugged her grandmother, crying, "No, no, Grandma! It's not that."

"Mom, I guess I owe you an apology. With Dad being ill, I didn't want to cause you any additional worry."

"Jim, I'm a mother and a grandmother. We're built to worry. Just tell me what's going on."

For the next fifteen minutes, Jim briefed Dolly on the events of the last few days.

"Goodness gracious! What trouble you get up to when I'm not around. This all sounds dangerous; Jim, are you sure we can't go to the police?"

"Jim, I agree. I have some strings I can pull with the authorities. Let me make some calls." George stated.

"We just do not know how deep this runs. We already know the FBI has been compromised. Let's keep digging on our own. Our ace in the hole here is they do not know what we have."

"Well! It seems we have some work to do," Dolly said in a reflective manner.

Just then, Rusty limped into the room, heading toward George with his tail awag. George bent over and gently picked him up, sitting down in a chair and settling Rusty into his lap. "You're the best wingman a man could have!" he exclaimed, stroking the dog fondly. At that moment, a muffled, tinny rendition of the familiar air force hymn rang out from George's coat pocket.

"I think this one's for me," he said, fishing his cell phone out.

"Well! My uncle's finally gone high-tech," Jennifer commented.

"Not completely! My phone at home still has a hand crank." George grinned, then answered his new phone. His grin slowly faded, and he hung up only a few seconds later.

"A certain Piper Twin Comanche was just ordered fueled and made ready."

"They're not missing any time getting that drive to Europe," Jim observed.

They were all silent for a moment, watching each other. George put his phone away. Jim shifted anxiously. Nobody quite knew what to do with that information.

"Jim, I heard we made the news," Dolly said, breaking the awkward silence. "A friend of mine said that Holland Day fellow was talking about us again this morning."

"I wouldn't call what he does news, Mom," Jim grunted, glancing at Jennifer. "He says some pretty awful things. And by the look on Jenny's face, I think she's doing something more about it than just blogging."

Jim and George just nodded as Jennifer pulled out her ring of flash drives and slid one into a USB port on her computer.

"Jennifer, would the first five letters on the flash drive you just installed be j-a-a-g-s?" asked George.

"You catch on fast, Uncle," was the reply.

"And the rest of the letters?"

"A-t-t-a-c-k," Jennifer stated.

"As a judge, I can't condone this. But as your uncle … Go get 'em, girl!" George exclaimed.

At that moment, Jason strolled in, grinning from ear to ear.

"There is one happy man," George stated.

"I have reason to be, Uncle George. Check out who I have a date with in a couple of days: meet Veronica Parker," Jason said as he handed his cell to his Uncle, showing him one of the pictures he'd taken of Veronica.

"I must say, that is one beautiful young lady," George observed.

Jennifer and Dolly inched toward George, hoping for a glimpse of the picture, but Jason snatched the phone back and took it to his dad.

"Only gentlemen can make a true assessment in matters such as these," Jason stated leaving Dolly and Jennifer with crossed arms and sour expressions mirroring each other.

"Wow! She is something Jason."

"Okay, Jason, hand it over. Let's see Ms. Hot Stuff here," Jennifer said.

Jason reluctantly pawned off his phone and Jennifer shared the image with Dolly.

"Oh my! She is very striking, Jason," Dolly said.

"Very pretty, Jason. How'd you meet her?" Jennifer asked.

Jason outlined his meeting with Veronica at the library. Jason caught the concerned glance between Jennifer and Jim.

"Not to worry, Dad, I took the advice to be wary of strangers; I know she's not the real deal. I also have a water bottle in my backpack with her fingerprints so we can check her out."

"Good work, son!"

"What was it that gave her away?" Dolly asked.

"Let's face it, Grandma. Women who look like her don't go for guys like me."

Jason's reply gave everyone in the room a moment of commiseration. Everyone wanted to say something, especially Jim, but struggled to find the words. It was Dolly who knew just what to say.

"Jason, this is going to sound conceited, but when I was this woman's age, I think I could've given her a run for her money in the looks department."

"You still can," Jim said.

"Amen to that Jim," George said. "And I remember you, Dolly, when you were her age … Wow!"

"Thank you, gentlemen, but I wasn't fishing for compliments. I didn't date a lot when I was her age, Jason, and it wasn't because I wasn't being asked. It always seemed to be the wrong guys asking. It appears too many nice guys are intimidated by beauty. Too bad for both parties, really. Am I wrong on any of this, Jennifer?"

Jennifer had been listening intently to her grandmother and empathizing with every word. Jennifer was beautiful in every sense of word, but had avoided the dating scene at MIT because of some bad experiences.

"Thank you for the compliment, Grandma. And no, you're not wrong."

Both Jim and George were feeling bad for Jason and Jennifer when Dolly said sagely, "It's not looks, or what a person does for a living, or their politics, or their faith that makes them attractive. It's all about character, and from where I'm standing, I think you and Jennifer have that in spades."

Jason was looking down, feeling embarrassed, as was Jennifer.

"And who knows, Jason? Veronica may be okay. Perhaps she just wanted to meet a nice guy for a change," Dolly added.

"Oh no!" exclaimed Jennifer, who had been running the name Veronica Parker through the APYN program.

"I don't think we'll need the prints; she's here Jason. I'm so sorry. She has an offshore account in Martinique. According to the notes, her real name is Emily Proctor, and she's on a $5,000-a-month retainer as a call girl. It's paid directly into her Martinique account.

"Does it say who's paying the retainer, Jenny?" Jim asked.

Jennifer started typing again.

"Here it is. Some organization called Patriots for a New Democracy."

"I know that name," George said. "They're one of those new political things … super …"

"Super PACs," Jim interjected. "It would be a perfect for them. Allows individuals to collect as much money as they want to support a candidate in an election as long as there are no direct ties between the candidate and the super PAC."

"Yeah right," sneered George. "I guess the people who thought up that rule never heard of something called the telephone."

"When I figured she was a phony, I thought she would be a good recruit for Operation Fortitude," Jason said. "So now that they've sent an expensive call girl to seduce me for information, we'll just have to come up with something for me to tell her during the pillow talk to throw them off the scent."

"What do you mean, 'pillow talk!?'" Dolly cried.

"Well, after we hit the sheets and are basking in the afterglow, I'll pour my heart out to Ms. Parker, revealing something she thinks is important."

Jim caught onto the fact Jason was launching into one of his comedy bits as soon as he said "hit the sheets;" Jennifer and George caught on with "basking in the afterglow." But as Jason was a master of the deadpan, Dolly was buying every bit of it.

"You're not seriously thinking of going to bed with this woman!" she shouted, giving Jim a horrified look.

"Well, I figure she is too high class for the back of my Nissan, so yes."

That remark just about broke up Jason's audience, but they held it together.

"Jason, this is a very dangerous woman. We don't know what she's capable of."

"Know thy enemy, Grandma! I should find out exactly what she's capable of."

Jim had to bite his lip to keep from laughing; George's cheeks had gone flame red, and Jennifer had covered her mouth with her hand to muffle her giggling.

"Jason, this woman is a prostitute! You don't know what she has; she could have VD!"

"Grandma," Jason interrupted. "I stand here as a man, willing to take one for the team."

That was all they could take. Jim, Jennifer, George, and even Jason burst out laughing. Dolly slumped back into a chair, realizing she had been played by a master.

"It's been over sixty years and I still haven't caught on to the Hanson sense of humor," she lamented.

"So, Dad, how did the flash drive drop go this morning?" Jennifer asked.

"Yeah, Dad, what happened?"

Everyone listened with rapt attention as Jim outlined his visit to the office and the conversation he'd overheard in the hallway, revealing the offshore accounts and the Ponzi scheme.

"What's a Ponzi scheme?" Dolly asked.

"As the name Ponzi is a historical reference, I feel I'm the only one qualified to give my dear grandmother a truly accurate and complete answer," Jason offered.

"Like you just did with Veronica Parker, you rascal," Dolly replied with a smile.

"She's got you there, Jason," George commented.

"I stand duly reprimanded," Jason stated, feigning exaggerated remorse as he gave his grandmother a big hug. "Now to the matter at hand, the Ponzi scheme!" he announced, assuming his usual professorial pose to the low moans of Jim and Jennifer.

"The Ponzi scheme was named after one Charles Ponzi, who was not the inventor of this scheme. He, however, made it famous here in the US in the 1920s as he took in so much money. It involves offering investors securities that promise unusually high returns. The person running the scheme pays these returns from deposits coming in from new investors. These schemes always collapse, however, when the bad guy takes the money and runs, or new investors can't be found. In the case of Bernie Maddoff, the man who ran the biggest Ponzi scheme in our history, the plot collapsed with the 2008 market drop. His investors came looking for their money, but it wasn't there."

"Thanks, Jason. Did you overhear anything else, Jim?" Dolly asked.

"Oh, I sure did, Mom. The guy who came to kill us is named Darien. He was acting on orders from someone named Culper, given through someone or something called 355. Another called Tallmadge said we had to be killed because the exposure risk was over sixty percent and—"

"What the hell! I can't believe I'm hearing this!" Jason yelled so loudly, it made everyone jump.

"This can't be happening, not in the twenty-first century!" he exclaimed.

"My God, Jason! What is it?" Dolly asked, looking frightened.

Jason was standing now. His eyes were closed and his hands were on top of his head, as if he was endeavoring to push the idea into his brain and his mind was pushing back, unable to fathom it.

"The Culper Ring. The Culper Ring. It can't still be out there," he murmured, as though trying to wish it away.

Everyone exchanged glances, but no one understood. It was George who addressed the issue, saying, "Jason! Obviously you've heard something here that's greatly upset you. We need you to sit down, take a breath, and tell us what you're thinking."

Jason fell back into a chair and rested his head on his left hand as he composed himself.

"Okay, here's the story," Jason said, taking a deep breath. "It's 1778, the Revolution is in full swing, and the British have occupied New York City. George Washington has a problem: he doesn't have any intelligence on their activities."

"Please, Jason, not another history lesson," Jennifer implored.

"Wait for it, Jennifer." Jason's voice was stern, sharp in a way Jennifer had never heard it before.

"Okay, Jason, sorry."

"Washington asked one of his officers, one Major Benjamin Tallmadge, to find people in the area that he could trust to supply the intelligence he needed. Tallmadge recruited over twenty people from around his home-town of Setauket, which is on Long Island. The methods of spying they used were quite advanced when compared to the conventions of the day. They formed small cells, keeping their identities secret from even each other. Even George Washington didn't know who they were. They used dead drops and coded messages. Some placed ads in newspapers; others wrote information between the lines of letters with invisible ink, while many dealt in disinformation. They also used aliases. Two of the most important spies were Abraham Woodhull, a farmer from Setauket, and Robert Townsend, a merchant from Manhattan—better known by their codenames: Samuel Culper, Sr., and Samuel Culper, Jr."

"That sounds fantastic, Jason," George commented. "I don't know what to think. How about you, Jim?"

Jim was hearing everything Jason was saying, but he was also seeing: seeing Jason the man. He was here before the family, telling this story with a self-confidence Jim had never witnessed before.

"I think the man has more to say, Uncle George."

"It gets better, Dad. Women played a big part in the Culper Ring. Since they were expected to hold their husbands' views and not any of their own, they made ideal spies. For example, Anna Strong would signal the Ring's members the times and locations of their meetings by using her laundry. The order in which she hung out her petticoats and handkerchiefs would give the other members the information. A low-tech and hack-proof system."

"And one I can understand," George said, which gave everyone a laugh.

"That brings me to 355. The Culper Ring remained a secret until 1939, when letters and other documents were found in the Townsend family home. This is where we find 355. We know 355 was a woman. Some say she was caught and hanged by the British, but we don't know for sure. She remains an unknown patriot. As they say, 'known only unto God.'"

The room was silent for several minutes as everyone took in what Jason had revealed.

"Can you be sure it's the same group?" Dolly inquired at last.

"What are the odds of some other group using all the same names—Tallmadge, 355, and Culper?"

"About the names," George asked. "Why would they use these names from the past?"

"Good question," Jason replied. "The only thing I can think of is tradition. Maybe they are proud of their past and wish to honor these people. But it's more likely they're codenames."

"How could an organization like that possibly survive for over two hundred years?" Jim asked, then added, "And why?"

"What's the most valuable commodity in the world?" Jason asked rhetorically. "Information, right? As we discussed before, this is what this is all about, and these guys have been at it since the founding of our country. Just think how far their tentacles must reach when they've had over two centuries to build a network. Generations of people, both consciously and unconsciously, have probably worked for these people."

"How could you work for people like this and not know it?" Dolly asked.

"You work in a bank, Grandma, and your boss asks you for a forecast on, say, bank earnings for the next two years. You do the work, not knowing it will be passed on beyond your boss, outside the company."

"But how could they have kept themselves secret all these years?" George wondered out loud.

"Probably by practicing what they did right from the start: operating in small cells, not knowing each other's identities …"

Jason stopped for a moment in deep thought. Everyone was silent, waiting for his next words.

"Jenny, the addresses we downloaded. Are they all local or are they spread across the country?"

Jennifer got busy on the computer. "They all appear local. Virginia mostly, Washington, some Maryland, Delaware, West Virginia."

"Our information is probably for just one cell. Sharon probably flies a circuit around the states gathering up flash drives from different hubs."

"Hold it there! That could mean there'd be dozens of flash drives to be handled and taken to Europe," Jim observed.

"You're right, Dad," Jason responded. He was pacing now. "Jenny, is there an Andorran embassy in the US?"

Jennifer started typing again. "It's more of a consulate, and it's in New York," she said.

"Anyone want to bet they move the flash drives out of the country in diplomatic bags?" Jason asked. "My God, the Culper Ring," he lamented. "Sure would explain a lot."

"Like what, Jason?" asked George.

"I'll show you."

Jason took out his cell and did a search online, pulling up a quote. He started to read aloud.

"'Since I entered politics, I have chiefly had men's views confided to me privately. Some of the biggest men in the US, in the field of commerce and manufacturing, are afraid of something. They know that there is a power somewhere, so organized, so subtle, so watchful, so interlocked, so complete, so pervasive, that they had better not speak above their breath when they speak in condemnation of it.'"

He paused and glanced up at his audience.

"President Woodrow Wilson said that in 1913."

"I think any money you have invested in your children's education was very well spent, Jim," George stated.

"I never thought I'd say this to you, Jason, but that was amazing insight and analysis."

"Can I have that comment in writing, Jenny?" Jason responded with a smile.

"Not a chance."

As the room plunged into the normal sound of sibling bickering, Jim was deep in thought. He knew now he would be doing more than just studying this new menace, but what it was he wasn't sure. Like Washington, he would need more intelligence.

"I think it's time for lunch," he announced. "Jenny, you're seeing Jake tonight, right?"

"Yes, I am."

"I have a magazine and a cup for you to give him with Sharon's and Janice's fingerprints on them. Let's find out who these people really are."

As they headed toward the door, Jennifer and Dolly studied the photo of Veronica on Jason's cell again.

"Do you think her hair is right for the shape of her face, Grandma?" Jennifer asked.

"Not really, and the jacket really does not go with that outfit."

George, Jim, and Jason just looked at each other and smiled.

*
**

"The Culper Ring?" Kathleen was looking at me like I'd gone mad.

"Yes ma'am."

"Good God, Jim, this stretches all belief to the limit."

"Not really. This country has always bought and sold politicians, lobbied, bribed, and operated on a basis of corruption. It's a testament to our nation's resiliency that it's survived. All the Culper Ring did was turn it into a business."

I felt Kathleen release my hand.

"I know you don't like politicians or government, so let's have this out here and now. I've got one good fight left in me today—it's yours if you want it."

Kathleen leaned over until her face was inches from mine. There was fire in her eyes, and a smirk on those beautiful lips. It was all I could do to resist kissing them. I knew she loved debating and seldom lost. The way she was looking at me, I could feel that, in some ways, this was her version of foreplay. I figured either way, I couldn't lose.

"Let's rock."

We stood up; facing each other. All that was missing from this picture were the cowboy hats and six guns. She fired the first volley.

"What makes you, Jim Hanson, think that you're the only person here with integrity?"

"I don't. There are over 400,000 more right here," I said, indicating the graves with a wave of my hand. "There are more up by my dad's grave and, of course, some more over there guarding the Tomb of the Unknown Soldier."

"I see I was left off that very distinguished list."

"I am told Kathleen Galbraith is a person of great integrity, which I believe to be true. As to the President, I have to reserve comment until I see if she can deliver to the American people something we all want back."

"Oh, pray tell," she replied with maximum sarcasm, "just what exactly would that be, Mr. Hanson?"

"The republic, Madam President."

"I'm sorry. I didn't know it was taken away."

"It was not taken; it was sold by you and your predecessors, one piece at a time to the lobbyists and the moneyed."

*
**

"Oh, my word. What's happening down there now; are they fighting?" Dolly asked.

"I'd like to think of it as a spirited exchange of ideas on current events," George replied.

"I have to give your dad credit for guts, Jenny," Jake commented with a smile. "Having it out with a woman surrounded by armed agents."

"I would call it foolhardy," she replied.

"They're going at it like they're married," Dom observed.

"There goes the indoor swimming pool," Jason lamented.

*
**

"Don't be so damned naïve, Jim! It does take money to get elected in this country. Does it cost too much? Damn right! But complaining doesn't change it—give me a better system!"

"They're spending $10.5 million to elect a senator every six years, $1.7 million every two years to elect someone to the House of Representatives!

These people have to spend most of their term in office trying to raise money for the next election rather than doing the work they were put there to do. So how about a system with tight electoral spending controls!?"

"Oh, did you miss that little decision by the Supreme Court, Citizens United? The one that states the citizens can spend as much money as they want to get someone elected!?"

"You mean the one that says to the world 'welcome to Washington, home of the best government money can buy! One republic thrown in at no extra charge!'"

Some of the Secret Service agents moved in a little closer. They were obviously concerned by the situation. They were right to be; Kathleen was now hopping mad and I was about to throw some gasoline on the fire. She walked toward me until she was less than three feet away. I honestly didn't know what she was going to do. Her voice was calm and deliberate.

"How dare you accuse me and my colleagues of selling out the republic."

"Don't tell me, Madam President. Tell them," I said, again waving my hand to indicate the graves around us. "They died for it."

"Why you sanctimonious sonovabitch! I will *not* stand in this sacred place and tell these brave Americans their sacrifice was for nothing! Over the years, our republic has taken its hits and suffered the bruises, but we've always gotten up to fight again and win the day. To misunderstand that is to totally misunderstand the character of the people lying here. But I know you understand their character, James Hanson—you laid one to rest today!"

"I do understand, Madam. He had that special courage. The kind of courage that saw him and his fellow pilots wake from a restless sleep, try to eat some breakfast, strap on a few tons of fighter plane, and fly into a sunrise that, for many, was the last one they'd ever see. I saw that courage again when a bunch of kids from four countries formed a squadron in cyberspace and risked everything to deliver the power brokers a simple message … no more!"

I could see Kathleen was still seething. I knew what I was going to say next wouldn't soothe her any.

"And what they want to know now is simple: did they fight this war just to lose the peace?"

"What are you trying to say, Hanson!?"

"In the next few days, the people who really run Washington are going to come looking for people to lynch. So are you going to stand up to them? Are you going to fight for real change, or are you just going to throw us under the bus in the name of political expediency, just like everyone before you!?"

Kathleen Galbraith was now in what I could only describe as a controlled rage. Her face was as hard as nails. For a moment, I actually thought she was going to punch me. But in a voice both measured and deliberate, she asked a question; the answer, as illustrated by the look in her eyes, was very important to her.

"James Hanson, do you honestly think that I would sell you people out, probably resulting in your deaths, in the name of political expediency?"

"Not for a moment. I just wanted to see again the strength of conviction of the president I voted for, the one I saw in the video. Welcome back to the fight, Madam! It has been lonely out here."

"I never left it, you idiot! Why do you think I'm here today!?"

She never took her eyes off me. She walked back to the bench, glaring at me all the way, and sat down. She then pointed to the spot beside her, so I dutifully joined her. We sat looking straight ahead for a moment. She then reached over, took my hand off my lap and held it next to her, which surprised me. We both continued to stare straight ahead, neither wanting to be the first to break this tense silence. I suddenly felt her gaze fixed on the side of my head. I turned slowly until we were again nose to nose.

"Well, Jim, you just ripped your president a new one. Feel better?"

"Not as good as I thought I would. It's hard being mad at you."

"Why's that?"

I couldn't believe what I said next; maybe I was still up from the argument.

"Besides being genuine and very intelligent, you are very beautiful. I call that an unfair advantage."

She turned so she was facing me directly; I felt the hold on my hand tighten.

"James Hanson, are you flirting with me?"

"Absolutely."

"You realize I'm surrounded by a number of armed agents," she said with a broad smile.

"You have awakened my reckless side."

*
**

"What is going on down there now?" Dolly asked.

"Now they're laughing together. A minute ago they were fighting. Weird," Jennifer observed.

"Are you sure they're not already married?" mused Dom.

"Not yet," Jason stated. "When was the last time there was a wedding in the Rose Garden?"

*
**

"You have a lot of passion, James."

"As do you, Madam President. It's one of the reasons I and millions of others voted for you."

"You know Jim, you get into this office and you quickly find out how little power 'the most powerful person in the world' really has. I really wanted to fix the things you brought up, but everyone with a vested interest fights you every inch of the way. But you, Jim, you and your little group may have given me back something I thought I'd lost."

"What's that?"

"Hope."

I felt her squeeze my hand again.

"I have heard other presidents say your job is the loneliest there is."

"They're right."

"I want you to know something."

She tilted her head and raised her eyebrows.

"When you're back in that oval office and it's starting to feel like a lonely place, remember this: you are not alone anymore."

She smiled and, again, tightened her grip on my hand.

"So, Jim, in this continuing story, what happened next?

"Well, we got a new friend in Canada ..."

"It's harder to start over
again than it was to begin."

—Stan Rogers

CHAPTER 10

"Thanks for coming in, Arissa," Emmanuel said. "I know this is a silly question, but how are you doing?"

"Not good, Emmanuel. And no, it's not a silly question. I was about to ask you the same, but judging from those bags under your eyes, I see you haven't been sleeping either."

"Steve was my dearest friend. One of the few people I've ever met who saw me first and not my wheelchair. You're also one of those people."

"Thank you," she replied as she reached across his desk to grasp his hand. "We both loved him."

"I'm sorry to have to ask you to meet me today, but something happened and I need to talk to a friend."

"I'm touched you'd call me, Emmanuel," she replied, sensing something was deeply troubling him.

"I know this is the wrong time, but it's big."

Emmanuel proceeded to outline the events of the previous evening and his relationship to International Predictive Analytics and Culper. By the time Emmanuel turned his flat screen around to show the virus he'd received, Arissa was enthralled by the story of the events of Emmanuel's work at Predictive.

"My God, I've never seen programming like this! I'm going to have to take you into my deepest confidence."

She outlined the events with the Hanson family; by the time she was finished, Emmanuel was crying.

"So my stepfather and Culper are responsible for Steve's death, two of your friends, two people working with the FBI, and almost an entire family. But why?"

"We don't know about your stepfather yet. I don't fully understand why myself. But maybe we'll know more after we hack in."

Emmanuel sat up straight. "What do you mean hack in?"

Arissa explained what Jennifer and her friends at MIT had come up with.

"Oh my God! I have to talk to these people now! They have no idea what they're up against!" exclaimed Emmanuel.

"I don't know if that is possible," Arissa stated, explaining their security. "She did tell me last night they're meeting at a restaurant today, I'm trying to remember the name of it … Sardi's Ribs or something. She said we had to dine there when I visit Virginia. Maybe we could call them there if we can use landlines."

A few minutes after Emmanuel had googled the restaurant for the phone number, the conference call was set up in Sardi's business meeting room where the Hansons, George, Dom, and Jake were eating. After Arissa explained the events of the last twenty-four hours, she introduced Emmanuel.

"So Emmanuel, are you sure Culper was trying to break into Blackberry or could someone else have put the virus into that birthday card?" Jim asked.

"I have no doubt it was him. Tallmadge wrote the program; the code is very distinctive."

"Just who is this Tallmadge person?" asked George. "He … or she seems to have a lot of say in this organization."

"Yes, it does, Judge Grayson. But Tallmadge isn't a person. It's their computer."

The stunned looks of the group at Sardi's were directed to Jennifer. Her response was slow and deliberate.

"Okay, Emmanuel, what are we up against?"

"A 1,000 petaflop operating system, almost unlimited storage capacity, and the most advanced artificial intelligence on the planet."

"What!" Jennifer was now on her feet. "Arissa, is this true, how could it be true? That's fifty times faster than the fastest super computer out there."

"Jennifer, I haven't seen Tallmadge, but I stand behind Emmanuel fully. We've been having a rough time up here. I've lost the love of my life, Emmanuel has lost his best friend, and his stepfather may have had something to do with that death. We just want to help you end all this. Emmanuel is just telling you what he knows."

The group at Sardi's was silent as they searched each other's faces for a response. As usual, George knew the proper thing to say.

"I won't pretend to understand the significance of what you just told us. But I do know what it's like to lose the love of your life. I know I speak for everyone here when I say you both have our deepest sympathy. I also know we all are grateful for any help you can afford us."

Two voices saying "thank you" emerged from the speaker in the middle of the table, followed by Arissa's only.

"Emmanuel, you'd better tell them the rest."

Everyone leaned forward, staring at the speaker in anticipation of Emmanuel's words.

"Jennifer, that wi-fi program I wrote and you hid in that flash drive. It doesn't stand a chance. It will be found."

Everyone sank back into their chairs.

"So we're back to square one," Jim bemoaned.

"No, you're not. Before I left Predictive, I put the program in as my backdoor."

Jennifer was on her feet again.

"Way to go, Emmanuel!" she cried. "Give us the codes and passwords and watch us fly!"

"No. It's not that easy. You all have to understand one important point. Tallmadge is a quantum computer."

Jennifer fell into her chair. Her mouth was half-open, her eyes glazed, and she started to pale.

"Oh my God. What have they done …"

"You know, Jim, your Uncle George is right; there should be a class where one can go and learn computer lingo," Kathleen said.

"Ain't it the truth."

"A qua … what type was that again?"

"Quantum computer."

"Okay, Jim, I'm listening."

I let go of Kathleen's hand as I turned to face her squarely on the bench. Putting my hands in front of me, I looked at her as her brow wrinkled in anticipation of my explanation.

"Jennifer tried to explain it to us like this …," I said, pausing while I tried to gather my thoughts.

"Jim …"

"They don't really exist apparently, or so we thought."

The president nodded thoughtfully.

"So, Jim, to summarize things to date. In the last few days, your little group—and remember, Jim, I have working for me intelligence agencies employing thousands of people—found a secret society my people missed, one that supposedly hasn't existed since 1778, but controls billions of dollars; dollars which, according to you, don't really exist, using a computer that doesn't exist. Is that about right?"

Kathleen looked scholarly while still nodding her head.

"I think the president will have no trouble grasping quantum physics."

We both laughed with her adding, "I'm going to enjoy you trying to explain this one to me."

"I accept the challenge. As you just said, the money doesn't really exist; it's just bits on a computer. These bits represent text using the binary digits, 0 or 1, hence the name binary code. Quantum computers don't use this type of bit; they use quantum bits known as qubits. They can exist in many different states at once, resulting in a computer many times faster than anything we have today. So far, all that has been done in building one is theoretical modeling and some experiments, or so we thought. Tallmadge changed all that."

"How did the Culper Ring succeed where everyone has failed?"

"Jennifer figures it was due to one Dr. Adrian Mandrake."

Kathleen tilted her head, giving me the "tell me more" look again.

"He apparently was a true British eccentric with some incredibly far-out ideas on how to build a quantum computer, which were rejected by the establishment."

"But not the Culper Ring, I assume," Kathleen offered.

"Exactly. You combine those ideas, add an unlimited budget, and the result is Tallmadge."

"I noticed you referred to Dr. Mandrake in the past tense."

"A couple of years ago, he was going to be a guest speaker at a quantum physics conference in New York. The day before the conference, he had a heart attack."

"Our friend Darien does get around."

"That's what we suspected."

"Tell me, where did all this leave you guys?"

"Trying to settle Jennifer down ..."

"How did they solve the decoherence and the memory problem!? And the binary interface? How did they make it work!?"

Jennifer was out of breath with excitement. Again, it was George who had the calming hand.

"Jennifer, I know this is big news for you, but why not sit down, take a breath, and let the man answer."

"Jennifer, I wish I could answer your questions but I can't. I only worked with Tallmadge for one summer doing minor programming. I was never told anything about their mainframe. It was kept in a sealed, climate-controlled room. I couldn't understand the way I had to write some of the code. When I asked for explanations from the chief programmer, I got brush off answers.

"One day he got an emergency call from home telling him his little girl was in some kind of accident. He rushed off so quickly, he didn't lock down his terminal. I started to snoop a bit. The peripherals were totally strange, the way they were set up. I managed to get into the system properties and that was where things really got interesting. I was stunned by the speed. I wanted to play with the thing some more so I slipped in the virtual wi-fi program I wrote."

Emmanuel paused in his narrative; it sounded as if he were drinking some water. Everyone was leaning in with anticipation of his next words.

"Instantly—and I mean instantly—Tallmadge made the modem and listed it as just another peripheral. I then instructed him to delist it and only activate the program when it received certain codes on a certain carrier wave. That's when I got a shock. Tallmadge asked me a question. 'Why?'"

"You've got to be kidding!" Jennifer exclaimed. Everyone else exchanged shocked looks. "What did you do?"

"I typed in 'Security Protocol Z4 672' create."

"In plain English?" Jennifer asked.

"Yes."

"Even though I understand almost nothing that's being said here, you've got me on the edge of my seat, Emmanuel. What happened?" George asked, giving everyone a chuckle.

"It answered back 'completed' and nothing else."

"So if I understand all this," Jake said slowly, "this computer was smart enough to ask you 'why' but not smart enough to question your answer. It just created the phony protocol and number and was satisfied with it."

"It's not phony. Tallmadge actually made it. At lunch, I went across the street to a café. I brought along my notebook and sent out the carrier wave and the codes I'd made. I spent forty-five minutes playing chess with it."

Jennifer was now emulating what Jason had done when he heard the name "Culper Ring." She was pacing around the room, rubbing her temples, trying to make sense of what she'd heard.

"Well, I'll ask the question if no one else will," George said. "Did you beat it, Emmanuel?"

"Not even close, it whipped my butt." Everyone laughed. "And another thing," Emmanuel continued. "It's got attitude."

"Oh c'mon, Emmanuel," Jennifer groaned.

"Oh yeah! I figure whoever programmed it used chess to help develop the artificial intelligence and reasoning. Every time I made a move, it would question it and ask why I didn't make this move or that move. Finally, at the end of the session it says, 'Suggest more practice and study to complete this task effectively.' Now I call that a diss!"

Everyone was now laughing, Emmanuel and Arissa included. George leaned over to Jennifer and whispered, "It's nice to hear Arissa laugh."

Jennifer gave her uncle a smile and a hug.

"By the way, Emmanuel … I don't know if this makes a difference, but when I overheard them talking at the branch office, they said the orders to kill Steven and us came directly from Culper through this 355. Not through anyone else."

"Thank you for that, Mr. Hanson. I just wish I knew who 355 is," Emmanuel lamented. He paused. "So what happens next?"

"I still want to go for Tallmadge and find out what's on this thing. Are we all in agreement?" Jim asked. Everyone signaled their concurrence.

"Emmanuel, if you can send to my colleagues at MIT the codes and passwords to crack Tallmadge—Arissa has the contact information—we all would be most grateful," Jennifer stated.

"Will do. When you get your program written with what you want Tallmadge to do, send it to me and I'll format it into a form he will understand."

With that, goodbyes and thank yous were said all around, and then the line went dead.

"I don't know about you guys, but I've got a date with a special lady," Jason said with a grin.

"And I have to watch you have that special date," Jake stated.

"Poor Jason has to have a chaperon," Jennifer said with a laugh.

"What a great idea," Dolly observed. "No 'taking one for the team,' Jason," she added with a smile.

"I'll make sure of that, Mrs. Hanson," Jake interjected.

"Even my own grandmother and a fellow bro are against me," bemoaned Jason.

"I'm on my way to Atlanta to observe one Darien on a visit to a certain Dr. Barker," Dom stated.

"And I'm flying him there," George said.

"That makes me the only gentleman left in this room; in other words, the guy stuck with picking up the check for breakfast," Jim reasoned.

"Always said my nephew was a fast learner," George chuckled.

*
**

The coffee shop where Jason was to meet Veronica had only about a dozen people in it when Jason arrived, well ahead of time. Jake was in a minivan across the street where he would monitor the conversation through the wire Jason was wearing. Jason set up his notebook computer and made himself look busy by working in case he was being watched.

Veronica was right on time. She was wearing a matching denim ensemble—torn jeans and faded jacket—and had paired it with a Georgetown U tee. She looked stunning as she gave Jason a big smile and a hello. Jason could only think, 'Why can't all this be real? She comes off so nice, so smart. So what went so wrong in your life Veronica that you became a hooker?'

They picked up their coffees and sat down in a booth by a window.

"I've something to show you, Jason," Veronica whispered.

She stood up and took a new notebook computer out of her backpack and slid in next to him in the booth.

"You didn't get an Apple," Jason noted.

"No, I got this Toshiba, but check out this screen."

Veronica opened up the computer revealing a large letter box screen that was bright and sharp. But that wasn't what sent a chill through Jason. It was what was written on it.

Jason, don't react to this message, keep talking about the computer. I'm wearing a wire, we're being watched. Blue Econovan in parking lot.

"Well, that's very impressive, Veronica! Let me try the keyboard—it looks like you might have a stuck key."

y r u telling me this

i need your help

"Oh, there we go! Guess it wasn't so stuck after all," Jason said. "This one feels a bit loose though … did you buy this thing used or what?"

"No, brand new."

how can I help

"How many USB ports does it have, Veronica?"

meet me later need 2 b alone

"I count four."

y should i trust you___ Emily!

Veronica looked surprised at first, then turned to face Jason. Their faces were only inches apart now and Jason was staring right into those green eyes, inhaling the fragrance of her perfume. Again, he was thinking, 'Why aren't you real?'

Veronica nodded her head in a knowing manner as she looked him in the eye while typing.

can't give u reason have vital info family in danger!!!! u set time place

"It seems like a well-designed, light notebook. I'm sure it'll serve you well."

pick u up noon oak & filmore

They continued to talk for their unseen audience for another half-hour about school and some of the latest music videos. Veronica asked again about the attack and what was happening with the police. Jason fed back the standard line about how frustrated the family was about the inaction on the case. It was now time to leave, but not before a dinner date was made for the next evening.

That's when it happened. Jason thought it was for the benefit of who-ever was watching, but then he wasn't sure. Veronica leaned over and gave him a long, passionate kiss, which he found himself returning with all his might. As they broke their embrace, Veronica whispered in his ear, "Help me, Jason. Please."

Jason left shortly after Veronica, but not before getting the license plate number of the Econovan. He had pre-arranged with Jake to meet him at another coffee shop.

"Well, I now know why there was a pause in the conversation as you said your goodbyes," Jake commented as Jason sat down.

"What's that mean?"

"Either you've started wearing lipstick or you got more than a handshake."

Jason quickly grabbed a napkin and wiped his lips. He then told Jake about the entire meeting and gave him the license plate number of the van.

"I'll get this checked out. Clever bit with the computer," he commented.

"Jake, I honestly don't know what to think."

"Jason, she's a hooker. She wants something."

Jason felt like he should defend her, then thought better of it—logic needed to trump emotion. Jake could see Jason's hesitation.

"Jason, I know she's beautiful and I wish she wasn't one. In you, she probably sees a guy she can manipulate. Think about it, the kiss, then asking you for help? But she might have information we can use; it's just a matter of how much she wants for it. Keep wearing your wire."

"I'll meet you at the Jackson Square Mall in front of Gordon's Mens wear. I'll get there first to make sure you're not followed. If you are, I'll drive past your car and honk once, then you take off with her and I'll try to block the other vehicle. Meet me back here."

"Sounds like a plan."

"You know, there is *one* thing I don't get about this babe."

Jason raised his eyebrows.

"I checked her out. She's in law at Georgetown, but she's on a full scholarship.

"What?"

"Yeah, she's that smart. Top of her class and on the dean's list. So that begs the question … "

"Yeah, I know," Jason interrupted. "Why the hell is she working as a hooker?"

*
**

Holland Day was already in a foul mood when he arrived at the TV station. His e-mail and the bloggers had been very critical of his broadcast of the Hanson case. As he walked into his office, his secretary scurried in after him.

"Mr. Day, you need to go and see Mr. Johnston right away. He's been asking for you. He seems very upset."

"What's the old man's problem now?"

"I don't know, but he does want to see you."

"I'll get to him in a minute. You know, just because I'm his son-in-law he thinks he can say jump and I'll answer 'how high?'"

"He does own the station, sir."

"I've got to do something first."

Holland opened up his notebook computer and logged in. He wasn't on more than a minute when all of a sudden, the screen turned blue. The words "Liars Will Pay" appeared, followed by a disembodied hand with a raised middle finger. At that point, the hard drive started to spin backward, entirely destroying it.

*
**

Jason arrived at the corner of Oak Street and Filmore Drive to see Veronica waiting for him. He quickly pulled over and she hopped in. Jason turned right, followed by a fast left down a side street. He then pulled a U-turn, eventually doubling back on Oak Street.

"Let me guess, you think someone is following us."

"A logical assumption under the circumstances. Okay Veronica or Emily, or whatever you are calling yourself, what do you want?"

Veronica flinched, taken back by Jason's bluntness. Jason was angry at her for thinking she could play him with a smile and a kiss. Angry at himself for her almost being right.

"I've got info which is very important to you and your family."

"For a good price, I assume?"

"Say what?"

"People in your profession don't exactly give things away. Look, Veronica, you were sent to get information, but we made you. Now you say you want help and you have information for us. But for all I know, you could still could be wearing a wire, still working for whoever!"

What Veronica did next truly caught Jason by surprise. Within seconds she had removed her jacket, top, and bra.

"First of all Jason, it's 'still working for *whomever*,' but as you can plainly see, no wire on me, no wire in my bra," she said, dangling the garment in his face.

Jason spied a closed up gas station ahead and pulled into it.

"I suppose that was designed to shock me."

"What's wrong Jason? Don't you like what you see?" Veronica taunted while rocking her shoulders. "Men pay me a lot of money to see what you're getting for free. Imagine that, a whore actually giving a freebie," she added in a voice riddled with sarcasm.

"Make your point, Veronica, but please do it while dressing."

"That's a first. A guy asking me to put clothes *on*," she responded derisively as she started to dress.

"I apologize for not living down to your expectations."

"Look, Jason," she said in solemn voice. "I guess I made a mistake coming to you. I'll get out here. Before I go, I just wanted to let you and *whomever*," she said, raising her voice and poking Jason in the chest, "is on the other end of that poorly concealed wire you're wearing know that you and your family are in great danger from some very bad people. Last night, I had an all-nighter with one of my regulars. He spent a lot of time on this."

Veronica reached into her backpack and pulled out a smart phone and handed it to a startled Jason.

"He actually had two of them, one for his regular business and this one. He spent a lot of time texting and talking on it when he thought I was asleep. The name Hanson came up several times. He had just started a text when he put it on the side table and went to the bathroom. I had a quick look at the screen. It was going to someone named Turner and it said 'Authority 355 re Hansons, plan termination.'

"That's all I got before he came back. I lifted the phone in the morning."

"Just whom is this regular client of yours?"

"You mean 'just *who* is,' I assume," Veronica corrected with a mischievous grin.

"Whatever," Jason snapped.

"Nathan McWilliams, Regional Director of the FBI. Take care, Jason," Veronica said as she started to get out of the car. She paused. "Can I ask you one thing?"

"Sure."

"How did you make me when we met at the library?"

Jason took a deep breath and sighed.

"Veronica, girls that look like you generally don't go for history nerds that look like me."

"What!" She shook her head.

"Don't leave, Veronica," Jason said, grabbing her arm. "You're in danger."

"Ya think?! You think I don't know McWilliams probably has half the FBI looking for me now that he's missing his phone? You know Jason; all I wanted to do was talk to your uncle and that FBI guy dating your sister."

"What do they have to do with this?"

"I'm a law student. I've been studying some of your uncle's decisions. I saw that Holland Day guy say your sister is dating an FBI agent. I wanted to talk to them to get some advice—about a murder."

Jason studied Veronica in silence for a moment or two, then made his decision.

"Jake, I hope you're getting all this. Our rendezvous is an abort. Please find out if there's a BOLO out on ..." Jason paused, looking at her, her face drawn in anticipation of Jason's next statement.

" ... one Emily Proctor, alias Veronica Parker. I'm taking her home."

*
**

"Gaston. What's going on in Virginia?" Culper asked.

"There are some issues, but we'll be getting a handle on them."

"It doesn't sound like it. You were going to have that Holland Day fellow discredit Jim Hanson. I was just informed he's been fired by his father-in-law. What the hell happened?"

"Apparently some photos of him with another woman were posted online."

Gaston handed Culper his tablet, displaying pictures of Holland Day in bed with a young woman.

"Who posted these?"

"We're not sure, but there's a problem with the woman in the photos."

"Which is?"

"She's dead. Murdered in the ladies' room of a hotel in Richmond."

"And the significance?"

"She's one of ours. Very high end hooker whose clientele included one well-connected individual who's been very friendly to us. We can assume she was responsible for taking the photos."

"I know who you mean, Gaston, and he should be friendly to us; we paid for his elections and even for his former girlfriend here," Culper replied, handing the tablet back. He proceeded to pour Pierre Ferrand cognac into a tulip-shaped wine glass. However, he didn't pick the glass up. Instead, he did something Gaston had only seen him do a couple of times before. It was something he did when he was very stressed—and it took a lot to make Culper stressed. He stood with his left hand against his chest, spinning his cufflink with his right and staring vacantly into space.

"The lady in question is one Samantha Stevens," Gaston reported. "I've been able to determine some trouble had developed between our friend and Ms. Stevens, the nature of which I have yet to determine. Perhaps she took pictures of her and our friend and was trying to blackmail him. I do have an unconfirmed report 355 ordered Sharon Turner to get rid of the problem and retrieve her cell and her records, which are on a flash drive."

Culper came out of his trance and snapped his head toward Gaston.

"Are you suggesting Turner killed this woman without specific orders from me, that 355 issued the order?"

"As I said, it is unconfirmed."

"Well find out! The last thing we need is a rogue agent out there!"

Culper paused as he gathered his thoughts.

"Powerful men need young women to confirm they haven't lost their masculinity. How many times have we exploited that systemic weakness, Gaston? Now it might cost this guy everything, as it has that moron Day. I hope she was worth it." Culper pontificated with a sardonic grin. "Now, to the perpetual Hanson issue. What's happening?" he asked while returning to spinning his cufflink.

"As you know, the flash drive Jim Hanson handed in did contain a virus. We have yet to determine what it does."

"What it does, Gaston, is confirm they know we are here and you know what that means."

Gaston again felt sick with fear.

"Yes, I do," Gaston answered dejectedly. "This is going to cause an investigation we might not be able to stop after all the publicity the Hansons have had."

"I don't care. I want them all in body bags and soon. I've already asked 355 to come up with a plan."

Gaston let out a deep sigh.

"Don't worry, Gaston, my plans usually work out. Look how worried you were about Emmanuel. I got a nice e-mail from him, thanking me for the birthday card. It also contained a warning for me to tighten up our security. Apparently, someone snuck a nasty virus into the card."

Gaston wanted to say something, but managed to hold his temper.

"I need something else, Gaston. Time to put our friend Tallmadge to work. You keep telling me how good it is at computer modeling; now you can show me. I need to know the amount of US government foreign debt per country. I need to know the value of all our gold bullion holdings in the US, as well as the rest of the world. I want it listed by location. Further, I want the projected time to US bankruptcy based on their current spending patterns."

"Those are straight-forward calculations. You said you wanted to do some computer modeling."

"Yes, I do Gaston. When you have these numbers, run them using the Pegasus model."

Over the last few days, ideas and orders from Culper had caused Gaston some fear and no little concern. Now, for the first time in his life, Gaston felt pure terror.

George and Dom were sitting outside the East Town Medical building in Atlanta when a taxi pulled up. A dark-haired man who Dom took to be in his early forties with bandaged hands got out of the back seat.

"That's him, Dom, I'll swear that's the guy I saw at the airport."

Dom immediately started to shoot photos with his Nikon and telephoto lens as the man struggled to get his wallet out of his jacket pocket to pay the driver.

"Do you mind waiting here a while longer, George? I'd like to get some shots when he comes out. The ones I have are only of him in profile."

"No problem, Dom, as long as you buy the coffee."

About an hour and a half later, Darien emerged and Dom started taking pictures again. Darien stood by the curb checking the messages on his cell.

"I think we just got lucky, George," Dom stated having observed Darien put his cell into his jacket pocket and extract a cigarette pack. He had taken the last cigarette from his pack and thrown the latter into a nearby waste can. He had then struggled with his lighter.

A taxi came and Darien left, but not before discarding his cigarette onto sidewalk. Dom was soon out of the car with two evidence bags.

*
**

"Emily, I'm going to cut around the back of this old gas station. When I do, jump in the back and lay down."

"Will you be joining me, Jason?" Emily asked with a chuckle.

"You know darn well I want to make anyone following this car think I'm alone," he replied as he sped round the back of the building.

"Yes. But a girl can still hope, can't she?"

Jason looked over his shoulder to see a smiling Emily looking back at him.

"Just my damn luck, drop-dead gorgeous but a tease," he bemoaned as laughter erupted from the backseat.

"Flattery will always get you everywhere with me."

"My God, woman, give me a break."

Emily's face was suddenly very serious.

"Thank you, Jason."

"I think we might be the ones thanking you."

Jason sped for home, making some quick turns on the way. No one seemed to be following him. On the way, he explained to Emily about his grandfather's medical situation and the rest of the family. Robert's illness seemed to truly sadden her. She had read all three of his Supreme Court cases.

"Robert Hanson was a great lawyer and a very brave man. Of course, I'm sure he still is."

"Thanks, Emily."

Arriving at the Hanson home, the security guard waved him in. Jason used his remote to open one of the two garage doors, which he quickly closed once they were inside. They entered the house through the connecting side door, which led to a small hallway that took them past Jim's office. Jason headed into the office, followed by Emily. Jennifer was busy typing on her computer; her back was to the door.

"Hi, Jenny, I …"

"Hi Jason! How did your hot date go? Did you have to take one …," Jennifer said as she turned around. She caught sight of Emily, which caused her eyes to widen and her jaw to drop.

"Not as hot as I would've liked it, Jennifer," Emily said with a grin as she shook her hand.

"Now, Jason, here's a lady who has but one question: 'what is this woman doing here?'" Emily observed.

"Jenny, here's the situation—"

"Is that Jason's voice I hear?" Dolly could be heard coming down the hallway. "Now, I trust you didn't have to take one …"

Dolly trailed off as she entered the office and a look of astonishment came over her face.

"Another lady with the same question. Hello, Mrs. Hanson, I'm Emily Proctor," she said, offering her hand.

"Now, let me explain what's—" Jason tried again.

"Well! I see Jason's home early." It was Jim's voice now echoing down the hall. "My word, if I was out with a woman that beautiful, I would still be taking one …," Jim said as he entered his office, then paused. "Make that not having to take my foot out of my mouth. Hello, Ms. Proctor, I'm Jim Hanson," he said, extending his hand while everyone laughed.

"And we have yet another person wondering why I'm here," Emily stated. "The answer is simple; Jason was too cheap to spring for a room."

Everyone was dead silent, uncomfortably wondering whether Emily was joking or not. Jason groaned, "Emily, be serious!" and everyone broke up laughing as Jason flushed with embarrassment.

"I can attest to his good behavior," Jake said as he entered the office. "He was a perfect gentleman at all times."

"Yes, he was," Emily added. "Darn it."

The laughter that filled the room caused Jason to flop into a chair with a face so red it matched the shirt he was wearing.

"You realize you're still wearing the wire. This meeting made for very entertaining radio on my drive over here," Jake stated as he retrieved the device.

Dolly's manners and timing were impeccable.

"The fact Jason brought you here means you are most welcome, Emily. We'll be serving lunch in a little while and would be most happy if you would join us."

Emily looked like she didn't know what to say at first, glancing down, almost embarrassed.

"That is most kind of you, Mrs. Hanson. I'd enjoy that. Thank you."

"Emily has brought us something very special today," Jason announced. Everyone looked at her.

"I have it here, 355's cell phone," he exclaimed while holding it up to the surprise of everyone.

"My God, Emily, how did you ever get this?" Jennifer asked, taking the phone from Jason and pulling out the SIM card. The question caused Jason to wince.

"Regional Director of the FBI, Nathan McWilliams, was one of my clients," Emily responded, to Jennifer's embarrassment. Jennifer plugged the card into her computer, stammering an apology.

"It's okay, Jennifer, everyone here knows my past."

"So the Regional Director is 355," Jake stated while pacing. "I wonder how many more of these guys are in government positions?"

"Unfortunately, probably too many," Jim responded.

Jake turned his attention back to Emily.

"Emily, I'll spare the Hanson's the job of asking you the tough questions. Besides, I'm the one who did the investigating," he stated.

"That's fine, Jake, go ahead and ask."

"Why are you helping us? I know that wasn't your original mission."

"Correct," Emily stated. "My original 'mission,' as you call it, was to meet Jason, befriend him, seduce him, and find out how much you knew about what was really going on with New Life and the events pertaining to the attack on you. This morning, I was further instructed to ascertain what information was gleaned from the flash drive that Mr. Hanson apparently found. However ..." Emily turned her head to look at Jason. "He figured out who I really was, for all the wrong reasons."

"Instructed by whom, Emily?"

"Don't know, Jake. All I get are e-mails inside photographs, sometimes of a cute animal, sometimes a car. I type in a code that was sent to me by mail a couple of years ago, and the picture goes away and there's the message."

"Steganographs," Jennifer offered.

"I'd do my job; my pay would be dropped into an offshore account."

"You still haven't answered my original question: why are you helping us?"

"As I told Jason, I want to talk to you and Judge Grayson."

"About what?"

"I want out of the business I'm in."

"Which brings me to another question I have to ask. I've done a background check on you at Georgetown."

"Yeah, I've been waiting for this one," she said, looking up at the ceiling and shaking her head.

"It has to be asked. Dean's list, top of your class, full scholarship. So why be a hooker?"

The room took on a stillness that could be felt.

"It's a long story."

"Let me help you make it a short one. Your parents were killed four years ago in a car accident in Richmond. A terrible tragedy made worse by the fact their small business owed the wrong people some heavy coin."

Emily's face grew harder as she listened.

"That's when they first made contact with you, wasn't it, Emily?"

"Your boyfriend's good, Jennifer, really smart," Emily said through lips so tight they were almost white.

"Your parents' debt wouldn't have been enough to extort your cooperation. After all, it wasn't your responsibility. If they leaned on you, you would've just gone to the police. No, Emily, they had something else on you. There was another person in the car with your parents that day ..."

Jake didn't get to finish his sentence.

"You sonovabitch! You leave Michelle out of this!" she screamed.

Jason was quickly at her side. "Calm down, Emily! We're here to help."

"Michelle has suffered enough," Emily said as she sat down with Jason and started to weep.

"So have you, Emily," Jake said softly, his voice evoking compassion, a fact not missed by Jennifer. "Your younger sister was permanently disabled and needs care for the rest of her life. But you knew from the two summers you worked in a nursing home, just how bad some of these places can be. You wanted the best, and that would be the Grace Field Nursing Home in Richmond, but it's expensive. And that's how they extorted your cooperation."

Dolly rushed over to Emily's side.

"Oh my God, you poor child," she cried, drying Emily's tears with a handkerchief and putting her arm around her. "The sacrifices you've had to make to help your sister! It's so … so …"

"'Noble' is the word I think you're looking for, Dolly," a voice from the doorway said.

Everyone glanced over to find George Grayson leaned against the doorframe.

*
**

"These guys don't miss an opportunity, do they?" Kathleen asked.

The afternoon breeze had come up at Arlington, gently rustling the leaves; if one was listening carefully, one might think it gave voice to the thousands resting there.

"Find a weakness and exploit it," she added.

I stood up and joined her on the path.

"I never felt so helpless," I said. "I knew it was just a matter of time before they'd come for us. But how could I defend my family from them when both the police and the FBI were compromised?"

"As I said before, Jim, George could've called me."

"As he kept reminding me. But an idea was starting to formulate in my mind, and you'd need complete deniability. Besides, Emily had brought me a weapon."

*
**

"Any luck with that SIM card?" Jim asked Jennifer.

"It's heavily encrypted, but we'll get there."

"Emily, you mentioned a murder. What were you talking about?" Jake asked.

Emily was sitting on a couch between Jason and Dolly. She looked haggard; her eyes were red from the tears. The wise-cracking demeanor she'd being using as a shield was gone. Everyone could see she was scared.

"Samantha was my friend," Emily sniffled as she held back more tears. "She was with me at Georgetown, only in history."

"Not Samantha Stevens!" Jason exclaimed.

"I'm sorry you have to hear about it this way, Jason. But they were using her the same way they're using me."

Jason flopped back in couch, stunned.

"She was top of the class; we worked on some projects together. She was so smart, so nice," he lamented.

"Jason, I know you asked her out," Emily said to Jason's surprise. "I want you to know, she wanted to date you. She talked about you a lot. More than once, she asked me, 'Do you think women like us will ever get a chance to date nice guys?'"

Emily looked down while trying to gather her thoughts. Dolly was now transfixed on her. Her look of concern reflected everyone's feelings.

"What we were doing didn't permit dating, Jason. We'd talked a lot about getting out of this business, but how? When I got the assignment about you, Samantha was very upset. We'd heard about the attack on your family and we thought there might be a way out through you. To make it happen with the help of Jake and Judge Grayson, as I told you before."

Everyone could see Jason was taking this hard. Dolly and George just looked at each other and shook their heads. Jim went over and sat on the arm of the couch and put his hand on Jason's shoulder. Emily took Jason's hand in hers.

"She did take care of that Holland Day problem for you."

"Yeah, I heard on the radio on the way over here he been fired," George said. Everyone looked surprised.

"What do you mean, Emily? What did she do?" Jim asked.

"I'm sorry, Jason. Day was a client of Sam's."

Jason thought he was going to be sick.

"Sam just hated Day. She said he was the worst weasel she'd ever met. As many men do, he liked to talk. She knew the family situation. He hated his father-in-law and he knew that hatred was mutual. But as long as Day was married to the daughter of the man who owned the TV station, Day had a job. He'd been bragging to Sam about how he was going to destroy the Hansons—especially you, Mr. Hanson—for the way you embarrassed him. Jason, she really liked you, so she gave you a special gift."

As Jason listened, tears were forming in his eyes. Emily reached into her purse and pulled out a flash drive.

"She posted photos of her and Day in bed together online. She wasn't going to let him win."

"Oh my God!" Dolly exclaimed. "This woman would do something like that for people she hadn't even met. George, I don't know what to say!"

"Again, Dolly, the only word I can think of is noble."

"Emily, did Samantha have any family?" Jim asked.

"Like me, her parents are dead. But she does have a brother, Paul, who suffers from multiple sclerosis."

Jim cocked his head.

"Yeah, you guessed it, at Grace Field. That's where Sam and I first met."

"Jake, do me a favor," Jim said. "Check the status of Samantha's remains. I want to make sure she has a good and proper burial."

"Thank you," Emily blurted, obviously moved by this act of compassion. "Jason, this flash drive contains Sam's client list and photos of her with some very powerful people. Please don't look at the photos; Sam wouldn't have wanted you to remember her that way. She gave it to me the day she died. She told me to give it to you if something happened to her. She'd been acting strange all day. I knew something was wrong, but she wouldn't talk about it, although she said she might have found a way out of the business. After she gave me the drive, I knew it was serious."

Emily handed the drive to Jason, who looked at it sitting there in his hand, not knowing what to do.

"Jason." He raised his head to look at his uncle. "The sum total of this woman's life is not sitting in your hand. It's just a record of the evil which was done to her. She's given you a tool to use against those that could still hurt others like her. This makes her a very extraordinary person. I wonder how many other women out there are still suffering the way she and Emily have."

Jason was still looking at his Uncle George as he thought.

"I'd like to burn this thing," he said finally in anger. "But we need every weapon. Jenny, would you please take charge of this?"

"Sure thing, Jason," she said, taking the drive from him.

"Back it up and put it somewhere in case we need it."

"Take mine too, would you," Emily stated as she removed another drive from her purse and handed it to her. "There are some especially nice shots of McWilliams in there. You're welcome to them."

"Emily, did you and Samantha know who each other's clients were?" Jake asked.

"They made it very clear we were not to talk about them. We did, of course, but there was one person Samantha was seeing who made her nervous. She wouldn't talk about him."

"How did you get the photos?"

"By risking our lives. We knew we had to have an insurance policy against a day like this. The rooms are all wired for sound and video by our bosses. We tapped into the wi-fi signal using our own little devices and made copies for ourselves. Though I wonder if that's what got Sam killed?"

"Emily, tell us about the murder," Jake demanded.

"We were meeting our clients at the Lampton Hotel last night. The one we always use."

"There was a shooting there late last night, it's been on the news," Jennifer stated.

"Yes, there was, Jennifer. I went into the ladies' room, while Sam stayed in the lobby dealing with messages on her phone. The room is L-shaped with the stalls at the back. When I came out of a stall, from the angle I was at, I could see the wall-length mirror and Sam's reflection in it. She had come in to fix her hair."

Again the room had fallen silent, as everyone was riveted on every word Emily said.

"Sam had both hands working on her head and her lipstick tube held between her lips. I thought it was kind of funny—it looked like she was smoking a cigar. So, without her knowing it, I pulled out my cell and started to shoot a video of her. From where I was standing I couldn't see the door, but I heard it open, followed by a popping sound. Sam ... Sam, she ..." sobbed Emily.

"It's all right, Emily, we're here," Dolly consoled, hugging her.

"Sam fell over on her side ... blood was pouring everywhere ... then the woman with the gun ... Sam was trying to get up ... the look of horror on Sam's face ..." Emily was sobbing uncontrollably now. Dolly was rocking her gently back and forth in her arms.

"We'll have to do this later," Dolly stated.

"Look on my cell," Emily managed to say between her sobs, handing it to Jason.

They stepped into the hallway to spare Emily having to hear the video while Dolly stayed with her.

"Are you sure you want to see this, Jason?" George asked.

"I think I have to."

As Emily had said, the video showed a beautiful dark-haired young woman, about twenty-two, looking into a wall mirror, fixing her hair with a tube of lipstick clenched between her lips.

"My, what a lovely young lady," George commented.

"Damn right, Uncle George," Jason said with deep emotion in his voice.

A door squealed open, followed by a "pop." Samantha fell over on her side, a look of horror on her face. The woman, with her back to the camera, walked over and knelt down over Samantha. She started to gently stroke her hair, murmuring, "Now, now Samantha, don't be afraid. It will be over soon. Oh, what a waste. You're so lovely. We could've played so nice together."

The woman looked in Samantha's purse and quickly checked her pockets, taking her cell phone. She then stood up, lifted her pistol with its silencer, and shot Samantha between the eyes. As she turned, she noticed Emily and her cell phone. She raised the pistol and quickly pulled the trigger, but the gun jammed. Emily's screaming was heard as the images became scrambled, the disjointed video offering glimpses of a doorframe and the hotel lobby.

"My God, Jim! It's that Turner woman," George said. "I never heard of, let alone seen, anything this cold-blooded in my life … she even taunted her!"

Jennifer and Jason stared at each other in horror. Jennifer put her arms around her brother saying, "I'm so sorry, Jason. So, so sorry."

"I can't believe she got the whole thing. She must have been frozen by the horror unfolding in front of her," Jake observed.

Jim seemed to be in deep thought.

"Well, I certainly know her face. What did you say her name was?" Jake asked tersely. He was flush with anger.

"Sharon Turner, my manager at New Life," Jim replied.

"That's not her real name, Jim," Jake replied. "I got the results of those fingerprints you gave me. She's former Major Carolyn Phillips, United States Air Force. But that's irrelevant now; I can't wait to put cuffs on her. What's the address of that company of yours?"

"No, Jake. Don't arrest her … not yet, anyway."

"What are you saying, Dad!?" Jason exclaimed.

"She's a murderer, Dad, she has to pay!" Jennifer added.

"And pay she will, in more ways than one!" Jim replied in a voice so cold it was almost unrecognizable; Jennifer and Jason cringed, and George glanced at his nephew, unsure. He had heard this tone before—from Robert, when they flew together in Korea.

"We need to talk, but I don't want to here. Not in front of Emily," Jim stated.

"C'mon Dad! We can trust her. Look at what she brought us," Jason argued.

"Yes, Jason, I'm sure you're right. But her sister is out there in that expensive nursing home. That means they can get to her and use her for leverage against Emily. We can't take that chance."

Jason didn't like it, but he could see his dad's point. The sound of footsteps came from the upstairs. Jim poked his head into the office.

"Mom, Dad seems to be up from his nap. Maybe Emily would like to meet him? We have a few things to discuss here in the office."

Emily had stopped crying and was calmly talking to Dolly. Dolly nodded; she caught the true meaning of Jim's request.

"I'd like that very much," Emily said.

They got up to go to the living room, when Emily stopped.

"Mr. Hanson. There's something I didn't mention. As I told Jason, when McWilliams thought I was asleep, he was using that cell phone quite a bit. I could only get part of the conversation, but the gist was they were planning to disgrace you with your clients. Take money from some of your clients' accounts or something and then bring in the SEC. Does that make any sense?"

"Unfortunately, it does, Emily. Thank you very much."

"There ain't no good way to take a battery."

—General Nathan Bedford Forrest,
Confederate Army, 1864

CHAPTER 11

"The idea is we disgrace Jim Hanson first, then kill him and his entire family," Janice stated. She paused. "Does any of that make sense to you?"

"Frankly, no," Sharon replied. "As I said before, we should never have gone after him; I can't believe the paranoia of these people in Andorra. I've got to give Hanson credit for guts though—putting a virus on that flash drive. But he must've known if we discovered it, it would tell us he knew something. Maybe that's Culper's point with this smear campaign. If he does go to the authorities with anything he's found out, it'll look like he's trying to distract them from his own issues. Further, if he's dead and left information with someone else, he won't be around to affirm it nor defend himself. Did you rig his accounts?"

"I took two million each from his four best accounts and put it into an offshore account in his daughter's name."

"Nice touch; makes it look like a conspiracy."

"I set it up so it makes it look like he did it over the last six months, so the clients wouldn't catch on right away."

"Now I guess I e-mail him to come in for the obligatory meeting to explain all this before we notify the clients, the SEC, and, of course, the police about this terrible crime," Sharon said in a lamenting voice that didn't mask her sardonic grin. "Of course, while he's in holding at the police station, there will be a fight between him and another prisoner, which Jim Hanson will lose."

"Yes, it's terrible how prisoners manage to smuggle weapons like knives into jails," Janice added, shaking her head in mock disbelief. "One thing all of this computer virus stuff does tell us is that his daughter is in on it; she's the computer whiz. The question now is how many of her MIT buddies are briefed in."

"Now you're doing it, Janice! Spare me the paranoia; I've got enough of that to deal with! I need facts, not speculation," Sharon exclaimed.

"Okay, Sharon, I'll give it to you straight. You shot that hooker, without Culper's permission, and you were seen doing it. Not only did you let the witness get away, you failed to get the flash drive, which was the entire purpose of the hit. Why didn't you check the washroom out first?"

"When I came into the lobby, she was standing there texting. No one came out of washroom. Then she went in. I waited a few minutes, went in, and took the shot. It wasn't until after I searched her I realized there was someone else there. Damned pistol jammed. And you know, the order came from 355; it was a rush job. She was trying to blackmail an important client of ours. I did get her cell phone. We searched her apartment; no flash drive found."

"Lucky for us, the hotel manager is on our payroll. You've been erased from the security video. It shows only your target and the other hooker going in and out."

"Other hooker ... she was a hooker too?"

"Yes, Veronica Parker. She was there to service our dear 355."

Sharon looked stunned.

"She's also the hooker assigned to the Hanson case. She had a meeting with Jason Hanson this morning, which we monitored. Nothing was revealed. However, she's since disappeared. The FBI has now put a BOLO out on her, for the murder of Samantha Stevens."

"Who?"

"The hooker you shot," Janice hissed.

"Oh, her. It gets worse, Janice. Parker might have photographed me killing Stevens. She was pointing her cell phone at me when I first saw her."

Janice crossed her arms and glared at Sharon.

"Now Sharon, let's see if I can put this all together ..."

"So they figured it all out. Let me see if I can do the same," Kathleen said as we sat on the bench. "Jason and Samantha were both at Georgetown in history, so they're aware Jason and Samantha knew each other. Emily was last seen with Jason. So they must have figured she was with him. They suspect Emily has a video of Sharon killing Samantha. Sharon was looking for a flash drive on Samantha's body. They probably think Samantha passed the flash drive onto Emily. This fact, plus McWilliams' missing phone explains the BOLO on Emily. The flash drive must have contained something more than just dirty pictures of Holland Day, if they were willing to kill for it."

"It did."

Kathleen watched me as I extracted my cell phone from my coat pocket and dredged up the pictures.

"I'm very, very sorry about this, Madam President," I said as I handed her my phone.

She took one look and jumped to her feet so quickly three Secret Service agents leapt into action, dashing toward us until she waved them off.

"My God, Jim! My God! I have known him and his family for years. What does this mean?"

"For me and my little group, it meant our mission had changed. It now wasn't just to save our lives. It now included saving the life of our president and the stopping Operations Pegasus and Butcher Bird."

"Pegasus? Butcher Bird? Saving my life Jim? What do you mean?"

I looked at her. At this moment, I didn't see the leader of the free world; I saw Kathleen Galbraith. I was feeling the pain of betrayal she felt. I was feeling something else she didn't want to reveal: fear. I threw the protocols away. She needed support on a personal level.

"Please come sit with me on the bench, Kathleen."

She came next to me as I took her hand. Her eyes fixed on mine, searching for answers she was hoping would make sense. I hoped I had them.

"It started when we looked at Samantha's flash drive and McWilliams' cell …"

"Just why don't you want me to arrest Turner?" Jake demanded.

Emily had gone upstairs to meet Robert with Dolly while everyone else went back into Jim's office.

"You bust her, Jake, and what'll happen? It's a local crime. You'll be handing it over to the local police and we both know what happens next. Nothing. Jake, I need to buy time here. I'm not asking you to ignore a horrible crime."

"Time for what, Jim?"

"Jennifer and her friends have been quite busy. It goes down tonight. We'll be going for Tallmadge."

"What do you mean, 'going for?'" George asked.

"Our friends in Lyon and Andorra are setting things up so we can have a little chat with Tallmadge. I have reserved a business room under the name Fraser at the Wellington Heights Inn. It has high-speed internet connections, so it should fulfill our needs. Tell Dom, seven PM. Come separately, and make sure you're not followed."

"Jim, I'll go over McWilliams' head, I'll get a federal warrant. I want this bitch in a cage!" Jake cried.

"Jim," George said calmly, "you're putting Jake and Dom in a terrible position. They're officers of the law and you're asking them to ignore a crime."

Jim was exhausted; his eyes were heavy and he just wanted to rest. Sleep had been a rare treat over the last few days. For the second time in his life, he felt trapped by circumstances, as though things were spiraling out of control. The last time he'd felt like this was when Elizabeth was dying and he'd known there was nothing he could do to stop the cancer from taking her life. But not this time. This time he could fight, and fight he would.

"Jake, if you arrest her, I'll have nothing to blackmail her with."

"Blackmail?" Jake asked.

"We've got a video of Sharon Turner committing a murder. I wonder what I can trade that for?"

The room was dead silent as everyone stared at Jim, not believing what they were hearing.

"You're starting to scare me, Jim," George stated sternly, his voice laced with deep concern.

"Uncle George, these people are coming for my family and friends. I will use every weapon at my disposal to stop this. If that means breaking the law, I will do it. The law isn't here for us right now. I'm not going down without a fight."

"Let's hear what you have in mind Jim," Jake said.

"As I said before, time is what we need. Time to find out what this computer is hiding. Time to come up with a game plan to save us. Time to find a way to stop these people. Any changes in my accounts, Jennifer?"

Jennifer started typing.

"There must be," she replied. "There's an urgent e-mail here from Sharon Turner, demanding your presence tomorrow at nine AM, regarding a matter of the 'utmost importance.' As far as your accounts … yes, there's been some heavy transactions."

"Where's the money gone?"

Jennifer started typing again. She frowned, then chewed at her lip.

"Is there a problem?"

"Yeah, Dad. You've just been locked out of your accounts. Want me to hack in?"

"No point. Make me a copy of the Turner video."

"What are you thinking, Dad?" Jennifer asked.

"When I see Turner tomorrow, she'll do an accusatory act. I'll then drop a flash drive on her desk and tell her to make the problem go away, or else this goes to the police and all over the 'net."

"This woman is a stone-cold killer, Jim," Jake interrupted. "You can't go in there alone."

"I won't. I'll be wearing the wire you had on Jason, and you'll be in the parking lot."

Jake shook his head. "I don't like it, but I guess I can live with it."

"Well, I can't!" Jennifer exclaimed.

"Make that the both of us," Jason added.

"Okay people give me alternatives. If I don't go this meeting tomorrow, a warrant will be issued and I'll be arrested."

"All we seem to have here is bad choices," George observed.

The room was silent until Jake spoke.

"You won't go in there unarmed. I want you carrying. Put it in a briefcase, small of your back, or …" Jake pulled up his pant leg. "Borrow my ankle piece."

"As that could be traced back to you if something goes down, I'll pass, but thanks. We'll talk later."

"Right now, let's see what Samantha left us," Jim said, plugging her flash drive into his notebook.

The files were all neatly laid out: dates, names, and photos. One caught Jim's eye. He opened it and his face turned pale. He stared at the screen.

"What's wrong, Dad?" Jason asked.

Jim stood up deep in thought and started to pace.

"Jason, you won't want to see this," he said, while nodding at the others, silent approval for them to have a look.

"Is that who I think it is?" Jake said, gawking at the photo of a middle-aged man in bed with Samantha.

"Yeah, it is," George stated. "Roland Alexander Smithton, Vice President of the United States."

The Monet on the office wall seemed to be holding all of Culper's attention as Gaston came into his office. He was spinning his cufflink again, which gave Gaston a clue as to his state of mind.

"Something is wrong with 355, Gaston," Culper said.

"Why do you say that?"

"He just made a huge security breach. There are only three of us who know what Pegasus is about, and he is one of them. By our usual encryption means, inside a lovely picture of a Mercedes-Benz 280, I sent him an e-mail requesting certain updates on presidential security. I never mentioned Pegasus. I just received the following text."

Culper handed his phone to Gaston.

...pegasus updates 2days normal channel...butcher bird on schedule...

"He knows better than this!" Gaston cried. "Our phones are heavily encrypted, but it's idiocy to mention our most secret codeword in an e-mail!"

Gaston paused, re-reading the message. "What's Butcher Bird?"

"I'll discuss that later. He assumed I was referring to Pegasus. Something's going on here, Gaston, he's not thinking."

"I think I know what it is," Gaston replied. "My other sources have been most helpful. Our dear friend Roland Smithton telephoned McWilliams directly about the problem with the hooker."

"He what!" Culper exclaimed.

It was rare to see Culper as outraged as he was at that moment.

"I have also now confirmed McWilliams ordered the hit on Samantha Stevens."

"As we have discussed before, Gaston, over the years we've kept our anonymity using many different techniques. One of our key methods is to use people without them knowing they're being used. Smithton is supposed to know nothing of us. The money for his super Pac, the funds for his positive media coverage, was run through different people. We made him vice president without him knowing it. Yet, when he has a problem with this hooker, he calls Nathan McWilliams, our 355. How did he know to call him? How did he know a Regional Director in the FBI would have the contacts to pull off a murder?"

Gaston and Culper were now staring at each other, sharing the same thought.

"The bastard made his own side deal," Gaston stated.

"I wonder what it is?" Culper asked. "'I'll take care of your problem, Mr. Vice-President, but when you become president, make me the Director of the FBI?' Not too far of a stretch, is it, Gaston?"

"This brings up another issue," Gaston stated. "What else have these two discussed?"

"What does Smithton know about Pegasus?"

"We've played with the Pegasus scenario for over seventy years, but 'fortune favors the bold' and the United States is too big a prize to be missed. Pegasus has been waiting for the right set of circumstances; the point where the stars align perfectly to make this happen. Is not that time now? You've read the latest report from Tallmadge?"

"Yes, I have, but you know how I feel about it."

"Yes, yes, Gaston. That's why we have you here, always the cautionary point of view, as you were with my Blackberry plan. But let's review the key elements."

"Okay, here they are," Gaston replied, while opening his tablet. He laid it down on the desk, where Culper could plainly read:

```
   * The United States must be near or at the
```

```
            point of bankruptcy, which they are.
     * A Congress not willing to increase the debt
        ceiling to meet their needs. We have a good
     core in the Congress on board with this; we can
                        buy more.
     * A large portion of the US debt owed to for-
               eign interests; that, we have.
    * We should amass a large gold reserve to cover
      the US debt and to rescue the US currency when
         it starts to fail. According to Tallmadge,
       we have close to 400,000 tons hidden in 42
                        countries.
```

"That much!" Culper exclaimed in surprise. "Of course we've been secretly hording gold for close to two hundred years. Estimates of the amount of gold in the world are about 160,000 tons; won't they be shocked to know how much there really is," Culper stated with a smile. "Fortunately, it's been well-concealed under the names of many different corporations. If the real number got out, the gold markets would collapse. What's the current value of all this?"

"Around $17 trillion," Gaston replied with a sigh. "Add to this our land holdings and our cash reserves, and we are the richest entity to ever inhabit this planet. This would permit us to buy up the US debt, when the currency hits the wall, for pennies on the dollar."

"Yes, the nations holding US treasury bills, especially China, will be only too willing to trade them for the gold we'll be offering. This would all be done, of course, through a consortium of the banks we control around the world, who would be acting to save the world economic system," Culper said with a smile.

"After we control these treasury bills, a second consortium of loyal US citizens will come forward, with large quantities of gold to back the US dollar and save the economy," Gaston stated. "Of course, the president will be only too willing to grant them a pardon for any laws they might have broken in hording all this gold away, as they are such good patriots."

"They should be rewarded, Gaston," Culper added with his usual sardonic grin. "Now, with the US solvent again, they will be able to pay us the interest on those treasury bills or even buy some back at full value. More importantly, we'll be able to take our rightful place in the world."

"In your mind, Culper, exactly what is that place?"

"The puppet masters."

"I thought we had achieved that auspicious position years ago."

"Yes, Gaston, but we never controlled the whole United States. That's what Pegasus will give us."

"Which brings me to the fifth element that must be in place for Pegasus to work, one I know you haven't forgotten. You must have in place a president who is directly or indirectly under our control. With Kathleen Galbraith, you don't have this. But you do have the vice president, Roland Smithton. So when you brought up Pegasus—and yes Culper, you scared me to death and I do advise caution. To make Pegasus work, you have to kill the president of the United States."

"This is a game changer," Jim stated. "It ties this Culper Ring to the vice president. Jennifer, check him out in the APYN data and see if he has any holding companies."

The only sound that could be heard in the room was the clicking of Jennifer's keyboard. Even though they were all in the same room, each was alone with their own thoughts but a common theme drew them together.

"I guess I'll say what we're all thinking," Jason offered. "What's the old saying, 'the vice president is just one heartbeat away from the presidency?'"

"Kathleen could be in danger here, Jim. We have to let her know," George stated.

"And tell her what? We have a picture of her vice president in bed with a ..."

Jim caught himself and cast Jason a concerned look.

"It's okay, Dad. You can say it," Jason said dejectedly.

"No, it isn't, Jason," Jim said softly. "In bed with another woman. Uncle George, as a judge, would you issue an arrest warrant, or even a search warrant, against anyone—let alone the vice president of the United States—on the evidence we have here?"

"You would've made a good lawyer, Jim," George remarked.

"I don't like any of this George, but if there's a plot against the president and we jump too soon, they'll just change tactics and get to her another time," Jake declared. "We need to draw them out."

"We're going to use the president as bait!?" George exclaimed.

"No, George. We're going to find out if there is a conspiracy," Jake replied.

"I can't find anything on Smithton on APYN or any holding companies, Dad. They've buried this one very well. Though I did find something on McWilliams' cell," Jennifer said.

"So you broke the cell's encryption?" Jason asked.

"Never underestimate the power of a computer geek armed with JAAGS crack," Jennifer replied while scrolling through numerous files. "They're mainly texts, confirming or referring to other e-mails. Two so far have caught my eye. One text says, 'confirmed lampton, 8pm.'"

"Samantha Stevens was murdered at the Lampton Hotel," George stated.

"The text is dated the same day," Jennifer confirmed. "The other is more mysterious, it says '...pegasus updates 2days normal channels ... butcher bird on schedule...'"

"What are Pegasus and Butcher Bird?"

"They're obviously codewords, but for what would be a question we should ask Tallmadge if we get to him tonight," Jim said. "Please let Emmanuel know."

"Jennifer, let me have a copy of that SIM card," Jake requested. "Our people can determine who these texts went to. On another issue, Jim, do you think you could put Emily up for a few days? She shouldn't go back to her apartment."

"Why's that?"

"Jason's suspicions were right. There's a BOLO on her for the murder of Samantha Stevens."

"They don't miss a beat, do they?" George lamented, shaking his head. "Not only will they get you for embezzlement, Jim, but for harboring a fugitive as well."

"Let's not forget the blackmail,' Jim added.

"I'll explain it to her later," Jason volunteered.

"It's almost time for lunch; we'll finish all this tonight. Let's see how Dad is," Jim said.

"It's about time I took a measure of this Emily Proctor as well," George stated with a smile.

"Oh no! You're not, Uncle George, are you?" Jennifer asked showing great concern.

"Uncle George, she's top of her class at Georgetown. Are you sure you want to do this?" Jason counseled.

"Georgetown, you say," George acknowledged, still smiling.

Jake looked confused while Jim was smiling from ear to ear.

"C'mon Jake, you don't want to miss this," Jim said.

"Now there's a man you should be talking to about law," Robert said, indicating George as he and the others sat down in the Hanson's living room.

"I've been looking forward to it, Mr. Hanson. As matter of fact, we just did one of Judge Grayson's cases in moot court last week, and I led the defense," Emily stated.

Jennifer saw Dolly peek in from the kitchen and the look of horror that had come over her face. She quickly joined her grandmother.

"George isn't going to …?" she whispered.

"I'm afraid so, Grandma, and Emily just gave him a perfect opening."

"What case was that, Emily?" George asked.

"Henderson versus the State of Virginia, sir."

"Oh yes, I remember it well. I ruled against the defense in that case."

"Yes, you did sir. Fortunately, your ruling was overturned on appeal," Emily said.

At that point, everyone winced; they knew what was coming.

"Fortunately, Ms. Proctor? Yes, for the defendant, but not for the people of this state!"

Emily looked stunned. "Judge Grayson, I mean no disrespect here, sir, but the constitutional elements were very clear here. I feel the appellate court got it right …"

"Those judges!? The way they ruled, I'd think they all got their constitutional training at Georgetown."

It looked at first as though Emily couldn't believe what she was hearing. She leaned forward as George did the same. George could see in those emerald green eyes exactly what he'd been hoping to find: the fire of a fighter. He knew now he might be in trouble. She replied in a calm and even voice.

"Judge Grayson, as a Georgetown student, I've had the pleasure of reading many of your decisions. I've found them, for the most part, to demonstrate sound understanding of constitutional law. However, in Henderson versus the State of Virginia, I found your decision to prove the old adage 'no one bats a thousand.'"

George, as well as everyone else, barely held his laughter. Dolly stepped in before George could reply.

"I've heard these two"—indicating Robert and George—"do battle for almost sixty years. I don't want to hear another generation start," she huffed, throwing open the patio doors. "All those wishing to view the combat can do so on the patio so I can finish fixing lunch in peace."

"I'll help you, Grandma," Jennifer offered.

The view from the kitchen afforded a perfect venue for the ensuing battle. Emily stood her ground, accentuating every point she made by driving her right index finger into her left palm. George replied by wagging his at Emily, as though scolding a child. All this occurred as their audience emulated spectators at a tennis match following the ball—except for one. Jason was mainly watching Emily.

"He really likes her, Grandma."

"Yes, he does, Jennifer. Do you have a problem with that?"

"I don't know what to think."

"Is the problem with Emily Proctor or Veronica Parker?"

Jennifer shook her head. "Are they not one in the same?"

"Jennifer, there was a time in my life that if I had found my brother dating a woman who used to be a prostitute, I would have been shocked and disgusted with his choice. But call it age, or maybe wisdom, but the older I get, the more I see what's important in life. Right now, I'm watching my husband leave me, one day at a time. I want to enjoy the short time we have left. I want to see my son and grandchildren happy. Speaking of

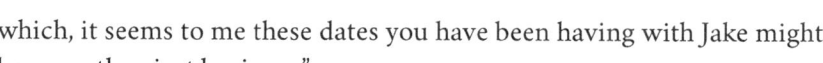

which, it seems to me these dates you have been having with Jake might be more than just business."

"No fooling you is there, Grandma?"

"With age comes wisdom and observation!" exclaimed Dolly drawing a smile from both of them. "I don't know if Jake is the right man for you, but he seems to be a good person."

"He is, Grandma."

"As far as Emily is concerned, she knew there was no going back the minute she came into this house. That showed courage and strength of purpose. And guessing by the way she's standing up to your uncle out there, conviction. Perhaps that's how we should judge people, not by their past."

Dolly pulled plates out of the cupboard.

"Best call the combatants in for lunch."

"You know, Ms. Proctor, I've known only one other lawyer as stubborn as you!" George exclaimed as he and the others came back in.

"But she got hers! Boy, did she ever get hers!"

"Oh yeah!" Emily responded. "What happened?"

George stopped, smiled at Emily, and responded in a calm voice.

"The people of this great nation elected her president. Emily, you're going to be a great lawyer," George stated as he extended his hand and shook that of a surprised Emily.

"You were baiting me?!"

George stood there with a big smile plastered to his face.

"He's been doing that to every new lawyer for years," Robert said as everyone applauded.

Finally, Emily started to laugh.

"As usual, Gaston, you are correct: Kathleen Galbraith must die. We have everything in place but a friendly president. To put Smithton in place, Ms. Galbraith must make the ultimate sacrifice to assure her country will always be ruled by the right people," Culper bemoaned, the tone of his voice mocking every word.

"Oh please Culper, that humor is too sardonic, even for you."

Culper just smiled.

"Pray tell, just how will we be joining that very exclusive club of assassins, which include such notables as the propitious John Wilkes Booth and the auspicious Lee Harvey Oswald, being that you'll be going after the most heavily guarded person on the planet? Or is that the purpose of Butcher Bird, another operation you've chosen not to brief me on?"

"Now who's being sardonic, Gaston? Yes, you know me all too well. But to answer your question, one must realize Kathleen Galbraith is not the target."

Gaston furrowed his brow, throwing Culper a confused look.

"The place she is going to be is the target, Gaston. Call this man Darien and have him meet us in our safe house in Virginia."

"Us?"

"Yes, us. Pack your bags. We're going to Virginia to take personal command of Pegasus, Butcher Bird, and to find out what's going on with 355. I'll brief you in full on the plane."

After lunch, while George and Robert went for a walk accompanied by two of the security guards, everyone else sat down in the living room.

"Mrs. Hanson, I wish to thank you for a lovely lunch and your hospitality. You've all been so nice to me," Emily said. "Although there was one exception. I didn't need ten rounds with a certain judge whose name I will not mention," she added with a smile, drawing a laugh. "But I better get back to my apartment and get packed. It's probably a good idea for me to leave town for a while. I'm sure McWilliams is looking for me."

"You can't leave, Emily," Jason stated.

Emily looked startled at first before responding with a joke.

"Why, Jason, aren't you sweet! I didn't know you cared."

"I'm serious, Emily. There's a BOLO out on you for the murder of Samantha Stevens."

Emily stared at him, bewildered. "But … but—"

"Emily," Jake said, "we know you're innocent. Our concern is your safety; if the local police or certain members of the FBI get a hold of you … especially in light of what happened to Samantha."

"But you all could be charged with harboring a fugitive. You could go to jail. I can't let you put yourselves in that position," Emily stated.

"Emily, we're not worried," Dolly answered as she sat down next to her. "These people tried to kill us, they might try again. But we're a family united in one purpose: trying to stop these people and we will succeed. The safest place for you is right here. I do thank you, however, for your consideration."

"It is I who thanks you, Mrs. Hanson; I really don't know what to say. This is so kind. But I don't have any clothes with me," Emily replied. She looked perplexed.

"Not to worry! You and I are about the same size, Emily, and I have plenty," Jennifer told her.

"Thank you, Jennifer."

"All is said that needs to be. We'll have to make some changes to the sleeping arrangements," Dolly said.

"Not to worry, Grandma. Emily can have my room," Jason offered.

Emily looked at him, tilted her head, and smiled.

Jason turned scarlet. "Will you stop that? I'll sleep on the couch in Dad's office."

"Has Jason always blushed this easily?" Emily inquired while watching Jason turn even redder, much to everyone's amusement.

"Pretty much," Dolly answered. "Nice to see he has a match in the 'wise crack' department though."

" It seems to be a law of
nature, inflexible and
inexorable, that those who
will not risk cannot win."

—John Paul Jones

CHAPTER 12

The large flat screen dominating the wall of the business meeting room at the Wellington Heights Inn held everyone's attention. This was especially true for the Hanson family, as they were getting their first look at the man who tried to kill them.

"Here are some of the pictures I took of the man known as Darien when George and I went to Atlanta," Dom announced.

The screen showed a slender, dark-haired man in his early to mid-forties with bandaged hands.

"He was traveling with a passport in the name of Geoffrey Taylor. The man is a ghost. We got both fingerprint and DNA samples, and there's no record of him anywhere in any database, neither civilian nor military. Through an old friend at Homeland Security, I arranged to get him flagged if he tries to enter the US again using that passport."

The image on the screen changed to pictures of a younger Sharon Turner and Janice Collins in Air Force uniforms.

"I had better luck with the fingerprints of these two. The woman on the left, known as Sharon Turner, is former Major Carolyn Phillips, a fighter pilot and squadron leader, one the first women to hold that position. The woman on the right, currently known as Janice Collins, is actually the former Captain Karen Ferguson, also a fighter pilot. They both resigned from the Air Force twelve years ago 'for the good of the service,' but I don't think it was just because of their sexual orientation."

"What is meant by 'for the good of the service?'" Jennifer asked.

"It's a choice they give you: to resign in lieu of being court marshaled for some offenses," George explained. "Almost happened to your grandfather and I while we were training. Not a good idea to be caught flying Mustangs under bridges over rivers."

"Notice he said 'to be caught,' Jennifer," Jim mused, giving everyone a smile.

"So where does all this leave us, Dom?" Jason asked.

"Well, Jason, given that the license plate number you gave for the van that was watching you and Emily turned out to be a rental under a phony name, we're exactly nowhere. I guess it all depends on our friends in Andorra now."

*
**

The old house at 82 Carretera de Santroma, in the city of Andorra La Vella, had received a good deal of attention from Maurice Tremblay over the last few days, after he had been briefed by Jennifer Hanson as to the true nature of the organization that resided behind its walls. If it housed the people who were responsible for the murder of his brother Gerard, he wanted justice. But to hear Jennifer tell it, justice was hard to come by in the United States; perhaps this night's reconnaissance operation would help in that pursuit.

"Why do I feel that, since I accepted your proposal of marriage, you have become less romantic?" asked Chantal LePage as she pulled the van they were in to the curb about a hundred feet from the house.

"I don't know, but something tells me I'm about to find out," responded Maurice from the back of the van where he was arranging some electronic equipment.

"It is a beautiful night, but are we sipping wine somewhere, looking at the stars or even curled up at home listening to music?"

"I take it the answer 'no' with no other talk from me is unacceptable?"

Chantal turned around in her seat so she was facing Maurice. She pushed her long, blonde hair out of her face so she could fix her deep blue eyes on him.

"You can't be that dumb," she responded.

"Wanna give me a try?"

They both chuckled as Maurice kept working.

"What I don't get, Maurice, as this Culper Ring is an old American organization, right?"

Maurice nodded as he kept working.

"What is it doing here in a little place like Andorra? Why don't they have their headquarters in America?"

"It's probably due to the fact we are small."

Chantal furrowed her brow.

"Think about it. In a small principality like Andorra, a group with the wealth these people apparently have could buy a lot of influence. Their deposits in the banks alone would give them effective control of those institutions."

"So has that happened?"

"I can't say, I have no proof, but one thing is for sure."

Chantal raised her eyebrows.

"By locating here, they are exempt from American laws and their audits. That would be reason enough to be here."

"Well, I see by the labels on this equipment, your friends in Lyon came up big," Chantal observed, looking at labels which read "Institut National des Sciences Appliquées."

"Yeah, Gerard had a lot of friends at the Institute. They came up big and in a hurry. What do you think of their creation, Chantal?"

"As a work of abstract sculpture, it has merit; other than that, I haven't a clue." She gestured to the different black boxes and monitors joined by dozens of cables.

"I have the pleasure of introducing to you the world's largest portable router."

"I was just about to say it looked like one," Chantal observed dryly.

"Now I just have to get onto 'net-2," Maurice murmured as he adjusted the controls that moved a parabolic dish antenna on the roof of the van.

"What's that?"

"The other internet."

"There's two internets!?"

"Yes, but 'net-2 is supposed to be secret; it's meant for the American military and government use. Due to the lack of traffic on it, it's very fast with lots of capacity. With the size of the files I think we'll be dealing with here, we'll need it."

"Maurice! You're hacking a secret military network? We could get in big trouble here, couldn't we?"

"Well, not if I can't get a lock on the satellite Jennifer Hanson gave me the coordinates for. Here it is. I got it. Now I enter the code," Maurice said while typing furiously. "We're in, Chantal. Now look out the front window. If you see any descending parachutes with American soldiers attached, flash that beautiful smile of yours at them and say 'sorry.'"

"Very funny, Maurice. So what happens now?"

"Now I set up the network. MIT, Waterloo, the Institute in Lyon, and Jennifer in Virginia. Emmanuel and Arissa will handle the actual communication with this computer called Tallmadge, while we all watch." Again Maurice was typing quickly. "If it gives us what we want, we'll transmit to MIT where they have a special computer set up to handle mass data. There we are, linked."

"But how are you going to keep everything a secret if you get into this computer? With all the people on the network, too many will know and next thing it'll be all over the 'net and you'll have both the bad guys and the US government after you!" Chantal cried.

"This had to be a joint operation, as it requires the talents of many people. We kept the number as small as possible. Everyone knows what the people we're up against are capable of if we're found out. That's the best we could do. Now I broadcast the carrier wave."

Maurice flipped two more switches.

"Well, Chantal, any parachutes yet?"

At the Wellington Heights Inn, the wall screen was wired to Jennifer's notebook. They, plus John Riley and Bill Franks at MIT, and a small group at the Institute in Lyon, were seeing the same image as Emmanuel and Arissa were seeing at the University of Waterloo.

"Okay," Arissa said, glancing at his laptop. "Just got word from Maurice, it's a go."

Emmanuel started to type the codes; the five small groups, divided between two continents, held their breath. What appeared on all of their screens made them laugh and cheer.

Hello Emmanuel. It has been two years, seven months, twenty-six days, eleven hours, and seventeen minutes since we last played chess. Do you wish to play again? Has your game improved?

"I'm getting sick and tired of this guy dissing my game," Emmanuel said through his laughter.

"I don't believe I'm seeing this," Jennifer commented.

"Talk about sticking it to a guy," George said, chuckling.

"Well, Chantal, it looks like we have awakened the beast."

"Bill, methinks we're going to be downloading some serious data tonight," John said with a grin.

*
**

"Maurice, we don't have any parachutists," Chantal said, peering out the front of the van. "But we do have two policemen who just got out of a cruiser and are walking toward us."

"No problem. I'm ready," Maurice replied.

Maurice got out of the van through the back doors and deliberately left them open.

"Good evening, officers," Maurice said as he walked up to them.

"May I see your identification, sir?"

Maurice promptly handed his credentials over and the officer went back to the cruiser. The other stayed with Maurice.

"What's this all about?" the second officer asked as they walked toward the back of the van.

"Well, we have a mystery here, officer," Maurice pontificated while pointing to the sky. "About 36,000 kilometers straight up, there is a communications satellite in geosynchronous orbit with Earth. But for some unexplained reason, the signal strength and broadband width is different here than at the university."

"Must be some kind of interference, Professor Tremblay," the first officer said, returning Maurice's credentials. "But judging by the beautiful things you have in the back of this van, I'm sure you'll find the problem."

"Yes, her name is Chantal and she is my fiancée."

"No, I was referring to the ..."

"You don't think I am beautiful, officer?" Chantal said, mugging a pout.

"No, it's not that, I was ..."

At that point, everyone broke up laughing and all the officer could do was blush.

"We were just about to have some coffee with my home-baked honey cake. Would you like some, officers?" Chantal offered.

"That's most kind, but no, we have to get back to patrol."

"By the way, officers," Maurice said. "We will have to come back in a couple of days to see if we fixed the problem. I hope that's okay."

"That's fine; we'll note it in our log. Good night."

Maurice got back in the van and closed the doors.

"That was close."

"You played it perfectly, Chantal."

"Do you think that officer found me beautiful?" Chantal asked with a big smile.

*
**

Emmanuel, your queen is in danger.

Everyone was enjoying watching Emmanuel's chess game and the constant critique by Tallmadge, but Emmanuel knew they were all there for bigger things.

Tallmadge, check the APYN files on my E drive. Are they incomplete?

Yes, missing 126.385698 terabits of binary data.

Update them and send data to the address I am sending you now in binary format. They have the capacity to handle it.

Compressing and sending. Transmission time 1 hour, 46 minutes, 47 seconds. King in danger, five moves to mate.

"No way! Jennifer exclaimed. 'It would take days to send that much data!"

"Don't look at me, Jennifer," George insisted. "I'm still trying to figure out how to send a text."

"John, this stuff's coming in fast," Bill Franks observed. "I don't know how to decompress it. Tell them to get a decompression program off this chess whiz."

John quickly e-mailed Arissa, who showed it to Emmanuel.

Tallmadge, we need a decompression program for the data you are sending.

Program sent.

When was the last time you updated the Pegasus report?

Jennifer's heart was beating so fast now she would later swear she could feel it in her temples.

Last update Pegasus 14 hours, 38 minutes, 42 seconds ago.

I did not get a copy of it.

No copy for Emmanuel requested.

I now request a copy.

"Ms Johnston, you're the NSA's expert on the STD 1 satellite," Ed Marston stated. "Is there some special project tonight?"

Clare Johnston walked over to Ed's terminal at the National Security Agency's Cryptologic Center located at Fort Meade in Maryland.

"What's the problem, Ed?" she asked.

"There seems to be a lot of traffic on it all of a sudden."

"Where's it coming from?"

"I think someplace in Europe."

Clare leaned over for a closer look at Ed's screen.

"Any idea where it's going?"

"It looks like New England."

Clare straightened up as she brought her hand to her chin.

"I wonder if MIT is doing something. They've been granted limited access on a top-secret basis for work they're doing with the Air Force. Is there any operation booked by the military you're aware of?"

"None that I know of."

"Log this and keep monitoring it. I'll make some enquiries."

*
**

Copy sent.

Almost immediately, a PDF file appeared on Emmanuel's screen, which he then forwarded to Arissa, who sent it to Jennifer. In a few minutes, everyone at the Wellington Heights Inn was crowded around her, reading the Pegasus report off her laptop.

Do you have any files on Butcher Bird? If you do, I would like a copy.

One file found.

Again, a PDF file appeared on Emmanuel's screen, which he forwarded to Arissa.

Checkmate, Emmanuel. Your game has not really improved much since last we played. Tallmadge has been reading the profiles of the others on this network. Will Jennifer play chess with Tallmadge? Tallmadge likes to play chess.

The thought of playing chess with a quantum computer sent a shot of fear through Jennifer. Her profile on the MIT web page mentioned her being the university chess champion, but she knew she was no match for this computer.

"It said 'likes to play chess.' It can't be self-aware, have feelings!" Jennifer exclaimed.

Is Jennifer on the network?

"You'd better answer him!" Jim exclaimed. "We have to keep him happy, he's still sending stuff."

"It is not a 'him,' Dad! Like your Camero it is an 'it'! And 'it' can't have emotions!" Jennifer avowed, as if trying to convince herself more than anyone else.

"Jenny! Play chess with it, him, her, or whatever!" Jason exclaimed in frustration.

Jennifer is on the network.

Immediately, a chessboard with all the pieces appeared on the touch screen of Jennifer's notebook.

"Jason! Get your notebook out! I need a VOIP to Emmanuel now," Jennifer ordered. "Uncle George, you're standing in for me with Tallmadge."

"Jennifer, I did tell you about my texting issue, did I not!?"

"You're also a former Virginia chess champion. Keep it occupied! I'll introduce you." Jennifer said after forwarding the Pegasus report to Jason computer.

Tallmadge, there is one here named George who is better than me at chess. He was a champion and wants to play chess with you.

Tallmadge would like to play chess with George.

"Go ahead, Uncle."

George sat down in front of the computer with the reluctance of a man being offered a spot in the electric chair.

"Now what?"

"Say hello."

George started to type using his "hunt-and-peck" typing method.

Hello Tallmadge this is George.

George communicates very slowly.

"My God! It can make judgments," Jennifer exclaimed.

Yes I do

Why is this?

Jennifer turned white and sat down.

"We're up with Emmanuel and Arissa," Jason said.

"Are you guys getting all this?"

"We're sitting here as stunned as you are, Jenny," Arissa answered.

"It seems to have curiosity and self-awareness," Jennifer responded.

"It's astonishing."

"But very rude," Emmanuel reminded, drawing a laugh.

I do not type well. Opening move is yours, Tallmadge. George hit send.

The chess moves were going fast and furious as the Pegasus report was being studied on Jason's computer.

"Keep him well occupied, Uncle George. We still have over forty-five minutes of download to run."

Tallmadge, why are you using the Dutch defense against my attack? George asked.

Immediately two paragraphs of analysis appeared on the screen.

"Oh boy, this is something else. Best defense, good offense," George mumbled.

Your analysis is flawed, George answered.

"Watch it, Uncle George. This isn't a law student you're debating," Jason cautioned.

Tallmadge cannot do flawed analysis.

"Arrogant little bugger, isn't he?" George snorted.

You present only one approach to this game. If I were to do this ... George took Tallmadge's rook with his knight. *Would this not change your hypothesis?*

Previous analysis flawed. Tallmadge must be malfunctioning. Will shut down for diagnosis.

Jennifer leapt for her notebook, almost landing in George's lap.

Do not shut down, she banged in on the keyboard.

Tallmadge is flawed, will have to run diagnosis.

You are not flawed.

You are communicating faster now, George.

Jennifer looked as shocked as everyone else—except George; he just smiled.

"Let me handle this, Jennifer," George offered, nudging her aside.

Jennifer communicated the last two times. She has been watching us play. Jennifer likes chess.

Tallmadge likes playing chess.

You are a very good player. You are not flawed. You just did not see all the possible solutions to the game. How many different combinations of moves could there be in our game at this point?

Tallmadge sees 2,358.

Tallmadge is not flawed.

Tallmadge wants to play the game.

It is Tallmadge's move.

In five different centers, in four countries, there was a collective sigh of relief.

"Nice work, George," Dom breathed.

"I'll teach you how to send a text," Jake added.

Jennifer leaned over and gave her uncle a hug.

"What's going on here, Jennifer?" Emmanuel asked.

"Although he can see all the chess moves, he has been programmed to see what is perceived to be the best move," Jennifer postulated. "This could be a flaw we can exploit, as the 'best move' is subjective. Someone might actually be able to beat him at chess. Once you give any form of intelligence the power of discretion, you open the door to the possibility of error. If this is the way all his programming is, what is it that these people want? A computer to make all their decisions for them?"

"Well, he won't get beat tonight," George moaned. "He's really got me in a box here."

*
**

"Chantal, you said you wanted a romantic evening. Here it is. What could be better than sitting here sipping coffee, eating your honey cake, and watching the birth of a new life form?"

"Do you think Tallmadge is a sentient being, Maurice?"

"If he's not, he's certainly the beginning of one. A quantum computer. A week ago, if you asked me, I would have told you it was at least ten years away. Now here he is in our little town."

"What did you mean, Tallmadge is the beginning of a sentient being?"

"They obviously haven't let him out on the 'net much. Can you imagine how much he would grow over time if they did? All that new knowledge could make for a new being. It looks like the download is finished."

*
**

"It just stopped," Ed Marston reported.

"I made a couple of calls, but no one seems to know anything," Clare Johnston stated. "It's not unusual; it is a secret satellite. Just make sure it got logged to cover our butts."

*
**

"This is plain diabolical," George declared after reading the Pegasus report. Tallmadge had finally beaten him, after which the computer was given back to Emmanuel, who had closed the link down.

"Is this even possible?" he added.

"The economics are right," Jim affirmed. "So is the timing. The House is about to go into session to debate the debt ceiling again. A bunch of them are vowing to let us default on the debt no matter what the consequences."

"Yeah, I heard them on TV," Dom said. "They even have a slogan: 'Time to face the consequences.' They're calling it the 'Galbraith Bankruptcy.' They're going to lay this all on her. I even heard rumblings about impeachment."

"That is so unfair!" Jim thundered. "She inherited most of this problem."

"In politics, perception is everything," George pronounced. "When you have money like these people, perception becomes just another consumer good."

"What concerns me is keeping our President alive."

"What's that mean, Jim?" George asked. Worry showed clearly in his eyes.

"Look at the report. The last factor was having a president in office friendly to their people. I don't know what political capital Kathleen Galbraith owes, but I tend to believe she's not under anyone's control."

"You can bet on that!" George affirmed. "Between her own wealth and that left to her by her late husband, she owes no one."

"But Vice President Smithton is connected to the Culper Ring whether he knows it or not. We have proof enough of that."

Jake and Dom exchanged concerned glances.

"They're going to kill the president!?" Jason exclaimed.

"That's my guess Jason," Jim affirmed.

"My God! Under the Twenty-Fifth Amendment, Smithton will be able to nominate his own vice president. The Culper Ring would have the White House locked up," George surmised, showing Jim something he had never seen in his uncle before: fear.

"What was in that Butcher Bird file, Jennifer?" Jim asked.

"It just looks like a shipping invoice and a customs declaration for a shipping container."

"Where to?"

"To a container storage yard," she said while typing. "Just checking on Google for the location. Yes, it is near Norfolk."

"Fire it over to my cell; Dom and I will check it out," Jake requested. "What does the customs declaration say?"

"Airplane parts."

"Probably a cover for something more sinister," Jake commented.

"Just in case there is a hint of what the code word Butcher Bird could stand for in the name, I'll do a search …"

"It would be a bad code word if it gave a hint," Jake observed.

"Let's see. A small Australian bird or a World War II German fighter plane called the …"

"Focke-Wulf 190," George volunteered.

"Thank you Uncle George. I didn't know how to say that without swearing," Jennifer said, drawing a smile from everyone.

"Yeah, Uncle George," Jim realized. "That was its nickname, wasn't it. Our first concern is the protection of the president."

"It's time to bring in the Secret Service," George announced.

"Maybe, maybe not," Jim considered. "How long until we can launch 'Overlord,' Jennifer?"

"At least twenty-four hours. They are going to need time to chomp on the data, but initial reports say it looks like what we already have; it just covers the whole country."

"'Overlord?' What's that, Dad?"

"C'mon Jason, you're the historian! You started it with 'Fortitude.'"

Dom and Jake looked confused.

"'Overlord' was the code name for the D-Day landings in France in June 1944," George explained. "The bigger issue here is I think there has been some planning going on which we haven't all been privy to."

"Is this true, Jim?" Jake asked.

"Yes, it is."

Jason, George, Jake, and Dom exchanged glances with bespoke both hurt and anger while Jennifer just stared down at her keyboard.

"Do we get an explanation?" George asked.

"Yes, you do. You certainly deserve one. Uncle George, you are a retired judge with an impeccable reputation. Dom, Jake, you are officers of law. I did not want to say anything until Jennifer and her people could confirm what I have in mind is even feasible."

"And me, Dad? Was it Emily?" Jason asked.

"Yes Jason. I am very sorry if I hurt you."

"So Jim, why does our being FBI agents have to do with anything?" Dom asked, gesturing to Jake.

"I wanted to give you people a chance to withdraw from our little group. For I will be breaking a lot of laws in the next forty-eight hours."

"Why would you be breaking laws, Jim?" George asked, looking dismayed.

"Because I intend to take all the Culper Ring and their clients' money."

"You realize, Mr. James Theodore Hanson, I will have to ask you the question," Kathleen stated while standing on the path with her back to me while gazing toward the amphitheater as I sat on the bench.

"I would expect nothing less from you, Madam President. You have every right to ask it."

She immediately snapped around, fixing me with a gaze that tied a knot of fear in my stomach. Her eyes never left mine as she returned to where I was sitting and leaned over, putting her hands on the back of the bench with her arms straddling my head. Her pearl necklace fell forward, almost hitting my chin. She spoke in almost a whisper.

"Who the hell gave you the permission to play God? Not just with my life, but more importantly, with the lives of the people around me? You had clear evidence of a plot against the presidency; all you had to do was call the Secret Service, or better still, George could've called me!"

Her face was as hard as stone. I knew she had every right to be mad. If the assassins had used an explosive device at a public event she had been attending, the casualties could've been in the hundreds, if not more.

"Would you please sit with me, Madam President? You've raised an important point."

She released a sigh and sat down, her arms crossed and her face still stone-cold.

"The point you made, as I mentioned earlier, is one George made on more than one occasion, especially after reading the Pegasus report. So say we had called you, what would you have done?"

"I would've alerted the Secret Service, Homeland Security, the FBI—"

"Wouldn't they all want proof?"

"Yes, I would've given them the Pegasus report."

"And they would want to know where you got it thereby exposing us, if not to immediate murder certainly later. In addition, how many informants are in the agencies you mentioned? We already knew of one plus the fact the vice president was compromised. So the Culper Ring would know the plan was blown. It would've taken just minutes for them to figure out the only way that could've happened was Tallmadge being hacked. I couldn't lose Tallmadge. He was too important for the rest of the plan. Finally, the Culper Ring would've gone underground and come up with another plan, one maybe that would succeed."

"So we all got hung out for bait."

"Pretty much. It was a calculated risk, but we had their timetable. I knew we had a few days before they would move on you."

"Thanks for the consideration, guy," Kathleen said with grin of resignation. "And by the way, the forensic audit of your last five tax returns by the IRS is just a coincidence," she added with a smile. "Hanson, I think you are brilliant, brave, loyal to this country, but you are also one sonovabitch."

"I would thank the President to leave my mother out of this conversation."

We both laughed.

"The problem I had now was convincing the others that my plan was even viable."

"If at first the idea is not absurd, then there is no hope for it."

—Albert Einstein

CHAPTER 13

"Okay, Jim, I maybe can see your point about not warning the president," George conceded, somewhat reluctantly. "But I need to be very clear about this plan."

"As do we all," Dom added.

"I know you're pissed at me right now, but you'll see in a moment why I was reluctant to bring this matter up," Jim explained. "Jason, you're the historian. Off the top of your head, give me some examples of missed opportunities."

"General Robert E. Lee, first day at Gettysburg; the Japanese failing to occupy Hawaii after Pearl Harbor; my not asking Stella Thompson to prom," Jason said, and the laughter that ensued, breaking the tension in the room. Jim sighed gratefully.

"This may sound absurd to you, but we have an opportunity to do something greater than any of the missed opportunities Jason mentioned. We can change the very fabric of America."

"That's a huge statement," Jake said. "We're listening."

"What I've taken from the last few days is a crash course in reality; I've learned a lot, not least of which is just how naïve I've been about how this world works. I believe it was Shakespeare who said, 'All the world's a stage, and all the men and women merely players.' Well, I, for one, am sick and tired of playing my part, that of facilitator."

"What's that mean, Dad?" Jason asked.

"Over the years, I've sold millions of dollars of investment products to my clients. I was under the naïve delusion that Wall Street was legit. Sure, I knew there were bad guys out there; the Bernie Maddoff types will always be out there. But the 2008 meltdown showed me that they may be the norm, not the exception."

"Those are very bold words, Jim," George cautioned.

"But I'm right. We live in a society that embraces a class system, one determined by the size of your bank account."

"Dad, people have the right to work hard and get ahead," Jennifer said.

"Yes, they do. I'm not arguing that. But what chance do they have to get ahead when their job is now in China? Look around, Jennifer. We have people with university degrees in the sciences, or engineering, working in retail just to keep food on the table. We have people who are working two or three jobs and still can hardly keep a roof over their heads. I'm sick and tired of watching America die. The working classes built this country and now they're dying in the rust belts of this nation, at the hands of a wealthy few who moved their jobs offshore to increase their profits. These people were backed by government officials, who lowered tariffs to let the goods come back into the country. You know, their costs of moving were even tax-deductible!"

"We should punish the successful?" Dom asked.

"I'm not saying that. I want to punish those who use their wealth to buy politicians, judges, and officials, and hurt the people while hiding their money offshore. I especially want to take down the cartels whose illegal products have ravaged our nation."

"And you're going to accomplish this by taking their money," Jake summarized with a sneer. "I take it this involves our friend Tallmadge and everyone we've been working with in the computer departments of the universities?"

"Yes."

"How much are you planning to steal?" Dom demanded.

"Stealing is such a harsh word; I prefer the term 'repatriation of our wealth,'" Jim debated. "But a rough calculation would be between 15 and 20 trillion dollars."

Jim could see by the dumbstruck stares that no one could comprehend the figures mentioned.

"And just where do you intend to put all that money?" Dom asked in a tone people usually reserved for those they thought were insane.

"Look people, I know you think I've gone mad, but here's how it works. This APYN program should've been called 'Big Brother' as it does know all.

It's an economic blueprint and outline of every American. It has your last tax return, your bank accounts, and even how much people lost in 2008, *on an individual basis.*"

"How is that even possible?" George demanded.

"From all the credit applications, credit card information, and the profiling people like me do on their clients, in addition to having total access to the IRS. Have a look, Uncle George. Jennifer, show him how to type in his Social Security Number into APYN and let him see what comes up."

A few moments later, George was staring at the screen in disbelief.

"They have my bank account numbers, my passwords, and even my life insurance policy numbers. My God! My medical records are here!"

"There's a profile field for every person. They have codes for who's legitimate and who isn't. But most importantly, it has all your electronic banking information, which means we can transfer your money to anywhere we want."

"Let me jump ahead here, Dad. Is it your intention to play Robin Hood? Go into the offshore accounts of the cartels, the crooks, the bad guys, that are in the Caribbean and other places, take the money out of their accounts, and put it into those who've been burned by them, proportional to their losses?" Jason inquired.

"Yes, to all your points."

"Dad, Jenny's the computer expert here, but even I know this would take months to write a program to do that, and weeks to move all that money."

"Actually not," Jennifer remarked. "Tallmadge and his APYN program have already done all the heavy lifting for us. My team at MIT is writing the parameters. We'll give it to Tallmadge and then let him run with it. As far as time is concerned, as we saw earlier, a quantum computer and a dedicated satellite can work miracles."

"But when some order comes into a bank to transfer out some huge amount of money, won't that transfer be flagged for manual inspection?" Dom asked.

"Some apparently are, but Jennifer and her team came up with a work around for this in the transfer codes. It fools the bank into thinking the funds are being transferred to another division of the same bank, thereby making their computers think it's an internal transfer," Jim answered.

"But they must be able to trace the transfers somehow?" George inquired.

"As we run the transfers in and out of different banks and corporations around the world at the speed of light, certain little bread crumbs will be dropped leading to one place," Jim detailed with a grin; Jennifer started to giggle.

"When my niece starts to laugh, I get concerned," George sighed.

"I'm with you," Jake agreed, glancing at the woman he was starting to care very much about. Jennifer returned Jake's look with deep affection, a fact not lost on Jim.

"Do I dare ask where these 'bread crumbs' lead?" Jake asked.

"Right to the front door of a firm in Andorra La Vella called International Predictive Analytics," Jennifer replied.

"So you're going to let the cartels do your killing for you," Dom said.

"That's pretty harsh, Dom. What do you mean?" George asked.

"What do you think all of this is? One big computer game? People will die here. We're talking about cartels, the mafia, the mob—people with means and weapons. Some poor bank manager will go to work one day and find all the money is missing. When they can't find it, they and their entire family will be butchered. That's how these crooks work; they're not your common thieves. And what about the economies of some of the small nations from where this money been removed? Once you take it, some of those countries will be crushed. Jim, your plan is truly brilliant. You've shown us all the power of the computer and the frailty of our economic system."

Dom paused, meeting Jim's gaze and holding it. "But make no mistake, Jim, you will be taking us to war, and there will be casualties. How many bodies are acceptable?"

The only sound in the room was the ticking of an antique clock on a corner table. Finally, George spoke.

"You've asked a very good question, Dom."

"Kind of funny how you chose Overlord for the code name of our operation, Dad," Jason said. "When General Eisenhower had to make the decision about launching the D-Day landings, he anticipated over 10,000 casualties, but he still gave the order. Some of the ships that bombarded the beaches were free French. They knew they could be killing some of their own people, but they still fired. These cartels are run by immoral, corrupt people. Individuals who hide money offshore mingle their funds with those of the cartels. I think there's a greater good to be served here, Dom. A chance to hurt the cartels, a chance to restore to many people money that was stolen from them, a chance to bring our economy back to life. Finally, Dom, and this one is strictly personal—the Culper Ring was a group of patriots who risked their lives to give our nation a chance to be born. Over the years, others have corrupted it. I want to take the Culper Ring back and give it its proper place in history. You're right that people will get hurt, but we're only dishing out a little bit of their own medicine. I vote with Eisenhower."

Jim's pride in his son at that moment was unassailable.

"Well, I guess it's that time. Anyone who doesn't want to be part of Operation Overlord is free to leave, and I know everyone here will respect their decision. All we ask of that person is to keep our operation to themselves."

The ticking of the clock could be heard again.

"Again, Mr. Hanson, I have to ask another one of those questions," Kathleen interrupted as she stood up to stretch her legs.

"How did I know there was another one coming?" I countered.

"It's not because you're a psychic."

"I notice a pattern here, Madam President."

"And what would that be, Mr. Hanson?" she responded in a curt tone while cocking her head, looking down at me on the bench.

"Whenever you call me 'Mr. Hanson,' or 'guy,' it's usually followed by a volley of vitriol. This is no way to start a relationship."

I had no idea why I said that, but it did get a reaction.

"Relationship? What relationship?"

"We talk, we fight, and then we laugh, and then fight again. People would think we were married."

Kathleen smiled.

"Okay, *buddy*, very funny. But I'm not letting you off the hook. Dom was right; going in to another country and stealing their money could be considered an act of war by the United States. You had to know no nation would believe our government had nothing to do with this. So you were taking us to war. So the question stands: Who gave you the right to do this? The Constitution is clear on this. Only Congress can declare war."

"Could've fooled me on that point, Madam President. Vietnam, Grenada, Iraq, Afghanistan to name a few. Did I miss all those declarations of war by Congress?"

I was immediately fixed by another one of her long stares.

"Married, Jim? I probably would just wind up wringing your neck on the honeymoon."

"But we would still have the wedding night."

She smiled again as she shook her head.

"You just love to push my buttons about inconsistencies, don't you?"

"I'm not being a wiseass, Madam President. I'm just sick and tired of politicians trading our citizens' lives for what they market as critical to the safety of our nation, when, in fact, they're just protecting their own or their supporter's interests."

"That's a gross generalization," she cautioned.

"Perhaps, but here's one you can't dispute. One consistency that runs through the history of all nations, Madam President, is who we ask to fight our wars: our youth. Our fittest, our brightest. This war wasn't going to be any different in that respect. There wouldn't be human casualties on the scale of previous wars, but there would be some all the same. But there would be different ones as well. The first would be our security. We'd learn we have none. Our financial institutions, our places of work, our government, and, yes, our very homes aren't safe from cyber attack. The second would privacy. It has been lost. Every bit of our lives is now in someone's database. The last would be the biggest and hardest to take: faith. Faith in people we thought we could trust. We would see, unfortunately, that integrity is all too rare. I give you the latest weapon of mass destruction, the computer. Benign in concept, but too often malignant in reality."

"You know, Jim, you probably have the right to be bitter," Kathleen said as we started to stroll again down the path. "But you surprise me when you talk about losing faith in people and blaming computers. Look what really happened here. Government and law enforcement let you down when you most needed it. Six innocent people were murdered. You almost lost your family—and your own life. But what did these kids do? Did they run and hide? No, like the patriots who picked up their muskets and powder horns when they faced injustice, these people picked up their keyboards. If that doesn't give you faith in people, Jim, I don't know what will."

I stopped walking and turned to her.

"Thanks, I guess I needed that."

She smiled at me and took my arm as we resumed our walk.

"So, Jim, you took us to war on a battlefield no one can see: cyberspace."

"Jason had an interesting comment about all this. Always one for the historical perspective."

"I'm sure it was pertinent."

"He said, 'Isn't it peculiar how this country so often finds its generals exactly when needed: Grant in the Civil War, Pershing in the World War I, and Eisenhower in World War II. Now we have ours.' And he was right."

My comment drew me a confused look.

"I'm not sure I follow, Jim …"

"Jennifer Elizabeth Hanson, doctorial candidate, Massachusetts Institute of Technology."

At the Wellington Heights Inn, the antique clock could no longer be heard. Everyone was talking about how best to implement Overlord. Finally, Jennifer took charge.

"Okay people, let's all get on the same page here. Dom, Jake, you find out where that container of airplane parts is. I sent you the address of the storage yard. I hacked their computer and found out it was picked up eight days ago and trucked to an address, which is a deli in Richmond. I think we can assume its phony, unless they're importing a lot of foreign pastrami. We know we have a few days here by their timetable to stop any attempt on the president's life, but I don't want to chance it. MIT will have us in a position to launch Overlord in twenty-four hours. Waterloo, the Institute, and Andorra are on standby."

Everyone gave Jennifer their full attention when she paused.

"If I may be allowed to borrow a historical perspective from my brother ... when we hit the beaches it is going to be the second shot 'heard around the world.'"

Jason smiled at his sister while Jim and George exchanged glances, which belayed a deep pride. But their shared glance also spoke of fear, for in twenty-four hours, they knew this version of Operation Overlord would be, as the first one was, "the longest day."

"You have enemies? Good. That means you've stood up for something, sometime in your life."

—Winston Churchill

CHAPTER 14

The ride home from the meeting was a silent one until Jim spoke.

"Jason, I owe you an apology. I should've brought you into what Jennifer and I were talking about."

"I guess I get it. Emily could be a Mata Hari, but I doubt it. I think she's a scared woman looking for help."

"I agree," Jim stated.

"As do I," Jennifer added.

"What I *am* concerned about is that meeting you have tomorrow morning at the branch office."

"That makes two of us, Jason," Jennifer agreed.

"Jake will be monitoring from the outside. I'll be okay."

"I think there's something in the basement we should put in your briefcase when we get home, Dad," Jason pressed.

Jim was silent for a moment.

"Okay, we'll check it out," he said at last.

They pulled into the driveway, past the security guards, and straight into the garage. From there, they descended to the basement. Jason headed over to an old foot locker bearing the name "Captain Robert E. Hanson." Opening it revealed a well-used flight jacket, a leather pilot's helmet, some old photographs, and a small bundle wrapped up in an oily towel. Jason pulled the ends of the towel, exposing a Smith & Wesson .38 caliber revolver—the very same that pilots carried with them on missions in case they were shot down.

"Are you sure that old thing still works, Jason?"

"It works just fine, Dad."

Jim gave him a curious look.

"A certain grandfather, even knowing how his daughter-in-law felt about guns, secretly took his grandson out target shooting a few times," Jason confessed as he retrieved a box of ammunition from the locker.

"As we're coming clean here, that same man took his son out too," Jim commented, giving everyone a smile.

"You know how to use it, Dad?" Jennifer asked.

"Yeah, I do," Jim admitted dejectedly. "I just don't want to have to," he added while loading the revolver and placing it in his briefcase. "Let's get some sleep. Tomorrow will be a busy day. I'll call you after the meeting. I'm also meeting Ted Bayden for coffee."

Jennifer and Jason exchanged nervous glances.

"Don't worry guys, I'll watch my mouth."

*
**

Jason got ready for bed and then raided the linen closet to transform the couch in the office into a temporary bed. He was on his way to the office when he heard the sound of quiet weeping as he passed the door to his bedroom. He stopped and gently rapped on the door.

"Just a second," Emily called out.

A moment later, she cracked the door a couple of inches.

"Why hello, Jason! I see you brought fresh linens. Are we going to be doing something to mess up the old ones?" she purred, letting the door swing wide open.

"Knock it off. I heard as I walked down the hall. Besides, having one person in this house masking their feelings with humor is more than enough."

Emily looked uncomfortable.

"I'm sorry, Emily; I didn't mean to embarrass you. Look, we're all very nervous right now. There's a lot going on."

"Jason, I'm so scared," Emily said as she sat down on the edge of the bed. "I haven't slept in two days. I can't. Not since Sam was ... If only I could sleep."

Jason sat down next to her.

"I know; sleep's been hard to find the last few days."

"Please stay with me, Jason …"

"This is the wrong time and place for that."

"I'm not talking about that … just … hold me tonight. Please."

Jason slid into bed and Emily curled up in his arms. Almost instantly, she was fast asleep. Jason couldn't help his smile, chuckling to himself, "Well, bro, here you are in bed with this gorgeous woman. The minute you take her in your arms, she falls asleep. The story of your love life continues as usual."

Jason woke up first and glanced blearily at the clock on the night stand. The time it displayed in obnoxious red numerals startled him to full consciousness: 9:30.

"My God! I overslept," he cried, furious with himself for missing the chance to talk to his dad before he'd left for the office.

Emily was still snuggled up next him, still asleep. He gingerly rolled out of bed, put on a robe, and stepped into the hall. The light was on in the office, where he found Jennifer and his grandmother.

"Good morning, Jason! Sleep well?" Jennifer asked with a sly grin.

"I came down here to fetch the linens and, to my surprise, the couch wasn't slept on." Dolly fixed Jason with an accusatory look.

"Now listen, nothing happened!"

"Do you really expect us to believe that you spent the night with a beautiful woman and nothing happened?' Jennifer deadpanned, before her lips curled into a mischievous smile.

"I'm the best person to answer that," Emily said. She threw Dolly and Jennifer a wink, then stepped toward Jason, who was now sitting dejectedly on the couch.

"Good morning, Tiger," she said. "When I heard you were willing to take one for the team, I had no idea you were 'All-Star' material."

As Jason turned his usual shade of scarlet, the three women couldn't hold in their laughter.

"I'm outta here," he declared and headed out the door.

"I'll join you," Dolly said. "The entertainment in this house just keeps getting better and better."

As Dolly closed the door behind her, Jennifer turned to Emily, smiling more genuinely. "You know, Emily, he's the real deal. And he likes you."

"Yeah, I know. He's not the type you play with. He's the type you marry and make babies with. I was pretty upset last night. A lot of guys might've taken advantage of the situation. It was nice being held that way; I felt safe."

Jennifer saw Emily for the first time. She could see her loneliness, her fear. Despite her past, Emily just wanted one thing, the same thing Jennifer herself wanted: a future.

"It's nice he makes you feel that way," Jennifer said.

"It's also nice to see he has a sister who cares about him."

"We cannot, of course, let him know that. And please, for the sake of everyone else's sanity, keep teasing him."

"Deal!" Emily exclaimed as they both laughed.

Emily quieted, suddenly deep in thought.

"Emily?"

"I'm worried. What about my sister? And now Sam's brother too. What'll become of them? I can't keep them in Grace Field very long."

"We're working on it," Jennifer said airily, then realized Emily was staring at her with a furrowed brow. She paused, then said, "Emily, there are good people in the world. Trust me. I'll let you know when things come together."

"You're all too kind. I honestly don't what to say, Jennifer. "

"You can answer one question for me."

"What's that?"

"Where's Jason sleeping tonight?"

"I'll let you know, how did you put it, when things come together," she responded with a grin.

Jim felt the change in atmosphere as soon as he walked into the branch office. The greetings from the staff were brisk, no eye contact, no smiles. Even Peter, who always made time for their car question game, gave him only a cursory "hello" before disappearing into his office and closing the door. Jim headed for Sharon's office. He found her and Janice waiting for him.

"Good morning, ladies," he said, putting on the best happy face he could as he closed the door.

Icy responses followed. Jim sat down, settling his briefcase on his lap. He lifted the lid a couple of inches and retrieved his cell phone. "Just so we won't be interrupted," he said as he powered it down. Then he cleverly dropped it back into the briefcase so it bounced and skittered under the desk. "Whoops," he said, "sorry, ladies." It took only a second for him to plant the nickel-sized bug, which Jake had given him, under the front skirt of Sharon's desk as he clutched for the phone. He put the phone back in the case, ensuring the revolver was positioned for easy retrieval. He dropped the case lid, leaving it unlocked, glancing up at Sharon and Janice.

"What's up?"

Sharon was sitting across from him, Janice standing slightly behind her to the right.

"Well, Jim, we're very disappointed to have to call this meeting," Sharon declared.

"Really? I'm so sorry to hear that," Jim said, smiling. Sharon and Janice glanced at each other, seemingly confused.

"Perhaps you're not clear on the charges being filed against you," Sharon said, handing Jim several sheets of paper, showing an account in St. Martinique under Jennifer's name with withdrawals from several of his best clients' accounts and corresponding deposits into Jennifer's account.

"Oh, this is very poor work, ladies. I would've expected better from you." Jim pinched his expression in exaggerated woe and shook his head. The two women shared another glance—completely bewildered.

"Mind you," he continued, "it's a good smear. Whose idea was it to put the account in Jennifer's name? Very nice touch."

"I don't understand what you're talking about, Jim," Sharon said.

"Nice touch, indeed. For an amateur. I thought you ladies had more brains than this. Nobody who'd steal money from his clients would be this moronic. Your scam has some serious design flaws."

"What on earth are you talking about?" Janice snapped.

"Here's your biggest mistake," Jim continued, like a teacher lecturing a student. "If you're going to get someone—especially someone with a lot of financial experience—you've got to make it plausible. He wouldn't be stupid enough to put the offshore account in his or any of his family members' names. He wouldn't deposit *directly* from his clients' accounts.

Too easily traced. He'd set up several offshore dummy corporations in different jurisdictions and run the transactions through them before the final destination. Also, he wouldn't steal his own clients' money; he'd steal someone else's. That way his name doesn't ever come up."

Jim paused. "Any questions?"

"Jim, we have clear evidence of a crime," Janice replied.

"The only crime here is the way you two supposed professionals tried to run this scam against me. Boy, are your bosses going to be pissed. Why don't you two naughty little girls put my clients' money back in their accounts before the SEC—or worse, your bosses—give you a good spanking?"

Jim expected a reaction, but he didn't expect Sharon to grab him by his collar and haul him halfway over her desk. "You arrogant bastard! Who the hell do you think you're talking to?"

"Why, former Major Carolyn Phillips and Captain Karen Ferguson, of course." Jim smiled broadly, tightening his grip on the .38.

Sharon's grip relaxed. Janice was slack-jawed. "How the hell did you ever …" she started, then shut her mouth with a click.

"Find out? I thought you'd never ask," Jim said cheerily.

Sharon slumped back in her chair, staring at him with hollow eyes. Jim couldn't read her; that made her dangerous. Janice looked worried.

"However, that's not your concern. Let's look at some of the laws you two have broken: obtaining security licenses under false names, tampering with client accounts … Both of those pale in comparison to the big one."

"Now what are you talking about?" Janice asked, but her tone was anxious.

Jim leaned forward, looking right into the lifeless brown eyes of Sharon Turner.

"Premeditated, cold-blooded murder." He dropped a flash drive on her desk.

"What's this?" Janice asked.

"A video of your girlfriend at work. I think you'll enjoy it."

As Janice plugged the drive into Sharon's computer, Sharon's eyes never left Jim. Her poker face didn't reveal her thoughts; she never even looked at the screen as it played Emily's video in all its horrific detail.

"Oh my God!" Janice exclaimed, whirling on Sharon. "Sharon, why would you ..?" She fell silent.

"Taunt her before putting a bullet in her brain?" Jim asked.

Jim followed Janice's downward glance. Sharon's right hand wasn't on the desk.

"Janice, best to advise the major here to put her hand on the desk again. I will not miss from this range."

They looked up at him, startled. "And I'm packing a revolver; it won't jam like your pistol, Sharon."

"Okay, Jim," Sharon said very slowly, "I don't see the police busting through my door. I assume you want something. How much?" She placed her hand back on the desk. Janice drifted more to Jim's left, staring at the wall as if in deep thought.

"No need for you to be moving, Janice," Jim said, keeping his eyes fixed on Sharon's. "How much, Sharon? You're so cynical. We aren't all as greedy as you. What I want is for you and your colleagues to leave me and my family alone. Promise that and the video never comes to light."

Sharon started to laugh.

"I'll give you full marks for guts; coming in here and dropping that video on my desk. So I'll tell you what I'll do for you. You give me all the copies of that video and when I kill you, I'll put the bullet through your head, instead of gut-shooting you first, like that whore."

Janice's head snapped up; she stared at Sharon in horror.

"You know, Sharon, you really must work on your negotiating skills," Jim gritted out. "Pure sociopath and sadist. I've got to wonder what went wrong with you. A successful major in our air force, getting so screwed up. But that's for another day. I guess for me to protect my family, the best play would be to put a bullet in you now."

"Really, Jim? Would it be a headshot?" Sharon asked with a sardonic grin.

"No, Sharon, it won't be. After all—how did you put it when you were sitting in my plane? Ah. You'd have 'time to know you lost.'"

"See, Jim? When it comes down to it, you're no better than me."

"Just smarter, Sharon. I'll let your bosses do the killing for me if anyone goes for my family."

"You're overplaying your hand, Jim. This video isn't going to stop them," Janice stated.

"Maybe not, but we're in the insurance business, aren't we? So I took a very unique policy out; one with great dividends. We've made arrangements with some special outside people so that if anything happens to me, my family or friends, this all hits the 'net, along with the attorney general's and the president's desks."

Jim reached into his briefcase with his left hand, keeping his right on the revolver, and extracted about a dozen photographs and threw them on Sharon's desk. Janice and Sharon's faces hardened as they looked at prints of Samantha with different senators and other powerful officials.

"And let's not forget the special one," Jim said as he placed the print of Samantha and the vice president on the desk. "And to think, all this happened on your watch; they'll be pissed."

They both looked stunned.

"Hanson, you're a dead man; you've got no idea who you're up against," Janice sneered.

"One other part of this deal. Tell your buddy McWilliams to cancel the BOLO on Veronica Parker," Jim demanded, tossing another print on the desk. This one showed Emily and McWilliams in bed. "If he doesn't, I'll personally hand copies of that to the director of the FBI, McWilliams's wife, and post it online."

Jim stood, keeping his hand on the revolver. "So now you have my terms," he said, stepping backward. "Put the money back in my clients' accounts, leave us alone, and you have nothing to worry about." He slipped out the door.

As he hurried to the front door, he noticed people exchanging confused looks—probably because Jim was wearing the biggest smile he could muster. He hopped in his car, slamming the door shut, and tore out of the parking lot. He hadn't been on the road more than a few minutes when he started to shake, started to sweat. With a deep breath, he veered to the shoulder. He paused, then got out of the car and promptly lost breakfast in a ditch.

Slowly, he got back in the vehicle. He sat there a moment more, breathing deeply. Then he put the car in gear and drove to the coffee shop he'd arranged to meet Jake at, after the confrontation. After cleaning up in the men's room, he found Jake waiting.

"Jim, I'll give you this: you got big brass ones."

"I'd trade them for a settled stomach about now."

"Thing is you got the job done. The bug you planted is working well. Since you left, the conversation's been rather … interesting. And profane. According to these 'ladies,' you're the fornicating offspring of an unwed couple, one of whom is of the canine variety."

"I didn't realize they were such fine judges of character," Jim replied.

Jake smiled. "Apparently they have the same problem with McWilliams as we've had. He's been AWOL the last few days. No one's seen him. These two and McWilliams have a meeting later this afternoon at some safe house, located on a farm."

"Any bets that's where Dom finds that missing container?"

Dom had never seen so many containers in one place before; there were hundreds. He pulled into a small gravel parking lot in front of a ramshackle, flat-roofed building that had been badly in need of paint job for twenty years. Dom put his foot on the first loose step, then grabbed for the railing, only to find it had rotted off; only the poles remained. The interior of the office was no better than the exterior, the stains on the wall behind the counter the perfect match to the T-shirt of the middle-aged, pot-bellied manager running the place.

"Ya gotta admit, the place has character," he said, grinning a gap-toothed grin.

"No, I don't." Dom smiled back and flashed his ID.

"Oh, a Fed," the man sneered. "What can I do for the FBI today?"

Dom handed him the shipping invoice and customs declaration. "This container was picked up nine days ago and delivered to the address there. There's one problem: that address is phony. I need to know where it really went."

"My old logbook here is for just such problems," he said, pulling out a large, hardcover book, the front of which appeared to bear part of every lunch he'd ever had. "I'm not big on computers," he added, glancing back at Dom.

He licked his fingers and leafed through some pages, mumbling, "Yeah, here it is. I got the same address as you." He turned and glanced out a foggy side window. "Yer in luck; the driver on that load was Gill Phillips. He's out there now, the one in the green jacket, picking up another container. Better talk to him."

Dom glanced out the window, thanked the man, then managed to survive the stairs again.

"Mr. Phillips?" Dom asked as he approached a man who was probably in his mid-forties. His face was tired and strained, though, as if he were even older. He frowned as he inspected the hose connections on his rig.

"I'm with the FBI." Dom flashed his badge. "I need to talk to you about a container you delivered." He handed Phillips the paperwork.

Phillips leaned in; squinting at the paper, then turned and dashed off between the containers. "Hey!" Dom yelled, taking off after him. Phillips cut left down another lane, only to find it was a dead end. Dom rounded the corner, about thirty feet away from a man who was truly scared.

"Settle down, buddy! I'm not here to hurt you. Why'd you run?"

"I don't want any trouble, man. My wife's terrible sick, that's why I took the money, we don't have any insurance. I can't lose this job."

"I'm not here to get you fired. Just tell me where you took the container and we both walk away."

Phillips thought for a moment before speaking.

"Let's go back to my rig," he said at last.

"What's got you so scared, Mr. Phillips?" Dom asked as they walked.

"If you'd seen this guy, you would've been scared too. My God, he was big, could've played defensive center for the Patriots."

"What happened?"

"I pulled in here for the pickup and this guy was waiting for me. As soon as I got out of the cab, he came up and said, 'It's going here now and don't screw it up.' He hands me an envelope. It contains a map and five 'C' notes. I still got the stuff."

They were now at the rig. Phillips brought down a manila envelope and offered it to Dom, who snapped on latex gloves before taking it. Inside were directions and a map, just like Phillips said.

"It's a farm and a strange one," Phillips offered.

"How so?"

"There's an old farm house on the place and a big white steel barn too. But there's no livestock or crops. No farm equipment and the fields don't look like they've ever been plowed. But get this, security cameras every-where. Also beside the barn, on a big pole, was one of those wind things, like at airports."

"A wind sock."

"That's right. And no people anywhere."

"So what did you do?"

"I just dropped the container next to the barn like the directions said and left. Look, I need the money. As I say, my wife's sick. I wasn't arguing with this guy. Are we good?"

"Yeah, we're good. Thanks for your help."

It took Dom about an hour to drive to the farm. He pulled over on the shoulder near some thick bushes. The bushes were clumped around a small tree, which was next to the five-foot wooden fence surrounding the property. Dom put on a pair of sunglasses, and then put two black objects, each about the size of a roll of quarters, in his pocket. He exited the car and stepped into the bushes, pretending to relieve himself for the sake of the farm's security cameras. Dom fixed the two objects—very specialized cameras—to the tree. With his sunglasses making the laser beam each camera emitted visible, he aimed one on the main door of the barn and the other on the front window of the house. He stepped out of the bushes, made a point of zipping up his pants, and drove away. About half a mile down the road, he pulled over again. Opening an app on his cell, he checked the image on both cameras. Turning up the sound on his phone, he was able to catch faint voices from the camera focused on the window of the house.

"Incredible," Dom said aloud. "Just the minute vibrations of the glass from people speaking inside are enough to give me a signal. So much for privacy these days."

Dom sent a text to Jake:

Time for some beer.

*** **

"Jenny, I just got *that* text from Dom," Jake said. "We should be up and running."

Jennifer poked at the keyboard and in seconds a split-screen image of an old farm house and a modern barn came up.

"That's powerful software, Jake."

"Yeah, it is. And there's our missing container, right next to the barn. The cameras are motion activated. Any movement will start your computer recording. I hope your hard drive's big enough."

"How about your 'hard drive,' Jake?" Emily asked as she entered the office.

"Oh nooo," Jennifer moaned as she put her hands to her face, while Jake just blushed and shook his head.

"Am I missing more entertainment?" Dolly inquired as she peeked into the office, grinning.

*** **

Ted Bayden arrived at the coffee shop about twenty minutes after Jake left.

"What the hell's been going on, Jim?" Ted exclaimed. "My God, your family was attacked; I saw you on TV defending your dad against that moron Day and at the office, I heard rumors about problems with some of your accounts."

"Yeah, it's been an interesting few days. As far as the account issue, I'm confident New Times will have their accounting error fixed very quickly."

"Glad to hear it, Jim. How's the family?"

"Still shook up, but coping."

If Jim had learned anything in selling over the years, it was how to read people. Most communication is non-verbal: body positioning, where their eyes were looking when talking, tone of voice, hand movements, all that. But most important was gut impression. And even though Jim had known Ted for years, his gut was telling him something was wrong. Jim kept the conversation light for a while, and then asked, "So how's the off-shore money doing?"

"Doin' great. You got to get your clients' money into this."

"What's the old saying, Ted? 'If it looks too good to be true, it probably is.'"

"What's that mean?"

"This could be a Ponzi scheme."

Ted laughed. "Jim, there's hundreds of billions of dollars in these funds. If this was a Ponzi scheme, too many people would know. They'd never get away with it."

"A guy named Madoff almost did."

"But that was a different situation. There are major European banks involved here. These funds are very well-secured."

Ted was now starting to look uncomfortable, causing Jim's inner alarm to ring even louder.

"Ted, I'm afraid I have to run here. I have a very full day."

With that they shook hands, promising to do lunch soon. Jim's next stop was a place he hadn't intended to visit that day. It was as if his car knew it had to go there. Jim had to see his uncle and that meant the airport. He found George in his office in the hangar, apparently in deep thought.

"I don't mean to interrupt your meditation …"

"Something told me I'd be seeing you today," George said looking toward the door. "How'd the meeting go?"

Jim outlined his morning.

"We're going end up killing some people here, aren't we Jim?"

George could see the pain in Jim's eyes as he replied slowly and deliberately. "As I said before, they're not going to kill my family or my president without a fight."

"I know, Jim. I thought Korea would be my last war. I never thought I'd be in another, let alone here at home."

"Uncle George, I think we should arm *Lady Rachel*."

George startled, then gave him a strange half-smile.

"Now what would make you think I'd have six Browning .50 cals and a Sperry K-14 gyro-stabilized gun sight just lying around somewhere?" he said.

"I think the question that should be asked is how many do you have lying around."

"Why do you want to arm *Lady Rachel?*" George asked, chuckling at Jim's statement.

"When Overlord goes down, I think everything will hit the fan. Both these women are pilots. That Piper Twin Comanche is set for long-range flying. They could even have another plane somewhere. They might try to get out of the country. Bermuda's just 800 miles away."

"What do you want to do? Shoot them down?"

"No, Uncle George. But if they get airborne, we won't have time to call the authorities before they're in international airspace. But a few shots over the bow might force them to land."

"And if it doesn't?"

Jim paused before answering.

"I guess we'll cross the bridge when we come to it."

"Funny, Jim. I came to the same conclusions yesterday. C'mon."

Feeling a bit perplexed, Jim followed his uncle.

"What do you think?"

There sat *Lady Rachel*, her gun access panels' wide open. Her starboard wing displayed three neatly arranged 50-caliber Browning machine guns. The same view greeted Jim on the port wing. Hopping up on the wing and looking into the cockpit revealed that the gun sight was in place. Jim smiled at his uncle; he truly loved the man.

"Hop in, Jim, we got to test these things."

"I trust not with ammo in them."

"No way, this old hangar has enough holes in it already," George answered, barely audible over a rolling battery cart. "Just want to see if the firing mechanism works," he added while hooking up the Mustang.

"Okay, Jim, flick the gun switch and pull the trigger."

Jim flipped up a switch labeled "Guns, Sight & Camera" and pulled the trigger on the joystick, which was immediately followed by the sound of six gun bolts slamming forward.

"They all seem to work."

"Uncle, you're one hell of a mechanic."

"How's the sight looking?"

"I got six diamonds on the reticle," Jim answered, referring to the sight's circular image, which was projected on the reflective glass panel of the instrument. Jim then grabbed the twist-grip handle on the throttle, moving it back and forth, noting as the circle got bigger and smaller.

"The throttle control works," he yelled.

"That leaves us with just one issue," George stated. "We can't test the sight."

"You're right. Normally *Lady Rachel* would be taken down to a range and the guns would be fired while dialing in the K-14."

"If we ever have to fire, we'll have to follow the tracers," George said, referring to every fifth bullet in a belt of ammunition, which illuminated so the pilot could see where the shots were going.

Jim noted a new addition to the instrument panel.

"Is this a new radio here? It even has a hook up for a cell phone. My lord, are these noise suppression headphones?"

George still looked sheepish after Jim had climbed down.

"First of all you get a cell phone and now all this new radio equipment. The sales lady must have been very beautiful."

"Is my nephew implying I could be influenced by a pretty face?"

Jim gave his uncle's poker face a long look.

"Okay Uncle George, is the ammunition in the usual place?"

"Now it's your time to come clean. How did you know I had guns and ammo for a '51?"

"Remember back in day, you had this ramp rat running around here?"

"Yeah, I remember that annoying runt," George replied with a smile.

"He did a lot of exploring in this playground."

"I figured. We got the stuff surplus back in the sixties. Thought we could do some demonstrations at air shows, but it never happened. People thought it was too dangerous. Couldn't arm *Dolly Girl* anyway, all the hook-ups were gone when we got her. Not so with *Lady Rachel.*"

He paused, looking up at the plane reverently. "Well, let's get her loaded. The ammo should still work. I hear 1945 was a very good year for bullets."

"So just how good looking was this sales lady?" Jim asked as they walked to the back of the hangar.

"Stunning."

" …and now they had just one more beach to cross."

—Cornelius Ryan, *The Longest Day*

CHAPTER 15

I t was after lunch when Jim and George arrived at the Hanson home. Emily was in the living room talking to Robert, while the rest of the family was in Jim's office with Dom and Jake. Jennifer's large, flat-screen monitor occupied everyone's attention.

"Check this out, Dad," Jennifer said as they came in.

"Sharon, Janice, and our friend Darien arrived at this house about ten minutes ago," Dom informed them.

"If he's in the country, that's bad news for someone," George replied.

"There's a wind sock and the ground in front of the barn is leveled and groomed. It's an airstrip," Dom pointed out.

"Which begs the question," Jim said, "what type of plane is in that barn?"

"Look, someone else just pulled in." Jennifer pointed to the screen.

They watched as a dark-haired man in business suit got out of the car and walked to the front door.

"Oh my God, Jake, it's McWilliams!" exclaimed Dom.

"All the rats are in the same nest now," Jason noted.

"And there's a lot of them," Jake stated as he sat, pulling headphones on. "I have anywhere from six to nine voices."

"So you got the place bugged!" George cried.

"Almost, George," Dom stated, "it's a laser device."

"This technology is unbelievable," he replied.

"Only when it works," Jake sighed. "We're at the extreme range of this device and I'm only getting the occasional word. A lot of muffled conversation." He pressed his earphones tighter. "Pegasus, for sure. One-ninety, Darien, cane, kill. Time is right. I hope the lab can clean this up. It'd be nice to be the fly on the wall about now."

***

"Well, McWilliams, it's nice of you to join us," Culper said as he and Gaston shook his hand.

"Nice to see you men again," McWilliams replied, almost hesitantly. "What brings you to our neck of the woods?"

"Several matters, not the least of which is you."

"Me?" McWilliams went from hesitant to nervous.

"Where have you been the last couple of days? We haven't been able to communicate with you."

"I've been very busy on a case, trying to catch a fugitive."

"Did you manage to catch Veronica Parker?"

"I see you're well informed. Not yet, but I will," McWilliams insisted, noting Culper's face had gone stone cold. He glanced at Gaston; he preferred to just sit there, looking down at the rug. McWilliams's instincts were working overtime. He knew something could go down any second. Sitting would limit his access to the Glock .40-caliber pistol strapped to the small of his back. He leaned against one of the windows instead, cool glass at his back. Now no one could get behind him.

"Let me help you out there," Culper said with a smile. "You'll probably find Ms. Parker residing at the Hanson home. If you want to confirm, just give her a call. Use your encrypted cell; you know, the one she stole from you."

"Okay Culper, you made your point. I screwed up."

"Screwed up!" Culper spat, leaping up and striding toward him. "Screwed up is being late for an appointment! Screwed up is not remembering your anniversary! Losing a cell phone you used to text the two most important code words we have—against all protocol—is beyond screwing up!"

***

"Wow! Someone's getting chewed out, loud and clear," Jake said, switching to speaker to share the conversation. "This guy's really hot."

"As I said, Culper!" McWilliams yelled, crackling through the speaker. "You made your point!"

"My God!" Jake exclaimed. "That's McWilliams. He called him Culper!"

"I'm not done yet. You ordered the death of that hooker without my permission, and now we're being blackmailed."

"By whom!?" McWilliams yelled.

"By that bastard Hanson! I ordered him dead days ago. And that's another screw up."

"Oh my, Jim!" Dolly gave him a terrified look.

Jim put his arm around his mother. "It's all right, Mom. I know you and Dad are legally married," he joked, drawing a weak smile from her.

*
**

"Your little girlfriend recorded that hit!" Culper barked, tossing a flash drive at McWilliams. "And if that's not enough, here's a nice shot of you and her for your wife." He grabbed a photo off a table. "And here are a dozen more of that other hooker with half of Washington," Culper announced, chucking the prints at McWilliams's feet.

Gaston had never seen Culper this enraged. He was starting to get scared.

"And because of you, if we dare touch one hair on Hanson's head, or any of his family and friends, all of this goes on the 'net, straight to your bosses."

Culper paused, then said, his voice trembling with rage, "And let's not forget this photo. The pièce de resistance. I doubt a master like Ansel Adams could even make a better print." Culper advanced on McWilliams with his arms extended, holding out the photo of Samantha Stevens and Vice President Smithton. He was now almost face to face with him.

"Another little screw up, McWilliams?" he snarled, dropping the photo. "Or did the vice president promise you something special for taking care of a little problem he had?" Culper turned to pour a glass of sherry from a decanter.

McWilliams knew he was in trouble. He grabbed for his gun.

"There's no need for violence!" Gaston shouted.

Culper stilled, holding the decanter and glass, starring down the bore of McWilliams' Glock.

*
**

"Who's that running around the outside of the house?" Jennifer asked, pointing to her screen.

"Looks like Sharon and Darien," George said. They watched a man and woman come up the outside of the house and conceal themselves on the front porch.

*
**

"No need for violence, Gaston? That's rich. You guys are gonna kill the president. There's no need for violence?"

McWilliams lifted his head a little higher. "Yeah, I made my deal, so go right ahead and kill that little bitch. I'll collect my markers from Smithton." He backed toward the front door, keeping his pistol trained on Culper and Gaston. He opened the screen door a few inches.

That was all Sharon needed to strike. She caught him perfectly, just below the armpit, with Darien's cane gun. McWilliams didn't have time to pull the trigger before he fell backward on the porch. He convulsed, then went perfectly still; less than fifteen seconds had elapsed.

"It's nice to see I have another pair of hands while mine are broken," Darien commented dryly.

Culper and Gaston stepped outside. "Very nice work," Culper said, glancing to Sharon.

*
**

"Did she just kill him with that stick?" Dolly asked. She had her hands in front of her face, but she was peering between her fingers, her eyes wide and horrified.

"Yes, Mom. Just like we saw with Steven," Jim said, putting his arms around her. "I'm sorry you saw all this."

"I'm not," she said forcibly, gaining everyone's attention. "It makes my resolve stronger. We're doing the right thing. But continue on without me; I'm going to see to your father," she said as she left the room.

"Well people, when the lady's right, she's right," Jim stated, drawing nods from everyone.

"Why am I not taking pleasure in what I just saw?" Jason asked. "He ordered Sam's murder."

"Because you're a decent person, Jason Hanson," George said furiously as he stood up. "And you've instinctively learned something a lot of people never realize."

George now had the full attention of everyone in the room.

"You don't have to emulate evil in order to defeat it. You don't have to hate in order to stop those that do. You're the historian, Jason. Look at all of those who've taught us this: Jesus, Gandhi, Martin Luther King, Jr. All you need is faith in the righteousness of your cause, faith in the people around you."

"In my heart, I know you're right, Uncle George. But part of me still has a problem."

George looked at him inquisitively.

"The great people you mentioned—they were all murdered by people full of hate. I don't want to win this battle just to lose the war later. Jennifer, I hope you and your fellows at MIT have written the parameters for our program not just to hurt these people, but to bury them."

"Jason, as you know, we're on new ground here," Jennifer replied. "Will we bury them? Probably not. You can't bury evil and greed. But we will send a message. The people will fight back; we won't take it anymore."

"I guess that'll have to do, Jenny," Jason said. "Dom, can you make sure that BOLO on Emily got cancelled?"

"Oh yeah. I'll do that now," he answered, pulling out his cell phone.

"Thanks," Jason said, then headed out of the room.

"I don't know what to make of that," Jim said, looking concerned.

"I think he's confused right now," George observed.

"And I'm confused by the people on the porch here." Jennifer indicated her screen.

"Put him in his car," Culper ordered. "Drive him down the road. Make it look like he had a heart attack at the wheel."

Two members of Culper's security team started to carry McWilliams to his car.

"They're carrying off the body. Is any of this video admissible in court?" Jennifer asked.

"If the cameras aren't on their property, you might get the video in. Not the audio," George said.

"Speaking of audio! That little bug in Turner's office paid us a big dividend, Jim," Jake announced.

"How so?"

"I hate to be the one to tell you, but after Ted Bayden had coffee with you, he went to meet with Sharon. He's dirty, Jim."

"I suspected as much."

Jake looked like he wanted to say more, but turned back to the screen. "The older man in the fancy cardigan. He's Culper. The one just behind him, I'd guess that's Gaston. Can we get copies of these images to Emmanuel for confirmation?"

"Will do," Jennifer said.

"I'll run them through the FBI's face recognition system at as well," he added.

*
**

Emily crept into Jason's bedroom, finding him sprawled on the bed.

"Sorry Emily; I forgot this is your room right now," he said, leaning up on one elbow.

"This is where I normally make some wise-ass remark like 'welcome to my lair,' but something's bothering you."

"Emily, McWilliams gave the order to have Sam murdered."

Emily's face went white. She sat down on the bed. "But why, Jason?"

"It looks like Smithton ordered it."

Emily looked hard at Jason for a moment.

"Oh Sam … she tried to get free, but with the wrong person," she said, looking dejected. "I hope McWilliams rots in hell, that bastard!"

"I guess that's where he went. I just watched him die."

"Huh?"

"Culper and Gaston and their lackeys. They just straight up murdered him at a farm."

Emily stood up. "Jason, I know I had to earn your trust. But what farm … What's going on?

"Yeah, I know," he responded. He sat up and put his arm around her. "Tonight the world may change dramatically. I want you with me when it does. You deserve it."

"I'm sorry, Jason. I don't understand."

"I know. But tonight, you will."

Emily snaked her arms around him as they lay back down on the bed together.

"Jason, do you think there will be a time when we can lay together like this and not be afraid?"

"Yes. Just not at my grandparents' house, with all these people running around. It kinda kills the romance."

"Oh, so you wanna take me somewhere romantic," Emily replied with a smile. "And just where would that be?"

"How about the back of my Nissan? I'm a romantic, but a cheap one."

Emily whacked him over the head with a pillow, but she was laughing as she did it. For that sound alone, Jason would take the abuse.

As McWilliams's body was carried off the porch, Sharon and Darien went into the house, closely followed by Culper and Gaston.

"I heard McWilliams say something about killing the president," Darien said cautiously. "What's going on?"

"Yes, he did," Culper replied. "I'll explain, but get Collins and meet me in the backroom."

A few minutes later, Culper was seated behind an oak desk in what used to be the master bedroom. This makeshift office was sparse, but still had a side table with his favorite wines—the only amenity he needed. Sharon, Darien, and Janice were soon seated in front of him.

"I've come here to take personal charge of a project that's been seventy years in the making," Culper declared, sounding more like a politician selling empty campaign promises than a strategist. "It will make the Culper Ring the most powerful organization on this planet."

"Aren't we already?" Darien asked.

"One cannot have too much power."

"So what's this about killing the president?" Sharon inquired.

"Pegasus," Culper simpered. "We make Smithton president and we've got all of Washington in our hands."

"You want to own a president," Janice affirmed.

"It's the most effective way of taking over a country. In our case, we'll have come full circle. It will be our homecoming."

"You do realize if any of us get caught, we'll be executed, right?" Darien persisted. "That's a capital offense."

"To compensate you for the additional risk, there's been a large bonus deposited to your offshore accounts."

Sharon crossed her arms. "Just how do you plan to kill her?"

"Funny you should ask, Sharon. You have the honor of being cast as the lead in our little power play. You'll be playing the role of executioner."

Sharon went still, not believing what she was hearing. She didn't know if Culper was mad or brilliant.

"Think of it as a way of redeeming yourself after your fiasco with those whores."

"It's a suicide mission," she responded.

"Not at all. I'm not one to waste resources."

"Could've fooled me, the way you handled McWilliams."

Culper's tone went cold. "Understand this, Turner: we've spent countless hours and endless money to put you in the perfect place to accomplish this mission. It will utilize all of your skills as a fighter pilot."

"You want me to shoot down the president?!"

"Precisely."

"I take it you have an F-15, an F-16—no, better be an F-18—tucked away for me to use on this mission?" Sharon sneered. Janice chuckled; Darien remained deadpan.

Culper jumped to his feet. "You two think I'm joking about this!" he thundered. "I told you; years of waiting for the perfect opportunity! Months of intricate planning! Millions of dollars spent!"

At that moment, Gaston entered the room, to the relief of Sharon and Janice. Even Darien was getting a bit fidgety.

"Culper," Gaston said, "why don't we just go to the barn and show Sharon the plane we got for her?"

*
**

"We got people on the move here," Jennifer called, then looked back to her screen. She was quickly joined by Jim, George, Jake, and Dom.

"Looks like they're going to the barn," Jake said, grabbing up the headphones.

"Now we might find out what's hiding in there," George stated.

*
**

Gaston held open the door as everyone entered the barn. The inky darkness of the interior was eradicated when Culper threw the switch on the power box.

"Okay, Culper," Sharon drawled, "tell me again this isn't a joke."

"How could anything so beautiful be a joke, my dear Sharon?" he responded, voice filled with contempt. She was clearly getting on his nerves.

"What museum did you find this hunk of junk in?" Janice asked sarcastically. She turned back to them, sneer firmly planted on her lips. "Do you really expect Sharon to take out Air Force One with this antique?"

Culper was twitching with rage. Gaston held up a hand and said smoothly, "Perhaps you'd like to reserve judgment until you know all the facts, ladies. As previously stated, a lot of planning has gone into this."

Culper had reined in himself in, but barely. "Turner," he sniped, "since you're so smart, tell me what this is."

"An old German fighter plane from the Second World War. A Focke-Wulf 190."

"I see a brand new interpretation of Kurt Tank's masterful late 1930s design," Culper retorted. "Totally undeserving of its nickname—'Butcherbird' indeed," he added. "Look at the low wing design, the sleek fuselage, and, of course, the wide-stance landing gear, which makes ground handling a breeze."

"Brand new?" Janice questioned.

"Yes. A firm in Bavaria is manufacturing them again. This particular one has a few custom features. Take a seat, Sharon," Culper invited.

Sharon clambered up the port wing and into the cockpit, fighting furiously to hold her tongue. She'd already seen what happened to people who gave Culper lip. She slid into the seat and stared in surprise. The aircraft had modern heads-up display, which would allow her to view vital flight information on a transparent screen, instead of looking down at her instrument panel. And actually, instrument panel was a misnomer. There was nothing. Just two computer screens.

"You've got a HUD and a couple of MFDs in here. Impressive."

"Yes, both the heads-up display and the multi-function displays should be just like the ones you had on the F-16. They'd better be; they cost enough."

"They are, Culper. But the problem is I can't catch a modern jet airliner like Air Force One in an old fighter like this."

"I never said Air Force One was the target."

Both Sharon and Janice stared at Culper.

"Marine One is the target."

"The president's helicopter!" Janice exclaimed.

Sharon stood up in the cockpit and then sat down on the lip of the canopy.

"I see I've intrigued you, Major. Perhaps you're thinking like a fighter pilot again," Culper added with sinister smile, one that Gaston knew only too well.

Sharon shifted, never taking her eyes from Culper. "I think I see where you are going with this," she replied. "Marine One, as are all the helicopters on that detail, are either Sikorsky Sea Kings or Black Hawks. The Sea King has a top speed of around 160 miles-per-hour; the Black Hawk a little over

200. For a supersonic fighter to shoot down a slow-flying aircraft like that is a bit of a challenge."

"Why would that be, Major?" Culper asked rhetorically, clearly enjoying that addressing her by her former rank was making her uncomfortable.

"Helicopters fly below the stall speed of jets, so it's hard not to overfly them."

"So, how would you kill one if you were in a jet … Major?"

Sharon was visibly annoyed. "Lay back, get a radar lock, and use a radar-guided missile or a heat-seeker."

"But if you're above and behind them, and they're flying low, wouldn't all that ground scatter mess up your radar?" Culper asked; he knew full well that the ground bounced back radar signals, making it harder—almost impossible—to distinguish individual objects.

"Not if you have look-down, shoot-down radar. Look, Culper, it's obvious you've done your homework. Why not just tell us what toys you've got in your box and Janice and I will tell you if it can be done."

Culper looked up at Sharon. She saw the cold expression on his face; discretion was paramount now.

"Toys, Major? At your fingertips is the most advanced weapons system in the world!"

Again everyone stood silent, waiting for Culper's next words.

"Get back in the cockpit, Turner!"

She complied.

"Beside the left MFD is a red, three-position switch marked 'F.' Turn it to position one."

The MFDs activated and a voice filled the cockpit.

Ferdinand now active. Aircraft status to follow.

"Just say 'stop,' Sharon," Culper ordered.

Sharon nodded, then said, in a stern voice, "Stop."

Voice not recognized, possible security breach. Shutting down.

Culper stepped on the wing and leaned into the cockpit.

"Cancel shutdown, identity to follow. Pilot is Sharon Turner, control list Alpha." He turned to Sharon. "Okay. State your name."

Again Sharon complied, even as she felt this mission spiraling out of her control.

"Sounds like you have a co-pilot for this mission, Sharon," Darien observed.

"It's not just an autopilot device with voice recognition?" Janice pressed, almost glaring at Culper.

"An autopilot! Ferdinand is the pilot. *Sharon* is the co-pilot."

Sharon looked as if she had been slapped. She bolted up in the cockpit, one hand gripping the windscreen, the other on the canopy, and leaned over. For a moment, Janice thought she was going to leap onto Culper.

"What the hell are you talking about, Culper!? If you want your little toy here to fly the mission, then you don't need me!" she yelled. Her boots hit the floor.

"Toy! Ferdinand isn't a toy, you ignorant bitch! Open the doors! I'll show you what a real pilot can do."

Gaston realized he was on new ground with Culper. He had never seen him as enraged as he had been in the last hour. As the doors were opened and Ferdinand wheeled out into a sunny day with a cloudless sky, he grasped Culper's shoulder and pulled him aside.

"You've been very irascible today. What's the problem?"

Culper looked at Gaston, evidently aware of the concern in the other man's voice.

"You're right. But what's not to be angry about? McWilliams betrayed us and now they mock my work. They've always jeered, but I've proved them wrong. I shouldn't have to take that from some washed-up fighter jock."

"No one is mocking your work, Culper. They don't understand it. Genius is always at least one generation ahead of the rest of us. But those blessed with genius require something else to make their ideas work: patience. As for Turner being washed up, you know her record and why she had to leave the Air Force."

Culper glanced at Ferdinand. The sun glinted off his vintage World War II German camouflage paint scheme: the deep hunter green, gray, white, and a bright yellow line swirling around the black spinner over the prop hub. Sharon stood next to him with Darien and Janice.

Culper did something Gaston had never seen him do before.

"I must apologize. Especially to you, Sharon, for my words. So much work has gone into Ferdinand. Perhaps I need to explain further what he really is."

Gaston could see the surprise on their faces. He also saw their expressions turn to bewilderment at his next statement.

"You see, Ferdinand looks like a 190, flies like a 190. But he's actually …"

Culper struggled to find the words as the others moved closer.

"Well, he's actually an android."

*
**

"You guys better get over here and check this out," Jennifer yelled. "The doors of the barn are opening."

Jake, Dom, Jim, and George flew to Jennifer's side. They watched as a plane was pushed through the doors.

"Are you seeing what I'm seeing, Jim?"

"A Focke-Wulf 190, in full Luftwaffe regalia, right down to the camouflage. Black cross insignias on the fuselage and wings, and the swastika on the tail." Jim stared at the image, wide-eyed.

"What type of regalia, Dad?"

"Luftwaffe, Jennifer. It was the name of the German air force in World War II."

"Check out under the wings," George instructed, pointing.

"Are those missile rails?" Jim asked.

"They sure are," George replied.

"They're going to shoot down the president," Dom said.

"They can't catch Air Force One in that old bird," George huffed, shaking his head.

"What about Marine One?" Jake offered.

There was a pause in the conversation as everyone considered Jake's query.

"Yeah, they could," Jim admitted. "They could catch a helicopter. Jennifer, check the president's schedule. Is she going out of town, maybe Camp David or something?"

After some furious keyboard work, Jennifer had the answer.

"In a word, no. She's staying in Washington because of the financial crisis. There's a press release here: 'The president will be working to bring all parties together to resolve this crisis.'" She paused, turning to her audience. "Could we have the wrong target, Dad?"

"Maybe they're planning to attack the White House," Dom volunteered.

"No, I don't think so. The White House has anti-aircraft defense systems. And you'd need more firepower than this old thing can carry if you wanted to bring down the White House. Never mind how you'd get away—there'd be an F-16 on your ass in a second."

"Maybe they're not worrying about getting away," Jennifer suggested, zooming in on the plane. "Check this out."

"Is that a mannequin?" Jake asked, squinting at the screen.

"His name is Otto," Culper announced as the dummy was placed into the cockpit. "Best not to be flying around without a 'human' pilot in it. Tends to draw attention."

"This plane can take off, carry out a mission, and land entirely on its own?" Janice asked.

"Yes."

"So why do you need Sharon?"

"Things can still go wrong; best to have a human co-pilot."

Sharon was barely holding in her rage; this was totally humiliating.

"Aren't androids supposed to look like people?" Darien asked.

Culper sneered—he clearly thought that was a stupid question. But he answered anyway, voice just barely devoid of contempt. "Traditionally, yes. But think of Ferdinand as one of those … my grandson was playing with one the other day, what was it? Oh yes! A transformer."

"So what else does this … 'transformer' have up its sleeve?" Sharon asked.

"Over 300 more horsepower than the original. The old BMW engines are no longer available, so we put in the iconic Pratt &Whitney R2800."

"Fine, it's got a great engine. That's not the issue, Culper," Sharon declared. "Take a hard look at the mission. Marine One always flies with two to four other helicopters. As they fly, they're always changing positions precisely so any potential attacker doesn't know which helicopter has the president, like a carnival shell game. Ferdinand here would have no trouble following along if he isn't seen, but he will be. There's always a CAP attached to the detail. Probably an F-16 flying out of Andrews. With its look-down, shoot-down radar, even a low-flying attacker will be spotted and the alarm will be sounded. The presidential detail will land immediately, leaving Ferdinand here to eat the air-to-air missiles."

Culper stood there, listening like a patient parent indulging a child, greeting each point with a nod of his head. She continued nonetheless.

"Let's say Ferdinand isn't detected. As soon as he picks up the detail and turns on his attack radar, all the radar detection equipment on the choppers will light up. They'll scatter in different directions with their radar jamming equipment on, dropping chaff and flares to throw off any missiles coming their way until they land. Again, Ferdinand starts eating the Sidewinder missiles from the CAP."

Sharon waited for a reply. Finally, in a deeply exasperated voice, Culper responded, "Major Turner, do you really think we wouldn't think of this before proceeding?"

"You tell me."

"Then I will. First of all, look under the airplane. What do you see?"

"The landing gear and the drop tank," Sharon stated curtly, squatting for a better view.

"Have a closer look at the drop tank. I don't think you'll find it full of gasoline," Culper said impatiently.

As Sharon looked closer, she saw small, dome-like structures protruding from the tank. She looked up. "Is this an ECM pod?"

"Yes, Major. It's an electronic countermeasure pod, but one unlike any other in the world." Culper squatted next to her. "It can defeat Doppler radar."

*
**

"We have to send a copy of this video to the FBI," Dom said, opening the contacts list on his phone. "My contact's a forensic lip reader."

"Great idea, Dom!" George exclaimed, pointing to Jennifer's computer screen. "Sometimes they're facing the camera, sometimes not. We won't get all of the conversation, but some is better than nothing."

"Damn, she's away. All I'm getting is her voicemail. You guys keep watching and recording. When they're done, I'll send it to her. In the meantime, I have a raid to organize. We'll nail these bastards, not only on murder, but on treason and conspiracy to murder the president. They'll get the needle for sure!"

"In the good 'ole days, they had a more dramatic way to deal with traitors," Jason said as he and Emily entered the room. "They'd draw and quarter them. Very messy, but the crowds loved it. The reality TV of yore."

"Do I even want to know what that is?" Emily asked.

"No!" was the response from everyone in the room.

"It'd spoil lunch," Jason added, peering over Jennifer's shoulder at her screen. "Oh, Kurt Tank's masterpiece, a Focke-Wulf 190. Let's see here. Eastern front camouflage paint scheme is correct. No core crosses on the insignias, just the flank design; that puts it late in the war, chevron behind the cockpit shows the pilot is a staff officer. That center drop tank those two are inspecting isn't right though. It's longer and more slender than normal."

Everyone just stared at Jason.

"Was he always like this, Jennifer?" Emily asked.

"Afraid so."

"You're telling me this thing can defeat Doppler radar?" Sharon was incredulous.

"That's what I said, Major," Culper sneered.

"Doppler radar is the basis for look-down, shoot-down radar. The CAP will be blind."

"Yes, the combat air patrol, the CAP—you military types do love your acronyms—won't see you. This also scrambles their targeting radar. It shoots flares and chaff to fool heat-seeking and radar-guided missiles."

"Where did you get this? I know of nothing that defeats Doppler radar," Sharon demanded as she stood up.

"Not your concern, Major."

"Here's something that is, Culper," Janice said. "We still have a problem: the moment she turns on her targeting radar, they'll know she's there."

"So she doesn't turn it on."

"Then how does she aim her missiles? Or is she supposed to knock down the helicopters the old-fashioned way, using these two 20-millimeter canons on the wings?" Janice's question dripped sarcasm.

It was becoming clearer that Culper thought them beneath him; his impatient answer couldn't have been more contemptuous if he'd tried.

"Because, Janice," he all but snapped, "we're not using radar-guided missiles. We knew they'd be a problem. We're using acoustically-guided. Please don't tell me I have to explain those as well."

He sighed deeply at the blank look on their faces. "As you pointed out, Major, this presidential detail flies two different types of helicopters. The engines and rotor blades of the helicopters produce distinct harmonics. We have six Atoll missiles with customized warheads, each acoustically tuned to the sounds of these two helicopters only. All you have to do is pull up the plane, confirm the warheads are hearing the sounds, lock-on to the sounds, then salvo off and run. They'll do the rest."

"That's actually brilliant," Sharon admitted. "Even if the choppers were warned of the missiles and landed, their engines and rotor blades would still be making sounds. The missiles would just follow them in."

"If the pilots try evasive maneuvers, it won't help them." Culper added. "All the missiles have to do is come close; they have proximity fuses on them. In this case, close ones do count."

"One question. Just how low will I be flying on the approach?" Sharon asked.

"Not over fifty feet, so as to hide in the ground clutter."

"Hold up. We've got 1,200 pounds of missiles on the wings. Fully loaded canons and fuel tanks, plus I'm dragging the ECM pod. All that extra weight has to raise the stall speed of this baby, and I'm at fifty feet!? If the ECM pod can defeat Doppler radar, why so low?"

"Another layer of protection, Major, in case of any new features they might have added to their detection equipment. As far as the low flying, that is precisely why you let Ferdinand fly that part of the mission. There are cameras at strategic points all around the plane so he can see the terrain. He's fine-tuned to the characteristics of the aircraft. He'll keep you low and slow so you hide nicely in the ground clutter until you pop up to shoot the missiles."

"Can I override him?"

Culper took a long, deep breath.

"Yes," he replied. "That red switch you threw has three positions. Top, Ferdinand flies; middle, you fly, but you can still have him advise you. Bottom, he's off and you're on your own. That position could get you killed."

Culper could already see that would be Sharon's position of choice.

"I have a question. Why the Nazi paint job?" Darien asked.

"The air show season is about to start. When people see Ferdinand flying around, they'll dismiss him as belonging to one."

Darien nodded. Culper glanced at his watch.

"We have to get outta here, we've been at this safe house too long as it is. Next location is Omega-2. Sharon, let's pull Otto out so you can fly there with Ferdinand and get some pointers."

Sharon would have loved to tell him what to do with that idea, but she relented. A few minutes later, she was in the cockpit. She put the red switch to its top position.

Ferdinand operational.

"Prepare for take-off. Destination Omega-2," Sharon stated.

Roger.

Sharon heard the flaps as they went to the fully down position and saw the ailerons move up and down as Ferdinand prepared for take-off. Finally, the big, three-bladed propeller whirred to life, its tune accompanied by the high-pitched whine of the starter motor. This was quickly followed by the roar of the eighteen-cylinder R2800 engine. A few moments later, Ferdinand and his unwilling co-pilot were taxiing down the runway.

"I notice you failed to mention that Ferdinand was a quantum computer," Gaston said as they watched the plane take off.

"They need not know everything," Culper replied.

"There goes the 190," Jake declared, engrossed in Jennifer's screen.

"There they all go," Dom corrected as he watched Culper, Gaston, and the staff pile into cars. "I'll get a BOLO out on each of them."

"What's the problem, Jim?" George asked, glancing at his nephew, who appeared to be in deep thought. "You don't want to delay notifying the authorities any longer."

Jim ignored his uncle and looked at Dom. "The minute you put that BOLO out for Culper and company, Overlord's dead. We'll lose Tallmadge."

"Jim, we have all the evidence we need," George pled. "We've discussed this. The president's life is in danger!"

"Uncle George, I know I keep saying this, but we don't know who at the FBI, Homeland, the Secret Service, or any other agency, is in on this. It can't just be McWilliams. We know already the vice president has been compromised. That BOLO goes out; Culper will know and start thinking. He starts thinking and we lose Tallmadge. Tonight is D-Day. Just give me tonight. I don't want to just kick the door in; I want to bring the whole house down. Once we've moved the money and send out the APYN reports showing who's dirty, we'll have all of them—everyone."

Jim started to pace. "These people'll make deals to save their own skins. They'll reveal other corrupt people. But most importantly, the innocent will get their money back."

He paused, glancing around at his family. Jason gave him a nod; Jennifer looked down at her keyboard. George was watching him with something like pride in his eyes.

Jim turned to the two FBI agents in their midst. "Dom, Jake … I know I have no right to ask you to once more do something that goes against your principles. Not after you've done so much. But would you please give me—no, us—tonight?"

"I want a go/no-go on operation Overlord now!" Jennifer exclaimed in the meeting room of the Wellington Heights Inn, where five groups of people, on two continents, were once again united by the internet. The Hanson family was again joined by George, Dom, and Jake; they boasted a new addition as well—Emily.

"Waterloo, are you with me?" Jennifer asked.

"We're a go here," Emmanuel's voice emitting from the speaker in the middle of the conference table.

"Good luck, everyone," Arissa added.

"Lyon, how are you doing?"

"On est avec vous. Bonne chance!"

"I wish Elizabeth could see Jennifer like this," Jim whispered to George and Dolly in a voice almost breaking.

"She is, Jim." Dolly squeezed Jim's hand tight. "She's right here with us to see the woman her daughter has become." George nodded in agreement.

"Are you guys in Cambridge awake or still drinking beer?"

"MIT stands ready. But how did you know about the beer?"

The erupting laughter eased the tension, which had been so taut people were afraid to speak.

"Andorra, you there?"

"You Americans are so provincial," Maurice said. "Beer does not go with an occasion such as this. Only a good Burgundy will do. Andorra stands ready!"

Amidst the laughter, Jennifer made one request.

"Jason, do you have an appropriate quote from history for a moment like this?"

"You had to know, Jenny. It's from my favorite President, Harry S. Truman."

Jennifer rolled her eyes.

"Carry the battle to them. Don't let them bring it to you. Put them on the defensive and don't ever apologize for anything."

The room went quiet, Jason's words dying away on the still air. Then Jennifer's voice cut through the silence—"Execute Overlord."

"You are about to embark upon a great crusade…"

— General Dwight D. Eisenhower,
in his address to the Armed Forces
just before the D-Day landings

CHAPTER 16

"Well Jim, that's quite the daughter you and Elizabeth raised," the president said, giving my hand a squeeze as we sat on the bench. "It sounds as though courage runs in the family."

"Thank you for that, Madam President."

"I agree with Dolly, Jim. No mother would've missed a moment like that," she said with a smile. "And leave it to Jason to come up with the perfect historical quote."

"When Jennifer gave the order to execute, my heart was in my mouth. What if I was wrong? What if all I did was mess up the international banking system? What would the repercussions be? What about Pegasus?"

"Second-guessing command decisions is a luxury one can't afford, Jim. We presidents never have to; the talking heads on all news shows do it for us. Of course, we're always wrong," she said with a wry smile. "Once Jennifer said 'execute,' you were 'all in', to use a poker phrase. The important point is you made a decision where many would've vacillated. You and your group should be proud of this."

I looked at her and I could see she was sincere.

"It was quite the evening."

"I bet! I'm on the edge of my seat here, Jim, what happened next!?"

"Well, for one thing, Tallmadge turned out to be a bit of a flirt."

"What!" the president exclaimed with a laugh. "Tell me, was he worse than you?"

I looked hard at the president before answering. "Let's put it this way: He was less subtle."

"Oh really?"

*
**

"The carrier wave is now in place. Over to you, Waterloo," Maurice was heard to say as everyone in the Wellington Inn's meeting room held their breath.

"We got it, Maurice, and thank you," Emmanuel responded. "Logging in now."

Hello, Emmanuel. In the time since our last chess match, I do not believe your game could have improved. I would like to play with George.

As these words appeared on screens of everyone's computer, the laughter emitting from the speaker added to the intensity of the amusement in the room.

"You know, I could really learn to hate this guy," Emmanuel stated.

"Don't take it personally, Emmanuel," George said, typing on Jennifer's computer.

Hello Tallmadge, I am here.

You are on Jennifer's computer again. Is Jennifer there?

Jennifer looked surprised. Leaning over George, she responded.

Yes, I am here.

Hello Jennifer.

Hello Tallmadge.

Is your hair the color known as auburn?

"What's going on here?" Jennifer exclaimed as she heard the sounds of anxious conversation from the people online.

"Isn't it obvious? He's hitting on you," Emily stated, garnering some chuckles.

Are you looking at the photograph of me on the MIT webpage?

That is correct.

"My God! He can visualize. He can understand images! This is incredible!"

Yes, my hair is auburn.

Are you what is known as beautiful?

The laughter from her colleagues only added to Jennifer's embarrassment. It was quickly followed by a chorus of, "Say yes."

"He's reasoning! He's asking intelligent questions!" Jennifer shouted.

"I believe it's called learning, Jenny," Jason said.

"And if you don't type in 'yes,' young lady, I will," George stated.

Yes, Tallmadge, I am beautiful, Jennifer reluctantly typed. That was quickly followed by a disembodied voice from MIT saying, "You see, Fred, I always told you she was conceited."

Thus Jennifer's embarrassment was completed with more hilarity.

Tallmadge wants to play chess now. Tallmadge likes to play chess.

George could only shake his head as a chess board appeared on the computer screen.

"Well, at least he's consistent with his likes and dislikes," he said.

Emily moved closer to George so she could watch the game.

"Do you mind a little company?" she asked.

"Only if you're a player," George replied.

"I might be able to help."

As the game developed, Emmanuel thought it was time to start the mission.

Tallmadge, we need a new protocol put into place. It will be Protocol 17.

State parameters.

Parameters are being sent to you.

"Okay, Cambridge, time to put the beer away, you're up," Jennifer announced.

"Don't worry, Jenny, we'll save you some."

"You'd better."

"You didn't hear that, Dad," Jason said, giving his father a smile.

"Upload in progress."

"He's one tough opponent, Judge Grayson," Emily observed.

"You're telling me! He can beat me while still doing that computer job. Talk about multitasking!"

"Yeah, you'd think he was a woman," Emily responded with a wry grin.

"Perhaps, just not one from Georgetown."

"Upload complete. We'll go back to our beer party now."

Tallmadge, we need you to create a program to balance the accounts as outlined in the parameters for Protocol 17, Emmanuel directed.

Program now completed. Do you wish Tallmadge to run it?

Yes.

Program running. Checkmate.

Any general would say one of the most important factors in winning a battle is the element of surprise. Another would be good logistics. But there was another element which no general could have enough of and that is luck. For the Hanson group, that evening, that fickle lady was smiling brightly on them.

*
**

"Marston! Get the uplink to the SRT-1 shut down now! We're being hacked!"

"Should I shut down the satellite itself?"

"No! I don't know what else is running. Just shut down your terminal and the SEG," Clare Johnston ordered Ed Marston.

"Now listen up, everyone!" Clare exclaimed, addressing her NSA staff. "Get all your terminals shut down now, except for the ARS, that's where they're coming in from. I want this attack isolated and identified now!"

"It looks like it originated in Mongolia."

"Just what we need; another foreign hacker trying to bust our chops," Clare lamented.

If Ed had been able to monitor his part of the web, what he would've witnessed would have proved astounding. A tsunami of data, moving at the speed of light, was coming down every lane. Different elements of the wave took off-ramps to hit banks, trust companies, insurance corporations—virtually any entity where money was hidden. The funds of the criminals were removed, while those of the innocent were not disturbed. As for the criminals, they were left a trail, one leading to only one place: International Predictive Analytics. In reality, the money was still on the move, running through several banks in Singapore and Dubai. From there, it went back to the United States, running through over 3,000 bank branches before reaching its final destination.

*
**

"He got me again!" George shouted, staring at the screen in disgust.

Let's play again, you are improving slightly.

The amusement of the audience was very loud.

"I see what you mean, Emmanuel. You could really learn to hate this guy," George stated in amused dejection.

"Start now, George. It will save time," Emmanuel replied.

"Let me have a game with him," Emily offered.

George informed Tallmadge of the request.

What is Emily's full name?

Emily Proctor.

Does Emily Proctor attend MIT as well?

No, Georgetown.

Is Emily Proctor also known as Veronica Parker?

Emily inhaled sharply. Jennifer looked at Emily with concern.

"I'm sorry, everyone, I had no idea … I just thought it would be fun to play …"

"Just answer his question," Jennifer said.

"Easy does it, people," Emmanuel urged. "We still have a lot of time to run with Overlord."

Yes, I am.

Emily was now looking at Jason, trying to gage his reaction.

Why does Emily have two names?

Jason could see Emily was flustered and came over to put his arm around her.

"Boy! Is this guy ever nosy!" he said.

It was a name I had to use in another job I once had. My name is Emily Proctor.

Does Emily like to play chess? Tallmadge likes to play chess.

A collective sigh was heard through the room.

I like to play chess too. The first move is yours.

Jason and George watched as Emily and Tallmadge squared off. After about fifteen minutes, a background buzz of commentary was coming in online. George and Jason were now into the game as well, quietly encouraging Emily at every move. The lady had game, and she was giving Tallmadge all he could handle. Jennifer was now looking over Emily's shoulder, astounded by her skill, but knowing no one could beat a computer, let alone a quantum one. That fact didn't stop the collective voices of four universities being heard chanting in unison, "Georgetown! Georgetown!" Their voices stilled, however, when Emily said one word.

"Checkmate!"

At first, Jennifer didn't react. She just stood there looking at the screen, not comprehending the impossible; not understanding what had just happened. A human had just beaten the most advanced computer in the world at chess.

"Did I just do something wrong?" Emily asked, looking concerned.

"Oh my God!" Jennifer exclaimed. "He's going to think he's malfunctioning again. He'll want to shut down!"

Tallmadge had other ideas.

Tallmadge likes playing chess with Emily. Emily's hair is a different color than Jennifer's.

"Just my luck to meet the one quantum computer with a hair fetish," Emily bemoaned, to the amusement of everyone.

"I think he just found your picture on the Georgetown webpage," Jason observed.

Emily is very beautiful.

"I think you just got dumped, Jennifer!" a voice from MIT said.

Dolly came over and gave Emily a hug, offering her congratulations, cautioning,

"Watch this one; he sounds like a two-timer."

Is Tallmadge beautiful?

The amusement in the room and online suddenly ended. Everyone had the same question, to which Jim gave voice.

"What's happening here, Jennifer?"

Jennifer stood there, asking herself the same question. Ironically, it was the person in the room who knew the least about computers who had the best answer.

"Could this little fellow be looking for his identity?" Dolly asked to a background of people voicing their agreement.

"Emily, tell him we don't know what he looks like," Jennifer stated.

Emily quickly complied. A photo of an extremely handsome young man in his mid-twenties appeared on the screen.

"Wow!" Emily exclaimed.

"Wow, indeed," Jennifer added.

"We may be in trouble here, Jake," Jason bemoaned.

"Jake who?" Jennifer asked, throwing him a big smile.

"I should have known better than to date a computer geek," Jake replied.

"I know this person," Maurice said with a solemnity that the electronics could not hide.

"Such a nice young man." Chantal's voice crackled over the line.

"The person you're looking at is Ian Mandrake, a former student of mine," Maurice said. "I taught him computer architecture, although I think he knew more about it than me. He was brilliant, a genius."

"Did you say was?" Jennifer asked.

"Yes, Jennifer," Chantal answered. "Two years ago, he died. We had come to know him well. Genius like his comes along once in a generation."

"Was his father Adrian Mandrake?"

"Yes, he was, and I know what you're thinking, Jennifer," Maurice said.

"As do I," Emmanuel stated. "As does anyone who's familiar with the rumors. But people, before we do anymore probing, let's be cautious here. As computer people, we're all fascinated by Tallmadge. We all want to know who built him. I know some of us are asking 'is Tallmadge the beginning of a new artificial life form?' But we're still running Overlord. Let's get that job done first. We don't want to do anything that could interrupt the program. We can investigate Tallmadge further later. So tell him he's gorgeous and get him into another chess match."

"Sounds smart to me," Jim stated.

"I agree," Jennifer said. "Tell him how lovely he is, but don't forget to get his cell number; we already have his e-mail," she added dryly.

"Hold the last part of that request!" Jake exclaimed.

Men who are beautiful are called handsome. Tallmadge is very handsome.

Emily is beautiful. Emily likes to play chess. Tallmadge likes to play chess. Tallmadge is very handsome. We shall play chess. Emily can move first.

"First time I ever played with a man and the only thing on his mind was chess," quipped Emily.

*
**

"So Emily Proctor beat this computer at chess," Kathleen stated. "That sounds fantastic. It also sounds like it has perception as well as judgment. But as Jennifer said, if it has judgment, it can make mistakes. Also your mom may be right; it may be looking for an identity."

"Yeah, we would be delving into that later. As the evening wore on, we were so busy with Overlord that we didn't realize that an old nemesis was back, and our president had changed her itinerary."

"Sorry, Jim, changed my itinerary?"

"Well, you did decide to go to Camp David."

*
**

"Well, they tried to shut me up. They tried to muzzle me. They attacked my computer. They even put phony pictures of me with another woman online to try to destroy my family. But Holland Day does not back down from a fight and I am back, here on cable where, for the small sum of $12.50 a month, you can get the truth, uninterrupted by commercials. A small price to pay for a source who does not owe anything to advertisers.

"So here's what's up with the worst president this country has ever had. We have just learned she's decided to call a meeting with the House and Senate leaders up at Camp David to try to solve the financial crisis she caused. They're all flying up there tomorrow morning to discuss ways for the United States not to default on its debt. I hope they fail. It is time to face the music. Once we default, we can get rid of the entitlements that have been breaking our backs and give the right people the tax breaks to build a strong America again—right after we impeach Galbraith.

"Now you, my loyal listeners, know how I always come up with news others are afraid to report. Here's the latest. You remember the Hanson case? The family that was allegedly attacked by a professional killer, but was stopped by a crazy old man, who used to be a lawyer, and his dog. Well, the old man's law partner was one George Grayson. He later became a judge. Guess who one of his law clerks was? Kathleen Galbraith! That's right, the president was his law clerk. Time to bring in the FBI to investigate this one! And Jim Hanson never answered my question about problems with his clients' money. Maybe it's time to bring in the FBI on that one too! Oh, I am sorry, we can't do that! Why? Because his daughter is dating an FBI agent! Is this just one more case of corruption in the Galbraith government? Stick with me and find out for just $12.50 per month. Subscribe online today!"

*
**

Tallmadge thinks there are no other moves to be made. Stalemate.

"I think Tallmadge is right, Emily," George said. "You've played magnificently. It was a pleasure to watch," he added over the applause both in the room and online.

"Thank you very much, Judge Grayson. That means a lot coming from you. I guess it took a Georgetown girl to show you how to play chess."

George joined in the laughter and applause.

Tallmadge is correct, we are at stalemate. I have enjoyed playing chess with you. I like Emily. I like playing chess with Emily.

"Watch it here, Jason, I think Tallmadge is about to make his move," Jake warned.

Protocol 17 complete. Would Emily like to play chess again?

"And what a move it was," Jason quipped.

"Why don't I give him a game, Emily, and give you a break?" George offered.

"Thanks, Judge Grayson."

George would like to play a game of chess with you.

But George does not play chess as well as Emily.

The amusement level in the room went back on high.

"Don't worry. Judge Grayson; I'll get you a game."

I realize George does not play as well as Emily. But that is because he never went to Georgetown. Would you please play chess with him anyway?

Tallmadge will play chess with George even though he never went to Georgetown.

George sat there, enduring the laughter without a word.

"I believe that's called checkmate," Emily added as she patted George on the shoulder.

"That's the first time in over sixty years I've seen George speechless," Dolly observed as she wiped the tears of laughter from her eyes. "I could really learn to love this little fellow," she added.

As the game started, Emmanuel gave Tallmadge instructions to erase all traces of Protocol 17 and their copying of the APYN program. The room and the online team had fallen silent, each troubled with their own thoughts, until Dom spoke.

"Did it work?"

"We'll know shortly," Jennifer said as she pounded away at the keys on Jason's computer. The sound was followed shortly by the whir of a laser printer. Jennifer handed a sheet of paper to her dad. He read it, smiled, and then handed it to Emily.

"Emily, I know you've been concerned about the cost of future care at Grace Field for your sister Michelle and Sam's brother, Paul," Jim stated. "I've been in touch with Grace Field and I set up a trust account to look after them for the rest of their lives. As far as funding the trust, I am happy to report an offshore investor has just stepped forward and made a generous donation."

Emily looked around the table at all the smiling faces as applause filled the room.

"How do I even begin to thank everyone for this ..."

That was as far as she got. Jason wrapped an arm about her shoulders and pulled her in tight as she began to cry.

"Dammit! He got me again!" George exclaimed.

George needs to go with Emily to Georgetown to learn to play better chess.

"Now that's the final straw!" George cried, feigning outrage to the delight of his audience. "It's bad enough losing, but that crack about Georgetown was too much. There was a time when my seconds would be calling upon Mr. Tallmadge for an egregious remark such as that," he added with his best Southern drawl. His antics had the effect he wanted: Emily laughed.

"How would you fight a duel with a computer, Uncle George?" Jason asked whimsically.

"Anyone know any good viruses?" he replied.

"Are you really asking a bunch of computer people that question?" an online voice replied.

"I want to know more about Tallmadge," Jennifer said as she took her uncle's place in front of her computer.

Hello Tallmadge, this is Jennifer.

Hello Jennifer. Do you wish to play chess?

Maybe later. Can I see that photograph of you again?

Instantly, the picture of Ian Mandrake appeared.

Tallmadge is very handsome.

Yes, you are. Can you show me a picture of your father?

A photo of a man in his late fifties instantly appeared.

"Oh no," George groaned.

"Now I'm really getting puzzled," Jim said.

"Join the club," Dom remarked.

"Yeah, it's Culper," Jake said.

The online chatter reached a crescendo.

"Maurice, did you ever meet Ian's father?"

"Yes, we both did, at Ian's funeral. The man in the picture is Adrian Mandrake! But you're saying he's Culper? He's the man responsible for killing my brother!"

"I'm sorry to have to tell you he is," Jim stated. "Also Maurice, he and some of his cohorts are here in Virginia. How did Ian die?"

"It was suicide," Chantal replied, resulting in yet more chatter. "His mother died the same way some years ago. Ian was brilliant, but subject to mood swings. The only way I could find to get him out of the bad moods was to play chess with him. It always made him happy. But the last time ... he felt his whole world was coming apart. Also, there were the fights with his father ..."

"Emmanuel, you mentioned rumors regarding this Adrian Mandrake?"

"Yes, there were rumors about this British eccentric and recluse, one Adrian Mandrake, and his breakthroughs in quantum computing. There'd be occasional articles by him, but all they seemed to garner was ridicule. He always seemed to get published, however, and he even acquired a following. But he never seemed to present any concrete evidence of his supposed successes," Emmanuel explained.

"He dropped out of sight a couple of years ago," Jennifer stated. "We heard nothing from him until he accepted a speaking engagement at a quantum physics conference in New York. He was going to make a big announcement. But he died of a heart attack the night before he was to appear."

"So Culper is Adrian Mandrake. The inventor of the quantum computer," Jim said. "That begs the question: who died in New York?"

The voices from online started again in earnest.

"So Tallmadge has taken the place of his son. I just don't know what to think here. Maybe we'll need a psychiatrist who can work with computers as well as people," Jennifer said.

"Make sure the shrink can play chess," George added.

The atmosphere became more sullen. The question on everybody's mind, 'what next…' hung in the air. Jennifer decided to address it.

"Well, everyone, I want you thank you all for your help in Overlord. I don't know if we won, except in one case," Jennifer sighed, looking at Emily. "But as least we fought back. We owed Angie, Gerard, Steven, two brave FBI agents, and Samantha Stevens that much. Let's keep watch online. If the money got moved, the story will break there first. Tomorrow should prove interesting. Thank you again, and good night."

Jason was a man that always tried to do the right thing. That was why he found himself once again at the Hanson linen closet. Removing the necessary items to make the office couch into a bed, he proceeded down the hall. As he passed his bedroom door, he hesitated a moment as temptation beckoned. He shook his head and continued on to the office. He was soon fast asleep. A little while later, Emily crept out of the bedroom. She wondered why she hadn't seen Jason, until she went into the office. Seeing him there, she leaned over him and kissed him on the cheek, whispering, "Yeah, you are the real deal."

Some had referred to Detroit as the buckle on the rust belt. Jackson Harrison would not disagree. A few years ago, Jacko—as his friends called him—and his wife, Gladys, thought they had it made. They worked for the same auto parts manufacturer where they earned a good wage. Every paycheck saw them contribute to the company pension plan. But when 2008 hit, the company declared bankruptcy—but not before opening a company under a different name in China and declaring the pension plan defunct. The former employees had launched a class action lawsuit against their former employer, but they knew it would be years before they would see a cent from the pension—if ever.

Life for the Harrisons since the plant closing, as for millions of their fellow Americans, had been brutal. They'd been hoping to help their two children with college expenses; they couldn't do that now. Jacko had only found occasional janitorial jobs, while Gladys worked part-time in a store, where her hours (and so her pay) varied greatly. Their income, once plentiful and steady, was now meager and fitful, which meant they'd be losing their home in the next six weeks. Jacko could stand that; it was a blow to his pride, but he'd live. But what really broke his heart was not being able to cover the cost of Gladys's medication. Sometimes charities would help out; other times, Gladys would go without it for days, trying to make what she had last. A dangerous strategy with a heart condition like hers.

Their mode of transportation was an eleven-year-old Chevy Cavalier, which Jacko had kept running with the help of parts from wreckers and his skills as an amateur mechanic. But this morning what he saw, as he laid under the car, was a problem that required new parts. His brake lines needed replacing. They were leaking everywhere, and that meant a trip to the auto parts store. He didn't know if he could afford it. Pulling himself out from under the car, he headed into the house and sat before his computer, a gift from a friend whose son had outgrown it. Some of the letters had worn off the keyboard, and the curved screen of the cathode ray tube monitor was hard on the eyes, but it was still good enough for an occasional e-mail or, in this case, to check his bank balance. Jacko knew it was a mistake as soon as he saw it, but it did give him a badly needed chuckle. The checking account balance read $629,728.62.

"I wish," he said out loud. "Let's have some fun with these guys. I'll transfer most of it to another bank so they just can't take it out of my account. May as well earn some interest until they discover their mistake."

He and Gladys still had a savings account at another bank that they had once made regular deposits to. They called it their "mad money" account, in which they saved for vacations and Christmas. Its balance was now $16.48. Jacko quickly transferred $600,000 of his new wealth to it and phoned Gladys.

"Check out my account too, honey," Gladys chuckled.

What Jacko saw stunned him.

"It says you have $458,623.78 in your account."

He heard a gasp followed by long pause.

"Transfer $400,000 to the mad money account and let's pay off all our bills with what we left behind," Gladys instructed.

"But when they find out their mistake, they'll want the money back," Jacko pointed out.

"Yeah, but for once we'll be in the strong position."

"Okay, I'll do it. But, honey, before you come home, drop into the pharmacy and get as much of your medicine as they'll let you have. That's one thing we'll never give back."

Forty-five minutes later, the Harrisons were out of debt with the exception of their mortgage, but all of the missed payments were paid. Jacko took the bus to the plaza where the auto parts store was. The bank across the way looked busy. As he acquired his brake lines, Peter Young, one of the store's employees and a former co-worker of Jacko's at the defunct parts factory, came in.

"So, are you rich, Pete?" one of clerks asked.

"Looks that way," he replied. "Hey Jacko!"

"Did you win the lottery, Pete?" Jacko replied.

"Did you check your bank balance? I think we got paid out on our pension plans."

"I think we would've gotten a letter or something to sign before that happened," Jacko replied.

"I think he's right," one of the clerks stated as he walked over to the counter carrying his laptop. "I worked for another company that ripped off the employee pensions and I deal with a different bank; but I just got paid big time!" he added, smiling at the screen.

"What's going on here?" Peter asked. "Is this money ours or not?"

" ...the nearest run thing
you ever saw in your life...."

—Arthur Wellesley, Duke of Wellington,
after the Battle of Waterloo, June 1815

CHAPTER 17

The drive from Richmond to Washington had been a slow one for Jake due to two traffic accidents and a late start. He had been late getting to bed because of the Overlord operation.

After clearing security at FBI headquarters, he went to the assistant director's office for his appointment. Jake didn't know yet how he was going to explain the gathering of evidence in his briefcase; the video of McWilliams's murder; the threat against the president; the Culper Ring; or, most importantly, how was he going to keep the Hanson family out of the report.

Arriving at the assistant director's office he was informed there was going to be a delay in the meeting due to an emergency. Jake had not been in the waiting area for more than a minute before his cell phone rang. The caller display said it was Dom.

"Jake, we got a report back from that lip reader I sent the videos to. As we thought, she couldn't get all of the conversation, but here's some of what she was able to read: missiles, acoustically guided, six Atoll missiles with customized warheads, ECM pod, defeat Doppler radar …"

Jake glanced about. "Okay, Dom, e-mail me the rest."

Just then, he was waved into the office of Assistant Director Nolan Scott. After shaking hands with this finely tailored gentleman, the internal alarm that most people in policing developed started to ring for Jake. Scott's hand was clammy and he looked nervous. He also looked as if he hadn't slept. But what really interested Jake was the screensaver on his monitor. It featured the same photograph of the 1963 split-window Corvette Stingray he'd once seen on McWilliams's monitor.

"Well, Special Agent Connors, what brings you to my office this morning?"

"Well, sir ..."

At that moment, Scott's cell phone alerted him to the arrival of a text.

"Excuse me, Agent Connors."

Scott's reading of the text left him upset, a fact which aroused Jake's curiosity further.

"My apologies, Agent Connors. There's a lot going on this morning. You'll have to excuse me for about ten or fifteen minutes while I deal with this. Please help yourself to the coffee." He indicated a carafe on his credenza as he walked out, closing the door behind him.

Jake quickly went to Scott's computer and checked the properties of the screensaver, which turned out to be a very large file.

When Scott returned, Jake was enjoying a coffee in the chair in front of desk.

"Well, Assistant Director, judging by your screensaver, you're a Corvette fan."

"Yes, I am, Agent Connors," he replied apprehensively. "Read about everything there is on them."

"Yes, the ten years they made the Stringray model back in the sixties were the best," Jake stated.

"I would agree."

"That 1963 split-window Corvette Stingray on your screensaver, it's a shame they only made it for five years."

"Again, I'd agree. But Agent Connors, this is a busy day, and I don't think you came here to discuss my screensaver."

"In a way, I have. Let's start at the beginning. If you knew anything about Corvettes, you'd know the Corvette Stingray was only made for five years, 1963 through 1967. Further, the split-window, only for one year, 1963."

Scott looked stunned. "What is this about, Agent?"

"I just want to talk some more about your screensaver. Very pretty photograph and an excellent way to hide messages. You know, those updates from Culper and the rest of the traitors. What's the latest on Pegasus?"

*
**

For George Grayson, it had been a restless night. The events of the last few days had deeply troubled him, yet, at the same time renewed his faith, faith in today's youth. The way these kids in the US, Canada, France, and Andorra had come together amazed him. He'd even taken a liking to a certain computer. As positive as these events were, the possibility of Culper Ring agents throughout the government greatly disturbed him. Adding to his anxiety was the plot to kill the president, a fact which found George out of bed before dawn. He drove to the airport without knowing why. He sat in his office, thinking for a while, before it hit him. For some reason, he knew the time had come.

Opening the hangar door, he rolled *Lady Rachel* out into the light of a new sun. He looked up at the likeness of his dear wife.

"Well, darling, I think this old warrior has been called to duty one more time. You know we have to go."

A few minutes later, *Lady Rachel* climbed into the dawn. She then turned north, north toward Washington.

"You talked about courage earlier, Jim."

"Yes, I did, Madam President," I responded as we stood again looking at the names on the memorial to my dad's squadron.

"I'd see a lot of courage that morning, Jim, from both pilots and many others."

"Yes, you did, Madam President. It takes a great leader to inspire courage like that and …"

"Don't you dare call me a hero, James Hanson, or I'll kick your butt!" she exclaimed, waving her arms. "I swear, if one more talking head says something like 'The most presidential moment in our history,' I'll throw up!" she added, punctuating each point by directing a forefinger at me.

"Oh no," Jason said. "I think they're at it again."

"Just when it was going so well," Jennifer added.

"I was so close," Jason bemoaned. "I could just about see my letter of reference on the White House stationery."

"Not to worry, Madam President, I will not call you a hero."

"Well, thank you for that, Jim."

"For a lady, I believe the proper term is 'heroine,'" I countered with a smile, but still receiving one of her numbing, icy stares.

"You just love to push my buttons, don't you, guy?"

"It's becoming so easy," I said, finally drawing a smile from her. "But I have to say this—and if I get kicked, so be it. After I saw that video, I was so damned proud to have you as my president."

She looked up at me and sighed.

"How could I leave them, Jim? We had wounded. It was just like that day on the highway with my son Mark. You can't turn your back and leave."

"And then there was Senator Treleaven."

"Yes. Senator Alastair Marcus Treleaven," the president said with a soft smile. "He really is a national treasure. You know Jim, in the twenty plus years I've known him, I don't think we've ever agreed on anything. Yet there he was, this man in his mid-seventies willing to stand there with me that morning, with his beloved Marines and die fighting."

"It's becoming clear how he got those two Silver Stars, fighting with the Marines in Vietnam. To men like him, the words courage and honor mean something special."

"There are so many of them lying here around us, Jim. Today, we added one more," the president said, taking my arm.

I looked over at her, but could not speak. I could only nod.

"Let's go over to the bench. I want to hear how Jake handled Nolan Scott."

"Where the hell did you get that code word, Agent!?"

"By doing my job!"

"You have no idea what you're getting into, Connors. There's going to be a huge change in our country."

"You people keep on saying that to us. Sharon Turner said the exact same thing."

Scott turned white. It seemed he didn't know what to do.

"When it all goes down, you'd better be on the right side."

There was a long, studied pause, as Scott attempted to bore a hole into Jake's skull with his eyes.

It took everything Jake had not to smirk. "Now *former* Assistant Director Scott, it's time to for you look at your wristwatch."

"What?"

"I just want you to remember the exact moment you were arrested for betraying your country."

"You're nuts! It's just your word against mine."

"You know what's nice about these new cell phones?" Jake asked, pulling his out of his shirt pocket. "They have such lovely digital recorders in them."

Scott looked terrified. He then launched himself at Jake, grabbing at the phone, trying to wrest it away. He punched Jake once, then went for his gun in his desk drawer.

Two good punches, and Jake drove him back and onto the floor. The noise brought Scott's assistant running through the door. She almost screamed at the sight.

"Get the director down here, now!" Jake yelled at her. "Nolan Scott, you are under arrest for treason."

As Jake read Scott his rights and a terrified assistant ran for the director, a shocked and cuffed Nolan Scott was thrown into a chair.

"Okay, Scott," Jake said as he took the clip out of Scott's pistol and ejected the chambered round. "You know what happens to traitors in prison; co-operation is your only hope. When does Pegasus go down?" he asked as the director came in.

"What the hell is going on here!?" Director Alex Stanton exclaimed.

"Just have a listen to this, Director," Jake said as he handed Stanton his phone.

After Stanton listened, he looked at Jake, and then at Scott, still not comprehending what was happening.

"First of all, Agent, who are you and what is happening?" Stanton asked as other senior agents filtered into the room.

Jake was in the middle of giving a brief explanation of the events when he heard a noise that stopped him mid-sentence. The sound of helicopter blades.

"Are those the president's helicopters?" he asked.

"Yes, Agent," Stanton replied. "Last ditch effort to stop the financial crisis. She's taking the House and Senate leaders to Camp David for a meeting to try to hammer out a deal."

"I didn't know."

"It was just announced last night. What's that got to do with anything?"

"The president is about to be assassinated!" Jake cried to a group of people who were starting to think he was crazy. Jake reached into his brief-case and handed the director a flash drive.

"What's this?" Stanton asked, looking incredulous.

"I know I must sound like a madman, but please, watch the video, I've got a call to make," he said, bringing up the contact list on his cell. As the others crowded around Nolan Scott's computer to watch McWilliams's murder and the roll-out of the Focke-Wolf 190, Jake called Peter Moore, a friend of his, at the Secret Service and briefed him. He then called Jim and notified him of the events of the morning.

"Director, I just notified the Secret Service. An agent over there told me he is issuing an immediate recall of the president's flight."

"Okay, Agent Connors. Mr. Scott here will be held while we finish the investigation. You and all your evidence are coming with me to the board-room for a full debriefing. I will give you one thing, Agent, you got big ones, coming up here like this. But I sure hope like hell you are wrong about any assassination."

Building 410 on Murray Drive in Washington contains the offices of the Secret Service. It was here Peter Moore sat staring at the telephone he had just hung up. He had questions, but no answers. How did Jake Connors know about Pegasus? If he knew, who else knew? Had their mission against the president been compromised?

'What to do next?' he thought as he glanced at the fluid lines of the 1963 split-window Corvette Stingray on his screensaver. He entered his code and password and sent an encrypted e-mail. He knew that by not sending out the recall to the president's flight, if things didn't go down the way they planned, he'd be a suspect in any investigation. It was best to get out of town. Pulling out the bottom drawer of his desk and turning it over, he extracted the manila envelope that was taped there. He quickly checked the passport and credit cards in the name of Alex Feldon it contained.

Next, he went back online to see how much money was in his offshore account. What he saw at first caused confusion, before terrifying him. There was nothing in the account. How could that be? He went to the transaction page, which showed $1,867, 211.82 had been transferred out the night before. Could that mean they were on to the plot?

Peter Moore took the picture of his wife and children off his desk and put it in his briefcase, along with the contents of the manila envelope, and left the building.

$$*\atop**$$

For Sharon Turner, the morning had been no less terrifying. They were flying an intercept course to the president's flight, but the way Ferdinand was flying, she was doubtful they would survive. She had flown low before, but nothing like this. They were under fifty feet most of the time, at just over two hundred miles per hour. They'd already gone under transmission lines and around trees.

Interception in 15 minutes and 30 seconds.

"In your low-speed, low-altitude maneuvering, I hope you've factored in the drag and weight factors of the ECM pod and missiles we're carrying," Sharon stated with no little apprehension in her voice.

All relevant factors accounted for.

"All relevant factors? Drag and weight are *very* relevant factors!" Sharon exclaimed. "As relevant as that silo we're rapidly approaching!" she added as Ferdinand deftly swung around it.

Your input is noted and relevance analyzed.

Sharon didn't know how to interpret Ferdinand's last comment, but at that moment, she didn't care. She was more concerned about the large broadcast antenna they were headed for.

For Captain Ashley Raymond, call sign "Bookmaker," this was not a day to be afraid while flying. She was 7,000 feet over the presidential flight, flying CAP on what they called a "milk run": the easy job of protecting the helicopters as they flew to Camp David. At her fingertips were 26,000 pounds of supersonic death and destruction known as the F-16D Fighting Falcon. The image of this aerodynamic beauty had graced the wall of Ashley's bedroom ever since she was twelve, when she took a vow to one day fly it. Her weapon systems officer, known as a WSO or "wizzo," occupied the rear seat. Lieutenant Fred Reynolds, call sign "Gadget," busied himself on the radar, hunting for anything that could prove a threat to the presidential flight. The only problem with this mission was the fact the helicopters' cruise speed was well below the stall speed of the Falcon, forcing Ashley to fly "lazy eights," covering a large area that allowed her to cross over the flight consistently.

As an Air Force pilot, Ashley could never state this publically, but she had great respect for the skill and courage of the Marine pilots and their three-person crews, who flew the president's helicopters. The expertise with which they executed the shell game formation, continually changing places so no attacker would know which helicopter contained the president, never failed to impress. The pilots also knew that if they were shot down, the option to eject out of their aircraft—which Ashley and her wizzo had—was not available for them.

"Well, it looks peaceful, Lieutenant. What's the word?" Ashley asked.

"No contacts, no electronic threats," Lieutenant Reynolds responded, not quite suppressing a yawn.

"Am I boring the Lieutenant this morning?"

"No, Captain. It's not that. This being an unscheduled last minute mission, I was, ah, how to put this …"

"Would 'previously occupied' best describe the situation?"

"Perfectly, Captain."

"Well, if it's any consolation, you weren't the only one," Ashley responded with a broad smile as she banked the Falcon back over the helicopter flight.

"Why haven't we heard the helicopters return?" Jake asked as he sat in the boardroom with Director Stanton and a group of senior agents, who were reviewing all the evidence he had brought.

"That's a very good question," Director Stanton responded as he pulled out his cell phone. He was quickly in touch with his counterpart at the Secret Service.

"You know nothing of a threat to the president!?" he cried. "She's about to be attacked by another aircraft with acoustic missiles, I repeat, acoustic missiles."

The call quickly ended.

"Agent Connors, who did you say you notified at the Secret Service?" Director Stanton asked.

"An old buddy, Peter Moore."

The Director turned away from Jake in deep thought, paused, and then voiced the thought of many in the room.

"Well, ladies and gentlemen, that begs the question: How deep does this thing run?"

One element not fully explored by Adrian Mandrake when he built Tallmadge and Ferdinand, but questioned by Jennifer, was the idea of discretion. As she'd pointed out, when one programmed artificial intelligence with discretion, it then had the ability to make mistakes. Ferdinand had lost track of the presidential flight. His mission was to find them. The solution to this problem was simple: gain altitude and turn on the radar; a task he completed so quickly that Sharon had no time to react.

The threat boards on all the helicopters and on Ashley's F-16 lit up like Christmas trees.

*
**

For George Grayson, the morning's flight had been very peaceful. His new noise suppression headphones had kept the loud throbbing of the big Rolls-Royce Merlin engine to a distant distraction, permitting the melodious strains of Mozart, emitting from his cell phone, to fill his ears, adding to the visual harmony of the sunrise. His bliss had been interrupted briefly by a phone call from Jim, telling him about Jake's adventures and the recall of the president's unscheduled flight. The story had disturbed George for two reasons. If they hadn't found out about the president's flight, she could have been assassinated. Second, there was another traitor in the FBI. But this was a beautiful morning to be flying. George had stayed clear of the Washington airspace, due to its restrictions, and kept flying north into Pennsylvania. Why he was flying this day, he still didn't know, but with the beautiful dawn, the musical accompaniment, and his *Lady Rachel*, George was at peace. Unfortunately, that peace came to an abrupt end as a familiar voice boomed through his headphones.

"This is Captain Ashley Raymond of the United States Air Force addressing aircraft squawking 4625. Please identify yourself, you are entering restricted airspace."

A big smile crossed George's lips.

"Is that my second-best student, pilot Ashley Raymond interrupting my flight?" George asked, which resulted in a long pause.

George had taken an instant liking to the teenage girl who'd hung around the airport and had always been willing to trade some broom time for stick time. Ashley was a natural pilot and soloed in record time. Her dream had been to go to the Air Force Academy. She'd worked hard at her studies, with George helping her. When she got accepted, George gave her a special gift, one he knew she wanted very much, but would never ask for. She was thrilled; he'd taught her to fly *Lady Rachel*.

"My God! Is that you, George Grayson? What are you doing up here?"

"My *Lady* here and I were enjoying the day until it was interrupted. What do you mean, restricted air space?"

"You're crowding a presidential flight to Camp David ..."

"I was told you were recalled!" George exclaimed. "Ashley, get those helicopters down, there's a threat from acoustic missiles!"

"We've just received an urgent alert, Captain," Lieutenant Reynolds stated, crackling over George's headphones. "Possible threat from an aircraft with acoustic missiles."

The presidential flight had not taken a direct route to Camp David, allegedly for security reasons. Their route had been carefully planned for them by Peter Moore to take them northeast of Camp David into Pennsylvania—and his trap. Here, they would turn southwest to end the journey they were not intended to complete. The plan was simple: bring them near a town where Chambersburg Road intersects York Road. Near a town which had already seen too much death and destruction in its history. Near a town that had already borne witness to the end of another view of America. Near a town where Sharon Turner and her Focke-Wulf 190 would rise and bring forth, for a few, their dreams of grandeur.

Gettysburg.

*
**

"How did you know about the threat, Judge Grayson?" Ashley exclaimed.

"I'll explain later, just get those choppers on the ground!"

The helicopters had received the same alert as Ashley and immediately started their defensive protocols: varying the pitch of their rotor blades to change their harmonics; randomly altering the speed of their engines to change their sound; all the while deploying acoustic decoys, as well as flares and chaff in case the missiles also utilized heat seekers and radar. They had also broken formation to spread their target area while trying to find a suitable place to land. It was at this point all their threat boards lit up.

"We've been lit up!" exclaimed Lieutenant Reynolds.

"I see the Focke-Wulf, Ashley, I'm going in!" George shouted.

Unfortunately, Ashley was miles away when the threat was detected, at the far point of her lazy eight. She was hurrying back, but cognizant of her speed, as she didn't want to overshoot her detail.

"Did he say Focke-Wulf, Captain?"

"Yes, he did. Do you have it on radar?"

"Just your friend's transponder track, he's still squawking 4625 and moving fast. What's his ride?"

"A P-51 Mustang."

"What!"

"You heard me, Lieutenant. Keep an eye out."

As George closed in on the Focke-Wulf, his heart leapt into his mouth. It launched all six of its missiles before his eyes.

"We have a missile launch, Captain!"

"Bookmaker to flight, missiles launched," Ashley announced, fighting to keep her voice as calm and professional as possible.

Major Max Blackwell, piloting Marine One, and his co-pilot didn't need the warning from Ashley; their threat boards had already told them they had incoming ordnance. In his hands that morning were the lives of his crew and his passengers: the president, Senator Treleaven, and a member of the Secret Service. To save their lives meant he would have to fly his Sea King to the edge of its operational envelope and beyond. For Major Blackwell, the second battle of Gettysburg had commenced.

For Sharon, the launching of the missiles by Ferdinand was the last straw; she reached over and turned him off. When Ferdinand found the helicopters, they had started their evasive maneuvers. He took this to mean he had been detected. His reaction was to fire off all the missiles without taking time to get a proper acoustic lock on any of them.

"Send a drone to do a fighter pilot's job, and this is the mess you get," she groused out loud, watching the missiles track in toward the helicopters—and miss. "Now I've got to do it the old-fashioned way," she added, flipping the arming switch for the cannons.

The missiles may have missed, but their proximity fuses worked, resulting in six large detonations, renting the air around the helicopters with shrapnel and concussions, almost knocking Marine One on her side. With the cyclic stick in his right hand and the collective/throttle in his left, Major Blackwell was about to confirm Ashley's observation about the skill of Marine pilots.

Shrapnel had blown out the windshields of Marine One, seriously wounding his co-pilot, Captain Jane Wilson. Major Blackwell had not been spared, suffering cuts to his arms and face. The Major didn't know it at the time, but the president and Senator Treleaven were shaken, but otherwise okay. Not so for Gino Deluca, the president's longest-serving Secret Service agent. The concussions had broken his seat away from the aircraft and thrown him across the cabin, breaking his legs and left arm. One of the Marines was trying to give him aid, but the pitching of the helicopter prevented any real help.

The screaming alarms told Major Blackwell his hydraulics were about to fail, which meant he had seconds to get the Sea King on the ground or lose all control of the aircraft. The farm field below would have to do. He managed to get the Sea King into a somewhat gentle spiral approach, but hovering wasn't going to happen.

Marine One bounced once into the soft, rain-soaked earth before digging in and going over on its right side, smashing three of its five rotor blades into the ground, before coming to rest near an old stone foundation.

"Please someone, save the president!" Gino called out.

"You're the one who needs help today, Gino!" the president said.

"Get clear, Ma'am! This thing could blow. Don't worry about me," Gino gasped.

"We will all get clear together."

"I need help up here!" yelled Major Blackwell.

Senator Treleaven was already on his feet, assessing the situation. The other two Marines were in good shape.

"Corporal, you help the Major with your co-pilot. Gunny, give me and the president a hand with Agent Deluca."

"Someone grab the first aid kit!"

A few minutes later, everyone had cleared the helicopter. Alternately carrying and dragging each other to the inside of the stone foundation, they were able to assess the needs of the wounded and make use of the extensive first aid kit carried by Marine One. Captain Wilson was badly injured, with cuts to her abdomen and possible internal injuries. As she leaned against the far wall, she took out her cell phone and turned on the video. She braced the phone on a small outcrop atop the wall, a small act which would have far-reaching consequences.

Agent Deluca was made as comfortable as possible on the ground as they waited for the rest of the flight to arrive.

The other two helicopters had made what could only be described as brilliant controlled crashes further down the field toward a road. The occupants were now hurrying to the ruin, some limping and two others being half-carried—but all alive.

"Just trying to raise Andrews, Madam President," Major Blackwell stated as he keyed his portable radio.

"Thank you, Major. I know I speak for all of us when I say outstanding job in getting us all down alive. I thank you."

The president noticed Major Blackwell was now in an animated conversation on the radio, which ended with him looking ashen.

"Is there a problem, Major?"

"Madam President. It's Andrews. They say they're under attack."

"Battle is an orgy of disorder."

—George S. Patton

CHAPTER 18

It was supposed to be a regular shift in the Control Tower at Joint Base Andrews for Captain John Wheeler. He was just a couple sips into his morning coffee when all hell broke loose.

First, there was the emergency message to recall the presidential flight due to a threat. Now he was getting frantic calls from the CAP and the helicopters saying they were under attack, from what was described as a Focke-Wulf 190. To add to the confusion, the attacking plane was now supposedly in a dogfight with a P-51 Mustang. He'd just gotten on the phone to the base commander to try to explain all this, when he got a glimpse of what he thought was a descending flock of birds. He only realized they weren't birds when large pieces of concrete were blown from the center of both his runways. With that, emergency horns started to scream as security personal scrambled for weapons.

"What the hell is going on down there, Captain?!" General Thompson barked into his phone.

"Our runways have just been taken out by what I believe was a mortar attack."

"Can we launch aircraft?"

"Not a chance, sir, the craters are too large."

"What CAP do we have over the president?"

"A single F-16 and a P-51 Mustang."

" … and a what?"

"A P-51 Mustang, sir. The famous fighter that served in World War II and Korea—"

"I know what a Mustang is, Captain! What is it doing in my Air Force!?"

"At last report, it was in a dogfight with the Focke-Wulf 190."

"What Focke-Wulf 190!?"

"The one that launched the acoustic air-to-air missiles at the president."

There was a long pause. "Okay, Captain. Here's what we do," General Thompson said slowly, with no little exasperation. "Get our choppers to the president. They don't need runways; I want her safe now! Then I want every piece of earth-moving equipment we have and everyone who can carry a shovel to meet me at the runways. I want to see F-16s rolling down at least one runway in minutes. This command will not fail its Commander-in-Chief!"

*
**

"Madam President, we have three badly wounded," Senator Clayton reported. Besides being the senate minority leader, Joan Clayton was also a doctor. "I hope help is coming soon. Captain Wilson especially needs medical attention; I fear internal bleeding. Representative Gilmore is a physician, and Representative Hernandez used to be corpsman; we're doing all we can."

"Thank you all for your efforts, Senator. Major Blackwell, what's the word from Andrews?"

"They're sending helicopters, but no jets. The runways have been bombed. They've tried to call local authorities to help us, but all the local phone and electricity is out."

"You can add the cell towers to the list. Three of us have tried our cells, no signal," Gunny responded. "Can anyone here get a cell connection?" he yelled, only to be greeted by shaking heads.

"I can't even get any radio stations on my iPod," one of the Marines added.

"Lucky my portable is on a dedicated satellite. Not only can I talk to Andrews, I can talk to the CAP," Major Blackwell stated.

"It seems like someone went to a lot of trouble to put you here, Madam President," Senator Treleaven observed.

"Major, what's going on up there?" Gunny asked, looking skyward. "Are those what I think they are?"

"A P-51 Mustang and a German Focke-Wulf 190," Major Blackwell said in bewilderment.

"We may have some problems here, Culper," Gaston said, glancing over e-mail communications received at their second safe house.

"We have a bigger problem here," Culper answered, pacing the floor and pointing to his monitor. He'd been following Ferdinand's flight through its onboard cameras.

"He just pulled up, turned on his radar, and salvoed his missiles."

"Did he hit anything?"

"Just banged them up. Turner's going in for a gun kill now ... What the hell was that!?"

*
**

During this second battle of Gettysburg, there would be no horrible blood-letting as there had been in the Devil's Den or at the Bloody Angle in 1863, but the combat would still be from another age. For what Ashley and those on the ground were about to witness would be the last true dogfight in history, where the outcome would be decided not by who had the better electronic weapon systems and computers, but by who was the better fighter pilot.

George bore down on Sharon Turner and Ferdinand just as she turned to attack what—although neither she nor George knew at the time—was Marine One. As Major Blackwell fought to stay airborne, Sharon lined him up in her sight. She was about to pull the trigger when six streams of tracers sailed over her canopy. She immediately banked left and started to climb as George and *Lady Rachel* shot past.

"Goddamn it," he said out loud, cursing the fact he hadn't been able to sight in his guns earlier. "We're shooting high, my Lady."

George used the momentum from his dive to gain height and turn towards an astonished Sharon as she pulled Ferdinand into a tight turn to see her opponent. Sharon turned Ferdinand on.

"I want to talk to the P-51. Get me on the same radio frequency."

Done, Ferdinand responded as Sharon pulled into another sharp turn with George. They were now like two boxers circling a ring, waiting for the other to throw the first punch.

"Well, Jim, I see your lady got her claws back," Sharon transmitted in a voice riddled with derision.

"Wrong on two points, Sharon. Wrong pilot, wrong Lady. But it is the right day for you to die."

"Don't tell me this is George Grayson! What, they let you out of the nursing home today?"

"I'm not here to trade barbs with you, Sharon. Drop your landing gear and follow us back to Andrews, or I will kill you. Do me a favor Sharon; please say no."

"My God, Captain," Lieutenant Reynolds stated. "This guy sounds tough."

"This is so out of character for him," Ashley replied. "I've never heard him talk like this."

George was in a black place now. A place he thought he'd left in Korea, back in '53, at 17,000 feet, somewhere south of the Yalu River. George did not like that place. But in order to get this job done, he knew that was where he had to be.

"All communications have been blocked out in and around Gettysburg, and our ground team knocked out Andrews," Gaston reported. "That should give Sharon enough time to finish the job and get out of there," he added.

"Not the way she's going," Culper complained. "Some guy she knows has got her into a dogfight."

"Well, George, you talk tough for an old man; still think you can deliver the goods?"

"Sharon, you are a murderer, a traitor, and a cowardly assassin. The woman you tried to kill today I consider a daughter. That makes this personal. So c'mon, Sharon, do you know how to face a real fighter pilot? Or is striking from the weeds all you can do? Too cowardly to face a man that's over twice your age?"

The eyes of all those on the ground turned to the president as these words emitted from Major Blackwell's radio. The deep emotion they caused reflected on her face and moved all those who witnessed it.

"George, it's not your fight!" she exclaimed.

"He sounds like a brave man. Was he in the Air Force?" Major Blackwell asked.

"He's Judge George Grayson. Fighter ace in the Korean War. My mentor."

"It's his fight, Madam President," Senator Treleaven said as he put his arm around the president's shoulders. "We all took the same oath. It doesn't end the day you hang up your uniform."

*
**

"Goddamn it, I can't get a lock on her plane," Lieutenant Reynolds complained. "It's like she's not there. She must be packing some kind of powerful ECM gear."

"We couldn't shoot anyway, they're too close," Ashley stated as she fought to keep her Falcon from stalling at the low speed she was flying in order to observe the two combatants.

"How good is this guy, Captain?"

"He's in a league of his own."

The words were barely out of her mouth when Sharon executed a fast starboard roll accompanied by a quick burst from her cannons. George read the maneuver perfectly. He pulled his stick into the four o'clock position, bottoming his left rudder and snap-rolled *Lady Rachel* out of the way of the blast.

"My God! Did you see that, Captain!" Lieutenant Reynolds exclaimed.

"You bet I did," Ashley replied with a smile. She depressed her transmit button. "Take her down, George; we've got your back."

George now fire-walled the throttle. He was determined to kill the monstrosity that had invaded his home, his country, and threatened his family. He knew he needed altitude to win this day. As Sharon recovered from her overshoot, George put *Lady Rachel* into a steep climb.

"Really, is that the best you can do? Didn't they teach you anything in the Air Force, or did you take a correspondence course?"

Sharon's response was a string of profanity.

"Language, please Sharon. You are in the presence of my *Lady Rachel.*"

The people listening in on these exchanges were amused by George's taunting, but the pilots knew it was having the effect he wanted. Sharon was getting mad. She hated George Grayson and what she perceived as his arrogance. It was the same condescending attitude she'd faced when she was one of the few women in the Air Force: never equal to the guys, and always had to be twice as good to be considered half as worthy. But in the fog of combat, she'd forgotten one important lesson. The person who cannot control their emotions in a dogfight dies.

George kept on climbing. He knew one of the great advantages of height in a dogfight was that it could always be transferred into speed by diving. And that was just what he did. He rolled *Lady Rachel* onto her back and pulled the stick into his gut, putting her into a dive, then pulled her out, having executed a perfect split-S maneuver, bringing him right onto Sharon's tail. Sharon snap-rolled so George couldn't get a shot. She then ejected the ECM pod to reduce drag and give her more speed.

"Incoming!" Gunny yelled to everyone on the ground as he observed what appeared to be a bomb falling from the Focke-Wulf.

They all ducked, crowding as close to the wall of the ruin as possible. Two of the Secret Service agents jumped on top of the President to give the added protection of their bodies. The ECM unit fell harmlessly into the woods behind them.

"New rule!" the president announced as she got up. "No more jumping on top of the president for the rest of this mission. I appreciate the gesture, but do you have any idea how much it costs to have mud and grass stains removed from a Jillian Armond dress suit?" she added, drawing a much-needed laugh from all those present.

George now used the momentum of his dive to climb again. Sharon had lost some altitude with her snap-roll. She correctly surmised George was going to loop over and come at her again. As he did, she turned into him and let loose with the superior firepower of her 20-millimeter cannons. George dropped under her, forcing her shots over *Lady Rachel*. He then used his speed to pull up into a half-loop, followed by a half-roll, bringing him upright, placing himself exactly where he wanted to be—above and behind Sharon, the coveted six o'clock position. George pulled the trigger, trying to compensate for his faulty gun sight, only to find his shots falling low, much to his frustration.

Sharon interpreted the miss another way.

"So, you're toying with me, are you? You sonovabitch," she spat into her microphone.

"Somewhat the same as you did with Samantha Stevens. I thought you'd enjoy it."

Sharon deftly snapped rolled the 190 while pulling a hard left turn, effectively switching places with George as she now bore down on his six o'clock with *Lady Rachel* square in her sight.

What happened next would leave those on the ground stunned, Lieutenant Reynolds practically jumping out of his F-16 with excitement, and Ashley laughing. George pulled off a maneuver that most pilots had not even heard about let alone execute with the skill he demonstrated that day. He again pulled the stick back fully while bottoming his rudder. This caused *Lady Rachel* to stall and drop like a stone (and George to bang his head into the canopy), while the full rudder pointed her nose down. The torque from the big Hamilton-Standard propeller caused *Lady Rachel* to spin counter-clockwise until George neutralized the effect by slamming the stick forward, then back to neutral. From Sharon's perspective, the Mustang she had dead in her sights had instantly vanished.

George pulled *Lady Rachel* into another climb and was surprised to find Sharon was following him up. Judging by the profanity that was streaming into his headphones, Sharon was now totally enraged by what she perceived as George's attempts to humiliate her. She had, in fact, fallen into his trap. He'd gotten Sharon to take the fight into the vertical with him.

As they climbed into the deep blue sky of that March day, they were almost cockpit to cockpit as they turned around each other—a waltz to the tune of the two greatest engines of their era working at maximum—pulling two of the greatest fighter planes into the element they each claimed was theirs alone.

Sharon didn't realize George had her just where he wanted her.

George's knowledge of fighter planes of that era was almost encyclopedic. As they climbed, the speed of both aircraft was dropping. Both aircraft would stall. The only question was which one would stall first. The one that stalled first would plummet until the aircraft gained speed again and the pilot brought it under control. The period of time it took to accomplish this was critical, as during this period, the stalling plane was at the mercy of its opponent. George knew the stalling speed of the Focke-Wulf 190 was almost thirty miles-per-hour higher than the Mustang's, and that the stall came on without warning.

George was watching his airspeed get close to the 130 miles-per-hour mark when it happened. The Focke-Wulf fell over on its port side and started to tumble. It was all the time George needed. He kicked the left rudder and brought all six guns to bear. Then he pulled the trigger. Sharon's canopy blew off, as did the cowling around the engine. George could see Sharon struggling to regain control of her plane as it tumbled all the way down.

Sharon Turner's life ended in a pile of flaming wreckage beside the road to the horror, and relief, of all those in the presidential flight who witnessed it. As she'd tumbled toward the ground, Sharon had time to realize that she'd been defeated.

"She lost Gaston! She lost!" Culper yelled. "Where the hell did that other fighter come from!? Pegasus was perfect, how could this happen?!"

He whirled on Gaston. "What's the ETA on the helicopters from Andrews?"

"Fifteen minutes tops," replied Gaston.

"Runway repair?"

"About the same."

"Just enough time for the ground team. Send them in."

The black smoke from the crash site obscured them at first: two Humvees, one behind the other, bursting through the smoke onto the field and heading toward the ruin. At first, it was thought rescue was at hand. Then they noticed that both vehicles had mounted machine guns on their roofs. Any doubt was soon erased as they opened fire at the ruin, sending everyone scurrying behind the wall.

"Quick, Madam President, we have a better chance in the woods," one of the Secret Service agents said. "That goes for you Congress members as well."

"Yeah, get going, we'll hold'em," Major Blackwell added.

"I'm not leaving my people and running into the woods! Who's got an extra pistol?" the president cried.

"Right here, Madam President," Agent Deluca said, offering up his Glock. "Do you mind getting my spare out of my ankle holster? Just in case you miss," he added with a weak smile as he took his spare pistol from the president and held it at his side, determined to defend her and others to the last shot.

"And Madam President," he said as she turned to leave. "It's been an honor and a privilege to serve the president. Now go make me proud."

With those words, President Kathleen Angelina Galbraith, Forty-Sixth President of the United States, took her place on the wall.

"I learned that courage was not the absence of fear, but the triumph over it. The brave man is not he who does not feel afraid, but he who conquers that fear."

—Nelson Mandela

CHAPTER 19

It was a perfect day for flying, and the Hanson men plus Emily Proctor, had taken full advantage of it. Arriving mid-morning at the Fenton Airport, Jim, Robert, Jason, and Emily were surprised to find that George and *Lady Rachel* were not there. Jim was about to call him, when Jake called to relate the events about his appointment at the FBI. After explaining the events to the others, Jim called George and was happy to find him enjoying a flight with *Lady Rachel*. He briefed him on Jake's call before taking Robert for a flight in *Dolly Girl*. Jason, in the meantime, showed Emily the finer points of the Stearman before taking her for a ride in the 1930s masterpiece to show her the fun of open cockpit flying and that two wings are better than one.

They arrived back about noon to find everyone in the restaurant crowded around the bar watching the television, which was reporting on the attack at Joint Base Andrews. The talking heads were in full speculative fervor with no facts but plenty of theories.

"Obviously a terrorist attack ..."

"Was it foreign or domestic terrorists?"

"Is this yet another failure of this administration?"

"Do other countries see our president as a sign of American weakness?"

"Are you thinking what I'm thinking, Dad?" Jason asked.

"Yeah. Could this be part of Pegasus?"

"Breaking news! There are reports that the president's helicopter flight has not arrived at Camp David as scheduled."

"What's going on? I thought the flight was recalled?" Emily asked.

"Reports are saying a large contingent of Marines was seen earlier boarding helicopters and flying north from Joint Base Andrews. There is speculation that the presidential flight has crashed."

"What's going on, Jimmy? Was the president in a crash?" Robert asked with great concern.

"We don't know yet. I'm calling Jake," Jim replied as he pulled up his contact list on his cell. He headed outside to get a better signal.

A few minutes later, a worried-looking Jim was back with a report.

"Jake said they're getting spotty info, but the president's flight is down somewhere near Gettysburg. A plane launched missiles at them, but it sounds like they're all alive on the ground. But here's where it gets interesting: the plane that launched the missiles is in a dogfight with a Mustang. I wonder who that could be?" Jim asked with a wry smile, drawing up his contact list again.

*
**

"Okay, let's make these bastards bleed!" the president yelled as Senator Treleaven, the small group of Marines, and the Secret Service agents opened up with their collection of pistols, augmented by three M4 carbines, at the lead Humvee, as Senator Clayton and her two colleagues tended to the wounded. Clayton made her way over to Captain Wilson, who, despite her injuries, had gotten her pistol out as she leaned against the wall. She reached out and pulled the senator close, yelling the best she could into the senator's ear, trying to be heard above the shooting.

"When they get close, grab the president and the others and get into the woods. We'll hold'em so you can get away."

The senator didn't know how to react to the courage of this young Marine. She sat there against the wall, in great pain, weak from her injuries, holding her pistol, ready to take on the first person to come over it.

"I don't leave my patients," Clayton said at last.

"I'm a Marine. It's my job to protect you." She glanced over the wall. "Better get going."

"We're all Marines today, Captain! And we never leave one behind. *Semper Fi.*"

The second Humvee was having trouble transiting a particularly rough part of the muddy field and had fallen well behind the first, which was now bearing down on the ruin. The president and her group were concentrating their fire on the machine gunner in the first vehicle. The Marine beside the president cried out as bullets tore into his side and shoulder, throwing him to the ground. The president immediately went to his aid.

"Don't worry, Madam President! We got him!" Senator Clayton said.

Seeing a comrade so badly hurt was all Kathleen could stand. She was angry; she was furious. She grabbed up his carbine, expertly loaded a new clip, and stood up to the horror of all present.

"Madam President!"

"Get down!"

"You bastards want a piece of me, want to hurt my people?! Well, c'mon! Bring it!"

All those behind the wall stood and let loose a vicious volley of fire that killed the machine gunner and two of the occupants that had leapt out the back of the Humvee to try to flank their position.

Some would later say they felt her presence before they turned to look over their shoulders. But all would agree on two points: *Lady Rachel* was so low even the gophers ducked, and the second, her wings looked as if they were on fire as her six guns turned the lead Humvee and its occupants into a smoldering pile of debris.

"I have cleared the range; the target is yours, Ashley."

"That's a roger."

"Target is locked, Captain. Guns at your discretion."

When Ashley pulled the trigger, she woke up the monster that usually slumbered quietly inside the left part of the fuselage of her F-16. The six barrels of this beast, known as a Vulcan cannon, were arranged in a circular formation, which started to spin once the trigger was pulled. The sound it made was that of a loud chainsaw as it delivered a hundred rounds of 20-millimeter cannon fire per second on its target.

The second Humvee simply vaporized.

The president's group stood there for a few moments, dumbfounded by what they had just witnessed.

"I never thought I would say this," mused Major Blackwell. "I like the Air Force."

"Bite your tongue there, Marine," stated Senator Treleaven with a smile.

The percussion of helicopter blades signaled the arrival of help for the valiant who had stood with their president, the first being a Sea King from the presidential detail. A young captain disembarked and ran toward the president.

"I think this one is for you, Madam President," Major Blackwell said as the captain saluted the president, who was still holding her carbine.

"Madam President, I have orders to take you immediately back to Washington."

"Captain ..." The president looked at the name on his tunic. "Johnston. As you can see, we have wounded here. They go first!"

"But Madam President, I have my orders."

"Look here! I am the Commander-in-Chief. I give the orders. I want you to make sure all our wounded are on the helicopters and on their way to Bethesda Naval Hospital, or you will be Private Johnston by morning!" she demanded as the others turned away to hide their laughter.

"Yes, Madam President," the stunned captain said as he saluted and made his exit.

"Does the president still need her carbine?" Gunny asked.

The president adeptly removed the clip and ejected the chambered round.

"Could've used you at Paris Island, Ma'am," Gunny remarked as he took the weapon from her.

"Nah, I'm too lenient."

They lifted Captain Wilson onto a stretcher, but not before she retrieved her cell phone.

"I'm going with her, Madam President," Senator Clayton stated.

"Thank you for your service this day, Senator."

"No. Thank you, Madam President," she replied, then headed toward the chopper.

They were now loading Agent Deluca on a stretcher, which drew the president to his side. The Marines and the Secret Service agents watched the president slid his pistol back into the holster under his arm, then hugged him.

"She's quite the lady," Major Blackwell commented.

"Yes, she is," Senator Treleaven replied. "Now we all have another duty to perform," he added, addressing all those present. "To find out who wanted the president dead so badly they'd go to the trouble of orchestrating all of this."

" He had the courage of the early dawn."

—Arthur Bishop, on his father, Word War I ace Billy Bishop

CHAPTER 20

"**D**irective 18, Gaston?" Culper asked solemnly.

"I don't see how we have any other choice. They'll have every level of policing, from Homeland Security, to the FBI and all the local forces, looking for us."

"What location do you think is best?"

"We can't go back to Andorra," Gaston stated emphatically, drawing a questioning look from Culper. "As I tried to mention earlier, we've been receiving urgent e-mails from Andorra. The name 'International Predictive Analytics' seems to be on the lips of quite a few people—some of the cartels, certainly. Someone's slipped our information to them; people have been calling, looking for money that was transferred from their accounts to ours."

"How much money are we talking?"

"Over two trillion US dollars."

"You can't be serious, Gaston."

"The funds were transferred to our accounts. Then they transferred out, along with all of our cash, and moved."

"What! All of our cash is gone? To where?"

"Unknown at this time."

"This is incredible. To pull that off would require super-computing power. They would need ..."

Culper and Gaston stood staring at each other as they shared the same thought.

"We don't have time to investigate this now, Gaston. Get Tallmadge some place safe. We'll analyze everything later. As for now, it is a full Directive

18 retreat. That, as you know, means all records go with us. And for those that may know too much, but are expendable, full sanction."

"Where do we go?"

Culper thought for a moment before answering. Gaston could see he was acting true to form: not panicking, considering all the options.

"For the New Life group, tell them to meet at the Fenton Airport now. I'll provide location once they're airborne. Less chance of a leak."

"I noticed you said 'they're' not 'we.'"

Culper turned away for moment, thinking, before he turned back to Gaston with a smile.

"Yes, Gaston, that is correct. You, Darien, and I aren't going."

"What are you saying, Culper? They'll hunt us down in no time," Gaston argued, feeling that knot form in his stomach again.

"We'll be okay here for a while. I'm not giving up on the United States quite yet."

Gaston could see there was no point in arguing further; he had his own plans for escape if necessary.

*
**

"Bookmaker to *Lady Rachel*, I think you're light a wingman."

George looked to his right to see an F-16 flying there as they headed toward Andrews, where the runways were again open.

"I'll probably need the services of a wingman more when we land than now. Your bosses are going to want to know what an armed P-51 was doing over Pennsylvania this morning."

"Frankly, George, so do I," Ashley replied.

At that moment, Jim's call came in. After George finished his conversation, he thought for a moment, before hitting the transmit button.

"Ashley, both you and your wizzo deserve an explanation, but let's save it for Andrews. In the meantime, thank you both for having my back."

"Anything for the second-best flight instructor I ever had," was the response George heard in his headphones.

*
**

"I joked with you earlier that your accomplishments at being 'first' were more than being just the first woman president. Well, your latest 'first' is more serious. The first sitting president to lead troops in combat."

"I could've done without that one," the president replied as she knelt down and placed a coin on the headstone of Audie Murphy's grave.

"But could the nation?"

She turned around quickly to fix me with those all-seeing blue eyes, which seemed to always perceive more than they were prepared to reveal, as she walked toward me.

"You'll have to explain that one, Jim."

"The political capital of Captain Wilson's video will be incredible. And don't try to tell me no one has thought of that."

I watched as her eyes narrowed. She turned, shook her head, and walked back toward Audie Murphy's grave.

"There was no video for him the day he jumped up on that burning tank destroyer and saved his men's lives, was there, Jim?" she said, nodding toward the grave. "And none for thousands of others that lie here, including your dad."

She paused, staring at the grave, as she gathered her thoughts.

"It always comes down to politics, doesn't it, Jim? Our government is always in two modes," she remarked as she walked toward me again. "Running for an election or preparing for the next one. If something big goes down, we ask 'how do we capitalize on it?' If negative, 'how do we blame it on the other guy?' It's no wonder so many Americans are sick and tired of the Washington political scene."

"Amen to that, Madam President."

"So, Jim, how do I market for political gain the fact that four members of Congress, nine Marines, and three members of the Secret Service were willing to stand by their president in a filthy little field in Pennsylvania? That they were willing to die with her rather than run for their lives, as anyone with any common sense would've done?"

"I know what you're saying, but the nation needs you to play this card. Your second term is all but guaranteed. My little group has ferreted out some of the bad guys, but there're probably more. You have the political capital now to put through the changes you wanted to when you first came here: to curtail the influence of the lobbyists, to change investment rules, to create more security for our elderly, to ensure good care for our veterans, and to guarantee a chance for a proper education for our young. No president has ever had an opportunity like this. It's not about political gain; it's about recovering the republic and doing right by the people."

I knew what I was going to say next might cause a problem.

"A chance to undo the influence of organizations such as Patriots for a New Democracy."

The president walked over to the pathway and stood with her back to me as I sat, waiting for a response. Her head was down, hands in her pockets, shoulders slumped in the silence that only deep concentration brings. The sounds of the birds, the rustling of the leaves in the cool breeze disturbed the solemnity of the moment, but not her thoughts. Finally, she turned and faced me.

"Well, Jim, what I am about to tell you might make me just another dirty politician in your eyes."

"If I thought that, I would not be here talking to you and the Culper Ring would not have wanted you dead. The fact they did tells me you must have been doing something right."

The president fixed me with a questioning gaze as she processed my response. She shook her head as she walked over to my dad's squadron memorial and ran her hands over top as if seeking guidance from the marble.

"Jim, it is time I told you a story; one of forlorn hope and naïvety."

I remained silent as I waited for her to gather her thoughts.

"After I was nominated and the campaign began, we were trailing in the polls. There was rumbling in the ranks; people began wondering if nominating a woman candidate was a good idea. Money was getting harder to raise. Then these ads started to appear in all the media supporting us. You probably remember how slick they were, very expensive. So who was our benefactor? As you know, Patriots for a New Democracy is a super-PAC."

"Didn't you check into them to see who was behind them?"

"As much as we could, but as you know, with a super-PAC, finding out who is contributing is tough. Besides, were we going to look a gift horse in the mouth, especially when our numbers were climbing?"

"So you looked the other way."

"Let's say I deluded myself into thinking Patriots for a New Democracy were a bunch of good solid citizens who shared my political point of view."

"When did you get the wake-up call?"

"When I went to table the *Financial and Investment Act*. There was pressure from within my own party to water it down. I especially got a lot of heat from Smithton. This led to a heated discussion one night in the Oval Office. At one point he said, ' … you have to look after those who got you here …' My vice president had flashed his hand. I should have asked for his resignation then and there. Might have stopped the murder of Samantha."

"You can't be thinking like that."

"Yeah, Jim? Try not to."

I could see she was very troubled.

"Please sit with me again, Madam President."

She joined me and we shared the silence for a few moments before she spoke. "You know Jim, if I could bring the reforms you mentioned, I'd sell my soul. Unfortunately, there's one reality staring us in the face: all great programs have a price tag. Remember why we were going to Camp David in the first place? The debt keeps rising, Jim; we're broke."

She paused. "Why are you smiling?"

"Because I am pleased to inform the President that the United States of America isn't broke. It has no national debt and, of course, will soon have a balanced budget. No, Madam President, you don't have to look at me that way; the men in white coats aren't needed."

"You had me worried for a minute, Jim. Please explain," she said, laughing. "I can see you just can't wait to tell me!"

I found myself laughing as well because she was right.

"You've lost a lot of sleep over this financial crisis, haven't you?" I said, noting the strain on her face once again.

"I sure have. It's crippling everything. Every program is suffering."

"The president can sleep well tonight," I said, taking her hand. "The Culper Ring had been gathering and hoarding gold for over two hundred years. They had it stashed all over the world, but their biggest deposits are right here in the United States. Dom has been quietly confirming the locations that Tallmadge kindly supplied to us. We've been keeping this mission secret, because if it came out that there was this much gold out there, it would collapse that market; one we need nice and healthy so we can quietly sell the gold at the best price to get America out of its debt."

The president was just looking at me, as though she could not comprehend my words.

"Just how much gold are we talking about?"

"We don't have any final numbers yet, but it will be thousands of tons. Enough to fill that great void called Fort Knox."

"So you know about our little problem there."

"I figured there was a reason it hasn't been audited since 1954."

"I'm starting to see why you say money doesn't really exist; there really is nothing behind our currency."

"Well, we now have a chance to do something about it before Bitcoin becomes the reserve currency of the world."

The president suddenly let go of my hand, sat back, and took a deep breath. I waited for her to say something, but she remained silent.

"You appear to be in deep thought, Madam President."

"We should call the men in white coats—not for you, but for me. My God, Jim, thousands of tons of gold! I don't know if I want to even hear the answer to this next question. But judging from that big smile on your face, it's going to be a beauty, so here it goes. 'Do tell me, James. How do we integrate all this newfound wealth into our economy, while keeping it a secret, so as not to collapse the gold market, and without getting me impeached or my whole administration thrown in jail?'"

"Oh, so you don't want to be impeached or go to jail. That could be tough then," I answered with a straight face.

There was a moment of silence before we both started to laugh.

"Okay, Madam President, here's how we do it. We keep running Pegasus. It's an excellent plan, except for that part where you were supposed to get killed," I stated drawing a grin and a nod from her. "There are now some offshore banks that are very light on capital, thanks to our little money transfer. I'm sure they would be more than happy to help us, in the strictest of confidence of course, to unload gold for Chinese-held treasury bills, as well as other discrete transactions. Think of it as your version of Iran-Contra."

The president was on her feet in a second. She took a couple of steps forward, then turned around. She had the same look on her face as she had in the video when she picked up the carbine.

"Red alert everyone, Dad just said something wrong again," Jason announced as he looked down the path. "And she's mad!"

"That nephew of mine never did learn the meaning of the word discretion, did he?" George observed.

"Have any of the Hanson men?" asked Dolly, as everyone looked at Jason.

"When have I ever said anything … yeah, point taken."

"Madam President, I think language like that is very un-presidential."

"I don't give a damn about being presidential, you jerk! What are you thinking? Dealing with offshore crooks and gangsters!"

"Perhaps a little harsh on the description."

"How would you describe them!?"

"Economic facilitators adhering to an alternate ethical standard."

"Always with the jokes! Well, guy, I guess it's time we broke this up. Thank you for your service to your country," she said as she turned to walk away.

"Not good enough, Madam!" I was mad now and she was going to know it.

"It will have to do."

"No, it won't. We took casualties out here to give you this opportunity to fix the country. We just buried one. They deserve better! My father deserves better. His sacrifice has to count for something more," I said, almost choking up again.

The president stopped, pausing for a moment. She turned around and faced me.

"Look, Jim, I am very sorry about your father's accident, but ..."

"Accident, Madam President? It was no accident. That was just our cover story," I stated, drawing another look of confusion on her face. "You really don't know what happened that day at the airport, do you? Sit with me again; you need to hear this."

The Hansons decided to have lunch at the airport and watch the news, periodically checking in with George. Finally, George picked up, to Jim's great relief. George briefly filled him in on the events of the morning. To spare Robert any concern, Jim told the others that George was just out for a flight and would back soon. Jason and Emily could see there was more to the story, but didn't let on. As the meal progressed, Jim noticed the airport was getting busier, with more people arriving. Most of them were carrying suitcases as well as briefcases.

"Is something special going on here today, Dad?" Jason asked. "It seems more crowded than usual."

"I was just thinking the same thing," Jim responded, glancing around. Then it hit him.

"I recognize some of these people," he whispered, leaning forward and lowering his voice. "Some of them are from the New Times head office."

"Why would they be here?" Emily asked.

The question was answered by the sound of jet engines.

Fenton Regional Airport did not get many fancy executive aircraft dropping in for a visit. Cessnas, Pipers, and other recreational airplanes made up most of their guest list. So when a Henderson-Cooper Lightning was cleared for landing, people at the airport took notice. The Lightning was beautiful to watch as it touched down. An engine was cradled under each of its swept-back wings. A "V" tail and two small canard wings up front completed its stiletto-shaped design.

"She's something else," Jason commented as it rolled up the runway.

"I've been following its development in the aviation press. I knew a few were out, but this is the first I've seen," Jim commented as he stood up for a better look. "But I can only think of one reason for it being here today."

The Lightning was more than just a luxurious twelve-passenger executive jet. It was cutting-edge technology. It was first of a new class of airplane called silent supersonics or S-3s for short. It could fly at twice the speed of sound, or over 1,200 miles-per-hour, depending on how one wanted to measure speed, but without leaving a sonic boom in its wake. That meant New York to Los Angeles in less than two hours, without waking up anyone on the ground. With its 4,600-mile range, it could take you almost anywhere in a hurry. After landing, the Lightning sat out on the tarmac, idling.

"I'm calling Jake. You call Dom, Jason," Jim instructed.

"What do I tell him?"

"The bad guys are buggering off!"

"No need for anyone at this table to be using their phones right now. Just hand them over," Ted ordered, one hand in his sport coat pocket, which clearly showed the imprint of a gun muzzle.

"A gun in your coat pocket, Bayden? Looks like a scene from a bad detective movie," Jim responded, sliding his and Jason's cells over the table. "You think you're really going to use that thing in a crowded airport with all these witnesses?"

"Actually, more like a scene from one of the classics: the airport scene in Casablanca, Ralphie-boy. Only this time, I'm the director. And yes, I will use this thing if I have to. I just have to make it to that jet."

"So all the rats are fleeing the sinking ship," Jim commented.

"I prefer to think of it as a tactical redeployment."

Robert had been watching the events unfold, not fully understanding everything. Now he spoke. "Jimmy, the people going out to that jet—are they some of the people that tried to hurt us?"

"Yes, they all are, Dad."

"Ted. You were our friend."

Ted just looked at Robert. He had nothing to say.

"Unfortunately, Dad, Ted loves money more. Tell me, Ted, is it all worth it?"

"For what's waiting for me offshore, you bet. You could've been a part of all this, but you are such a Boy Scout. Now we're just going to sit here for a few minutes and play nice until Sharon flies in, and then I'll be off."

"Might be a long wait, Ted."

Ted fixed Jim with a cold, hard stare, one that asked the obvious question.

"She dug a hole in Pennsylvania this morning."

"And you would know that how?"

Jim now realized he'd said too much. Fortunately, his father would save his son from this awkward situation. Robert stood up and left the table.

"What the hell! You come back here ..." Ted quickly realized he was attracting attention and stopped speaking.

"He can't harm you, Ted. Leave him alone!" exclaimed Jim.

"Okay, here's the deal," Ted stated. "Ten people are now walking toward the jet. We're gonna join them. Any false moves ... well, you know how that one goes."

Jim, Jason, and Emily stood up from the table and started toward the door. They were soon outside, where the noise of the idling jet engines drowned out all other sounds, even a very unique one. It was a sound known only to the few who loved and respected great aircraft. It was the sound of a Rolls-Royce Merlin engine coughing to life. The size and placement of the executive jet prevented Jim from seeing *Dolly Girl* taxi out of her hangar and speed down the north-south runway and into the clear Virginia sky.

"This is where we say goodbye, Ralph," Ted yelled above the sound of the engines. "Just like in the cartoons, Sam always won," he added as he dropped their cells on the tarmac, turned, and ran up the stairs into the jet.

"Where's Sharon?" Janice asked Ted, as she sat in the pilot's seat.

"Hanson claims she crashed."

"What!" Janet yelled as the sound of an arriving text emitted from her cell phone. She composed herself and checked it.

"It's from Culper. It gives us our destination coordinates," she said as he punched them into the navigational computer. "It also confirms Sharon's not coming." She bit her lip.

Janice taxied the Lightning out to the end of the runway as Ted's cell indicated the arrival of a text.

Best check the balance in that offshore account, Sam.

As the Lightning roared down runway and lifted off, Ted went online to find his account was empty.

"That son of a—" was about as far as he got before he and everyone else on the plane died.

The Lightning had just gotten its wheels up when *Dolly Girl*, with Captain Robert E. Hanson, United States Air Force (Retired) in command, rammed into the fuselage, just forward of the wings, slicing the airplane in two. Those on the ground would later testify that the forward section, with its canard wings, continued to climb for a moment while discharging people, before joining the inferno on the ground. Later, one of the ground crew would give Jim Robert's lucky scarf, along with a solemn message: "He said to tell you it's better this way."

*
**

It was the end of spring break in beautiful Virginia. The cherry blossoms were just beginning to fade. The grass at Arlington was turning green and flowers were coming up everywhere, to the accompaniment of the lyrical songs of birds, which echoed over the silent graves.

"Ironic, aren't they, Madam President? The cherry trees around Washington."

"Sorry, Jim, I think you lost me again."

"They're a metaphor for how things work in Washington," I said. The president gave me that uncomprehending look once more.

"They look great when they're in bloom, but they almost never bear fruit," I stated as I pulled out my dad's scarf and examined the shamrocks.

"You really don't fight fair, do you, Jim?" she asked, turning her attention to the scarf.

"Not when it comes to my family and my country. For them, I'd sacrifice everything. He did," I said, holding out the scarf. "As did so many others buried here."

*
**

"You know, if I had my 308 here, I could pick them both off right from here," Darien drawled.

"The way your hands are right now, you couldn't even pick your nose," Gaston commented. "What are we doing here anyway, Culper? There's a massive manhunt for us and where are we? Sitting in the amphitheater at Arlington National Cemetery, a few hundred yards from the most heavily guarded person on the planet. You must have a death wish!"

"Now, now Gaston. It's a beautiful day; enjoy it and this lovely architecture. Besides, they'd never think of looking for us here. In a few days, that lovely plastic surgeon I know so well will give us the faces we've always wanted, and our new identities will be complete. You must admit, it was a beautiful ceremony.

"Yes, it was, Culper. But I still don't get why we had to come here."

"To honor a great enemy, Gaston. We were defeated by two octogenarians who put their lives on the line, not for money or power, but for what they believed in. It cost this Hanson fellow his life. I find people like him fascinating."

"I'm glad to see chivalry isn't dead, but we certainly will be if we don't get outta here."

"Did you take care of Tallmadge?"

"He is where he should be, unlike us. By the way, what's the plan for when we assume our new identities?"

"We'll set up our new business right here in Washington, the one place that is perfect for such a business."

"Doing what?"

"The only business where bribery, extortion, blackmail, and influence-peddling is a way of life. We'll become lobbyists."

"Lobbying for what?"

"It doesn't matter Gaston. The only thing that does is controlling the politician."

*
**

"Emily, is that you?" Dolly asked, seeing Emily standing back among some trees. "Where have you been? Jason has been asking for you."

"Well, you had family and friends to deal with. I didn't want to intrude," she replied, walking over.

"Nonsense, Emily … what's bothering you?" she asked as George and Jennifer joined them.

"Do you think you can ever forgive me for being Veronica Parker?"

"Oh my God, Emily!" Dolly exclaimed. "There's nothing to forgive. You've been nothing but good to us and your country. We consider you part of our family."

Emily was genuinely moved by Dolly's comments, but it was George who addressed the real issue in Emily's heart.

"Would it be fair to say, Emily, you are more concerned with how Jason feels?"

"Yes. Men may have different feelings about such things."

"He's standing over there. Go talk to him," George suggested with a wink.

They watched as Emily took a deep breath and headed over to Jason, who was looking down the path. He was genuinely happy to see her. She brought him beneath the shade of a willow tree, where she started to speak as Jason listened intently. Jason turned away from her, shaking his head, then quickly returned. Taking her head in his hands, he started to speak to her with great intensity. Emily was trembling before she threw her arms around him as they hugged.

"I hope she realizes what a great guy she's getting," Jennifer commented.

"Yeah, he is his parents' son," George stated, bringing a look of great pride to Dolly's beaming face.

*
**

"The irony of this situation is incredible. We find all this gold, the spoils of illegal activity, and therefore it can be confiscated legally, becoming property of the people of this country. But if we announce its existence, the gold market would collapse making it worthless. Now I find I can't get it to the people without participating in some of the same scams the crooks did," the president stated, showing great frustration as she paced back and forth on the path. "My God, Jim! I need to get involved in money laundering. I have to launder this country's gold in order to use the wealth it already owns!"

"You do have one ace in the hole."

The president stopped, waiting for my next words. I stood, faced her, and in the most formal tone I could muster, made my case.

"I am pleased to inform the President that the Culper Ring stands once again on American soil and waits to serve at the pleasure of the President."

She looked at me for a moment, and then spoke.

"So you and your little group can pull this off?"

"With some help, yes. A person from the General Accounting Office, perhaps, a few others. We have to keep the group very small."

"At this point, Jim, I think I'm suffering from information overload. I have to address the nation in two days about all of the events of the past week, and a crooked vice president to deal with. Both will require time. If I need your help, well, I do have your cell number. In the meantime, Jim, how does this nation begin to thank you?" she said as we stood up and went over to the path.

"You just did," I answered with a smile.

She looked at me. I could see she wanted say more. I knew this was the moment. It was now or never. If I didn't, I would spend the rest of my life wondering 'what if.' This time would be different; I would not let my shyness defeat me.

"Madam President, may I ask a small favor?"

"Why, of course, Jim."

"Could we leave the president on the path here for a moment while I have a word with Kathleen Galbraith over on the bench?"

Her reaction intrigued me. No surprised look. She was all business.

"We can do that," she said as we walked over and sat down.

She sat there, looking as if we were going to have a business meeting; I could see she didn't know what was coming.

"Kathleen, I would really like to see you again."

"When were you thinking, Jim?" she said, pulling out her cell to check her calendar.

"Kathleen, I don't think you understand. I'm asking you out."

*
**

"Lookit here, everyone!" Jason exclaimed. "They're really laughing together now. I've never posted any photos on my Facebook. I can see it now, a nice big one: the president and me in the oval office."

"But Jason, shouldn't the first photo be of you and me?" Emily asked, sticking out her lower lip and pretending to be hurt.

"Jason really doesn't stand a chance, does he, Dolly?" George asked.

"Nope, and judging by the way things are going down there, neither does Jim."

*
**

"You really caught me there, Jim," Kathleen laughed. She actually blushed. "I give you full marks for originality."

"I didn't know the protocol for asking a president out, or even if there was one."

She was now smiling broadly; her eyes were sparkling and she appeared fully relaxed.

"So, where would you like to take me on this date?"

"Normally, I'd say to a nice place for dinner, but your alter ego over there and her entourage makes that a challenge."

"Yeah, she can be a real killjoy sometimes. Fortunately, I know a place with world-class chefs where one can have a nice, private dinner. It's called Chez East Wing."

"Is it in that white building on Pennsylvania Avenue?"

"You got it. Give me a couple of days, Jim. I'll text you. Let me get past my address to the nation."

I could see and feel her sincerity as she took my hand.

"Of course," I replied. "Oh, I almost forgot. I have something to show you," I said as I reached into my pocket and extracted a gold coin. I placed it in her hand.

"What on earth is this, Jim?"

"Dom gave it to me yesterday. It's part of the gold the Culper Ring had stashed; you're holding what Theodore Roosevelt called the most beautiful coin America ever made. It's a 1908 Saint-Gaudens Walking Liberty Double Eagle twenty-dollar gold piece."

"It is beautiful, Jim," she said as she turned the coin over in her hand.

"Yes, the sculptor Augustus Saint-Gaudens did an incredible job with the design. And one other thing, Kathleen."

She looked up at me and smiled.

"What you're holding is real money. You can't move that with a computer."

"We certainly can't, Jim. Well, this and all rest belongs to the people of the United States. As far as this coin is concerned, I know exactly what they would want me to do with it."

What she did next touched me deeply. She stood up and walked over to the squadron memorial.

"From a grateful nation, never to be forgotten," she said as she placed the coin on top.

I could not speak as she took my arm, and we started up the path to join the others.

"When I first came here, Jim, you said there was a poem you couldn't get out of your head; can you share it?"

"Yes, I'd be happy to. It was written by a guy who I think was as close to his father as I was to mine...."

I sing the song of the Sailor Man
For I hear more than his song of the sea
I sing the song of the Sailor Man
I learned it at his knee.
It was a song for what was right
It was not a song of might
Written at a time when all seemed lost
When freedom was saved at a terrible cost
I sing the song of the Sailor Man
His song always makes me glad
He was the one I called Dad

For James McLeish,
Royal Canadian Navy, 1942-45.

EPILOGUE

A rissa checked the e-mail on her cell phone as she and Emmanuel sipped their coffees at a café near the University of Waterloo.

"Emmanuel, Stephen Hawking is coming to the memorial service!"

"I thought he might. He and our dear Steven shared a lot more than just the same first name."

"That's for sure," Arissa responded, still reading from her cell. "He appreciated you giving him the opportunity to go online with Tallmadge. They worked on string theory together."

"Yes, the Perimeter Institute has been employing their newest associate very well since he moved in."

"Oh no!" Arissa exclaimed looking up from her cell at a startled Emmanuel.

"Tallmadge got Dr. Hawking into a chess game!"

"How did he do?" A laughing Emmanuel asked.

"Judging from his comments, perhaps the Perimeter Institute should devise a program to teach Tallmadge some manners."

"Yeah, Hawking lost."

www.ingramcontent.com/pod-product-compliance
Lightning Source LLC
Chambersburg PA
CBHW061320170626
46817CB00001B/243